The Curious Tale Of

CARTER NICHOLSWORTH

M FOX

Cider House Press

ISBN: 1461177111
ISBN-13: 9781461177111
Library of Congress Control Number: 2011930078
CreateSpace, North Charleston, SC

For the boys Kyle, Tanner, Tai and Holden.

Acknowledgements

A book doesn't just happen. Like in an old fashioned marionette, there are so many strings attached to the assorted body parts that without all of them operating as an integrated system, the gangly puppet has coordination issues. This is never more true than the in collaborative efforts required in the behind the scenes efforts of writing and producing a book.

Saying thank you, my mother used to remind me, is one of life's more important lessons. Mom had lots of lessons, this being one of her better ones.

So, thank you to all those whose efforts contributed to breathing life into Carter Nicholsworth and the substantial cast that joins him on stage.

Pam Brown, my editor and spiritual guide for her tireless work and encouragement as well as her indispensable technical skills and friendship.

Shari Griffith, whose tenacity, wonderful insights and instincts sanded rough edges, then tweaked good to better. Her dedication, commitment and unconditional love helped bring this book to life.

Tya Ates for her vision and talent in creating the art for the book cover.

Chris Faye for her imaginative interpretation of the map of Aeiea.

Lee Good who was there at the beginning when Carter was just an idea rolling around in my head. For her help at the early stages of birth.

Kathi Wittkamper and Mara Rockey for their invaluable editing and publishing expertise, and an evaluator with a razor-sharp scalpel who shall remain anonymous.

Last but certainly not least, the polisher. Renee Johnson, my invisible editor extraordinaire who in the final hours massaged subtle nuances to a smooth, clean read.

Thank you to my understanding family and friends—who have not seen much of me lately—for your patience, understanding and support.

*They who dream by day are cognizant of many things
which escape those who only dream at night.*
— *Edgar Allan Poe*
1809-1849

Table of Contents

Preface

It is not so much our common humanity that defines who we are. After all, no two people, or two things, are exactly alike, and everything is in a state of constant transition. Your left eye, for example, is different from your right. There is not one physical feature on one side of your body precisely replicated on the other. As a matter of fact, no anatomical feature, not tooth nor freckle, incorporated into your entire physical essence is the same as another.

Furthermore, identical twins are not identical. Two precision widgets rolling down the assembly line, stamped from the same die in a scientifically controlled environment are also dissimilar. With each stamping, some miniscule microscopic changes to the stamping die have occurred. In this particular case, the process responsible for the nonconforming widgets is friction.

The point I make is, everything in the Universe is uniquely different and, thanks to time, constantly changing.

I speak of these matters because of their relevance to both the story you are about to begin as well as the personal journey of your own life. No one has ever traveled the road you are taking because it is one of a kind and you are laying the road as you go.

But if we are all born unique, why do so many work so hard to deny their sacred birthright? Why suppress our specialness in order to conform and give the appearance of similarity? Could it be that fear of rejection or being judged keeps us strangers from our natural state of uniqueness? Is it not our own insecurities, doubts, and fears that undermine our experiencing the universal harmony of creative living?

What if you chose differently? You are, after all, co-author of your own story. What if you chose the courageous adventure of discovering just who you really are? Where would you begin? Perhaps a long walk in the woods or sitting without the possibility of interruption in a quiet, private location. A mirror is as good a place as any to begin. Look deep into your eyes. What you see before you is the physical miracle of the remarkable you, different as a single twinkling star amongst a night sky of countless stars. That's you—a true miracle in a Universe of infinite miracles.

Some come to the reality of their uniqueness not by choice. They are physically different or have other challenges that set them apart. We cannot always choose the circumstances of our lives, but each of us can choose our response to the unique set of challenges we face. It's in our own personal response to these tests that we find both our strength and our freedom. Discovering the light in these challenges opens the door to possibility. In other words, adversity is opportunity in disguise.

Everything, from a worm in the ground to a star in the sky, has energy. That energy will in time change form (the universal law of impermanence), but the energy will continue. The seed from a redwood carried away by a bird and passing through its digestive system becomes a seedling that grows over centuries of sunsets to a mighty tree. Impermanence never sleeps.

One day, the tree falls, but its energy is transferred back into the ground where the continuum of life recycles once again. And on it goes: energy, transition, transformation, and impermanence, a story without end.

· · · · · · ·

Celebrate your sacred uniqueness and wear it proudly. At the same time, know that forever you are also a connected and integral part of all there is.

Now open the door to possibility. Come along on a most unusual adventure and enjoy crossing over into The Curious Tale of Carter Nicholsworth.

"Nightmares are a strange journey into chaos. Have a nice trip."

Chapter 1
Wickedwood

Carter woke gasping for breath in the thick, sticky heat that filled his small second-floor bedroom. Sweat glazed his forehead, and the fine, rusty hair sprouting from his forearms tickled at the sleeves of his damp pajamas. A chilling shiver shook the length of Carter's body as he tugged at his mind to remember his terrifying dream.

· · · · · · ·

The long, blistering days of summer had begun to fray a bit around the edges. A surprise evening rainstorm had washed away a dry season's harvest of dust from leaves anticipating transition. Daylight pushed up snug against the night on this first day of September, and at Lake Mohegan Junior High in Upstate New York, school would be starting in less than a week.

An only child and achingly shy, Carter Nicholsworth spent far too much time standing in a secluded corner of insecurity, quietly examining the unremarkable condition of his sneakers.

Different from most boys his age living in rural Lake Mohegan, Carter preferred a good book and the isolation of solitude to the gritty, unfiltered noise of adolescence. More often than not, he wore an expression of disappointment on his face. Some might even say sadness. At best, there was a serious quality about him that weighed heavily on his young shoulders.

He was also awkward in the company of most adults, including his own parents, Howard and Cynthia Nicholsworth. Occasionally he wondered if at birth he had been given to the wrong set of parents, once complaining to his mother, "This is not the family I expected."

In short, Carter considered life to be one confusing jigsaw puzzle. Quite possibly, his logical conclusion might stem from an inability to piece together a bewildering jumble of life's contradictions.

When it came right down to it, he just didn't fit.

It was the legendary swath of woods pinched between the back of the Nicholsworths' split-level home and the twisting two-lane highway running north to Mahopac and south through Peekskill that provided a timid boy safe harbor from the battering uncertainties of youth. On more than one occasion Carter had toyed with the idea of running away, making the woods his home. He failed to understand his shapeless plan was nothing more than the playful teasing of a boy's imagination.

On this peculiar first day of September in Carter Nicholsworth's bedroom, morning had arrived on tiptoe, dressed in a cloak of mystery. As the veil of sleep was slowly lifted, Carter became aware of the silence. There was neither the usual chatter of birds greeting the new day nor the patter of parents readying for work. Not even the nagging whine of the ancient refrigerator complaining of the ravages of old age. Carter worried that perhaps while asleep he had lost his hearing. Nervously snapping his fingers, he assured himself that his generously proportioned ears were operating just fine.

Anatomically speaking, at least by giggles scattered amongst the insensitive whispers of his Lake Mohegan schoolmates, Carter Nicholsworth wasn't quite right.

Feet were about the only part of Carter that did seem rather ordinary. Perhaps it was his unusual physical appearance that gnawed at his self-confidence, undermining what otherwise might have been an easy place in the world. There was the red cluster of free-range freckles that had focused their attention on Carter's nose before splashing out across his cheeks. His exaggerated freckles were like a wide path of random stepping-stones lacking a final destination.

Then there was the issue of his ears. Located on each side of his head were ears that Carter believed were growing at a rate several times faster than the rest of him.

As if all that didn't produce enough unwanted attention, from atop Carter's head grew hair the color and texture of paprika thatch. Defying gravity, his stack of hair reached for the sky before finally, in a seeming fit of exhaustion, falling like a spent burst of fireworks fading into a summer's night.

Like a wonderful dessert, I have saved the best for last. Hunkered down in that untamed mess on Carter's head lived Nevermore, a small bird perched like a black cherry nestled at the summit of an ice cream sundae.

· · · · · · ·

It had been a particularly cold day last spring, gray with gale and rain, when Carter rescued a baby bird blown from its nest. The frightened bird was weak and soaked from feather to skin when Carter found it trembling under an umbrella of wild thistle.

"A raven!" He could barely contain his excitement at the discovery of the tiny clump of frightened feathers.

"This little blackbird will one day grow into a powerful and wise raven," Carter announced boldly to a disinterested wind preoccupied with punishing his unruly hair. Carefully scooping the shivering bird into the palms of his hands, he lifted it toward his face. Once at eye level, he spoke to the small bird in his most solemn voice. "You shall be able to talk and we will be inseparable friends. Now," he said, his tone deepening to underscore the seriousness of the moment, "in the spirit of my favorite poem, you will from here forward be known as *Nevermore*."

And so it was.

In the weeks that followed, Carter began his morning routine by first feeding his feathered friend from an eyedropper. The bird grew, but not much, and certainly not into a raven. Nevermore never did live up to the reputation of his namesake, remaining forevermore a small, common, garden-variety black bird. Although the little bird didn't speak, Carter was not all that disappointed. He would talk endlessly to his only friend, convinced that Nevermore could understand and respond with thoughts wired directly into his own mind, even if the bird could not make a sound. At least that's what he believed. Carter was smart, but it soon became evident to him that the little black bird was equally as smart.

Nevermore began his life with Carter in the comfortable lodgings of a shoebox lined with socks rescued from a fate of furniture polishing. Then one day without giving formal notice to his landlord, the little bird abruptly changed his housing arrangements, taking up residency in the unkempt penthouse of tangle growing atop the boy's head.

"Nevermore," Carter said in amazement, "I believe finding you was no accident. You were sent to me for some reason." Nevermore cocked his head, opening and closing his pointed beak several times as if trying to say something, but for all his effort, he remained silent.

. . . .

Carter sat straight up in bed as if hit by a bolt of lightning. "Silent," he said aloud into the semidarkness of his bedroom. Though unable to remember any details, the terror of the disturbing dream that had awakened him was still fresh in his mind. "Yes, that's it! Silence has some important connection to my dream." He glanced at his alarm clock. 6:35 a.m.

The night was in slow retreat. With his eyes now fully adjusted to his familiar environment, Carter noticed a light rain sheeting down his bedroom window. He watched as drops formed, fattened, then competed in a race to the wood sill below. Carter kicked at the mess of blankets that entangled his legs. Going to the window, he placed his face against cupped hands on cool glass.

Raindrops tapped the window then blurred as he focused through the dull light on an ancient oak standing at the woods' edge. With seemingly little effort, the tree's strong limbs reached upward, stretching toward a fleet of gunmetal-gray clouds sailing in formation across the sky. Carter believed the oak was something like a sentry protecting the forest from uninvited guests. He never dared enter the woods without first stopping to rub his hand three times in a clockwise motion against the tree's rutted trunk. This ritual was his sign of respect and signaled that he was a friend of the forest.

Dressed in a stretched-out turtleneck, the grungy sneakers his mother on several occasions had unsuccessfully attempted to dispose of, and a pair of large khaki shorts he would never grow into, Carter quickly left his bedroom anxious to get into the new day. With his "lookout" Nevermore at the bird's familiar post in the crow's nest of his hair, he bounced down the stairs located just beyond his bedroom.

Leaving his home through the back door and shielded by the porch's overhang, Carter watched the few remaining drops of last evening's storm being squeezed from the sky. From the north, an approaching grainy mist curled toward the forest. Morning was hard at work, struggling to force the night into the promise of a new day. Crossing the bog now occupying his lawn, Carter trudged toward the hedge that separated his back yard from the woods. A torn gap in the hedge splayed out like an open wound from the base of the shrubbery. This was Carter's port of entry.

Just beyond the hedge, the giant oak anticipated the arrival of Carter Nicholsworth. On the third rub of his hand on the tree's trunk, a most strange thing happened. From deep in the woods, a bone-chilling wind howling like a tortured cat came racing up toward him. The sudden gust pushed past what appeared as two silhouetted women dancing in a mad frenzy on the forest floor. At that moment Carter thought he heard what sounded like a deep sigh, then words spoken in a muffled whisper:

"You must stay

if on this day

you come our way."

The tree shuddered then groaned under the weight of the unsettling news while rattling leaves nervously gossiped the wind's cryptic warning. Carter reasoned the message was the creation of his imagination. "After all, isn't it sometimes hard to tell *what is* from *what isn't*? Surely this must be one of those what isn'ts," he said to Nevermore, his own voice tighter than usual as he attempted to reassure his shaken confidence.

No doubt a random hallucination, Nevermore telegraphed to Carter's mind. *Don't give it a second thought.*

Wrapping himself in that preferred reality, Carter took a long breath, pulled his narrow shoulders up high around his neck, and entered the forest of Wickedwood. Once in the woods, Carter traced a familiar, well-worn path. Remains of last night's rain, resembling miniature crystal soldiers safeguarding a shared secret, weighted the underbrush. The hanging raindrops seemed to wink at him as he passed.

Winding parallel to the highway, the trail rose steeply, veering sharply right then up a stiff embankment. An arid plateau was his reward for the climb, where a carpet of smooth, sun-bleached stone lay scattered across the high forest floor. In this part of Wickedwood, a few stunted trees appearing twisted over in pain clung desperately to life. They reminded Carter of the shriveling people who lived in the home for the dying where his mother worked part-time as a nurse.

Farther on up the trail the crest of a ridge came into view. Just off to the left, a massive outcropping of rock bulged up from the ground. Carter called the impressive formation Great Gray. About thirty feet above the forest floor, time had carved into the granite ridge a jutting under bite of a shelf with a wide view of the trail he had just walked. Often Carter would climb Great Gray and sit quietly on brittle pine needles littering the ledge while considering possibilities. He felt certain that many years ago Mohegan Indian scouts had routinely used this observation point to warn their people of impending danger. Once he found several small bones in a concealed crevice. Most people would think Carter's findings were the remains of a dead little creature. Not Carter Nicholsworth. He knew his discovery was the amputated fingers of an unfortunate Indian, captured and unmercifully tortured by an enemy.

Passing Great Gray and coming up and over the ridge's brow, Carter began his descent into a fragrant valley where the colors of the forest became more vibrant, as if they were ripening. The landscape was different here from the stagnant lethargy of the high forest whose poor soil could only support the malnourished of nature's neglected offerings. Trees grew in thick extended families in this dark corner of the forest where all was in constant transformation.

This was Carter's favorite part of Wickedwood. Parasol-capped mushrooms poked their brown painted heads from beneath a spongy floor of wet mulch. Sharing the space, a number of beetle-infested trees lay rotting where they had fallen, their energy returning to their source, only to transform once again.

In the background, the theme song of an ancient ritual of renewal had been playing over and over again since life first appeared on Earth. Amber oozed thick and sticky from festering wounds, while a marbled grayish-green fungus stacked the trees' wrinkled skin.

It all felt magical to Carter. Inhaling deeply, he smelled the sharp, pungent fragrances of life, death, and rebirth.

Before walking much farther he arrived at the edge of an imbedded granite stairway. Steps wound down a short but steep ravine to where large, wobbly rocks entered Sharptooth Creek. Cautiously Carter rock-hopped across the rain-swollen creek. The seasonal flow was too small to appear on any map except the one Carter had drawn and kept in his secret treasure chest. Sharptooth Creek had been given its name by Carter in honor of the thorny berry bush that athletically scaled the creek's steep banks, eager to take a painful bite out of any unsuspecting passerby. Often as he approached the creek, he would be greeted by the prattle of the small creatures nesting in the briar, but not on this day.

In the early morning light, a growing fog gathered at Carter's ankles as he casually whistle-walked along the path that was slowly disappearing behind him.

More than an hour had passed since Carter and Nevermore had first entered Wickedwood. He was now in the deepest, darkest part of the forest. *The center of the Universe*, thought Carter. Here some of the oldest trees in Wickedwood had assembled, each formally dressed in rich coats of emerald moss. The ancients grew long, scraggly beards of lichen that danced to the lyrics of an archaic poem long forgotten by humans. In their costumed splendor, the elders proudly boasted their elegance to the forest. At this point, the canopy was so dense that it cut off almost all light, and for that reason Carter didn't notice the fog just now beginning to tentatively climb his legs.

It was here that the largest, most long-lived tree in Wickedwood stood. Many years ago, a devastating wildfire had leapt through the forest, devouring all in its path with the exception of the old tree. But even the great tree couldn't entirely resist the fire's ravenous appetite, and it suffered a hollowing at the bottom of its immense trunk. A grotesque mouth of broken charred teeth, barely three feet high and less than two feet wide, opened at the tree's base. This gaping disfigurement served as entrance to Carter's place of refuge.

Earlier that summer Carter had stood with hands clasped behind his back studying the tree. "Needs eyes," Carter had said to Nevermore. Taking a deep breath, he had shifted his weight to his other leg. He squinted his own eyes. Nevermore was in total agreement. So, using tools borrowed from his father's workbench, Carter cut two round windows above and to each side of the half-moon entrance. Upon completion, he stood back to examine the tree. He was pleased with his work.

"A wood elf in need of a good dentist," he informed Nevermore, smiling.

"Hunters Hut" was the name Carter had chosen for his hideout. He liked the name and thought if there were hunters in the forest not any bigger than he, surely the tree would make a fine hut for them.

Inside Carter's shelter, a cozy space barely five feet in diameter and less than that in height served as the wellspring of a boy's imagination. Hunters Hut was loosely furnished with Carter's lifetime collection of assorted stuff. His third-grade class picture was nailed opposite the entrance above a stubby-armed corduroy TV bed pillow. The rust-colored bolster sat at the head of a plaid wool blanket. A three-legged footstool his mother had discarded and he had salvaged sat in front of two cinderblocks supporting a single wood plank. Piled randomly along the board, like so many stacks of his mother's Sunday morning pancakes, was a collection of Carter's favorite books. There was also a flashlight, a box of candles he had purchased at a yard sale with his allowance, and, of course, the centerpiece of his eclectic furnishings: his treasure chest.

The chest was actually a dark-skinned, tobacco-scented wood box that once housed cigars belonging to Carter's father. That was before he stopped smoking. Now the box contained a counterfeit Swiss army knife, the "finger bones" of the Mohegan Indian, matches, a small piece of granite rock Carter was sure contained gold, his hand-drawn map of Wickedwood, and a slip of paper saved from a Chinese fortune cookie. Crispy fortune cookies were the standard dessert served at the Sun Dragon Restaurant, a favorite eatery of the Nicholsworths in nearby Peekskill's Chinatown. The cookie was not memorable. The fortune, on the other hand, was. Written in bold red letters on curled yellowing paper were the curious words:

*"NIGHTMARES ARE A STRANGE JOURNEY INTO CHAOS . . .
HAVE A NICE TRIP"*

. . . .

Squatting at the entrance to Hunters Hut, Carter waddled into the cavity of the scorched tree. He quickly found his flashlight and focused its beam on his box of treasures sitting on the bookshelf. Placing two lit candles on the shelf, Carter stuffed the matches into his pocket. When he reached into the treasure chest, he felt drawn to the small strip of paper from the fortune cookie. Studying the puzzling words, Carter tumbled onto the blanket, tucking a rolled-up towel under his head. He lay there motionless on his back, trying to make sense of the fortune cookie's mysterious message. Spasms of candlelight danced across the burnt ceiling while this morning's frightening dream flirted just out of reach of his memory.

Distracted, Carter hadn't noticed the long, wispy fingers of fog just beginning to explore the interior of Hunters Hut. Not until the troupe of dancing images projected across the ceiling began to fade did Carter notice the cool breath of the unexpected intruder cautiously sneaking into the opening of the hollowed tree. Nevermore had been acting strangely, stretching, hopping from one foot to the other, and rapidly flapping his wings, but strange behavior was not all that uncommon for the small bird, so Carter hadn't been alarmed. Carelessly stuffing the fortune into the pocket of his shorts, he crawled to the entrance and looked out into the forest. Nothing. Absolutely nothing. Absence had swallowed the forest. In a puff of smoke, like a white rabbit gone missing from a magician's top hat, the forest had entirely disappeared—

Wickedwood was gone.

. . . .

Perhaps you should know something more of Wickedwood.

The forest had come to its name through a well-publicized trial held around these parts in 1683. The trial took place in Godswell, a small, inconspicuous village built by toiling, stoop-backed Puritan farmers at the edge of a small lake. The obscure little village, along with the surrounding farms that once economically supported the town, has long since vanished. Godswell itself is not important to this story. The whispered dark tale of what is now known as Wickedwood is.

Passed down through generations of Lake Mohegan's children, the story tells of twin sisters born with skin a soft shade of burnt butterscotch, hair of pure white, and eyes empty of all color. Left at a very young age to fend for themselves, the two had been abandoned in the forest under the tent of a tilted elm. The reclusive sisters survived by foraging for roots, mushrooms, and berries, making their permanent home in these very same woods.

Sometime around the sisters' twentieth year, the population of Godswell's cats began to noticeably decline. Under the cover of night, with a full moon to light their way, the twins would steal into the sleeping village of Godswell for the purpose of kidnapping the citizens' cats, returning to the woods with burlap bags squirming with their fresh catch. Later, in a mystical ceremony known only to them, and with the full moon looking on as a witness, the animals would be sacrificed while the sisters, singing in a language unfamiliar on Earth, danced wildly around a blazing fire.

Cats were one thing, but when one day a freckled-face farm boy with hair red as a blaze in the wood went missing, the citizens of Godswell finally had enough. The sisters were tracked to their shelter in the forest by an angry mob of villagers armed with pitchforks and captured. Justice, such as it was in those days, was swift. Refusing legal counsel, the accused were put on trial the very next day.

Mara and Magi were tried for witchcraft, blasphemy, and probable murder. The two wouldn't confess, claiming the dispatch of cats their only offense. They asserted no knowledge of witchcraft, blasphemy, or of the kidnapping of a boy, but the disbelieving jury's verdict was quick and unanimous.

"Guilty!" they condemned from the jurors' box, a safe distance from the bound sisters. "Guilty!" they shouted over and over, shaking their angry fists in the air. Mara and Magi laughed hysterically while clapping their hands in approval of the jury's impassioned performance.

As punishment for their crime, the sisters were ordered to be burned at the stake. "An eye for an eye," clamored the frightened citizens of Godswell. "They are daughters of the devil."

The woods were declared forbidden, haunted by Satan and the evil spirits of witches. From that day forward, the forest carried the name Wickedwood.

And so it was on a day born as dark as their fate, the bound sisters were dragged from the stocks at the foothold of Godswell's only church. Past the cemetery flanking the white clapboard church they went, then through the village's streets lined with the souls of the curious and morbid. They were marched to the edge of the woods where the sisters angrily growled their seething contempt at those gathered. The captors tied the sisters' arms and legs painfully behind their backs to a single tall stake that rose above their heads.

While flames from brush piled at their feet leapt to catch hold of their soiled gowns, the two swore their innocence and spat hatred, promising revenge on the jeering townspeople. In their agonized final words, the sisters cursed anyone who would ever dare enter the woods—so the story goes.

Oh, one other thing—the boy was never found.

· · · · · · ·

Carter Nicholsworth did not, however, believe in witches, nor did he believe that the forest was cursed, though most Lake Mohegan children did, and for that reason, young as well as older visitors to Wickedwood were somewhat rare. He knew the woods like the familiar sweet smell inside the cookie jar waiting for him at home. Carter believed he could easily make it back to his house even if he could not see the way.

It was about then that Carter remembered that when he had left his house earlier that morning, he hadn't told his parents where he was going, and come to think of it, he hadn't even seen them. He thought if he didn't return soon, there was a remote chance his parents might miss him. They might even begin to worry.

Although Carter dismissed that possibility, on further reflection he dutifully climbed out of Hunters Hut and began the walk home.

Almost immediately Carter was lost. He hadn't taken ten steps before sharply striking his knee on a large boulder. "Ow!" he cried out with surprised pain while grabbing his knee. Nevermore, who was on full alert anyway, was further jolted by the volume of Carter's voice. "Where did that come from?" Carter asked loudly while rubbing his sore knee. The rock was not located anywhere in his memory of the area surrounding his hideout. He turned to face Hunters Hut and took the few steps back to the ancient tree to better orient himself.

Bad news. The tree was gone. His heart quickly picked up its pace, and Carter felt a heat spreading throughout his body along with a deep drumming in his ears. He also felt a sick, bitter taste rising from the bottom of his throat.

"Not to worry," he said in a worried voice to Nevermore. It was hard to know whether Nevermore was worried, but the little bird sure was on the move, hopping about while practicing takeoffs and landings in the growing perspiration collecting under his red nest.

"Don't panic," Carter said, again attempting to reassure both of them. "It will only make things worse. I'm just a little confused, that's all. I need to calm down, relax. One thing is certain. If I tried to make it home in this fog, I would fall into a ravine and really hurt myself, or worse, break my neck. I think the best thing to do is stay right here. Just sit tight and wait for this miserable fog to lift. What do you think, Nevermore?"

If Nevermore was doing any thinking at this moment, he wasn't sharing.

And so Carter sat exactly where he was, not daring to take a step farther in any direction, and he waited . . . and waited.

· · · · · · ·

It seemed an eternity before Carter realized he could finally see the outline of his sneakers. He rubbed his eyes. He could faintly make out what appeared to be the images of broad-faced flowers drooping wearily from tall, arched stems directly in front of his face. *Strange,* he thought, trying to locate the flowers in his past reality, his mind preoccupied with the lifting fog. Any minute now he would be able to start back down the trail toward home.

Although the temperature was mild, Carter felt the sharp fingernails of a cold chill sweep up the small hairs on the back of his neck. The lifting fog revealed that there was no trail. Worse yet . . . there was no forest.

Carter sat frozen. Like Nevermore, his mouth moved, but no words came out. He stared beyond the large, swaying flowers across a great rolling green meadow. Not the familiar color green of Wickedwood, but more of a synthetic green. He remembered a color from a long ago misplaced crayon box.

"Chartreuse! I must be dreaming. This just can't be happening. Of course, it's just a dream, what else could it be? Wake up!" he ordered. "Wake up!" He pinched his arm until it was sore. Nothing changed. Tears filled his eyes. "I don't understand what's happening to me. How can this be? Where am I? Am I dead?" There was, of course, no response to any of his questions.

Slowly lifting his head while swiping at his tears with the heels of his hands, Carter stared up at a grid of enormous magenta tiles set in black grout. Two suns hung heavy over the meadow, one orb considerably bigger than Carter's only personal reference, the other about half again as large. The spheres burned fiercely red, reminding Carter of the round Chinese paper lanterns at the Sun Dragon restaurant.

Wherever he was, Carter understood that what he was seeing was not located anywhere near Lake Mohegan. It was at the end of this bewildering thought that his morning's dream came flooding back into his memory.

· · · · · · ·

Uneasily, Carter sat silent and still as a rock. He closed his eyes and opened his mind. In his dream he was flying, his thin arms stretched long at right angles from his body. Tilting first left then twisting right, he floated the updrafts. Like a hawk, he was gliding in a loose circular pattern, the cold winter air whooshing past his substantial ears, taking stinging, bird-like pecks at his cheeks. His vision blurred.

On the ground in a field far below lay an undistinguishable dark shadow. Sky and land was without boundary, a chalky smudge of charcoaled gradations—winter bleak.

As he wound his way downward, the shadowy object below grew. Without the horizon as a point of reference, Carter felt disoriented, unable to judge distance. Soon the figure on the ground began to take form. It was a human being lying face up in the field. What happened next almost caused Carter to fall from the sky. In that moment he realized the human figure lying on his back was a child.

It was himself!!!

Lying in the flattened brown grass, the boy's frozen expression was strangely peaceful. Large flakes of snow danced gracefully while making their silent descent. Snow created the appearance of a white lace bandana that crowned the boy's head. The snowfall intensified, beginning to obscure the boy's facial features. A confetti of ice drifted down to the boy's lips where it quickly melted, sliding into his open mouth. The mouth filled and overflowed.

In a matter of minutes, the blizzard had all but obscured the boy's body. Then, in that finite moment of transition held most delicately in a state of perfect balance, suspended in time and located at the outermost edge between here and there, the snow completely covered the boy.

Carter had disappeared.

Chapter 2
The Investigation

Police Detective Paul Leary didn't wear a uniform. To look at him closely, it would be difficult to know what he did for a living. He was a rather oval-shaped man in his late fifties. His thin, graying hair was combed over from the far left side of his head, just above his ear, to cover a prominently receding hairline. With a more traditional haircut, Detective Leary would better be described as bald. His skin tone matched the color of his little remaining hair, and it was apparent by the stains on his tie, in addition to the length of his belt, that here was a man who, upon completing one meal, began anticipating the next.

The Nicholsworth home was simple enough, furnished mostly, the detective imagined, by other people's leftovers. He allowed himself a small smile remembering his wife's addiction to garage sales. Moving cautiously from room to room, Detective Leary and two underlings thoroughly searched Carter's bedroom and the rest of the Nicholsworths' residence. When they were finished, the detective waved the younger officers off and instructed them to wait outside in their unmarked car.

"When was the last time you saw your son?"

Howard and Cynthia Nicholsworth sat across from the detective on the edge of their living room couch, their anxious faces turned toward each other as they considered the detective's question. "Yesterday," Cynthia said hesitantly, then, while shifting her eyes to the detective, she unconsciously reached toward the coffee table separating them and pushed a half-empty bowl of dusty peanuts in his direction. Leary sampled the skimpy hospitality of Cynthia Nicholsworth. Without looking down, the practiced policeman pulled a handful of nuts from the bowl and, losing not one to the floor, in one smooth motion stuffed them all into his mouth.

"What time yesterday, Mrs. Nicholsworth, and what was he doing?"

Carter's mother thought for a moment. She wasn't sure of the time and she was even less sure of what he was doing. "Well," she said slowly, "I believe that it was evening. Yes, that's it, sometime after dinner . . . and I believe he had mentioned something about a bath."

"I don't remember that," Howard Nicholsworth said.

"Of course you don't," snapped his wife, not turning her head to make eye contact with her husband. "You weren't here. You didn't get home until a few minutes before I had to leave for work at Sunset House. You know, Howard, actually you are never here when I need you."

"Now folks," interrupted the detective, clearing his throat of peanut residue. He shifted uncomfortably on a small chair that complained under his weight. "I know you're both experiencing a great deal of stress, so let's try to stay calm and focused."

Cynthia's arms were folded firmly against her chest, her mouth tight and thin. She did not look again at her husband for the rest of the interview.

"Mr. Nicholsworth, can you remember the last time you saw your son?"

"Well, let me see." Howard Nicholsworth studied the ceiling as if seeing it for the first time. Putting a hand to his chin, his index finger traced a horizontal path back and forth against his lower lip and his eyes narrowed. After thinking for a moment, he said slowly, "I believe it was Wednesday. Yes, Wednesday, I'm sure of it. I had an important early morning meeting scheduled at the office and I was having breakfast when he passed by the kitchen door. I saw him out of the corner of my eye and said, 'Hi, Carter,' and he said, 'Hi, Mr. Nicholsworth.' Funny kid, that Carter, calls me Mr. Nicholsworth. Yes, it was Wednesday morning, I'm sure of it."

"Do you know where he was going?"

"Well, I'm not so sure about that. School's out, you know. Could be going anywhere."

"He doesn't go *anywhere*," Mrs. Nicholsworth said, becoming increasingly irritated. She stared straight into the slumping hound dog eyes of Detective Leary as she spoke. "He only goes into the woods behind our house. I don't know what he does out there, but it seems like he's spending most of his time back in those woods. Personally I think the bird is the real problem. I told Howard to get rid of that bird."

"What bird?" Howard asked.

"Okay," said the detective, reaching for a second helping of stale peanuts. "I think we're getting off subject here. Do you think, folks, that there is a chance Carter might be out there in the woods right now?"

Howard Nicholsworth relocated his special spot on the ceiling and shrugged his shoulders as if the detective's question had never entered his mind. "I don't go into those woods anymore. No sir, I get poison ivy real easy. Used up an entire bottle of calamine lotion last time I went and had to take a whole week off from work . . . not happy about that." Unconsciously Howard scratched his left arm. "But if you want to go, by all means, be my guest. Also, best watch out for the boogie man." Howard flashed a cheesy smile and winked at the unamused detective.

· · · · · · ·

About an hour later, a search party led by an aging and considerably overweight police detective entered Wickedwood. The detective wondered why some people ever bothered to have children. He also wondered whether his wife was going to make honey-dipped cornbread for dinner tonight to go along with her famous chicken and dumplings recipe.

Detective Leary was a career policeman but growing weary of his work and approaching retirement. His hunch was that the missing boy was a runaway, the interview with the Nicholsworths only serving to reinforce his theory. In all his years on the Lake Mohegan police force there had never been one homicide. Although the kid's parents were, by his own definition, disconnected and a bit weird, since there were no signs of foul play or motive, the Nicholsworths did not appear to be "persons of interest."

Leary turned to the inexperienced young officer walking closest to him. "The kid's either out in these woods or he's a runner. We'll check the woods first, but if nothing pans out here, we'll give it the mandatory time, then, write it up and file it as a runaway."

The detective's wilted suit was soaked through with perspiration when he arrived out of breath at the hollowed tree. The two accompanying officers, who were in good physical condition, stood half smiling at each other. Nearby, the lead detective with one arm extended against the Hunters Hut, removed a dirty handkerchief from his pocket with his other hand. He blotted the sweat from his sagging face. A mess of limp hair had been rearranged on the side of his head revealing far more skin than the detective would have been comfortable exposing. Grabbing a flashlight then getting onto his hands and knees, the detective pushed a portion of his large frame into the tree's entrance. It was questionable whether his entire body would fit inside Hunters Hut. Detective Leary was not about to risk the embarrassment of getting stuck partway into the tree's opening or the possibility of missing tonight's dinner.

"Buddy," he called to the smaller of the two standing officers while backing out awkwardly from the den, "get in there and find something."

When Buddy finally emerged from Hunters Hut, he just shook his head. The search brought back a suitcase full of personal memories of his own childhood for Officer Benito "Buddy" Laggerio, but provided no clues as to the whereabouts of Carter Nicholsworth.

Daylight was beginning to fade when Detective Leary noticed the child-size footprints in the soft ground leading away from the tree. There were only a few, then nothing, nothing except for a small scrap of paper. The detective grunted as he bent to pick up the curling yellow paper.

"Nightmares are a strange journey into chaos. Have a nice trip."

Scratching his tender, sunburned head, Leary twice read the prophetic message from the Sun Dragon fortune cookie. The mere thought of Chinese food was making him hungry. Burying the small slip of paper next to the Milky Way wrapper in the pocket of his rumpled pants, Paul Leary shrugged his shoulders, ending his search of Wickedwood. Gesturing at the two police officers, the detective turned away from the tree and headed home for dinner.

Chapter 3
Aeiea

Carter felt overwhelmed by both the confusing images of his dream and the view that stretched out before him. Although his youth limited his life's experiences, the fact he had spent so much time exploring the playground of his imagination somewhat shielded his mind from a devastating reality. Wherever he was, it was not Earth.

Standing with hands on hips, Carter slowly turned in all directions surveying the landscape. There were no people, wild animals, insects, trees, mountains, or visible bodies of water. The meadow surrounded him, completely filling his vision. "What now?" Carter said with a deep sigh. Nevermore had no answers.

"Should I stay here and wait for someone to find me? If I leave, will I get lost?" He laughed aloud at the thought. Pointing his finger at the horizon, Carter closed his eyes and spun until dizzy. Opening his eyes, his finger pointed in the direction of the lesser sun that, like her big sister, hung pumpkin-orange against the magenta sky.

"Okay. That's it. We go that way."

Not very scientific, Nevermore groused.

With no further thought, Carter started walking toward the smaller disk. The intense color of the chartreuse meadow caused him to squint. He wished he had the sunglasses buried somewhere in the top drawer of his Lake Mohegan bedroom dresser.

Carter walked for what seemed a very long time. The two suns were beginning to swell and appeared ready to set the grasses on fire before falling into the far end of the meadow. It was about then that his stomach reminded him he had missed lunch. It was reasonable to figure there would most likely be no dinner as well. His empty belly grumbled its objection to his conclusion.

The meadow rolled out flat before him, while one edge tipped down to the left. A gurgle of running water came from that direction. Carter smiled with the realization that the running water brought the first sounds he had heard since arriving at wherever it was he was. Being quite thirsty, Carter maneuvered to the meadow's border and slid most of the way down the loosely graveled hill toward the sound of water.

There was no water. Instead, when Carter reached the dry creek bed, he discovered the source of the sound of running water. Almost his size, sitting hunched over a dry sandbar with its back to him, was a heavily warted, three-toed toad sipping a deep breath of air through a straw. The toad ballooned then dramatically tossed his head backward. Removing the straw, it gargled the sound of a running creek.

Carter was impressed. *That's quite a trick; the toad must be trying to fool his next meal into coming down here for a cool drink,* he thought. Twice more the toad repeated his creative impersonation.

"Did you know," croaked the toad in a rather haughty voice, not bothering to turn his head in Carter's direction, "we bloated, bumpy beasts can see as well behind us as we can in front of us? Call me Gus, or call me Russ. Long as it rhymes, it really doesn't matter. Some say that Croaker is mad as a hatter, but in fact I'm just a toadzical, the wayward son of a Wimzical. Impressive aren't I? Yummmm."

Carter tried to speak, but he was so nervous his trembling lips only mouthed a response.

"Rude, rude, rutabaga, Studebaker, I'll stick your lying tongue in a rusty old pasta maker! Yummmm," the toadzical crooned in a deep throaty voice.

"I'm s-s-s-sorry," Carter stammered. "I-I . . . didn't lie, I-I . . . didn't even say anything."

"Yeah, right," croaked the annoyed toad. "I . . . I . . . two 'I's. I should stomp your stomach and blow out your *two eyes.* Yes, that would be a good thing to do, and quite tasty too. *Two.* Yummmm."

"I didn't mean to be rude. I didn't mean to make you angry," said a frightened Carter, taking a step backward.

"*Mean . . . mean,*" said the toad. "Did you say 'mean'? Are you actually daring to imply that I am mean, or do you simply have a problem with my color green?"

"No, I—"

"Quiet!!!" yelled the mean, green, three-toed toad that officially went by the name of A. Croaker. Then, collecting his composure, very slowly and softly he said, "You know, I am quite hungry. Got any balonegry?"

Actually the toad was quite poor with the art of rhyme and was known to take extensive liberties in a failed attempt to perfect the difficult skill. His long tongue traced the line of his upper lip (do toads have lips?) before slipping silently back into his mouth.

"So am I," Carter replied. "I don't know what balonegry is. Did you—"

"Quiet! Quiet!! Quiet!!!" The toad had obviously come to the end of his severely challenged patience. "Who cares about youuuuu? I am the only one who counts around here. Why you're nothing but a . . . a . . . a . . . what exactly is it that you are anyway?"

"I'm a boy."

"Ahhhhh, a boy," said the toad, attempting to exhibit a persona of indifference. "Yes, of course, of course, a boy. I knew that. By the by—not that I am at all interested, but strictly as a matter of scientific inquiry, and furthering my intellectual and educational pursuits—are boys good to eat? A tasty treat?" The toad shot a sideways glimpse at Carter, wanting to be sure to catch the boy's reaction to his question.

"No," shuddered a horrified Carter, "they are terrible to eat . . . actually quite bony as well as painfully poisonous." He was, of course, not telling the truth; however, his heightened level of anxiety called for extraordinary measures. "I thought toads ate flies and things like that."

"Ahhhh, yes," replied the toad who smelled something like the rank mud in the shallows of Lake Mohegan, "and therein lies the problem. You see, once I dined on flies aplenty, but that was before being deported from Wimzi for the unspeakable crime of helping an old toad cross the road. Now, oh poor me, we're fresh out of the filthy flitterers here on Wimzi's border with Stanelhooven. I be groov'n."

"Stanelhooven, Wimzi are places? Where on Earth are Stanelhooven and Wimzi?"

"A better question might be, 'Where on Aeiea are Stanelhooven and Wimzi?' Well, Stanelhooven is precisely, to the fractional centimeter, equidistant between the Dweeg and Gushkin territories, to be exact, although I'm not at all sure, with the distinct possibility that my entire response was nothing more than pure manure," answered the toad.

"Actually, we are not in Stanelhooven," he continued. "We are in the northeast corner of Dweeg Territory, but I came up empty when trying to think of a word that would rhyme. As to the second and more complicated part of your question, the location of Wimzi is a tightly guarded secret known only to everyone. Enough of this. I am using up all of my precious strength on your foolish questions. Leave me alone or I'll eat your feet. Don't come back unless you're bringing me a big bag of bloody, black bugs. Out, out, drunken lout!" croaked the mean, green, three-toed toad. "Yummmm."

Carter turned and quickly, with hands and feet churning, scampered up the steep riverbank. About halfway, he heard the toad's woeful dirge, his voice husky and full of melancholy.

"Oh, when the flies fly north for their wintering, Croaker croaks loudest cuz he's a starvering . . ." and then the familiar impersonation of a running brook.

Carter had no intention of returning either with or without a bag of bugs. When he arrived back at the top of the bank, the meadow had blossomed into a field of purple poppies. Crossing through the chest-high flowers was at first most difficult. Carter tried not to step on or damage the beautiful flowers. Realizing he was making little progress, he soon gave up the effort to be careful. Although Carter was now tromping down the poppies, the graceful, long-necked flowers immediately bounced back, leaving no evidence of his passing.

Just as abruptly as the meadow had begun, it ended. Carter stood with his back to the neatly ordered field of poppies looking straight ahead at a long dirt road that disappeared into the horizon. Without hesitation he started down the road. Walking at a quick pace, he continued in the direction of the smaller of the two suns.

It seemed he had walked for many hours. Beads of sweat gathered then ran from the seclusion of Nevermore's nest, down across the open field of Carter's brow, tracing a familiar path down his face, tickling as they traveled. When at last he turned to see how far he had gone, the wall of poppies that had been at his back hours before was still just a few feet behind him.

"Did I miss something?" Carter asked Nevermore. His head began to throb as he considered the impossible. "Have I lost my mind, Nevermore?"

Dazed by his spinning mind, Carter could think of nothing else but to continue walking, although his stride was significantly shorter and slower.

Preoccupied with the confusing circumstances of his day, Carter was unsure of exactly how long he had been standing at the crossroads—six roads to be precise, splitting off from the main road he had been traveling.

A weathered post with six nailed arrows pointing in the direction of each road leaned from the ground. The arrows lacked any information regarding distance or, for that matter, failed to identify the name of any location.

"Great!" said a growingly annoyed Carter to Nevermore. "That certainly is helpful. Some brilliant engineer from the local department of transportation is obviously doing good work here, very good work indeed. Signage for those who don't read or don't care how far it is to where they are going or, for that matter, don't even care where they are going." His eyes shifted first left, then right, then left again, studying each road as if there was only one right choice.

Carter's frustration was interrupted when he noticed off in the distance billowing toward him a small coffee-stained cloud traveling one of the roads. Lowering himself into a densely clustered stand of fragrant brush decorating the road's sloped embankment, Carter waited.

Before too long, flailing down the road while running backwards and moving just ahead of the swarm of dust, came a goat-like creature with far more legs than it probably needed. In front of the animal (or behind, depending on how you see things), an overflowing grocery cart of this and that was harnessed to its sides. Transitioning the creature and cart were two wooden poles. The cart sported two side-view mirrors that enabled the creature to see behind him—or was it in front of him? Whatever.

Hooves, which you might expect at the ground level of the creature's legs, were also missing. Instead, paddle-like flippers flapped as it ran, far more resembling a duck's webbed feet than a goat's hooves. All this seemed quite odd to Carter. As the creature ran, it sang:

> *"I once knew a flea who swallowed a bee,*
> *The bee who stung the flea on the knee.*
> *The knee of the flea got as big as the bee,*
> *The bee who lived in the bumblebee tree . . ."*

Jumping from his hiding place onto the road as the creature neared, Carter held his arms directly over his head and shouted in his most authoritative voice, "STOP!!!"

Taken off guard, the surprised goat-thing pushed an assortment of legs outwards toward its front end where they noisily scraped the dirt road in a most unusual braking maneuver. Unfortunately, the speeding creature lost control and began a fishtailing skid from one side of the road to the other before completely losing its balance and becoming airborne.

"BOZO!!!" the creature yelled irritably at Carter as it flew past him.

In a wild theatrical finale of uncoordinated tumbling acrobatics, the creature finally came to rest against the side of a mossy boulder alongside the grocery cart that had broken free and now tilted precariously above him. The disoriented creature lay there for some time on its back, its multitude of legs like so many pick-up sticks thrust stiffly in every direction. It looked up at the purple sky with bug-wide eyes. Eventually the goat-thing glanced over at Carter who stood speechless, staring. Understandably embarrassed, the animal readjusted an odd headgear gizmo featuring a wraparound rear-view mirror, then scrambled to regain its floppy feet and some degree of dignity.

The creature's ears, unlike Carter's that were just simply large, were enormous. The weathered, leathery skin cascaded from the sides of the animal's head, draping its front-most legs to where the lower edges lay torn and ragged from dragging the ground. Just behind its nose, a single horn spiraled upwards. At the tip of the creature's curled accessory hung a bell, while a bright red scarf loosely wrapped its neck.

"Whyjadoit?" the goat-thing bellowed at Carter.

"I beg your pardon?"

"You beg? Well, now I must admit," responded the aggravated creature, shaking off its recently acquired layer of dirt, "I have never encountered a beggar before. I didn't even know what a beggar looked like, but as a recognized authority on the subject, I can say clearly and in all certainty that you, sir, are most certainly a beggar. As you can obviously see, I have no pockets to hold the spare change you so shamelessly seek. Fact is, all my money is tied up in equity investments and commercial real estate. In any event, I don't believe in giving to beggars. Get a job!"

"But I'm no beggar," responded an amused Carter.

"Excuse me, I distinctly heard you say, 'I beg.' It's really rather simple and doesn't require a degree from some fancy, high mucky-muck institution to figure out that if you beg you're guilty of being a beggar." The creature turned its head to address several birds feeding on the ground. "Ladies and gentlemen of the jury, I rest my case."

"Well, that is absolutely ridiculous. I was just using a manner of speech."

"Ahhhhhh, manners," said the creature, raising its thickly-knit eyebrows. "Well now, isn't that a whole new how do you do? You should also know that manners are another subject I am quite familiar with. Some, who shall remain nameless to safeguard their privacy, hold me in the highest regard, even considering me to be *the* authority on the subject. Therefore, sir, I must conclude it is my considered and highly suspect opinion that you, sir, are mannerless. You have obviously been . . . er . . . dismannered."

"Dismannered? Dismannered isn't even a word."

"Precisely correct, and you clearly make my point. Only someone who is mannerless or lacking character, would make an issue of that type of hurtful, unkind observation. Say, are you trying to distract me and not answer my question?"

"Well . . ." Carter said, "you have me so confused, it seems I've totally forgotten your question."

"Whyjadoit?"

"I be . . . ahhh . . . excuse me?"

"Whyjadoit, whyjadoit, whyjadoit???" The creature's crossed eyes bulged with frustration.

Shifting uncomfortably from one foot to the other Carter said, "Um, yes. Of course you are right, totally right. Say, can we change the subject?"

"Most certainly," responded the creature while taking a deep, calming breath. "I don't remember the subject anyway." Tapping a webbed foot against its bearded chin, the strange animal tried hard to think of another profound topic to discuss. Finally it said, "So what's up with the heron on your head?"

"That's not a herring," Carter answered. "Are you having trouble with your eyes?"

"Who said anything about a herring? Are you having trouble with your ears?"

"I am not having a problem with my ears, except perhaps for their size."

"Ah," the creature said, "when it comes to the size of ears, my rule of thumb is, the bigger the better."

Carter swallowed a laugh as the creature stumbled backwards, stepping on one of its dragging ears. "As I always say," it continued, "a heron on the head beats a thumbtack in bed. It's a good luck thing, you know, a heron on the head. Whereas a herring on your head is bad luck, yes, very bad luck indeed. Just about the worst luck you could possibly have.

"Had a dear old hairless uncle once upon a time who grew a herring from the top of his head," the goat-thing continued. "Uncle went to an outdoor concert one oven-hot day and forgot to put on his hat or sunscreen. Well, the unfortunate broiled herring curled up and croaked from the heat, putting quite the stink on Uncle's head.

"Soon Uncle became the only one left sitting in his section. He thought the putrid smell was caused by his upset stomach, probably the result of a moldy, custard-filled donut he had eaten earlier at the concert. After inhaling that disgusting dead fish for most of the afternoon, Uncle cut a beastly burp then tipped over on his green face, joining the deceased fried herring.

"Tragic and utterly unnecessary, wouldn't you say? I had earlier advised Uncle to see a dermatologist and to get that nasty thing removed. Oh, how I miss my dear old uncle," the creature cried. Removing the red scarf from its neck, it dabbed at its crossed eyes then noisily blew its nose into the scarf.

"Which reminds me," it said absently while examining the scarf's contents, "I missed breakfast this morning. As I always say, bad luck, those head herrings, oh yes, very bad luck indeed."

"Well," Carter informed, "it's neither a heron nor herring on my head, it's just Nevermore, a common garden-variety black bird."

From his nest, the small bird stared intently at the creature, not blinking an eye.

Re-tying its now sticky scarf around its neck, the creature said, "Ah yes, of course, the black bird," as if it had known all along and was now simply reuniting with an old lost friend. "I knew that."

There was an awkward moment of silence while the creature's eyes narrowed. Clearing its throat it spoke. "Excuse me." Turning, it reached back into the grocery cart, pulling assorted items from a collected jumble of junk. A random grab bag of this and that was tossed high into the air.

"Gotcha!" it shouted and hauled from the cart a heavy book with tattered cover entitled *Rumpledoerfler's Complete Graphic Encyclopedia of Twitters and Tweeters*. "Hmmmm," muttered the creature, thumbing the pages while ruffling its beard. "Just as I suspected. There is no such thing as a Common Garden-Variety Black Bird."

"Just look up 'black bird,'" Carter said.

"Do you take me for a fool? I did that as well, nothing there. You, my good sir, have an imitation bird on your hands, as well as your head. A charlatan. A fake. A fraud. A forgery. This thing that sprouts from your colorful crown is not as he would have you believe. This, sir, is a ruse, pure and simple, and I have exposed it. Tell me, my dear friend, was this imposter trying to sell you roofing and siding or maybe pork belly futures or perhaps one of those multi-purpose, slicing and dicing kitchen gadgets?"

"What is it with you? Nevermore is just an ordinary black bird and he is not trying to sell me anything."

"Hmmmm," came the skeptical response from the creature, resuming the fingering of its beard. "I probably should have looked under 'ordinary black bird.'"

Slowly shaking his head in disbelief, Carter said, "You are ridiculous."

"No, actually I'm Imalima. That would be 'lima' as in the green kidney-shaped bean. Since you have brought up the subject of beans, sir, I am quite fond of the little legumes as those can attest who have had the unfortunate displeasure of experiencing my company following my digestion of the gastronomical treat. Who are you?"

"Carter," said Carter. "Who are you?"

"I said Imalima," answered the goat-thing, mildly annoyed, then again repeating its name, this time slowly pronouncing each syllable, "I'm-a-lima."

"Sorry. So you're a lima . . . What's a lima?"

"No, no, no. Not *Whatsalima*, it's *Imalima*. It's not what I am, it's who I am—Imalima, get it? It's the *who* not the *what* of it . . . get it?"

"I get it," Carter said, who really did not. "But what's your name?"

The creature collapsed to the ground in a hairy heap and began to blubber, softly at first, then when Carter was slow to respond, louder and with far more emotion. Once again taking the scarf from its neck the goat-thing for a second time blew its nose into it.

"Do you enjoy tormenting me? Hasn't my life been hard enough? Oh, poor miserable Imalima," it sobbed, its large head just inches from the ground.

"Sorry," Carter said, "I think I understand. Imalima really is your name."

"Correcto," replied Imalima, inhaling a deep breath and brightening a bit. "My parents were expecting a turtleoster but got me instead. As you might imagine, they were quite disappointed. Naming me A. Imalima was their revenge."

"The name is a bit confusing," Carter admitted, ignoring for the moment his curiosity of turtleosters. "What happened to the 'A'?" Not waiting for an answer, he continued down his stream of questions. "Imalima is a good name. It actually has a nice ring to it. Speaking of rings, what's the purpose of the bell on the ring 'round your horn?"

"Oh, that's so I won't get lost. As long as I can hear the bell, I know where to find me."

"Well, I guess around here that makes perfect sense," Carter said. "Would it be impertinent of me to ask where you were going in such a rush?"

"Indeed it most certainly would. However, since I don't know what the word 'impertinent' means, I don't mind responding—I have no idea," answered Imalima.

"But you seemed in such a hurry, surely you were going somewhere."

"No, not really, but if what you just said is true, perhaps *you* could tell me where it is I am going."

With that, Imalima raised his head, sniffed the air then, looking seriously at Carter, said, "I can't believe the time."

"What time is it anyway?" Carter asked.

"Dunno," Imalima answered.

"But you said . . ."

"I know quite well what I said, but where I come from, you can't believe anything about anything. I was just making the point that I can't believe the time. Have I lost you?"

"I am so lost I wouldn't know where to begin even if I tried to answer your question."

"Gotta go, you know, or I'll miss it."

Re-harnessing himself to the grocery cart and adjusting his headgear, Imalima trotted off down the road—backwards, of course.

"Go where? Miss what?" shouted Carter after him.

"Haven't a clue," came Imalima's fading voice. "See you there." In another moment he was gone from sight.

. . . .

It is hard to know if the poor, unstable creature was just accident-prone or whether his clumsiness was not the by-product of some other, more ominous physiological or psychological defect. A trained therapist might conclude Imalima suffered from low self-esteem or perhaps some type of conflicted relationship with his inner self.

It is also a very strong possibility that while Imalima's head was rolling down the assembly line, rather than receiving the standard full scoop of brains, he instead received a production worker's warm breakfast of scrambled eggs. When you think about it, they kind of look the same, and if the worker happened to be in a rush, distracted, color blind, or just an individual with a quirky sense of humor, well, who knows what may have happened?

It is of no consequence. The unalterable fact remains that Imalima's mental dilapidation along with his unique assortment of body parts were obviously screwed together without benefit of an instruction book and not properly tightened down. This is likely where the expression "he has a screw loose" comes from.

And then there is the embarrassing matter of Imalima's criminal record. It just so happened that one day, quite by accident I might add, Imalima made the unfortunate mistake of telling the truth, a capital offense in Wimzi. This unforgivable indiscretion normally carries the death penalty or the absolute worst punishment of having to do the baked-on greasy dishes of Wimzi's lone politician, Senator A. Twit, for an entire month.

As luck would have it, on the day of Imalima's trial, a considerably lesser punishment of banishment was handed down by His Most Excellent of Excellencies, the detestable and dishonorable Judge A. Flembal. Actually the judge rendered two sentences. In addition to the banishment, Imalima was made to suffer the indignity of public humiliation. The usually ill-tempered judge was fortunately distracted and in one of his rare good moods. He was daydreaming in court, eagerly anticipating his very own fabulous unbirthday party that no one but he would be attending, since no one else was invited. Imagining eating his unbirthday cake alone, Judge Flembal spared Imalima's life and instead ordered him first confined to the stocks down by the jail, then deported.

Because of that simple chance coincidence of fate, Imalima was not hung.

The occasion of an unbirthday is cause for joyous celebration and, indeed, a very rare happening where, in the wobbly world of Wimzi, everyday is your birthday . . . except, of course, when it is not.

As to the business of an unbirthday, citizens of Wimzi are personally charged with the responsibility of maintaining an official organized, itemized, and notarized accounting of all their sneezes. Just as you might expect, having a cold or allergies is a good thing in Wimzi.

The three rules of unbirthdays are the following: A stifled eye-popping sneeze in a theater or library (against the law) doesn't count, cheating is encouraged, and lastly, an overspray of a fellow Wimzical with a vaporous mist of sneeze juice is considered good form and carries a bonus value of two extra points.

Just for the record, I believe the concept of an unbirthday did not originate in the territory of Wimzi. There are several rumors as to the holiday's inception, with one being that some time ago, a hatter, a hare, and a dormouse, who happened to be distant relations of Imalima's, had sent an invitation for the celebration of an unbirthday tea party to Imalima's family. It sounded like their kind of party, but the return address was from a land not on any map to be found in Wimzi. Deepest regrets were returned, but the idea of an unbirthday took root. Rules were written to give the holiday an original Wimzical twist, and the rest is history.

At the conclusion of his trial, a disgraced and shackled Imalima was led into the town square. With head bowed, he was urged up several steps onto a platform by a prodding pair of guards. His neck and four of his many legs were securely locked into a series of wood stocks. The creature's scraggly beard rested on a board, just inches from a bowl of freshly cut onions. Imalima spent much of the entire hot and miserable day in tears.

"Crybaby! Crybaby!" taunted the passing citizens of Wimzi. Elegant feathers, snatched from the tails of unsuspecting turtleosters, were generously provided for such occasions by the Wimzi Department of Injustice. The feathered instruments of torture were used to tickle the many webbed feet of the manacled prisoner by the two guards assigned the responsibility of seeing to it that Imalima received the maximum amount of discomfort possible. Compassion is also considered a serious crime in Wimzi.

Early the next morning the poor creature was taken from the stocks. Following the same two guards, his tormenters from the previous day, he walked in the direction of Wimzi's western border. Imalima moved slowly, his stiff legs suffering discomfort from his torturous stock experience.

"How 'bout a second chance?" he asked, trying hard to sound upbeat. His question was not directed particularly at either guard.

"Sorry," came the response from the taller of the two, who in fact was not sorry at all but rather enjoyed Imalima's miserable misfortune.

"We have our job to do whether we like it or not," added the shorter, who appeared sympathetic, but in reality liked his job a lot.

The banishment ceremony at the border was brief and perfunctory, containing a hard seed of unfriendliness. Imalima was informed that if he was ever found in the territory of Wimzi again he would be racked and stretched like taffy.

Then, without looking back or, to be accurate, looking forward since he was moving backward, Imalima quickly scooted over the border with no intention of ever returning to Wimzi.

Although he was a true Wimzical born in the territory of Wimzi, Imalima was now permanently banished from his homeland and, with his deportation, stripped of his first name, "A." Due to a tragic flaw in his genetic chemistry that resulted in moments of unintentional proper behavior—totally illegal, according to the laws of Wimzi—the creature was now homeless.

Like a wandering gypsy, Imalima traveled the territories, surviving on the generosity of the good citizens of Aeiea. The possibility that one day the convicted criminal might be welcomed home to Wimzi as a national hero was the furthest thing from his mind.

Chapter 4
From Bad to Worse

arter shaded his eyes from the glaring intensity of the two suns. Late afternoon held tightly to the day's heat. A smudged bank of gray-pink clouds stood unmoving, leaning against a backdrop of purple sky.

Following the same road Imalima had taken, Carter, with the little black bird comfortably nested in his hair, began walking. "Some event must be happening soon, Nevermore, for that creature to have run off in such a hurry. With all the possible choices of direction, it must have had a reason to pick this particular road. I know, I know, nothing makes much sense around here, but we need to go in some direction and what better choice do we have?"

By now, it should be evident that Carter was quite comfortable having one-way conversations with Nevermore. In fact as earlier mentioned, so intimate was Carter's relationship with Nevermore that he believed thoughts went directly from the bird's mind to his own.

Up ahead, a gathering of ring-necked palms, pushed by a late afternoon breeze, bowed and waved graceful fronds in a farewell gesture to the setting suns. At this point the road curved, neatly skirting the palms. So engrossed by the spectacle of the dueling suns, Carter, if not for Nevermore's warning, would have walked right into the barricade.

A series of sequential flashing yellow lights topped several striped sawhorses. The sign hanging from one of the sawhorses read *DEAD END. POSSIBLE DANGER UP AHEAD. DO NOT ENTER. NO HUNTING, FISHING, OR GOLD PANNING.* Along both sides of the road, a crowded grove of young trees stood bracketing the sawhorses. Just beyond the barrier, the road curved and disappeared from sight.

A second, considerably smaller sign on another sawhorse pointed to what appeared a much less hostile road with unlimited visibility. The smooth road dove straight into the horizon. This sign read: *ROAD TO HAPPINESS. THIS WAY TO EASY STREET.*

Carter, whose only earthly experience with adventure was limited to a prolific imagination nourished in the forest of Wickedwood, took a deep breath and climbed over the barrier that posted the warning sign. Which begs the question . . . why do a few courageous souls choose to risk the uncertainties of the road unknown over the predictable road of comfort and certainty?

After walking the road for quite some time, Carter began to erase the barricade's warnings from his mind. "Maybe someone was just trying to scare us from trespassing on their property," Carter said to Nevermore.

Hard to tell, came the voice passing through his mind. *It seems we've been cut adrift in unchartered waters where logic doesn't apply and isn't going to help us out much.* Nevermore, who on occasion could be accused of being an intellectual bore, twice stretched his wings before settling in again.

Although it was early evening, there was still a squeeze of light left in the day when Carter's daydreamed longings for simpler times were interrupted by the frantic flapping of Nevermore's wings. That was just a split second before he walked smack into a large canvas curtain stretched tightly between twin posts growing from the ground at opposite sides of the road. This was the second time in the same day Carter was caught napping. He was aware that daydreaming could be hazardous to his health especially wherever it was he was. Carter made a promise to himself to stay more alert.

The canvas was painted in great detail from its top all the way down to the bottom edge. Like a transfer of reality, cut and pasted from the natural world, the painting perfectly connected with the existing road and sky. Standing in front of the curtain, he marveled at how real it looked. The hard pack that he and Nevermore had been traveling continued seamlessly on the mural all the way to where it touched the sky.

Carter, who had been walking along the middle of the road, walked to the far side of the painting and peered around the curtain. The road continued on this side of the curtain as well, eventually disappearing into the horizon just as it did on the painted canvas. Looking back and forth from one side of the curtain to the other only added to his bewilderment.

"What's up with that? I mean, what's the point?" Carter's mind was overheating with confusion as he walked the short distance back to the middle of the road to re-examine the canvas. He stood there a few moments before finally returning to the curtain and ducking under.

"Impossible!" he shouted. The road was gone, and Carter found himself entirely surrounded by a wet, sour-smelling forest. Shafts of early afternoon light filtered lazily through the loose fabric of the forest's canopy.

"Wait a minute," he said to Nevermore. "On the other side of that curtain there was an open road, there was no forest, and it was beginning to get dark. When I looked around the curtain to this side, it was just more of the same, but when I went under . . . well, what if I just ducked back under to the road . . .?" When Carter went to lift the curtain it wouldn't budge. "Okay, we go to Plan B." He walked to what should have been the curtain's edge and kept walking and walking and . . . no edge. No way back.

Nevermore was becoming increasingly agitated in his red nest.

The mind is a funny thing. It assesses a constant flow of information then sends out signals as to what to do with that information. Every once in a while, the mind gets a case of the hiccups, and when that occurs, there is no telling what might happen next. This is often the stuff of dreams.

Carter was having one of those moments. He thought it interesting how one minute you could be standing in line at the movie theater wondering where that girl lives who you just caught smiling shyly at you. Then your mind might do the old switcheroo and have a little hiccup. After your eyes meet, you feel embarrassed and look down at your feet. The sidewalk you were standing on is gone and now you are balancing on a narrow ledge quickly crumbling beneath your feet. Slipping from the ledge running the length of a sheer granite wall, you fall hopelessly toward oblivion. Plummeting headfirst toward an outcropping of rock on the beach far below and with the moment of truth about to arrive . . . you find yourself lying in bed, waiting for your heart to slow—

Skip a dee doo dah—

A distant memory of the fortune from the Sun Dragon restaurant cookie came rushing back. Carter could reconcile the mischief of dreams, but deep down he knew this was no dream, unless . . .

What if his entire life was nothing more than a moment in someone else's dream? His mind trembled, quickly dismissing the strange thought.

Completely disoriented, Carter's attention went to one of the few remaining familiarities of his brief life: his body. His empty stomach was complaining loudly of neglect. Joining the growling grievance committee was his dry mouth.

"Food and water, Nevermore. We have to make that a priority. Keep your eyes peeled for anything that looks edible or something to drink and report back to me."

Aye, aye, Captain, came a thought down from the crow's nest.

There were no paths for Carter to follow. After searching the woods awhile longer, he came upon a small brook. Quickly lowering his face to the cool water, both Carter and the bird drank deeply. His thirst finally quenched, Carter sat, using the chiseled trunk of a huge tree as a make-shift backrest. Thin willowy vines hung from the tree's impressive limbs, reminding Carter of an old banyan tree he had seen a picture of in a *National Geographic* magazine. Different from the photograph in the periodical, this tree was showered with fragrant, orange flowers that trumpeted their beauty. Oval-shaped yellow fruit grew heavy from the giant's stressed branches. As Carter was soon to discover, the vines were actually fibrous roots growing from the limbs of the stout tree.

Driven by hunger, Carter picked a piece of the ripe fruit hanging from a low branch, smelled it, and took a small bite. Under different circumstances, perhaps Carter would have been more cautious. Perhaps he would have been more in tune with Nevermore, who was trying desperately to communicate with him. Then again, maybe not. He was after all so hungry he was willing to eat almost anything. Nevermore kept a wary eye on him. Feeling a bit tired after devouring several of the sweet fruit, Carter reclined under the tree. In a moment, he was fast asleep.

A repeated clunking sound wandered in and out of Carter's rambling dreams. While he napped, thick roots grew from the tree's muscular limbs, digging into the ground surrounding him. Carter woke to find himself imprisoned. He had no idea how long he had slept. Quickly jumping to his feet, he pulled with all his strength against the fibrous bars, but to no avail. Reaching up for Nevermore, his hand came away empty. The bird was gone.

"You broke the law," said a calm voice from above him.

Squinting, Carter looked up to see four skinny creatures of graduated length hanging upside down from a tree branch. The quartet dangled by their ringed tails just inches apart and looked something like a mix of mostly sloth with a little bit of possum thrown in. Normally sloths don't have tails, hanging instead from long limbs that terminate with three sharp claws, but Carter realized that nothing he had been experiencing recently could be mistaken for normal.

"Let me introduce ourselves," said the longest creature in a stiff, formal voice. "I'm A. Jerq, senior member of our talented family. My sisters from left to right are, in un-alphabetical order, A. Morun, A. Dummi, and last but certainly in my expert opinion least, we have A. Duhweeb. Everyone in Wimzi has 'A' for a first name except those unfortunate criminals who are banished, losing their privilege of a first name. Our second name is our middle name as well as our last name. We are quite keen on the law herein as you are about to find out."

"I believe you go by the name of Carter Nicholsworth, is that correct?" asked the creature closest to A. Jerq, peering over a small pair of reading glasses resting on the far end of its nose.

"Correct," Carter answered, "but how did you—"

"Just answer the question!" A. Morun yelled, pointing a curled claw at Carter.

"Just answer the question," the other sisters chimed in, repeating themselves over and over, louder with each repetition. The increasingly agitated sisters then began yelling at each other, "Just answer the question!"

Finally, in an attempt to restore order, A. Jerq pushed hard off the tree limb she hung from, causing her head to clunk against A. Morun's head who in turn clunked against A. Dummi's who then finally clunked with a hard vengeance against the noggin of A. Duhweeb.

"I will have order," came the annoyed voice of A. Jerq, "or I will clear the court."

The sisters mumbled a few inappropriate words under their breath then, resentfully, one by one, fell silent.

"Now, isn't that much better?" A. Jerq asked of her sisters in a syrupy-sweet condescending voice. The three mostly sloths did not respond, remaining perfectly still while glaring angrily at their big sister. A. Jerq returned her attention to Carter, flashing a toothy, insincere smile. "The court finds you guilty on all charges," she said without emotion.

"Guilty of what charges???" Carter shouted, unable to believe what he had just heard from the smug mostly-sloth.

"Guilty of what??? Guilty of what???" the sisters shouted up and down the line.

A. Jerq yelled, "Silence! Order in the court, or I will clear the chambers!"

Her sisters were having none of it this time. "Guilty of what?" they echoed back and forth at each other. Again and again A. Jerq smashed her head against A. Morun's who passed the beating down the line. And so it went, until finally, overcome with exhaustion and pain, the sisters' voices began to fade.

"Anyone got an aspirin?" A. Duhweeb asked, holding her head between two claws.

"Not a one," responded A. Morun who was also holding her swelling head. "However, I do believe I have an Ibuprofen somewhere in my pouch."

"Please," A. Jerq appealed in slow and deliberate cadence, "could the jury give me one small precious moment of silence while I pronounce my sentence on the defendant?"

"Your Honor," Carter asked, "what supposed law am I being accused of breaking?"

"No 'supposeds' about it. You broke it alright, broke it just as sure as a cracked speckled muke egg is a leaker," A. Jerq answered.

"Oh what I wouldn't do for a soft-poached muke egg on toast right now," lamented A. Dummi to A. Duhweeb.

"Aren't we supposed to question the defendant?" A. Morun asked.

Frustrated, A. Jerq crossed her limbs against her chest. "I just wanted to sentence him, but if you feel you have pertinent questions relating to this case, you may ask them."

With that, A. Morun unfurled a long length of paper that almost reached the ground. "Question number one: Do you have a lot of toys?"

Carter frowned, "I don't see what—"

"Question number two: Are you rich, famous, either, or neither?"

"Well," Carter responded, "you didn't give me a chance to answer the first question, and besides, I don't see what this has to do with anything."

"It has something to do with everything!" A. Morun shouted. "Besides, we are not here to listen to your answers; we are only interested in our questions and—"

"The law is the law," A. Jerq interrupted, "and in fairness, which is what we're all about, it applies equally and entirely as well as fundamentally to absolutely everyone . . . especially you."

"I am done with this defendant," A. Morun sneered. "Sentence him."

"Wait!" Carter shouted. "I haven't had a chance to defend myself."

The sisters looked questioningly at each other then huddled together. Heated words were exchanged, faces slapped, ears pulled, and noses pinched. After a few minutes of this absurdly bad behavior, which only a court in Wimzi could be proud of, A. Jerq composed herself and cleared her throat. "All right, defend yourself, but make it snappy."

"First, what crime am I accused of?"

"Truthiness!" A. Jerq shot back. Her sisters put their claws to their ears, their eyes rolling back in their heads.

Carter stood quietly for a moment, trying to understand the charge. "I'm sorry, I'm not sure I got that."

"Truthiness!" shouted A. Jerq once again, then repeated herself a third time, although this time slower, pronouncing each syllable. "Tru-thi-ness. What part of truthiness don't you understand? It is not only against the law in Wimzi to tell the truth, it is a capital offense. Besides, the name 'Carter' is not on the official list of acceptable names in Wimzi, so you are using the name of a fictitious, non-existent illegal alien, or at a minimum, you are a non-compliant individual, which is a second capital offense. Would you like to try for a third?"

"Kill him!!!" A. Dummi screamed.

Carter's head felt like it was stuffed with wet cotton. The words from the mostly-sloth sounded garbled, and there was a low buzzing noise in his ears. He shook his head to clear his mind.

Who are these ridiculous creatures anyway? Carter remembered falling asleep under a fruit tree and wondered at the possibility that all of this might be nothing more than a dream. It all seemed far too absurd to take any of it seriously; however, these were indeed strange times.

"This is a mockery of justice!" Carter shouted while pointing at the sloths. "I demand a lawyer!"

"Too bad for you," A. Jerq said in a subdued voice. "We no longer have lawyers in Wimzi, and we only have one semi-unofficial judge, that being our disrespected cousin, the dishonorable, disbarred, and definitely demented, Judge A. Flembal. Believe me, you're better off with us because, as we all know, the judge is as cracked as a leaky muke egg."

A. Duhweeb raised a claw. "I just thought of a third offense," she said proudly. "The defendant is additionally charged with trespassing, and for the purpose of handing down the maximum sentence, all charges are hereby officially bundled together. Yes, willful trespassing with the intent to create mischief and mayhem in a clearly posted 'No Trespassing' area is the bundled charge. He definitely disregarded the sign."

"Let's skin him," A. Morun suggested through a cruel smile.

"No, I have an even better idea!" A. Dummi shouted. "Just boil him. Boiling in his skin is best for bringing out the flavor."

"Now, now, let's not rush to judgment here," A. Jerq said in a calming voice. "Instead, let cooler heads prevail. I suggest the better choice would be to have the punishment fit the crime. In this case, the painless unscrewing of his legs would ensure that in the future Mr. Nicholsworth's compulsion to trespass in a posted 'No Trespassing' area would no longer be a temptation for him."

Carter felt lightheaded. He thought he might faint and his legs wobbled tenuously under him. Rapidly blinking his eyes while considering what A. Jerq had just stated, he soon found his voice.

"You know the sign you're referring to never used the words 'No Trespassing' and could easily be misinterpreted; therefore, under Murphy's Law, since you tied the three charges together, I must demand a mistrial declared and a dismissal of all charges at once."

It was true. The sign didn't actually say "No Trespassing." Other than that, he had no idea what craziness he was talking, but he did remember a saying he had once heard, "When in Rome," (in this case Wimzi) "do as the Romans do."

There was a moment of total silence. Judge and jury were completely caught off guard. The mostly-sloth creatures actually seemed at a loss for words. Narrowing their eyes they looked back and forth at each other. Again they huddled.

"We've reached a verdict," A. Jerq stated after lengthy deliberations. "This court finds you, Carter Nicholsworth, guilty on all counts because we believe you are lying and terminally insane. Congratulations." The sloth sisters politely applauded the jury's unanimous decision. "Guard, release the prisoner."

A fat, bristled hog wallowed noisily out of the brush. Flies swarmed the beast's large head, several practicing takeoffs and landings from the grunter's cheesy smile. He snorted loudly as he approached Carter's makeshift cell. Hanging from a chain attached to one of the few remaining buttons on a stained military jacket the hog had obviously outgrown was a large, tarnished key. He resembled a link sausage stuffed into his jacket casing. Wheezing heavily, the odorous beast opened the door to Carter's cell. The hog's watery, bloodshot eyes looked menacingly at Carter as the boy walked quickly past him, exiting the makeshift prison.

Without warning, the hog snuck in a sneeze, just missing a dodging Carter with the overspray. Wiping the sneeze juice that was collecting under his snout onto the forearm of his slick, snot-starched sleeve, the disappointed hog removed a small book and quill from the interior of his jacket and recorded just one sneeze.

"Drats, just missed. Sign here," ordered the grumpy guard, pushing the notebook at Carter.

"Where's my bird, Nevermore?" Carter politely asked the hog. The hog, without taking his eyes from Carter's, pointed at his bulging stomach.

"Ate 'im."

"You what???" screamed a horrified Carter.

"Aw," the hog said, "ain'tcha got no sense of humor? I was just joshin' ya. 'Sides, he looked too bony to even make a decent appetizer. He'z most likely just out for a stroll look'n for a stray worm to eat—I eat worms."

"Nice," Carter said.

"Excuse me," A. Jerq interrupted. "I certainly can appreciate the profoundness of your obviously very important conversation regarding your dietary preferences, but in the interest of expediency, I'd like to move on as we have a very busy court calendar ahead of us today. You're free to go." She waved a dismissive claw at Carter in a good-bye gesture.

"Go?" Carter asked. "Go where?"

Growing increasingly impatient, the sloth angrily answered, "I have just given you a 'get out of jail free' card. Go past go and collect two hundred domas for all I care. What a moron!!!"

"You have a problem with A. Morun???" A. Morun screamed at A. Jerq.

"I said moron, Morun!" yelled A. Jerq back at her sister.

Paying little attention to the mostly-sloth creatures that were back to brain banging, Carter headed off quickly in the direction of the sunlight that peeked into the forest. He hoped to catch up to Nevermore while putting as much distance as possible between himself, the mostly-sloth sisters, and the stinky hog.

His stomach was again rumbling. Time seemed to have lost meaning. Hours were slipping like water through a strainer. How long had it been since he left Lake Mohegan? Carter had no idea. On he walked. Finding Nevermore and something to eat consumed his mind. The little bird had on occasion taken off for a day or two, but that was back in Lake Mohegan where the bird was familiar with his environment.

"Come back, Nevermore, come back," Carter called, hoping the bird would hear him. Unconsciously, with the back of his hand, Carter swiped at a tear. On he went, though the day was closing in on him and he was feeling most weary and alone. When it became so dark he could safely travel no farther, he hastily made a bed of fallen leaves. Lying on his back before exhaustion carried him off to sleep, he whispered into the night, "Come back, Nevermore. I need you."

Chapter 5
Wiggonwoggen

Early the next morning Carter woke slowly from a fitful sleep. His swollen eyes fluttered open then crossed as they attempted to focus on an object centered on his forehead. Nevermore was back. The little bird explained he had been busy exploring and had found many a strange creature while flying his overhead investigation.

Surprised and happy to have his friend back, Carter was even happier when the smell of food cooking drifted into his awareness. Nevermore flew from Carter's brow a short distance in the direction of muffled voices coming from somewhere beyond them. The small black bird landed on a fallen tree protruding from a ridge. Carter sat straight up while back and forth several times went the bird between the ridge and Carter's shoulder.

You have to see this, thought Nevermore into Carter's mind.

Getting on his hands and knees, Carter quietly crawled to the lip of the ridge and carefully eased himself into a position where he could peek over the edge without being seen.

What came into view reminded Carter of a painting he had once seen while on a school field trip to a New York City art museum. The beautifully painted landscape was permanently engraved into his memory. Dragging his mind back to the present, Carter stared down into a valley that tumbled out onto a textured countryside of variations on green. In the deep pink morning sky, the twin suns played hide and seek with soft, nubby clouds. The panorama of the valley stretched across obsessively neat rows of freshly plowed farmland. The patchwork of double-spaced lines ran to the valley's edge, where they disappeared into stacked, sharply chiseled mountains.

A third of the way down from the mountain crowns, a semi-transparent mist, like a fairy's breath on a cold winter's morning, hung motionless from invisible wires connected to a domed, square-tiled ceiling. The view filled Carter with an overwhelming sense of awe, but it was the foreground that spoke loudest to him.

He saw approximately twenty large circus-style canvas tents each brightly colored and held in place by tall center and side poles. The tents were tightly pegged at their hems to the ground. Triangular flags waved proudly from the center and side poles, snapping crisply to the commands of a strong morning breeze.

"Do you think this is some sort of circus or carnival?" Carter asked.

Perhaps, or maybe some type of county fair.

"Well, whatever it is, there sure seems to be plenty of activity down there," Carter said excitedly. From a distance, there seemed to be a sense of normalcy, the first Carter had experienced since the fog had swallowed Hunters Hut and him along with it.

Crude empty wagons rested haphazardly across a large, flattened area of grass. Four wooden spoke wheels bore the weight of each wagon's frame while several tall supports along the outer rails rose from their flatbeds. The purpose of the supports was obviously to keep each wagon's contents from spilling. Carter thought the wagons' primary use was probably to haul hay.

A tandem team of curved, long-necked creatures that looked like distant cousins of the ostrich stood on thick, muscled legs. They were harnessed together by a shaft that ran between them and was hitched to each of the wagons. Instead of feathers, these animals had thick, curly coats of a mahogany-brown wool-like substance covering their bodies. Tangled knots of dreadlocks spilled from their heads, but perhaps most unique, mechanically speaking, were the creatures' knees. Each had an upper and lower knee bulging from both legs. When they moved, they did so in a halting, herky-jerky articulated motion. Carter found himself smiling as he watched them strut about. They looked like they were just learning to walk and could topple over at any moment. It was the first time Carter had smiled in quite a while, and it felt both vaguely familiar and definitely good.

Nevermore hopped down from his mess of a nest in Carter's hair onto the prone tree trunk where the bird could look directly into his eyes. It was all Carter could do to keep himself from laughing out loud. I mean really loud . . . the bird was smiling. Imagine that, a smiling bird. How can a bird smile? Don't ask me, I'm merely the storyteller. Anyway, the fact is, Nevermore was smiling.

"What is it?" asked an amused Carter. "My ears? My freckles? My hair?" Of course, Nevermore wasn't talking.

Looking back down into the valley, not very far from the large tents, Carter saw many lean-to structures. Observing no permanent buildings, he surmised that this might be where those who tended the farms slept.

In the fields of grass to the left of the tents were rows of stalls, some with awnings and some without. Overflowing baskets bragged an assortment of food. Shuffling from one vendor to another, a milling crowd wandered aimlessly amongst the stalls.

A short distance behind the tents was an oval running track, similar to the one at Lake Mohegan High School. A gathering crowd appeared to be anticipating some scheduled event.

"People, right, Nevermore?"

Proceed with caution was the response. Carter felt that was wise advice, but at the same time he was teased with mounting curiosity. Needing to get a closer look, Carter worked his way down the long hill. Keeping a low profile so as not to be noticed, he moved carefully from one tree to another until finally he was on level ground, right at the edge of the tree line. Venturing a quick look from behind the tree concealing him, he saw he was only a short distance from a small group of individuals who seemed about his age. Carter was uncertain who they were, but one thing he was sure of was these beings were not people.

On tiptoe Carter wound his way through the shadowed underbrush camouflaging his appearance. Now close enough to hear their animated voices, it turned out to be an undisciplined curious second look from behind a tree that proved his undoing.

· · · · · · ·

Serene had been expecting Carter and watched with amusement as he took extraordinary precautions not to be seen.

Carter's eyes locked onto Serene's, who stared back. Both stood for a moment, frozen in time, as if one of them dared to move, it would scare the other off. Finally Serene flinched, gesturing for Carter to come closer.

Tentatively and somewhat reluctantly, Carter gave up the marginal security of distance to sheepishly make his way toward the gathering.

The beings had many human-like features, such as their basic frame, yet there were some distinct differences. Aside from most being willowy thin, their skin was as white as talcum. Each sported several metal bands that wrapped or spiraled up their arms. They also wore lightweight sleeveless tunics that draped over tight ankle-length leggings ending just above their large but slender bare feet. Their heads were barely covered in a fine layer of hair, each in a different, vibrant color. Pointy ears were neatly framed by their colorful hair. The odd-looking beings had exaggerated, deeply set almond-shaped eyes without lashes or brows. The pupils of their eyes were the color of a translucent green sea, while perfectly formed lips turned up at the corners in a perpetual smile. From their graceful hands grew extra long fingers, with extra long fingernails matching the color of their eyes.

All of them looked pretty much genetically similar except for one who was very different.

Nevermore, in a defensive move to intimidate the strangers, puffed up his feathers and stretched as tall as he could in a failed attempt to appear fearsome. The beings didn't seem all that impressed with or frightened by the fluffy bird.

"Welcome," said the one who had made eye contact with Carter. The tone was warm and familiar, as if there had been a close relationship in the past. Hesitating for a moment, Carter found his voice.

"This here bird is my friend Nevermore," he said, pointing at his head. "My name is Carter Nicholsworth."

The creature, never taking focus from Carter's eyes, said, "Yes, we know."

"You know," responded Carter quickly. It was more of a statement than a question. After another moment of collecting his thoughts, he said, "Well, in that case, since you know who we are, perhaps you can tell us who you are, where we are, and how you know who we are."

"The first two requests are fairly easy, the third, a bit more complicated and will have to wait for an answer. My name is Serene, only child of Elderwiser. Let me introduce my friends."

One by one, pointing to each being, Serene called them by name. They each took a step forward, bowed deeply then stepped back. Politely, Carter answered every bow with an awkward bow of his own.

"Closest to me is Ushi, next to him is Herkifer, then the twins Ferbert and Fermond. After them is Lyke, then Retann, Lohden, Iat, Zebenuza, and Abogamento. We are Wiggwoggs, and you are in the territory of Wiggonwoggen, which is located on the orb of Aeiea under the twin sister suns Suva and Ahneese. You have just passed through Wimzi Territory, incredibly fortunate, I might add, to have made it out alive."

Carter stood motionless, without expression. The response from the stranger left more questions unanswered than answered. "Is an orb a planet?" he wondered. "And if so, where is Earth?"

"A little more of a geography lesson?" Serene offered.

"Sure, but could you please take it a little more slowly? This is all quite a bit overwhelming and an awful lot to digest."

The Wiggwogg reached deep into the interior of a rope-belted tunic, producing a folded map. "This may help." Serene sat on the ground, carefully undoing the old map. The other Wiggwoggs, taking their cue from Serene, also sat. Carter followed suit, sitting next to Serene.

"We are here, close to our northwestern border," Serene said, the long fingernail of an index finger pointing to their present location. "As you know from your recent experience, Wimzi Territory lies over here, just beyond our border and reality. To the south of Wimzi and west of Wiggonwoggen is Dweeg Territory then Stanelhooven, the Gushkin Territory, Bunnicloven, and the Dwarf Forest of Sarwinnia. South of us is the Esbolien Desert, the Land of Ferrins, LeMorte Forest, and even farther south, the Unexplored Territory. To the north is The Great Sea Valion and the island of Athulian." A few of the Wiggwoggs looked away upon the mention of the island and shifted uncomfortably.

"You will have a better sense of what is where in good time. I think that is enough school for now," Serene said, refolding the map. "You have been given much information to try to understand in a short time."

"Does your bracelet serve a purpose?" asked the Wiggwogg named Retann.

Carter looked down his arm. "Why, that's a wristwatch to tell what time it is. It measures time in hours, minutes, and seconds."

"We have no need for such a machine here on Aeiea as we have no knowledge of hours, minutes, or seconds," Retann said. "We eat when we are hungry and sleep when we are tired. We live outdoors and make our beds on the ground under shelters. Our intention is to always be in harmony with nature. If for some unusual reason we need to know the passing of time, we use the rhythm of sisters Suva and Ahneese to guide us."

With Serene in the lead, the group walked in the direction of the tents. The Wiggwogg in front of the band of friends strode with the apparent confidence of a leader. "Have you any idea," questioned Serene, "how you might have happened to be here?"

"Not a clue," Carter shot back, "but I have a sense you might have some ideas."

Serene immediately changed the subject. "How about we go to the races? You look like you could use some fun."

Skirting the tents, the group walked toward a large crowd of other Wiggwoggs pressed several deep along a wooden railing that circled the oval track. Making their way to an opening, Carter found himself standing in front of a well-groomed racetrack, watching a trotting parade of small, stubby, four-legged animals kick up dust as they passed.

"Baby hippos or maybe pygmies?" Carter inquired.

"I don't know what baby or pygmy hippos are. These are full-grown oomaduma from the Esbolien Desert, especially bred for racing."

Riding atop each beast sat a Wiggwogg youth, clinging to braided reins of coarse black hair growing from the thick necks of their oomaduma. An assortment of transparent glass beads woven into the braided neck hair of the beasts dazzled brightly in the afternoon light. Anxious jockeys sat bareback on their oomadumas, fidgeting with excitement while adjusting their goggles and gear.

A distinctive-looking Wiggwogg, dressed in a pair of snappy pinstriped knickers, a navy blazer, wide-brimmed straw hat, and bow tie stood unmoving at the starting line with megaphone in hand. Stuck in the headband of the Wiggwogg's hat was a card reading *OFFICIAL,* but his real name was J. Wally Boogieboozenboil. No one knew what the "J" stood for and most thought he had made it up to make himself appear important.

The animals lumbered back and forth across the starting line under the weight of their nervous riders, one actually coming over to the crowd of onlookers at the rail to see if possibly anyone was offering a special treat. Finally, with the oomaduma mostly lined up in reasonable order, J. Wally said into his megaphone, "Riders, steadyyyyyyyyy, readyyyyyyyyy, annnnnnnnnnnnnnd.........GO!!!"

The crowd cheered loudly, and in a great cloud of whirling dust, off thundered the oomaduma, most in the right direction. A few laggards trudged listlessly to the track's edge where they nibbled grass and brown-faced golden flowers. Frustrated jockeys in fancy, colorful shirts with large identifying numbers on their backs pulled hard at their reins and slapped loudly at the oomadumas' exposed flanks. Impossible-to-keep promises were whispered into the oomadumas' small, twitching ears. Some embarrassed jockeys spoke gentle, encouraging words to their mounts, while others simply yelled at their beasts in frustration. One emotional and obviously disappointed jockey simply buried his face in his oomaduma's wrinkled neck and wept.

It was all to no avail as some oomaduma obviously had a different agenda than their riders on this particular day.

Meanwhile, in the thick of things, three heavy-hoofed oomadumas bumped and jostled their way through much of the race and were now jockeying for position on the inside rail for the lead. The volume level of the crowd increased with anticipation as the animals charged with nostrils flaring around the final turn of the race and into the homestretch. At this point, the jockeys went for their whips.

Nevermore seemed to be enjoying the race as he hopped excitedly from one foot to the other while making a bigger mess of Carter's already messy hair. Surely this race would have held almost anyone's attention, but Carter's mind was spinning with so many unanswered questions.

"I'm sorry," he said, turning a serious face to Serene. "I'm preoccupied with so much I don't understand. It seems that more answers only lead to far more questions. You say I'm on Aeiea. Where is Aeiea? How did I get from Earth to Aeiea? More importantly, how do I get back? And certainly, not that it is at the top of my list of questions, but I am curious. Can you tell me something of Wimzi?"

"Oh yes," Serene replied. "It is no surprise that you have many questions, Carter. I think the best course would be to take it slowly, one small bite at a time, so you can better digest all the information. To your first question, Aeiea is the third orb of seven thrown by Suva at her younger sister, Ahneese, who had angered her by claiming to be the hotter of the two suns. You know how sisters can be.

"As to the location of Aeiea, it is located in the twenty-third solar system of the seventh galaxy. Getting you here was not easy, and I imagine getting you back may be even more difficult, but perhaps I speak out of turn."

Carter didn't quite know what to make of the bizarre information his mind was desperately attempting to process. "How do you know all this?" he eventually asked.

"Elderwiser," was Serene's single-word reply. After a brief hesitation allowing for Carter to catch up, Serene continued. "In regard to Wimzi, you are most fortunate to be standing here in Wiggonwoggen. Very few who happen in, happen out. Whatever your wildest mind can possibly imagine thrives in Wimzi. It is a land of lies and dead ends. Nothing is true or real. Masks and trick mirrors, stairs leading up to doors that open into walls, a place where up is down and in is out, where good is bad, and bad is good, where what is, isn't, where what was, wasn't, and what will be, won't. This is the mad, mind-twisting playground of Wimzi. If you know what's good for you, stay out."

Carter felt overwhelmed. "Can you help me . . .?" He hid his face in his hands. Taking a moment to compose himself, he looked up into Serene's soft green eyes and finished his question. "Can you help me find my way home? I don't know where to start. I don't even know if it's at all possible." Tears welled in Carter's eyes, blurring his vision.

"In a lifetime, sooner or later we are all faced with surrendering that which we hold closest to our hearts," Serene said. "Energy, dimensions, and forces you have no concept of are at work here. Nothing is for nothing. You are here for a reason, and like a bud opening to the promise of a flower, you cannot rush the bloom. There are always choices, none without consequences. However, choosing to fight against the perfect order of all things is an unwinnable battle. Better to relax and surrender to the lesson."

"But I'm just a boy," Carter said, feeling the unsteadiness of bewilderment in the context of Serene's words and the recent turn of events in his short life. "I have lost everything."

"No," Serene replied, wearing the Wiggwoggs' permanent smile. "You need to alter the way you see this situation. Your perception is your reality. By simply shifting your perception, you change your reality. You have not lost anything; rather, you have gained everything. You are so much more than you understand, and that is why you are here. The spirit can never be lost, only abandoned. On this journey, your spirit will help Suva and Ahneese light our path. You must trust me, Carter."

Lowering his shoulders while relaxing the muscles of his jaw, Carter felt the tension drain from his body. He even managed a half smile in appreciation for Serene's comforting presence.

"Let us have some food. You must be hungry." Serene led Carter and the band of Wiggwoggs toward a row of long tables laden with a wide assortment of cakes, fruits, and vegetables. Unfamiliar Wiggwoggs were milling about overflowing baskets of produce. They were bartering their services for food with farmers who stood behind their tables. Although Carter did not recognize any of the food, it all looked and smelled delicious.

Sitting at one of the many long tables with Serene and his band of Wiggwoggs, Carter ate until his swollen stomach hurt. The realization that several of the adult Wiggwoggs were staring at him and that he had nothing to offer as pay or trade for his meal discomfited him.

Watching Carter's awkward moment seemed to amuse Serene. "Don't worry, my friend. Remember I said nothing is for nothing?"

It was at this exact moment that Carter became aware of two things. First, he observed Serene often spoke in riddles. The second and more profound thing he noticed was that, in his relatively short life, Carter could not remember a single time of ever having been referred to as "my friend."

· · · · · · ·

Carter's unpracticed back muscles ached. Sweat made working with the slippery, smooth handle of the hoe difficult. Twice it flew from his hands—one time almost hitting Herkifer. Apologizing, an embarrassed Carter wiped his moist hands, which were growing a fresh crop of tender blisters, on his shorts. The ever-smiling Wiggwogg came over to Carter and without saying a word simply patted him on the shoulder.

Working hard with the Wiggwoggs, harvesting and stacking a variety of melons, some with greenish-yellow shiny skins, others with darker coverings that had the coarse texture of a mesh net, was how Carter spent the remainder of the hot afternoon. *At least I've done a hard day's work for my food,* he thought. *The "nothing is for nothing" riddle is solved.*

After an early dinner, Carter joined a number of Wiggwoggs who were building several lean-to sleeping shelters. The crude structures were hewn by axe from the freshly cut lower branches of trees surrounding the outer edges of the valley. A stiff frame of tree limbs was lashed together, set at a forty-five degree angle, tied then pegged taut to the ground. The criss-crossed roof of pine boughs was positioned onto the top of the frame and covered with dry hay that was also strewn on the floor of the lean-to. Bales of hay were stacked atop each other at both sides of the shelter to ward off the wind, and a rolled-up tarp to protect from rain was tied across the upper horizontal head frame limb, leaving the entrance wide open.

Cozy, thought Carter standing back from the entrance of the lean-to while admiring his handiwork. His mind did a backward flip landing him squarely in the familiar forest of Wickedwood, where he stood staring at the two windows he had just installed above and to each side of the perma-nently open mouth of the Hunters Hut.

It felt like a lifetime ago.

Late that night, with the remnant embers of a communal campfire still pulsing, Serene sat cross-legged in front of Carter's lean-to, watching the boy toss and turn in his fitful sleep.

Coiled tight as a snake ready to strike, then shooting his legs down and his arms out, Carter struggled with his demons. Spasms of fear poked at his thin body. In his dark dream, he ran frantically, stumbling over tree roots, at times falling hard to the ground and then, trying desperately to catch his breath, he scrambled to his hands and knees to regain his footing. The panic that held him prisoner made getting up to continue running seem impossible. When he finally was able to stand, his normally cooperative legs felt weighted. No matter how fast he ran, the calm women's voices whispering terror into his nightmare were gaining on him—

"You must stay,

if on this day,

you come our way."

Chapter 6
The Circle of Power

Flutters of red-orange light warmed the skin of Carter's eyelids, bringing him out of his troubled night's sleep. The morning was punctuated by the excited voices of children discovering gifts brought by the new day. Flower petals floated on the breath of a light breeze, scattering the fragrant ensembles on the ground as each bloom completed another cycle of life. A spray of young Wiggwoggs laughed and tumbled past the open end of Carter's lean-to, making their way down to a rolling green meadow. From around the edge of Carter's shelter peeked the face of Serene. "Do you swim?"

"I sure do," responded Carter, shaking off the cobwebs of his bad night. He considered himself a good swimmer, having learned to swim at the young age of five in the warm, algae-laced water of Lake Mohegan. Swimming was one of the few achievements that encouraged his otherwise fragile confidence.

"We are going to my favorite place to swim, but it will take half a day's running to get there. If you are up for it, follow me," called Serene, heading off in the direction the children had taken. Carter jumped up and ran after the Wiggwogg. The plush green meadow rolled on for quite a distance but eventually tired, fading first to a washed-out blond then to the subtle color of wheat. The pace was steady, but Carter was in good shape from climbing the hills of Wickedwood. He liked to run and had often thought that when he got into high school he would like to try out for the track team and be a long distance runner. All that seemed so far away and long ago.

Up ahead, Carter could see a swinging suspension bridge crossing a river. Once on the other side of the river the transition from grass to a mixture of sand and grass hindered Carter's speed. Eventually the topography leading down to a small beach at the water's edge transformed once again, this time to a clutter of loose rock. Worried about turning an ankle, Carter slowed, falling still farther behind Serene who, with confident agility, easily maneuvered over the minefield of rock.

Boulders snuggled together, leaving barely enough room between them to title this location a beach. Climbing a large boulder, Serene gestured to Carter, who was about thirty or so lengths behind, to catch up. In a few moments the two were standing side by side atop the rock, gazing out across a vast body of water. In the far distance, what appeared to Carter as an island hunkered low in the water like a stilled predator patiently lying in wait for its next meal.

Pointing at the dark body of land growing from the water, Serene informed Carter, "That is the island of Athulian, homeland of the Gootz. The sea before us, surrounding Athulian, is The Great Sea Valion."

Upon closer visual examination, Carter honed in on a spliced spine of foothills rising from the eastern edge of the island that led to a chain of mountains running the entire length of Athulian. A jagged stroke from an artist's pen separated mountains from the sky, drawing Carter's eye from one of the tallest peaks down to the sea. The entire face of the mountain range appeared dark and textured in mottled shades of charcoal while an ominous spirit of evil radiated from the island.

Pulled by curiosity to Athulian's mysterious and sullen presence, Carter felt his body tense. *Danger*, thought Nevermore into Carter's mind.

"I am going to tell you a story," said Serene, "and it may help to still some of the choppy waters you struggle to navigate. It is connected to the purpose of your being here on Aeiea. Come. Sit here next to me. This may take a bit of time."

Carter sat uneasily next to Serene atop the surface of the boulder, gazing out across the sea.

"At the close of the thirteenth era," Serene began, gently trying to calm Carter's feelings of apprehension, "there lived an isolated tribe of Wiggwoggs in the southeastern corner of Wiggonwoggen. Their physical appearance was very different from ours and they had a wild look about them. They were known as the Gootz. Secretive and nomadic, the Gootz chose to live independent and separate from the larger family of Wiggwoggs. Stealing from hardworking Wiggwogg farmers, the Gootz also foraged for their food in the surrounding forests of Wiggonwoggen. They followed a charismatic master who ruled over his cowering subjects with brutal intimidation. The leader of the Gootz, who now goes by the name of The Grinder, practiced the skills of dark deeds. He worshipped the power of control.

"The Circle of Power, entrusted to Elderwiser for safekeeping, was used as an instrument of harmony and abundance intended for all citizens of Aeiea to share. It is common knowledge throughout the territories of Aeiea that the Gootz leader snatched then betrayed this sacred gift once protected by the good Wiggwoggs of Wiggonwoggen.

"Physically, the Circle of Power is a very simple round gold medallion with raised letters on its surface from a language unknown anywhere on Aeiea," Serene continued. "The medallion was affixed to a gold chain and worn secretly by my father, Elderwiser, the wizard of Wiggonwoggen, around his neck and under his robes. He understood the importance of his responsibility. As instructed, he wore the medallion over his heart, only removing it briefly once a year to be returned for a ceremony of renewal at the sacred tulk tree.

"The specific day of the ceremony is always ushered in on the breath of the seasonal solstice marking the beginning of summer. It was customary upon his annual sojourn to the remote tulk tree that Elderwiser would remove the chain from around his neck and place the medallion in a small opening carved by time into the core of the tree. If anyone watching thought to retrieve the Circle of Power from inside the tree, they would have been surprised to find it missing, disappeared."

Carter was intrigued. Something here sounded vaguely familiar, although he could not quite figure out what it was. His mind fastened tightly onto Serene's unfolding story.

"Only a small number of Wiggwoggs sworn to the medallion's protection knew of the whereabouts of the beautiful tulk tree or of the sacred annual ritual. These most trusted of Wiggwogg elders were known as Elderwiser's Council. My father understood that power has the potential to be abused. Power must be handled very carefully, with great awareness, respect, and wisdom. In the wrong hands, this energy has the ability to be used for the most foul and wicked purposes, becoming a volatile agent of evil."

Serene moved closer to Carter as if the words about to be spoken might somehow be taken by a wayward gust of wind and find their way to unintended ears.

"The tulk tree blossoms but once a year with a single magnificent golden flower," continued Serene, "and the brief life of the bloom is over in less than an hour. In the drama's closing moments, a puff of smoke rises from the opening in the tree where the medallion has been placed. In that same moment, from high on a branch, a beautiful golden flower then blooms.

"Directly below the branch from where the golden flower blossomed, Elderwiser would sit quietly with his eyes closed, legs folded in the lotus position, arms resting on his legs, and his hands open to the sky. When it was ready, into the waiting hands of the wizard the withering flower floated. The golden flower was, as are all things, in transition. Now, in the hands of Elderwiser, the flower would continue its transformation into the Circle of Power.

"The rest of this tale has been stitched together from the many stories passed down through generations of Wiggwoggs," continued Serene. "I cannot swear to the reliability of what I am about to tell you, but over the years we have heard enough to piece together a reasonable chronology of events surrounding the loss of the Circle of Power.

"It appears that the leader of the Gootz, jealous of Elderwiser's stewarding of the Circle of Power, spent nearly three hundred years in tireless pursuit of the priceless necklace. His chief of spies whispered a host of rumors involving a golden medallion and an enchanted tree. The Grinder found the stories interesting enough, but in the spirit of eternal distrust, he decided the source of the stories was suspect and unreliable. He didn't attach much credibility to the accuracy of his agent's questionable information.

"It was quite by accident that one brilliant solstice morning while journeying along the River Sme, The Grinder happened upon the ancient and quite rare black tulk tree. He had never before seen such a tree. Standing at the tree's base, the leader of the Gootz was mesmerized. Was the tree growing so fast that the last time he had passed this part of the forest he had entirely missed seeing it because it was small and unremarkable? How was it possible that for all of his years wandering the forests of Aeiea he could possibly have missed a tree as unusual as this?

"Just prior to The Grinder's arrival at the tulk tree, Elderwiser and his Council had temporarily interrupted the sacred ceremony, abandoning the scene to investigate what sounded to them like the tread of an intruder. Elderwiser had already placed the medallion in its secret hiding place and the irreversible process had begun. They intended to be gone for only a moment or two, but in the heat of pursuit lost track, as Wiggwoggs often do, of how long they had been gone. Their search of the area proved unsuccessful. If there was an intruder, by the time the Wiggwoggs arrived, he had vanished. Unfortunately the Wiggwoggs had no idea as to the significance of their absence. As fate would have it, at this critical moment, the vulnerable treasure was left totally unprotected. That was a most regrettable mistake."

Carter held on tightly to every word as Serene continued.

"Fascinated by the breathtaking elegance of the tulk, the hungry Gootz scavenger inhaled the sweet-scented aroma coming from high up in the tree. Mistaking the precious flower growing from a lofty branch for a golden piece of fruit and driven by hunger, the Gootz leader began to scale the tree. Climbing through that small window of time left open by the unsuspecting Wiggwoggs, The Grinder finally arrived at the tree's limb where the fruit should have been. Instead, as he reached between the leafing branches to pick what he thought was something edible, a withering flower fell from the branch to the ground below. Unable to find the object of his climb, the frustrated Gootz leader cursed aloud and returned to the ground. He went over to kick the brown-flowered imposter but to his astonishment, in the place where the dead flower should have been, sister suns Suva and Ahneese had focused their attention on a golden chain with an attached medallion lying on the ground. The prize glistened brilliantly in the morning light. Picking up the chain, The Grinder examined it closely before realizing what amazing good fortune had just been delivered into his hands.

"Celebrating his stroke of luck while tightly grasping his treasure to his leathery lips, The Grinder temporarily forgot his hunger. He tauntingly thrust his dirty, sweat-streaked face in the direction of Suva and Ahneese and began howling his success at the twins like a wild beast. The leader of the Gootz had finally found his long-sought beloved, the Circle of Power.

"What he couldn't have known was that unless the medallion was worn constantly over the heart, its power would be compromised. He also was unaware that unless this ritual he had inadvertently stumbled upon was repeated annually on the summer solstice, his newly found treasure would eventually weaken and finally be reduced to a shadow of its original strength. In time, it would become little more than a handsome piece of jewelry. And that," informed Serene, "is exactly what is happening now, making the desperate leader of the Gootz even more dangerous. Out of fear of losing his precious medallion, upon reaching the island of Athulian, The Grinder took his prize and hid it away in a secret vault, never to be worn over his heart.

"The corruption of power led the immoral Gootz leader and his tribe to the addiction of insatiable material desires and impossible longings. More was never enough. What they gained in ill-gotten treasure, The Grinder has paid for dearly in the currency of conscience. Now they are morally bankrupt. The Gootz have lost any sense of happiness, and any of the small scraps of goodness they had managed to salvage are today entirely spent. Over time, the Gootz's greed and hunger for power has increased while the actual strength of the medallion has been on the wane. To compensate for the diminishing strength of the Circle of Power, the fearful Gootz, using sheer brutality, now attack their neighboring territories at will, plundering, torturing, and killing as they go. This is unacceptable. The Circle of Power must be returned to Elderwiser."

"Tell me more about Elderwiser," interrupted Carter.

"You shall know in due time. May I continue?" Serene asked in a mildly annoyed tone.

"Most certainly, I'm all ears," Carter replied. Smiling broadly, he pointed with index fingers from both hands at his exaggerated ears. "I thought you were through."

Serene's face softened. "The Circle of Power must be honored. In the wrong hands, as we have sadly witnessed, it has the potential for unspeakable consequences. It was some time later, on the night of the theft, that the Gootz leader along with his followers used the light generated by the Circle of Power to make their escape from Wiggonwoggen. Skirting the edge of the territory of Wimzi under the cover of a moonless night, their pilfered prize safely secured around the neck of the thief, they snuck out of

Wiggonwoggen. The leader of the Gootz and his community made their way to the uninhabited island of Athulian, where they settled. At first, it was quiet in the territories, but it was far from quiet on Athulian. The Gootz were busy building a number of castle fortresses, inventing weapons, and devising strategies from which to carry out ambitious plans.

"The stolen resources of conquered civilizations would be put to use building their utopian empire of Gootz supremacy. They saw the purpose of power as simply the means of achieving domination, their domination over all of Aeiea. Insatiable desires have created a population on Athulian without moral principles. Inbreeding has taken its toll on the mental as well as physical health of the Gootz but not on their inventive skills when it comes to the art of mayhem and butchery.

"There was a name on record for the Gootz leader during the time he was a citizen of Wiggonwoggen, but that name has long since been lost," Serene continued. "Since pulling up stakes and moving to the island of Athulian, the bloodthirsty Gootz leader has carried out many murderous attacks on nearby lands. His terrible cruelty and his disgusting body odor have struck fear and revulsion into the hearts of all citizens of Aeiea, except of course the Wimzicals, who fear nothing nor are disgusted by anything. The king of the Gootz earned through his brutal reputation his name The Grinder." Serene spoke his name in a hushed whisper, as if saying it aloud might somehow invoke a surprise visit from the dreaded Gootz leader.

After a moment's silence, Carter cleared his throat. "The Grinder," he repeated. "Well, this is all most interesting, and I must say, Serene, you are quite the storyteller, but what does any of this have to do with my situation?"

"I know that your being here is not by accident or coincidence," answered Serene. "You are here by intention. We have been waiting a very long time for your arrival, even before your most recent birth. It is now our destiny to reclaim that which was entrusted to and wrongfully taken from Elderwiser. If you want more information, and I'm sure you do, you will have to speak directly to Elderwiser. After all, he is the one who brought you here."

Chapter 7
Surprise

The rest of the day seemed to pass by Carter in slow motion as if in a dream. Feelings of hope then hopelessness washed over him, like Valion's waves rolling onto the beach's apron, pushing and pulling at a waterlogged gathering of driftwood. Sitting alone, he watched the Wiggwoggs splash and play in the shallow waters. Laughter coming from the sea seemed distant, echoing as if passing through a tunnel. Like a flat stone skimming the still early morning surface of Lake Mohegan, Carter's mind skipped through his memory of waking from his frightening dream. It seemed the key to much of the mystery that had become his life was now in the possession of Elderwiser.

Carter did swim, but it was more to prove to Serene his aquatic skills rather than to join in the fun. He swam in his shorts whereas the Wiggwoggs swam in their tunics and leggings. Serene was relaxed, enjoying the water.

Once back on the beach Serene turned to Carter and said, "For now, I have taken you as far as I can. When the time is right, you shall meet the wizard of Wiggonwoggen."

· · · · · · ·

"From the very beginning of known history in Wiggonwoggen," Serene told Carter one night, "Elderwiser has been the leader of the Wiggwoggs."

It had been several days since the beach excursion. Serene and Carter were now inseparable as their friendship deepened. The two youths sat facing each other just inside the entrance of Carter's lean-to. "It is believed by some that Elderwiser was not originally from Wiggonwoggen but rather came to the territory from the south, looking much as he does now, walking calmly out from the scorching sands of the Esbolien Desert. It is impossible to survive in that hostile desert for more than a few days even with food and water. Yet Elderwiser supposedly arrived in Wiggonwoggen empty handed and refreshed without thirst or hunger from those unforgiving wastelands.

"Others believe the master of the Wiggwoggs did not come from the Esbolien Desert at all but rather from the north," Serene continued. "Their story is that of a great fish who swam out of the River Sme and onto the river's bank one night at the site of the ancient tulk tree. Upon doing so, the mighty fish was instantly transformed by The Source into Elderwiser and entrusted with the responsibility of protecting the sacred gift of the Circle of Power. As a reward for his stewardship, Elderwiser was gifted with the power of a wizard and promised eternity.

"Now with the Circle of Power no longer in his trust, the promise has been undone," Serene said solemnly. "Elderwiser still has great strength and wisdom, but he is for the first time beginning to show physical signs that impermanence never sleeps. When asked which, if either, story is true, Elderwiser simply smiles and says he's too old and doesn't remember. I recall one time when I was young asking him where he came from. He picked me up and, holding me in his arms, looked upward and pointed his finger toward the sky. It's as if it's as much a mystery to him as it is to his questioners. I think you will be pleasantly surprised when you finally meet him."

With the story complete, and without invitation, Serene reached across the gap separating the two and awkwardly hugged Carter. "Friends," said the Wiggwogg, making a statement of intent.

"Friends," echoed Carter.

"That's good," Serene replied. "In the days ahead, we will need to be."

· · · · · · ·

Serene's history is also quite interesting and certainly worth the telling. So is that of the culture of Wiggonwoggen and the background of those who are considered the young leader's closest friends.

On rare occasions, when all the children of suns Suva and Ahneese lined up in the sky, one directly behind the other, it would signal the ritual time for Elderwiser to climb the sacred Mount Maluuk. The old wizard would make his pilgrimage all the way to the freezing summit of the tallest mountain in all the territories, where he would remain for twenty days and twenty nights. He would take no nourishment, and his only clothing was a simple lightweight robe that ended at his ankles. With the exception of his long staff, which he was never without, Elderwiser carried nothing.

One time Elderwiser actually stayed on the mountain for one hundred thirteen nights. When he did not return after a month, a rescue party was sent up the mountain to find him. For weeks the Wiggwoggs scoured every inch of the bleak, foreboding landscape. After thoroughly searching above and below every ledge and crevice on Mount Maluuk, the wizard was eventually given up for lost. It was thought the great leader of the Wiggwoggs would never be seen again.

Fate, however, had other plans. When Elderwiser finally did come down from the mountain, he was asked by the overjoyed Wiggwoggs how it was that they who had searched so long and hard could possibly have missed him. Elderwiser laughed and told the Wiggwoggs they had not missed him but actually passed right by him on more than one occasion, with several using his shoulder to help pull themselves up. He had not wanted to be found and so he disguised himself as just another boulder.

When the leader of the Wiggwoggs was finally ready to return home from Mount Maluuk, he carried a gift for the Wiggwoggs who had been grieving the loss of their spiritual leader. Claiming the present he proudly carried on his shoulders was a blessing given him by The Source, Elderwiser told the Wiggwoggs that the name of his gift was Serene.

The integrity of the leader of the Wiggwoggs had never been in doubt. No one questioned the circumstances or origin of Elderwiser's gift but rather simply accepted the generosity of the sage with loving hearts and abundant gratitude. Besides, the incident happened so long ago that the children of the children's children who witnessed the event had long since moved on and the only remaining memory of what actually happened was captured in the handed-down story.

Even though by appearance Serene had the physical features of a Wiggwogg and Elderwiser did not, Serene was acknowledged by all as the rightful heir of the ancient Wiggwogg. Serene was a natural leader and soon became a mentor to the youth of Wiggonwoggen. While the ageless Elderwiser remained forever old, Serene remained forever young. Now with the loss of the Circle of Power, all that was starting to change. Time had begun to nip at the heels of the great wizard.

It is common knowledge amongst all Aeieans that Wiggwoggs are by nature gentle beings, eating only that which grows from the ground. Just as surely as an oomaduma can't fly, unlike their neighboring Wimzicals, neither can a Wiggwogg lie. The citizens of Wiggonwoggen come easily to laughter and live a communal life as one big family helping one another as needed. They are good neighbors to the citizens of the other territories as well, trading fairly for their goods and services. If a Wiggwogg chooses to mate, their union is for life and beyond. Neither fear of punishment or reprisal in the afterworld are considerations in determining their standards of social behavior. Wiggwoggs do not worship desire or materialism in their simple lives. Their reward is abundance. Citizens of Wiggonwoggen are grateful for all they have and have all they need.

Because of their peaceful disposition, the Wiggwoggs had never acquired or ever felt the need for weapons of any kind, even to defend themselves. Some might consider this a bit naïve, but it had always worked for them in the past. A growing drumbeat of aggression spreading throughout the territories from the land of Athulian was beginning to cause the Wiggwoggs to reconsider. There was much debate on the subject with no immediate common resolution.

There is one other thing: Long ago when Elderwiser came down from Mount Maluuk with his surprise gift to the Wiggwoggs, he was so pleased at their loving acceptance of his offer that he gave the Wiggwoggs a second gift. Elderwiser shared one of his most closely guarded secrets—the secret of invisibility, and even more. He showed the Wiggwoggs how they too could turn themselves into a boulder as he had done while on the mountain or, for that matter, multiples of anything or anyone they set their mind to. They could also simply become invisible. The leader of the Wiggwoggs warned that this powerful magic was not to be used frivolously, for to do so would result in them being unable to return to who they were.

As for Serene's inner circle of friends, they all seemed to play easily and work hard together without complaint. The young Wiggwoggs who were there at Carter's first encounter with Serene were never far away from their leader. Carter had noticed how each was different from the other yet there seemed a common thread that bound them to their friendship. Without question, they were easy and accepting of Serene's leadership. Following Serene's direction, they welcomed Carter as one of them. A transfer student from a world away, the young Earthling was easily accepted into their fraternity.

Friendship was a whole new experience for Carter Nicholsworth but one with which he was growing increasingly comfortable.

· · · · · · ·

One day the group was playing a sport with a net and ball that reminded Carter of volleyball except in this game the large ball was about the size of a beach ball. Ushi, who was on the front line, jumped and hit the ball hard over the net. Serene, who had been playing opposite Ushi, had jumped to block the shot and took the full force of the spiked ball directly to the face. The Wiggwogg fell stunned to the ground. Immediately the other Wiggwoggs circled their fallen leader.

"Stand back!" Retann shouted. "Give her room to breathe."

"She needs water," Lyke yelled. Instantly Iat ran off to fetch water. Carter bent and cradled his friend's head in his arms while Ushi stood stunned at the net.

"Serene, can you hear me? Are you all right?" Carter asked. In a moment, Serene's eyes fluttered open. A collective sigh of relief went up from the group. It took just a little while longer before Carter's reality integrated the words he thought he had just heard spoken by Retann and Lyke. "Give her . . . she needs . . ." Did he really hear that?

Carter looked down into Serene's glazed eyes that appeared to be having a hard time focusing. "Are you a g-g-girl?" he asked haltingly. He tried to say the words without stammering but they got stuck in his throat and came out in a stutter.

"Well, I am a female," Serene confirmed. "What did you think?"

She had caught Carter in one of those moments when the mind decides to take an unannounced time out. He was staring down at Serene, his mouth hanging open. Just at the last moment, Carter sucked back the saliva that threatened to waterfall over his lower lip.

"What difference does it make?" she asked impatiently. Slowly and a bit wobbly, she sat up, rubbing her sore face.

"It makes a huge difference," Carter answered. "I never thought you might be a girl. You led me to believe . . . Why didn't you . . . ? I never thought that . . . It always seemed . . . You always looked . . ."

The Wiggwoggs stared at Carter, who seemed incapable of completing a sentence. I guess you could say that Carter's already taxed mind was in crisis, experiencing somewhat of a meltdown or, at best, a temporary malfunction. Rational thinking, never mind a finished sentence, was for the moment out of the question.

"Carter, what exactly is it you are trying to say?" Serene asked pensively.

Looking down at the ground while trying desperately to compose his thoughts, Carter finally said, "For some reason I never considered the possibility that you might be a girl. Not that there is anything wrong with girls. I just have never . . . well, before, I really didn't have any friends. Outside of my mother, a couple of aunts, one cousin, and a few teachers, I don't think I ever said more than ten words to a girl. Not that I'm prejudiced, because I'm not, I just really never understood . . . I don't know how . . ."

It was at about this moment that Carter's mouth gratefully shut down.

Serene got to her feet. "Let's see if I can help," she said, pacing back and forth while rotating her tender jaw. You could see her busy mind collecting and sorting her thoughts. When she finally stopped pacing, she turned just a few inches from where Carter was standing and looked straight into his eyes. "Stop me if I am not making sense or you disagree with what I am saying. I believe you are uncomfortable because your reality has been turned upside down. You have had quite a bit of that lately, and with your inexperience with friendship, you were just learning to trust. Now this.

"Well, Carter, nothing has really changed. There was no intentional deception. I am who I am, and you are who you are. Our friendship has been growing in spite of our obvious physical as well as spatial differences. Why not just relax and keep doing what we have been doing? It seemed to be working just fine, don't you agree?"

Yes, thought Nevermore to Carter. *Just fine. Don't get in the way of yourself and ruin the first real friendship of your life. I mean, besides me, of course.*

"You're right as usual, Nevermore," Carter said aloud. Serene squinted her eyes while looking sideways at Carter. No matter how many times she had overheard Carter's one-way conversations with Nevermore, she was always surprised when it happened, never ceasing to be amused at the process. As for Carter, his life had recently taken such a radical turn that to him little should have come as a surprise. Yet nothing could have prepared him for what lay just ahead.

Chapter 8
Take a Hike

By early evening a large number of Wiggwoggs had gathered and were milling about an open area behind the lean-tos. They talked in small groups or sat in a loose circle around the great communal campfire, singing. Warmed by the blazing fire and a full stomach, Carter took a cue from Serene, who beckoned with a sideways nod of her head and excused herself from two elder Wiggwoggs with whom she had been talking. Several others of Serene's gang also slipped out from the gathering, fading quietly into the shadowy forest surrounding the campgrounds. A trail partially covered by a thick carpet of mulching leaves still damp from an afternoon's rain squished underfoot.

The clan of Wiggwoggs and Carter quickly caught up with Serene, who had been waiting for them. Carter had not noticed earlier, but now became aware that each Wiggwogg was carrying a backpack and holding a tall walking stick. Without saying a word, Serene handed Carter an extra pack and his own walking stick.

Following Ushi and Serene, Carter and the other Wiggwoggs made their way deeper into the darkening forest. *What's happening?* Nevermore asked into Carter's mind. *Where are we going?*

"I would say by the looks of it we are going on a night hike."

"Shhhhhhhhhh," Serene whispered annoyed over her shoulder.

Ushi, who was in the lead, set the pace. He was the fastest runner of the group and could maintain a loping gait for long distances without tiring. The boy from Earth couldn't help noticing how gracefully the Wiggwogg navigated the overgrown forest path.

Carter thought that Ushi's broad forehead, long nose, and pointed ears somewhat resembled what a hairless wolf's face might look like. When the "Wolfwogg" smiled, which was not often, his two sharp upper canine teeth slightly overlapped his bottom lip.

Once, Ushi, who was the tallest of the adventurers, told Carter that he could hear things before they happened. He also mentioned that he did not talk much because he was too busy listening and you could not do both well at the same time. Maybe that's why it seemed Ushi was the hardest Wiggwogg to get to know. Seemingly withdrawn yet always focused and aware of his surroundings, Ushi had a highly evolved connection to the natural world.

"You learn from listening, not talking," Ushi instructed Carter. His intense eyes reflected his wisdom.

· · · · · · ·

As Ushi's exact origin is unknown, the factual genesis of the "Wolfwogg" is a mystery. There are rumors—and they are only that, rumors—that Ushi was not born of Wiggwogg parents at all. Of course, there is outrageous speculation as to exactly who his original parents might have been, but most stories have been dismissed as nothing more than nonsense.

Ushi personally had no recollection of time before the day he was discovered by a Wiggwogg farmer and his wife who had been working in their fields. The drenched couple had sought shelter from a sudden storm in a nearby cave. Cowering in the dark shadows at the back of the small cave was Ushi.

At the time, Ushi was about four or five years old. When the farmer attempted to comfort and pick him up, he was thanked for his efforts by being bitten on the hand. The farmer's wife, seeing the fear and hunger in the eyes of the wild creature, reached into her weather-protected picnic basket, drawing out two pieces of freshly baked bread spread with jam. Placing the bread at her feet, she stepped back. The hungry youngster ever so slowly approached with caution, then, in the blink of an eye, snatched the food. All in one motion, he turned then ran to the back end of the shallow cave where he noisily devoured the offerings without taking his distrusting eyes from the farmer and his wife.

"He is frightened, Taub," said the farmer's wife to her husband. "Who would abandon a young one like this? Have you heard anything at market of a missing Wiggwogg?"

The farmer had not.

The two Wiggwoggs returned daily at about the same time bringing more food. Before a month had passed, they were able to feed him by hand.

On a day that had dawned as ordinary as the day before, the youngster up and followed the farmer and his wife home. Over gently rolling green hills and through their freshly plowed field to their small, slightly tilted farmhouse the three traveled.

From that day forward, the good Wiggwogg farmers, who had not been blessed with a newborn of their own, raised the youth as if he had been theirs from birth. As the years passed and Ushi grew tall, he more and more took on some of the features and instincts of a wolf.

It was Serene who easily recognized the special quality of Ushi's character and his inborn ability to connect with the natural world.

On the day they first met, a wild oomaduma from the Esbolien Desert had made its way north to Wiggonwoggen in search for food. He had gotten into the neatly furrowed fields of Ushi's adoptive parents. Ushi had been alone and working the land when he came upon the oomaduma. The menacing, half-starved animal was big, and with a stream of flying saliva, it shook its angry head at Ushi, asserting its territorial authority. The smiling son of Taub the farmer, who would not be intimidated, walked straight up to the beast.

Serene, who had earlier been hiking along the River Sme, just happened to be walking the winding road past the farm when she came upon the scene. At that moment, Ushi's mind was preoccupied, focused on far bigger things, like the mad oomaduma standing directly in front of him.

The farmer's wife, who was now also Ushi's mother, was a witness to the confrontation. She called frantically from the front porch of the farmhouse for Ushi to run away from the beast. She tore off her apron, waving it frantically in the air to get Ushi's attention.

A great roar came from the depths of the hungry oomaduma, its splayed open mouth boasting several large broken or rotting teeth that nevertheless looked like they could do some serious damage. But Ushi didn't flinch. Holding his ground, he spoke with a calm reassuring voice to the beast, which at first was having nothing of it. The oomaduma snorted and stomped its front feet angrily on the softly tilled soil as if preparing to attack.

"You know, my father has worked quite hard plowing and planting these fields," Ushi informed the beast. "You are making quite the mess of it. Still, you are in no danger here and there is plenty of food to share if you will simply behave."

The oomaduma charged at Ushi, but only for a few feet before it abruptly stopped then backed up. It was attempting to frighten the adopted wolf-like Wiggwogg. Ushi held his ground, continuing in his soft voice to reassure the beast that he meant it no harm and that he understood why it might be angry. Slowly the animal ceased its aggressive posturing and snorting. Lowering its head while pawing the ground, the beast began to calm.

Ushi picked some sweet fruit from a nearby tree and offered it to the oomaduma, dropping it at the animal's feet. The creature devoured the handout in a single bite. After gathering more fruit in a basket and feeding it to the beast, Ushi led the wary oomaduma to a water trough where it drank deeply.

Not wanting to startle either the beast or the young farmer, Serene approached slowly from behind. Scenting the air but without turning around and putting his back to the oomaduma, Ushi said, looking straight ahead, "I have heard of you and seen you at market with friends. You are the one called Serene, aren't you?"

Not waiting for an answer from the surprised Wiggwogg, he continued, "My name is Ushi and I live here on this farm with my parents. About the oomaduma . . . there was little food or water in the desert where he lived, and the poor, wretched animal is simply trying to survive. I am happy to have been able to help."

That is how Serene and Ushi met. Their friendship slowly grew from the seeds of playful companionship. The rest is well-known Wiggwogg history.

Oh—as to the renegade oomaduma, Maurice, or Morris as some called him, the once-bony beast and expatriate of the Esbolien Desert, happily remained on the farm and got fat. He became Ushi's responsibility, and Ushi rode him daily to the public market, pulling a wagon brimming with fresh fruit and vegetables to be sold at his father's stall.

· · · · · · ·

Carter understood from Serene that Wiggwoggs could not lie, but what he did not understand was how something could be heard before it happened.

So much of what was happening did not make sense to the boy from Earth. It seemed to him that all things his short life's experiences had taught him were no longer relevant. At every turn, his reality was being challenged. Slowly, however, he was starting to get a little more comfortable with the insecurity of uncertainty.

Coming to a moonlit clearing, Serene took one of Carter's hands, Herkifer took the other, and together they joined hands with all the gathered Wiggwoggs in a tight circle. Maintaining silence and with their eyes closed, the tribe raised their heads toward the sky. Not knowing his role, but pleased to be included in what appeared to Carter as some type of Wiggwogg ritual, he thought better than to ask questions.

In a moment, still without a spoken word, the circle was broken and now, with Ushi resuming his position in the lead followed by Serene, Carter, Herkifer, Ferbert, Fermond, Lyke, Iat, Lohden, Retann, Abogamento, and, lastly, Zebenuza, the hikers once again set off down the trail.

Interesting, but not revealing, Nevermore said to Carter, referring to the ritual.

"Shhhhhhhhhh," Carter said to Nevermore.

"Shhhhhhhhhh," Serene said to Carter for a second time.

The identical twins, Ferbert and Fermond, for whatever reason things float in and out of a person's mind, drifted into Carter's awareness. One often began a sentence while the other finished it. One brother might begin to say something serious and the other would finish with something really amusing, frustrating the initiating sibling to no end. Carter wondered if perhaps there was only one of them and the other was simply some sort of a reflection in a mirror, an illusion. Maybe a joke the Wiggwoggs were playing on him.

None of the Wiggwoggs seemed to think of Ferbert and Fermond's verbal communications as unusual. One time when the twins, Serene, and Carter were playing a Wiggwogg card game called Blather, Ferbert began a sneeze and Fermond finished it. Serene, concentrating on the game, did not bother to look up from her hand. "Blessings," she said absent-mindedly while throwing down two cards and picking up two new ones from the deck.

Carter's mind skipped to a memory of how he had once asked Ferbert and Fermond for help telling the two of them apart. Looking puzzled, they answered the question with a question. "Why would you," began one. "Want to?" finished the other.

Carter thought for a moment, but nothing came to his mind. "Forget it," he replied. The subject never came up again, and somehow he never made a mistake with their names when addressing one of them individually, or if he did, neither thought it important enough to correct the error.

Interesting how, even when in the idle position, the mind likes to relentlessly chatter. A smile stole its way onto Carter's face, his own mind taking a sharp curve to the place in the dirt road where he had encountered the goat creature, Imalima, running backwards, of course. He wondered if Imalima had ever figured out where he was going and why he was in such a rush to get there.

So lost in his daydreams was Carter that he bumped hard into Serene. It was very dark and they had been walking for hours. With the exception of an occasional ray of light streaming from the moon, visibility was limited to a few feet. Up ahead, Ushi had smelled something. The Wiggwogg had abruptly stopped, and Carter, who had been following Serene closely so as not to get lost, could not stop his forward momentum in time and walked right into her. "Sorry," he said. The Wiggwogg's warm smile was forgiving.

Ushi, nose pointed skyward, turned slowly in several directions, inhaling the secrets of nature. "I smell rain," he announced to the others. Looking about, he saw a long shelf carved into a bank of rock just behind them. If his weather prediction was correct, the shelter would offer them protection while they slept. As he lowered one broad shoulder and then the other, his backpack slipped quickly to the ground.

Serene broke a long silence and said, "We will make camp here. We have traveled far enough for this night, and tomorrow will be a long day. We should be arriving at the River Sme sometime late in the afternoon. The goal is to get there and cross before dark. We could cross back at the bridge, but it takes us too far out of our way and we would have to double back."

"Serene, just where are we going? Is there a reason you're keeping the purpose of this hike a secret from me?" Carter could no longer hold back his curiosity.

"Soon, Carter, the pieces of the puzzle will begin to fall into place. Patience. By tomorrow night there will be answers. I promise. Now we need to rest.

Using rolled-up rain ponchos as pillows, the exhausted hikers slipped into tight cocoons of sleeping bags and one by one drifted off. To be sure, Carter had questions, so many questions, but he was becoming a good student while learning the important lessons of trust and patience. Tucking his apprehensions away for the time being, he followed the Wiggwoggs, surrendering this day to sleep.

· · · · · · ·

Carter and the small party of Wiggwoggs rose early with morning's first light. Ushi proved to be a good weather forecaster and was right about the rain. During the remainder of the night, a wild storm had poured non-stop from the sky, but now as morning was making its grand entrance, the storm took its cue and moved on.

After a quick breakfast of sweet hardcakes and a type of fruit tea, which both seemed to be a staple of the Wiggwoggs' diet, the adventurers packed their gear and cleaned up their campsite. Within the hour, they were back on the trail with Ushi once again assuming the lead position. The clan pushed on at a strong pace all day, skipping lunch and only stopping for an occasional short break. Much of the hike was spent along the narrow path that rimmed a steep canyon. The up side of the canyon's sheer wall was painted with dappled light created by the low afternoon angle of Suva and Ahneese. *Incredible view,* thought Carter to Nevermore as he looked across the open chasm.

Concentrate on where you're stepping, please. If you're not careful, you could kill the both of us, transmitted the silent bird into Carter's mind.

"Did you forget you can fly?"

Serene looked over her shoulder. "Are you talking to me?" she asked.

"Er . . . no, just Nevermore." Carter imagined Serene's disapproving expression.

Off in the distance, Carter heard the notes of a timeless and repetitious melody being sung by the lyrical harmonics of rushing water at the bottom of the canyon. He imagined frothy white water smashing against scrubbed rock, searching for options that would lead to the most direct route in a race to the sea.

Ushi turned in the direction of the river and guided the hikers in a steep descent toward the canyon's floor. The going was slow and tedious. A simple single misstep could cause an individual to become an unwilling participant in a small avalanche. Zebenuza actually did slip once, causing a mini landslide. Grimacing in pain as he swept passed his horrified companions who were unable to help, Zebenuza slid some twenty feet or so on his back before luckily grabbing hold of an exposed tree's root.

While catching his breath, Carter wiped the perspiration from his brow with his forearm. He now stood alongside Serene on a tall boulder just above the water. "That," Serene said loud enough to be heard over the water's thundering voice, "is the River Sme."

The previous night's storm had swollen the river to where it had flooded its banks and now ripped fiercely past them. Serene pointed toward a beautiful tree boasting a latticework of graceful branches, growing along the riprap hem of the river's far bank. The tree's thick, twisted trunk was different from any tree Carter had ever seen. "And that, my friend," she said through her perpetual smile, "is the ancient tulk tree." Serene then jumped down to the ground from the tall boulder and waved for Carter to follow as she headed toward a thin beach on the water's edge.

Considering the distance Serene had just jumped, Carter decided a more prudent descent better suited him. Scooting down the face of the boulder on his bottom, Carter then picked his way through a minefield of driftwood to the beach where Serene and the other Wiggwoggs stood waiting. Not more than a hundred feet up river, an accumulation of rock lurked from just above the water's surface. The group walked the beach to the location where the river's floor rose up out of the rushing water.

Pulling a rope from his belt, Lyke knotted a loop around the waist of each hiker in the order they had been walking, leaving approximately five feet between them. Lyke was known in Wiggonwoggen for his skill with rope. He could make any kind of a knot and place a lasso around anything his lariat could reach.

Lyke was the oldest of three brothers; his younger siblings were Retann and Lohden. The trio was practically inseparable. Lyke considered his brothers to be his best friends and was loyal to a fault. He would defend them against anyone, even if they were wrong. If Lyke said he would do something, you could rely on his word.

Retann, the middle brother, was smart and had an intelligent answer almost before a question was completed. Rather than a team player, Retann, who had the reputation of being quite quirky, preferred to work quietly alone while Lohden, the youngest of the band of Wiggwoggs, was more social and could sell reading glasses to a blind mouse. He had flashes of temper yet was the funniest of the group. If you wanted a good laugh you could always count on Lohden.

While Lyke tied the rope around the waists of each adventurer, Herkifer stood at a distance watching. He had concerns about crossing the river at this location but did not speak up because he didn't want to appear frightened. He believed his courage instilled a sense of confidence in his traveling companions.

Herkifer's most visible physical asset was his strength. He was built like a rectangular wood block, and his neck was wider than his head. His short legs were thick as fire hydrants. Although you might not guess it at first glance, he was known for his skills at climbing. His tunic modestly hid powerful legs, and his reputation amongst Wiggwoggs for scaling walls of rock was legendary.

As hard as he looked, Herkifer was probably the most soft-hearted of all the Wiggwoggs.

"We will cross here," Serene said to Carter.

"Isn't there another way?" Carter asked. A memory of the fun he had crossing the swinging bridge over the River Sme when he and the Wiggwoggs had recently gone for a swim skirted his mind. He looked at the unforgiving intensity of the rushing water smashing past them and at the long distance to the other side of the river. He was a good swimmer, but this would not be his first choice of water for a fun dip.

"Don't worry," reassured Serene. "I know this is dangerous, but we have crossed successfully before . . . although I don't remember the water being quite this high or the rapids nearly this fierce."

Serene's words did not carry the confidence Carter would have preferred hearing.

The surface of the River Sme played wildly under the domed grid of magenta sky throwing a fine spray of rainbow mist up toward the tulk tree. The thin film swept in and out of the tree's branches, bathing the tulk so that its reflected brilliance caused Carter to squint.

Ushi stepped almost knee high into the cold water before coming to the first rock. Cautiously Serene, Carter, and the rest of the Wiggwoggs followed, holding firm onto the rope stretched in front of them. Whipping quicksilver fast over and around rock, the water chewed at the unsteady legs of Carter and the Wiggwoggs. When Ushi was almost halfway across the river, Zebenuza, bringing up the rear, was about one-third into the swirling soup.

"Keep moving!" shouted Serene over her shoulder into the volume of the raging river. "Don't stare down at your feet! Just follow the steps of the one in front of you." Serene's instruction came a moment too late for Ferbert and Fermond.

"Uh," called out Ferbert.

"Oh," finished Fermond.

An echoing hypnotic song played by the River Sme had captivated the minds of the twin brothers, disconnecting sensation from their feet. They waved their extended arms frantically in circles, first in one direction then the other as they tried desperately to regain their balance. It was a losing battle. The rope that had become slack between them snapped taut as the twin brothers tumbled into the rushing river. First Ferbert's head went under, then Fermond's. Carter was panicked, frozen in the terror of the moment. Floundering in the rapids, the twins threatened to pull them all in. The scene seemed to Carter at first overwhelming, then in the next moment distant and unreal, like watching an unfolding disaster on the television evening news.

He braced himself as best he could.

Herkifer, who had been directly in front of the twins before they plunged into the turbulence, moved instantly into action. "Hold steady!" he shouted to all the hikers above the river's din. Ribbons of current raced to claim the bodies of the two brothers whose arms flailed in agitation and fright. The river wanted the twins, but not as badly as Herkifer did. He pulled with all his strength on the rope connecting his waist to those of Ferbert and Fermond, sustaining rope burns on the skin of both of his hands. Lyke, who had been behind the twins, pulled one of several ropes from his belt, quickly knotted a lasso on one, and threw it perfectly over one of Ferbert's extended arms.

The River Sme was not about to give up her catch so easily and even tried to coax the others into joining the twins for a swim. As Lyke was trying to pull the brothers toward him, the hungry river kept pulling them back, and for a while the water was winning. It was like trying to reel in two really big fish on one line against a ferocious current.

A dead tree rose up at an angle from beneath the river's surface not far from where Lyke was standing. The rope-master threw his end of the rope over a thick lower limb of the partially submerged tree. Winding the remaining length of rope around his wrists and hands, he pulled hard, using the tree for leverage.

"Help me, Herkifer!" Lyke called out. "I can't do it alone!" The strongest Wiggwogg cut the rope connecting himself to Carter, Serene, and Ushi. Holding tight to the section of rope leading to Ferbert so as to allow no slack, he made his way back over the rocks to Lyke. Together they pulled with all their strength against the unrelenting grasp of the stubborn, rushing river.

In the end, it was Herkifer and Lyke's uncompromising determination that won the fierce tug of war. Slowly, ever so slowly and with great reluctance, Sme surrendered her fresh catch of the day.

"Grab his leg, Herkifer!" Lyke cried out. Each hauled one of the twins from the river and tossed their dead weight, like sacks of grain, over the strong shoulders of Herkifer, one on each side for balance. "Hurry, hurry," came in ripples up and down the line of drenched hikers. Carter and the Wiggwoggs raced the remaining distance to the riverbank barely touching the surface of rocks.

Ferbert's and Fermond's pale, lifeless bodies were carried ashore by the weary Herkifer. They were gently laid out under the shade of the tulk tree in the center of the surrounding circle of friends. With their eyes closed, the twins seemed to be in a deep, peaceful sleep.

"Isn't anyone going to do anything?" Carter implored. His question was answered by silence. "All right then, stand back and give me some room," he ordered.

The Boy Scouts had been one of Howard and Cynthia Nicholsworth's many failed attempts to lure their son from the forest of Wickedwood. Carter had little interest in scouting rituals or most sports, but he did enjoy swimming. When an instructional class on swimming safety and CPR was offered by the Boy Scouts, he eagerly signed up. He won a merit badge for his skill and did so well he was asked to become a teaching assistant. True to the nature of his introversion, Carter had declined the offer.

"Serene, listen to me and watch what I do. You take Ferbert and I'll take Fermond." Carter quickly explained the technique of CPR as he immediately went to work on Fermond. Serene carefully followed Carter's instructions, observing his technique while working over Ferbert.

In a few moments, one after the other, the brother's bodies shuddered back to life. Fermond and Ferbert each gave up a good amount of the River Sme in the process. The other gathered Wiggwoggs stood silently by, looking back and forth at each other in disbelief.

From that moment forward, Carter's relationship with the Wiggwoggs was dramatically changed. He had earned their respect, confidence, and brotherhood. For his part, Carter just took a personal giant step up the ever-wobbly ladder of youthful self-esteem.

· · · · · · ·

Weary from their river adventure, the party stumbled the few yards up to the trunk of the tulk tree. It was early evening, but they were all too tired to eat. As darkness began to swallow the day, one after another, the adventurers drifted off into a deep sleep under the enchanted tree. The silence of the cool, starlit night was broken by the sound of a cracking branch from above.

"Hoo . . . hoohoooooo," called a voice. "*Who* . . ." came a question from high in the tree, "will join Serene on this sacred mission and *who* will not?"

Carter did not budge, but when his eyes finally adjusted to the dark, they shifted their focus to a branch high in the tulk. In the background, he could hear the constant low rumble of River Sme rolling past. Perched on the branch was a red owl.

A talking owl? wondered Carter. *How come that owl can talk, Nevermore, and you can't?* Either the little bird chose to ignore Carter's insensitive question or it did not have an answer. Rubbing his knuckles deep into his eyes while trying to clear the cobwebs of sleep, Carter sat up. When he looked again for the owl, it was gone. "Was that my imagination?" he whispered to Nevermore. This time his question was answered with a single word reply.

Nope.

"We're here, right on schedule, Father," Serene said. All the Wiggwoggs were already awake, most sitting cross-legged in a semi-circle several feet from the trunk of the tulk tree. Serene sat at the base of the tree facing Carter and the Wiggwoggs.

On the branch where the owl had perched now sat what appeared to be an old man. He was dressed in a long white robe revealing his bare feet at its hem. To Carter, he looked human. His hair was long and grew into his beard that rested on his chest. Most surprising to Carter was the color of the old man's hair. Like his beard, it was red with flecks of gray.

Weird, came down the thought of Nevermore. *What's up with that? Are you two related?*

"I trust your short hike was uneventful," said the old man to his audience.

"Other than an unscheduled swim, it went well enough, Father. Carter Nicholsworth is proving to have been a wise choice and has already been of great value. If not for him, we would already be two Wiggwoggs shy of the number before you." All eyes went to Carter who shifted uncomfortably on his seat on the ground.

"That must be Elderwiser," whispered Carter to Nevermore.

However did you become so smart? came the sarcastic response.

Elderwiser leapt with the agility of a monkey from one branch down to a lower one, then another, before finally jumping easily to the ground. He came over to where Serene was sitting at the base of the tulk and sat as close to her as he could. Serene turned her face to her father and the Wiggwogg wizard turned his to hers. He placed his two cupped hands between their faces, creating a short tunnel. Both sat there motionless for a few moments, staring into each other's eyes and far beyond. The River Sme seemed to hold its breath as a deep hush fell over the forest.

Turning his head to face the Wiggwoggs and Carter, Elderwiser spoke. His voice was thoughtful yet distant. "What I am about to ask of you is most difficult for me. I think it only fair you have an idea of the danger that most assuredly lies in wait for you. Then each of you must make a personal choice whether or not you will join Serene on this sacred mission to capture and return the Circle of Power for safekeeping in Wiggonwoggen. None of you are here by accident. Much thought has gone into the selection process, and I have personally picked each of you for reasons that, if you choose to participate, will become evident as the journey unfolds."

The old wizard stood and extended both arms horizontally from his body. Closing his eyes, he began to spin, slowly at first, but with each turn picking up speed until he was barely a blur. Just as Carter thought Elderwiser was about to lift off the ground, the spinning slowed until once again the leader of the Wiggwoggs stood steady and faced the group. His azure-colored eyes burned bright into the dark night with the intensity of a blue flame.

"I see a land I have never before walked. This place is fallow as nothing will grow in its poisoned ground. My nostrils are assaulted with the sickening stench of burnt and rotting flesh. I see a road cobbled out of sticky red crimson cruelty, leading to that land. I see the bones of those who have gone before you, stacked randomly like so many cords of wood alongside the shoulder of this road. I see half-starved monsters lurking just below the surface of Aeiea, waiting for you, and somewhere underneath a distant structure of stone, I see the Circle of Power."

Appearing exhausted, Elderwiser closed his eyes. Carter wondered if Serene or any of the other Wiggwoggs could hear his heart beating hard against the wall of his chest. While brothers Ferbert and Fermond quietly set about building a small campfire, the other young Wiggwoggs sat still as rocks, hanging onto the old wizard's every word.

Carter had waited to meet the leader of the Wiggwoggs, with Serene's promise of resolution to unanswered questions, yet here he was learning the lesson of patience. This was not the right moment to press his agenda. He relaxed and let go of his need to know now. It was at that precise moment that the old wizard turned and for the first time made eye contact with the young Earthling.

"Welcome, Carter Nicholsworth," said Elderwiser. With a warm smile, he bent at the waist and, reaching forward, took both of Carter's small hands in his own.

"'Why me?' you are probably wondering. The simple answer is, because of who you are. You are, more than most of your peers, comfortable with your uniqueness. It is your level of imagination and character, of which you understand little, that qualified you for this mission. You have no memory of me and that is as it should be. Your future, however, is a mystery even to me, but I can tell you one thing. It is intertwined with the fate of the Circle of Power. You are on loan to us for a brief moment in time and thus the urgency," Elderwiser said, his eyes scanning the cold sky, "but you must know that I cannot guarantee your safety, nor do I control your destiny."

Serene moved to Carter's side and rested her hand on his shoulder. "Relax, Carter," she said. "There is nothing in this moment to fear."

Changing the subject to diffuse the tension caused by his words, the old wizard's eyes shifted to Carter's scorch of red hair. "Perhaps you can introduce me to your little friend perched on your head."

"N-N-N-Nevermore," stuttered Carter, the name finally coming unstuck from his tongue.

The wizard released one of Carter's hands. He raised his arm toward the bird and Nevermore hopped easily from his nest onto Elderwiser's extended index finger. Bringing Nevermore to his eye level, Elderwiser slowly turned his hand while examining the little bird.

"Nevermore, gatekeeper of Carter's conscience," Elderwiser said, smiling. "Welcome to Aeiea. Would you like to hear a story?" The sage's eyes shifted back to his guest. Carter was so transfixed it was all he could do to affirmatively shake his head. Nevermore mimicked his master.

"Very well then." The old leader of the Wiggwoggs returned the bird to its red nest, closed his eyes, and raised his head toward the night.

"Long, long ago, before awareness or the illusion of time, a small sphere began to form deep in the infinite cosmos. The mass, like so many before, was created from a fine scattering of dust, blown from the open palms of The Source by her breath. It was to this newly formed celestial entity, third of nine from the twin sisters of light, that The Source offered the blessed gift of life and so was born Aeiea."

Summoning up his courage, Carter asked, "How far is Aeiea from Earth?"

"Irrelevant," was the smiling wizard's one-word response. "May I continue?"

"Sure." Carter's face reddened as he nodded awkwardly to hide his embarrassment.

"Words fail to describe the incredible pristine beauty of this globe. The Source eventually began stocking her celestial creation with a bountiful assortment of wildlife, one of which was an interesting and diverse species known as Aeieans. The first offspring of the original Aeieans was a child born with a golden necklace around its neck. Attached to the necklace was what appeared an ordinary circular medallion. In truth, the medallion was anything but *ordinary*.

"The Circle of Power, as the medallion is now referred to, is not in itself either good or evil. The medallion has two sides. One side is the power of light whose energy is of the heart."

"Listen closely, Carter," whispered Serene, "and you will come to know the importance of our mission."

"If the medallion is used with love as intended by The Source," Elderwiser said, "the Circle of Power will open the door to enlightenment. But as with all surfaces of form, the Circle of Power has another side. That is the side empty of light, the shadow side where a mighty force born of insatiable longing is always busy at work. If the Circle of Power is worn shadow-side out, it will attract the energy of fear and greed, driven by an ego that can never be satisfied."

Turning to Carter, Serene said solemnly, "This is how power works in partnership with envy to entice those who can never have enough."

"One night," Elderwiser said, "as the Aeiean child lay asleep under a star-filled sky, one of his younger siblings, who had been staring with envy far too long at the dark side of the medallion, became seduced by the energy of ego. Quietly, while his brother was deep in dreams, the child stole the medallion. Although the thief's identity has long since disappeared into the great void of obscurity, the power released from the abuse of trust began to grow and continues to do so until this very day, as does the constant struggle between the forces of good and evil."

Carter felt a chill slide up his back. Shaking off an involuntary shudder, he looked first at Serene's face, then back to Elderwiser's, both softly comforting in the campfire's orange glow.

"With that first theft of the Circle of Power, a curse was unleashed upon the thief and all who would follow him," the old wizard continued. "Those who chose to join the thief soon developed an affliction called 'jealously,' a lusting for the possessions of others. An insatiable desire for 'more' corrupted the spirit of those Aeieans. They were condemned by their choices to spend their lives with one foot in the past and the other in the future. The little peaceful orb caught a cold, small and manageable at first, but over time, the tiny infection grew into a nasty epidemic.

"Then one day, quite by accident and unbeknownst to its bearer, the medallion was lost. It happened while the thief was crossing the River Sme in search of 'more.' The medallion eventually became buried in mud just at the river's edge. Over time, the beautiful tulk tree grew from that very spot. And so it was on a beautiful summer solstice morning, upon waking from a most peculiar dream, I found myself sitting at the base of that tree looking up at a single golden flower. The rest is history."

Carter felt the weight of Elderwiser's story heavy on his shoulders. Looking down at the ground, he took a deep breath and released it slowly.

"Do not despair, Carter Nicholsworth," the wizard continued. "All is not lost. Some are coming awake. There is yet hope. The uncontaminated innocence of birth continues to live on in the spirit of every newborn, and therein is the promise for our once peaceful planet. Carter Nicholsworth, you have remained an innocent. You are of my family and one of a growing number of exceptional beings. I refer to these individuals as the enlightened ones blessed with the gift of goodness and abundant imagination, which for you, Carter, is your unique creative power. It is for that reason you have been summoned here."

Abruptly ending his story, as if anticipating urgency, Elderwiser once again found the boy's eyes with his own. Carter felt a second chill move up his back, spreading to his ears and cheeks. The story left so many unanswered questions.

A short, uncomfortable silence was broken by the sound of beating wings. First only a few, then others joined in until all the night's light was blown out by a windstorm of wings.

"Bats!" cried out Carter who could not make out the form of the invaders. The acrid smell of decaying flesh filled his nose. He felt the sting of sour bile rise in his throat. It reminded him of the time he had found a dead possum in the woods behind his home. Countless white maggots had crawled across the unseeing open eye of the animal and moved in a slow, curving column in and out of the stiff creature's gaping mouth.

Within moments the night was once again still.

"Not bats," Serene said softly. "Kenga. They are very large bird-like creatures loyal to the Gootz. Sometimes they carry on their backs small invading forces of Gootz from Athulian for hit-and-run attacks against the territories, but they are more often used simply for gathering intelligence. In other words, spies. I don't believe they were aware of our presence, but to be on the safe side we must assume that they saw us. Even if we were noticed, we would probably be seen as nothing more than just a group of lost hikers, too small to be a threat to the great power of the Gootz. In any case, from now on we must be extra careful. Because of our small number, we cannot afford to give away the element of surprise."

Elderwiser stepped out from the moonlit shadows. Starting at one end of the Wiggwoggs seated around the campfire, he moved slowly from one to another, touching his fingers to his lips before pressing them to the forehead of each. When he at last came to Carter, who was at the far end of the semi-circle, Elderwiser placed both his hands, gnarled with age, on the boy's shoulders.

"Your home is of another time, another place, Carter Nicholsworth. Wiggwoggs have no choice but to be in truth and to do what we believe to be for the common good of all. At this time the common good would best be served by our locating and regaining stewardship of the Circle of Power. We must also help you find the door to your destiny and see to it that the light is carried forward."

"But . . ." Carter's mind was spinning with more information than he was able to process. He felt overwhelmed, more confused than ever before.

"Understand the journey will not be an easy one. At every turn, your courage will be tested. You will encounter a sea of challenges that will confront your character. Much like your shadow, uncertainty will surely be your constant companion. Best to make friends with uncertainty rather than have it as your enemy.

"If I had the knowledge on how best to achieve your mission," continued Elderwiser, turning from Carter to address the rest of those gathered, "I would share it with you, but unfortunately I do not. I can see only so much. The rest is hidden behind a dark curtain. All I really own is my faith and this moment. The rest is water through a sieve. I have touched each of you with my faith. I can do nothing more. If you choose to return to the safety of home, step forward. There will be no shame. Otherwise the rest is up to you."

A moment of silence followed with the Wiggwoggs looking from one to the other, but all remained rooted where they stood. Carter considered Elderwiser's words and pondered his options. Where would he go? He felt he had no choice.

"All right then," the old wizard said. "I take it since no one moved you are all going with Serene. Seekers of The Circle, you must leave quickly. On the off chance the Kenga did see us and thought our gathering suspicious, it will not be long before they reach the island of Athulian and gossip their sighting to their masters."

Elderwiser completely wrapped himself from head to foot in his cloak. Once again he began to spin, this time so fast that his feet actually did lift off the ground. The old wizard's cloak fell empty to the place where he had just been standing, and as Carter looked up into the cool night, he saw a large red owl winging gracefully toward the moon.

Chapter 9
Reunion

Serene had hard choices to make. Ultimately all decisions were rooted in the same question: how best to get to the island of Athulian undetected, find the Circle of Power, and safely return to Wiggonwoggen with the medallion in her possession? She understood from Elderwiser that Carter was somehow irreplaceable as a member of the mission and that his personal fate was connected to the mission's success. The old wizard could not tell her more. Wizards are smart, but they don't know everything.

"Well, Elderwiser picked you for your creativity and imagination," Serene said. "What do you have to say?"

After a thoughtful moment Carter said, "As I see it, if there is a chance of success, it would go a long way if we could surprise the Gootz. Our small number is in our favor, so even if we're detected at some point, I don't think The Grinder would send the full force of his army against us. So I guess what I'm saying is, we stay low for as long as possible. If I've been in and out of Wimzi and am still alive, there is a chance we could all do the same."

"Perhaps, because you are not from Aeiea, you have some special immunity from the ways of Wimzi," Serene said. Carter just shrugged and looked at her, not knowing how to respond.

Serene understood that their group of explorers would inevitably have to cross The Great Sea Valion, but how and where was the question. If an inland route were chosen, they would have to spend time in Wimzi, an unpleasant and quite possibly deadly proposition. Traveling through

Dweeg Territory, Stanelhooven, then a quick sprint through the narrows of Wimzi seemed the best option. Walking in the shadows of the territory's forests would also make the most sense in an attempt to avoid the watchful eyes of Gootz spies. No doubt this route would give them the best chance for surprise.

That plan would easily be the smartest choice except for one really big problem: Wimzi. They would have to cross this "land of no return" where nothing was ever as it seemed. Serene knew of no travelers other than Carter who had ever come back from Wimzi. They would also have to take the time to build a boat somewhere on Wimzi's shore large enough to accommodate all of them in order to make the plan work. All that seemed a bit daunting. However, the other option of a long journey at sea in an attempt to bypass Wimzi while trying to evade sea serpents or being discovered by the Gootz seemed even more problematical.

Just maybe, if Carter could resist the forces at work in Wimzi, there was a chance that the Wiggwoggs accompanying him might be protected as well.

"I believe our options are limited as to how best to get to Athulian," Serene said to Carter. "Any final thoughts?"

"Since you asked," Carter replied, "I think we should stay on land as long as we can and spend as little time as possible on the sea. It's my opinion that we should cross Valion from Wimzi at the point closest to the island."

"Given our limited options, I believe what you say makes sense." Serene reached across the short distance separating her from Carter and shook his hand in agreement with his assessment.

· · · · · · ·

The leader of the Wiggwoggs believed the most likely place to find the Circle of Power was in Bludenbonz, the fortress castle of The Grinder. The well-guarded castle was built by The Grinder high atop a bluff that rose up from the sea on the westernmost tip of Athulian. The castle's name Bludenbonz (pronounced blood 'n' bones) came from the unique red mortar that went into building the showpiece of The Grinder's kingdom. It seems that an unusual combination of extracted blood and bones, a most reluctant donation from The Grinder's unfortunate victims, were the principal ingredients ground into a thick, soupy mix that bonded stone to stone in the fine, upscale castle.

The successful crossing by the adventurers would put them on the beach directly below Bludenbonz Castle. From there, Serene envisioned they would climb to the fortress, rescue the Circle of Power, and make their quick exit.

Serene called the others into a circle. Once all were seated, she took the map from inside her tunic and opened it.

"With the help of Carter," she explained to the others while tracing a line from where they were to their destination, "I have agreed on the best possible route to get us onto the island of Athulian."

Smiling gratefully at Carter, Serene refolded the map and, nodding her head, tucked it back into her tunic. "Done," she said. "Now let's now get some sleep. Tomorrow promises to be a most interesting day."

· · · · · · ·

Darkness was still upon them when Serene woke Carter, then each of the snoring Wiggwoggs. After their now familiar breakfast of hardcakes and tea, the friends sat in a close huddle to get the day's briefing from their leader. Serene invited Carter to sit next to her.

"I would trust Elderwiser with my life, as we all do, or we would not be here. You are each my father's choice for this mission so I am asking you to be prepared to sacrifice. Are you comfortable with that?"

Carter nodded hesitantly, not knowing what kind of sacrifice Serene was speaking of. His respect and friendship for the Wiggwogg leader was growing with each passing day. It was not by his conscious choice that his life had been turned upside down. He had not asked to be where he was, and yet he had the sense that this was the perfect place for him at this moment.

The plan was to stay inland. They would cross out of Wiggonwoggen and travel through the Valley of Dread in Dweeg Territory. Their route would then take them over Mourners Mountains and down into Stanelhooven. From there, Carter and the tribe of Wiggwoggs would finally arrive at the edge of Wimzi. That name alone was cause for Serene to shudder. If you were among the lucky few who entered and did not lose your life, then at minimum, surely you would lose your mind.

The only one Serene knew of who had escaped with both life and mind intact was Carter Nicholsworth. Could he do it again? Did Carter have some kind of protection against the wildly wicked ways of Wimzi? Was Elderwiser aware when he chose the young Earthling for this mission of Carter's apparent immunity to the dangerous absurdities of Wimzi? Perhaps whatever had given Carter amnesty would protect the rest of them as well.

"First things first," the young Wiggwogg leader informed her friends. "Since an inland route has been chosen, we must first cross back over the River Sme or we might accidently walk over the border into Wimzi."

Carter was not looking forward to repeating his recent experience with either the river or Wimzi. "Are there no other alternatives to crossing the river?" he asked.

"I'm afraid not. The weather has held, and Elderwiser told me of a place where we can safely cross." Then, turning to directly face the boy from Earth, Serene warned, "I make no promises, Carter. Our mission will be a difficult one. Most assuredly, uncertainty will be our constant companion, and even if we somehow manage to succeed, I don't know what lies ahead for any of us. None of this adventure will be easy. As we all too well know, just Wimzi alone is a bottomless well of madness. Those who fall in never climb out. It is an unforgiving world of illusion."

"Illusion," Carter repeated in a whisper. He tried to explain to Serene about a magician he had once watched on television. After several frustrating attempts to explain the concept of television, Carter shrugged his shoulders and said, "Forget it. I guess I don't understand the science of how television works well enough to describe it."

A headache was beginning to organize behind Carter's temples. His mind slipped back to his brief journey through Wimzi. Closing his eyes, he took a slow, deep breath. In the next moment, he saw himself sitting in a dark room. The only light came from the screen of a television sending out a stream of electric blue shadows flashing across his face.

"And now, ladies and gentlemen," came the announcer's voice, "a special program intended for the viewing pleasure of Carter Nicholsworth."

The screen filled with the vibrant colors of a cartoon. Carter's face contorted with uncontrollable laughter as he watched the antics played out on the TV. All of a sudden one of the cartoon characters, a smiling crab, reached through the glass screen and grabbed hold of Carter's red hair in its claw. Flapping a segmented fanned tail, the crab dragged him toward and into the television screen. Carter's body went rigid, his laughter ceased, his face frozen in horror. Before he knew what was happening, he was on the other side of the screen, being pulled along a beach by three cartoon crabs twice his size. Sand shoveled into his mouth and stung his eyes.

In the background, two bright red crabs stood alongside each other playing oversized guitars while a third crab opened and closed its claws above its head in sync with the sound track of clacking castanets and Latino music. Each of the crab musicians wore Carmen Miranda-style turbans laden with plastic fruit.

"Ain't no cookin' like Cajun cookin'," sang the crusty crustaceans in perfect harmony and with a forced south of the border twang. *"Oh, kid cakes tonight, kid cakes tonight, kid cakes 'n' beer. We're havin' kid cakes tonight. Oh, kid cakes 'n' beer. We're havin' kid cakes tonight."*

The fourth crab that had kidnapped Carter was now wearing a white chef's hat and matching full-length apron. Across the chest of the apron was the framed face of Carter Nicholsworth. Underneath was the word "MISSING." The crab chef stood over a large cauldron shaking spices with both claws into the steamy boil. Next he took an oar from a rowboat beached next to the cauldron and vigorously mixed his recipe while running his tongue across his exaggerated blue cartoon lips.

"What do you think, boys?" the chef asked. "Getting hungry for dinner? I could use a little help over here."

With a thumbs-up signal from the chef, the singing trio of crabs dropped their instruments and grabbed Carter's arms and legs in their claws. They swung him back and forth over the open-mouthed kettle, finally tossing him high into the air. Upon completion of an acrobatic somersaulting plunge toward the waiting pot, Carter landed with all fours fully extended, straddling the cooker. The surprised crabs abruptly ceased their singing. They looked back and forth at each other then together crawled onto Carter's back, trying to force him into the pot.

"Jump on him good and hard till he drops into the pot!" shouted one of the guitar-playing crustaceans. "He looks like he'll be tasty and tender."

"I'll take a drumstick," said the other guitar player.

"He doesn't have drumsticks," informed the crab who had been playing the castanets.

"Ok, then I'll just take the wings."

Up and down they madly jumped until Carter, in a desperate move made possible only through the art of the animator, easily swung his body to the side. The disappointed crabs that were left hanging in midair by Carter's deft maneuver plopped one after another into the boiling cauldron.

Pushing the oar through the bubbling brew, a smiling Carter sang:

"Oh, crab cakes tonight, crab cakes tonight. Oh, crab cakes and beer, we're havin' crab cakes tonight."

· · · · · · ·

Serene nudged Carter's arm. "Hello . . . anybody home? What is a crab cake anyway? You were mumbling something about crab cakes tonight."

Shaking the cobwebs from his mind, Carter apologized to Serene. "Sorry, I don't know where this headache came from, but it sure took me off to a strange place." He rubbed his eyes, trying to focus on the Wiggwogg.

"Be careful, Carter. Wimzi is so much more than a place on a map. Like a magnet, it can pull your mind into chaos. If you think about Wimzi for too long, it will pick up your thoughts and infect them with illusion." Serene's serious message was not lost on Carter. Her face seemed to age with her words of caution. "Come, let's break camp. It's time to go."

The Wiggwoggs and Carter gathered their equipment and cleaned the area so that any curious visitor would never know they had been there. Carter noticed that this "brushing down" process was a standard Wiggwogg procedure when breaking camp.

The formation they had been walking in since beginning their mission had one significant change. Following Ushi, who continued in the lead, was Serene, and now at her side was Carter. The symbolic change was not questioned or challenged but rather easily accepted by the Wiggwoggs.

Ushi sniffed the air. After a moment he set off in a westerly direction that would take them first back over the River Sme and then into the Valley of Dread. As promised by Elderwiser, their return trip across the river was rather easy. Upon reaching the water they discovered that a great tree had fallen, almost bridging the river, possibly the result of the recent storm. This lucky circumstance helped make their crossing uneventful.

The day seemed to stretch on as Carter struggled against the seduction of sleep softly singing an old familiar lullaby. He stumbled awake several times under the hot, impartial glare of sister suns Suva and Ahneese.

Rounding a wide curve on the trail, Ushi, with both arms raised, came to an abrupt halt. He crouched down, and the others followed his lead. Total silence. Carter looked beyond Ushi and noticed up ahead a single tree growing alongside the trail. Under the shade of the tree was a rickety bench, the apparent work of an inexperienced carpenter. The resulting product of the novice was a humpty-dumpty, cattywumpus structure, complete with countless skin-piercing splinters.

This was not your basic slide-over-and-make-room kind of bench. The letters *BUS SOTP* were freshly painted on a staked sign directly behind the bench. A wet paintbrush straddling the open mouth of a paint can drooled on the ground. It was not the tree, the misspelled sign, or the bench that was the source of Ushi's alarm, but rather the occupant sitting on the bench reading an upside-down newspaper in his lap. It was a familiar Wimzical.

Rising from his kneeling position, Carter also recognized the unusual creature he had earlier met at the crossroads and shouted excitedly, "Imalima, is that you?"

"None other," came the cautious reply. "Do I know you, sir?"

"Of course you do. Don't you remember me? We met when I surprised you at the crossroads a while ago. You were in quite a hurry at the time."

"Well, certainly I remember you. I never forget a face." The other Wiggwoggs had stood and joined Carter as he approached the bench. "You're the sneak who snuck mail from my letterbox. I feel it only fair to inform you, sir, I immediately reported the theft to the proper authorities, and now your face is prominently displayed on the walls of all the territories' post offices. There's a price on your head, Lalivar," an intense Imalima informed Carter.

"Lalivar? Who is Lalivar? My name is Carter. What are you talking about, Imalima?"

Imalima was standing on his hind legs. Folding first his newspaper then two uppermost legs across his chest, he glanced indignantly at Carter. "That's for you to know and for me to find out. Perhaps I have you confused with someone else."

"No perhaps about it," Carter said.

"Well then," Imalima replied, "don't you think, sir, you owe me a bit of an apology?"

"For what?" asked an incredulous Carter.

"For what you ask. How about, for starters, the intentional and blatantly malicious conspiratorial attempt to confuse me?"

"Oh brother," Carter groaned.

"Why not leave your brother out of it. This is just between you 'n me, pardner," droned Imalima while switching gears. It sounded to Carter as if he had slid into a rather poor attempt to imitate a western film actor's drawl. "No need to drag a fourth person into what's simply a barroom disagreement, if you catch my drift. How 'bout you 'n me just step outside a moment 'n settle this once 'n fer all?"

Nut job, came Nevermore's silent observation from the crow's nest of Carter's head.

"We *are* outside, in case you hadn't noticed," Carter reminded Imalima. "I don't know why I even bother to talk to you."

It was as if Carter had just delivered a low punch to the stomach of the multi-legged creature. All the air seemed to go out of him. His back hunched and he hung his skinny head on his chest while he drew in a single breath and exhaled deeply. "I must admit, I am not surprised by your comment." The cowboy persona was gone. "You're just like the rest of them. Hardly anyone talks to me. You hate me, don't you?"

"No," Carter answered defensively as a wave of heat flushed his cheeks. He felt responsibility for Imalima's outbreak of insecurity. "I don't hate you. We seem to have a communication problem, that's all."

Carter studied Imalima sitting on the bench. Something was different. It was then that Carter noticed one of the creature's many legs was loosely dangling against his body. "What happened to your leg, Imalima?" he asked.

Looking down dismissively at his useless dangling appendage Imalima said, "Oh, that thing. As you might imagine, it is a bit tricky running backwards. Unlike the advantage of some mothers, I don't happen to have the good fortune of eyes in the back of my head, so while running late as usual on my way from here to there—by the way, have you ever been to either place? 'Here' is rather monotonous, ruined by sprawl, you know, but 'there' is fabulous. One of my all-time favorite eateries is there in 'there.' If you enjoy museums and art galleries, 'there' is not to be missed. Anyway, where was I?"

"You were—"

"Of course, thank you for reminding me. So, running late as usual, on my way from here to there. I'm rolling along at a pretty good clip while minding my own business, when all of a sudden, legs go flying in all directions and I'm airborne. You know, it's just like A. Dummi to see me come tootling along and slip a rotten muke egg onto the road."

"Did you say a dummy probably slipped a rotten muke egg onto the road?" Carter questioned.

"No, I did not. I said A. Dummi probably slipped a rotten muke egg onto the road," answered Imalima.

"Well, that's what I just said," Carter responded.

"Did not."

"Did too."

"Didn't. Anyway, you're interrupting my story. Where was I?"

"You were—"

"Of course, thank you again for reminding me. So I take a tumble. My number three exterior and posterior leg on the windward side, that would be third one up from the bottom back leg on the left, does a complete three-sixty and snaps. What is commonly referred to in medical terminology as the fibulator bone is irreparably damaged, tragically leaving me with a terminal gimp. That, sir, in a nutshell, is the reason I am sitting at this here bus stop, waiting for the number twenty-seven bus."

Carter stood staring at Imalima while carefully weighing his response. To say there was a communication problem was an understatement, yet he didn't want to provoke or challenge the creature's obviously fragile mental state.

Having a conversation with Imalima is like tiptoeing through a trip-wired minefield in Cuckooville, Nevermore communicated into Carter's mind.

"Imalima, my friends and I have been traveling this narrow road for days now. This is the absolute first bus stop we have come across and we haven't seen one single bus. For that matter, with the exception of your grocery cart, we haven't even seen anything on wheels."

"Well, ha cha-cha. Of course you haven't seen a bus or bus stop. This is the first official, permit-authorized, and licensed bus stop on Aeiea. It's brand new. In reference to your not seeing a bus, I am not at all surprised. Why would you expect to see a bus if there were no bus stops? You appear somewhat confused, perhaps even a bit discombobulated. Let me guess, you are in the slow reading group in school? I hold no judgment of you as we all have our limitations. I will attempt to clarify a simple but obviously difficult for you to grasp concept.

"First you must have bus stops *then* you get buses. That's how it works. It's like, build it and they will come. Another possible and even better reason you might not yet have seen a bus on Aeiea is that they have yet to be invented, a minor and insignificant detail. As I always say, the devil's in the details. If and when they are invented, I will have already built a chain of bus stops all across Aeiea, coincidently, cornering the travel market. The Johnny Appleseed of bus stops, if you will."

"How do you know about Johnny Appleseed?" Carter asked.

"Who?"

"You said 'the Johnny Appleseed of bus stops.'"

"I said no such thing. Never heard of Mister Applesauce till you brought him up. Who is this John Hayseed fellow anyway?"

"But I distinctly . . . I . . . never mind."

"Right," said Imalima, plunging ahead. "So if I have the exclusive license for all the bus stops, the bus company will have to pay me a user's fee each time they stop at one of my bus stops. Why, I could sell franchises that would serve overpriced wieners and cold drinks to hungry and thirsty waiting suckers such as you. No insult intended."

Carter couldn't help himself. "Good idea, Imalima. If they have to wait for a bus to come along for as long as you will have to wait here, you are going to have a lot of hungry customers. Why, you could make an absolute fortune off of each franchise."

Go easy, came the message down from the nest. *Don't provoke him.*

"Maybe you're not as dumb as I thought you were," Imalima said. "Want to be my partner?"

"Ummmmm, no thanks, Imalima, I'll have to take a rain check. At the moment I have more important things on my mind. Keep me posted, though, for when you come up with your next brainstorm, will you?"

Enough is enough, said the black bird from on high. *It sounds like you're beginning to relate, and that could be a dangerous thing.*

"Oh, one other thing," said Carter. "While we're on the subject of buses, for future reference you need to spell 'Bus Stop' correctly on your signs."

Imalima turned to examine his handiwork. "It is spelled correctly," he announced. "It is you who is incorrect. Try standing on your head and see what you get," he said confidently.

Carter cocked his head and actually gave Imalima's suggestion a moment's consideration. "No," he said finally. "I don't think so."

"I see what you mean," said Imalima, staring at his sign. "If you stood on your head, then the word 'bus' would be incorrectly spelled. Very smart, very smart indeed. I like the way you think, Mr. Pennysworth."

"Nicholsworth," Carter corrected.

"Whatever . . . hmmmmm. If what you say is true, then by my calculations I believe you owe me four centicles."

"What?"

"Oh, never mind. Keep the change," said Imalima, feeling generous.

Serene and company were only too well acquainted with Imalima. Being in a near state of constant locomotion, Imalima had on numerous occasions bisected the byways of most of the territories, including Wiggonwoggen, leaving a wake of chaos in his path. Although estranged from his native land, there was no doubt Imalima was genetically pure Wimzical. Some time ago it was determined by the citizens of Wiggonwoggen that out of respect for Mental Health Week, it would be best if the curious expatriate of Wimzi was avoided. This discrimination only served to further isolate Imalima, which may have been a contributing factor to his already full-blossomed case of paranoia.

. . . .

A jumble of backpacks, along with other assorted traveling gear, was strewn about the ground as the tired travelers welcomed a long overdue break. Wiggwoggs also lay scattered in various positions on the soft, low-growing clover like so many pick-up sticks, observing with detached amusement the dysfunctional discourse between beast and boy. Eventually tiring of the entertainment and in the heat of a sultry mid-afternoon, one by one they fell asleep.

It was within the hour that the first of them began to stir. Like a slow-growing virus, the restlessness spread from one Wiggwogg to another. Carter eased out of a dream that had featured Imalima, and upon awakening, he quickly sought out Serene. He got right to the point.

"I've been thinking. I have both a concern and a possible fix," he ventured. "Someone could sneak up from behind and surprise us. If they were real quiet, they could take several of us before anyone became aware of what was happening. We are vulnerable to attack from the rear position. You may think this an unworkable suggestion, but I think it's a good one. Since Imalima goes backwards to go forwards, he could be our eyes in the back of our heads."

Serene's face scrunched into an expression of doubt. "I don't know. We have been warned about contact with Imalima. Once a Wimzical, always a Wimzical. We cannot afford to jeopardize this mission, yet your observation of our vulnerability is correct. As I have said, Elderwiser chose you for his own reasons. If I am asking you to trust me, I must likewise trust you. I guess if you feel strongly about this and will take responsibility for Imalima, we can give it a try. That is if you can convince Imalima to join us. He's quite the gypsy, you know."

After dinner and gathering their gear, the adventurers were once again on the march with one noticeable difference: the caboose position in their walking order was now filled by Imalima. It took some persuading as Imalima had some issues of ego in accepting his placement of last in the lineup. Carter had to promise him he would give the proposed partnership in Imalima's bus stop venture a second consideration once their mission was complete. Imalima had no idea what their mission was, and that continued secret was part of the deal Carter had made with Serene. Imalima was a long way from earning Serene's trust.

As for Carter's compromised integrity, the boy justified in his mind that his misleading promise of reconsideration of a business partnership was for good ends, and in this unique, one-time-only situation, the ends did justify the means. There was also the realistic probability that even if their mission was successful and both managed to survive, Imalima would by then have forgotten the deal or possibly offered the business arrangement to several others. It most certainly was a stretch of ethical boundaries, but Carter was reasonably comfortable with his decision.

Ushi had taken his usual position up front as he led the travelers into the night. The road had narrowed and they were walking single file. Carter found himself just behind Serene, staring at the Wiggwogg's heels as she moved sure-footedly through the dark. There was no visible path, and Carter wondered how they knew where they were going. The forest that earlier had provided them cover had now begun to turn gaunt. Soon rolling hills lit by a wide swath of pulsing stars completely replaced the forest.

The original plan was to have reached the edge of the Valley of Dread in Dweeg Territory by nightfall, then to make camp and enter the valley in the first light of day. But because of their encounter with Imalima, the group was now behind schedule and having to make up for lost time.

Not much was known of the Valley of Dread except rumors of a once-fertile land that now lay fallow. The sheer, almost vertical walls of the mountains running along the Dweeg Territory's distant border with Stanelhooven were passive observers of the persistent wind. Mourners Mountains had come to their name through a wailing wind carrying its message of sorrow to any listener. The mountains served as a protective fortress for the Dweeg from any attackers striking from the west. A grieving howl that constantly swept through the mountain passes had a long history of driving an inexperienced traveler mad.

Before the adventurers would reach the mountains, however, they would have to cross through the Valley of Dread on the northeastern corner of Dweeg Territory. On the other side of the mountain range, the wind was a stranger. Somewhere in the upper reaches of Mourners Mountains supposedly lay the isolated village of Millililli, home to the Minnininni. To the north, Stanelhooven was quiet and mostly empty of inhabitants who preferred the richer, loamy soils of the lowland Gushkin Territory.

To the north of the Gushkin Territory was the Dwarf Forest of Sarwinnia and Bunnicloven, a mostly flat land carpeted in purple-flowered clover. Bunnicloven was stocked with long-haired animals resembling rabbits. The "hoppsters," as Gushkins and "Hoovens" referred to them, had significant ears and a pouch located on their undercarriage much like a kangaroo's. Finishing off their odd features, a long, thin tail arched gracefully upward. Like cousin rabbit, they lived a busy communal life deep in a complicated labyrinth of burrowed warrens.

· · · · · · ·

Serene had once before been in Dweeg Territory, but in her travels she had not met a single Dweeg. The leader of the Wiggwoggs had heard they were peaceful and once enjoyed an agrarian lifestyle not unlike that of those who lived in Wiggonwoggen.

The Dweeg had a longstanding reputation for being good neighbors. Their submissive nature was reasonably secured by their topography. They were pretty much left to live out their simple farming lives working hard on the land in relative peace and happiness.

That was before The Grinder and his army of Gootz discovered the Oxbuk Pass, a narrow canyon winding through Mourners Mountains. That was also before The Grinder and his Gootz army invaded the Dweeg Territory. The Dweeg were unprepared for the brutality that swept over the land like locusts. Driven from their farms, the once easygoing spirit of the defeated Dweeg was broken.

When Dweeg Territory was invaded and more than one-third of the Dweeg population slaughtered, the traumatized inhabitants lost all hope. With many rounded up and taken off to Athulian to work as slaves, the Dweeg remaining in their territory had become emotionally cowed by their terror. It was a dark period in their history, referred to by the Dweeg as "the time of tears." Barely a handful now lived in the territory, whose fertile soil once supported strings of prospering small farms. The remaining population had since retreated to a series of chambers hidden deep in the lower elevations of Mourners Mountains. There the terrified Dweeg lived out their solitary existence in a state of constant insecurity, not daring to venture far from their well-concealed caves.

If the loathsome Gootz didn't physically hold the Dweeg prisoner, then their paralyzing fear of The Grinder most certainly did.

Chapter 10
The Grinder

Some time ago, when the door to the twenty-fourth era had just begun to close, The Grinder had begun experiencing a sense of restlessness. Looking about what was then the original Bludenbonz Castle, he felt discontent with what he saw. He thought his home was looking a bit shabby.

The bored Gootz leader ordered Athulian's ancient castle torn down and rebuilt with a new structure erected in the footprint of the old castle. There it would take its rightful place in the history of Aeiea as a monument to The Grinder's life. He knew it would take an untold number of hands working continuously around the clock close to one hundred years to rebuild his castle, but what's a century more or less to someone as important as The Grinder?

Dweeg slaves went meekly to their task and literally put their lives into their work. Generations of Dweeg came and went, as unnoticed as the evening's tide slipping onto the shore of Athulian. Mortar used to bind rock to rock was made from the ground-up bones of those slaughtered by The Grinder. The unfortunates were either victims of combat or legions of older indentured slaves who had been worn down by the years of cruelty, no longer able to keep up with younger workers.

When the new and improved Bludenbonz Castle was finally complete, in a rare move totally unbefitting a feared sadistic leader with his reputation, The Grinder declared a day of celebration. To show his appreciation of a job well done, The Grinder allowed the broken-spirited Dweeg slaves, both young and old, to sleep in on the morning of the celebration before being rousted for another day of work. Several of the more militant of The Grinder's generals, quietly, very quietly, questioned their leader's unprecedented generosity.

Only when Major General Kuk, the most indiscreet of the whisperers, was found hanging from a tree alongside the road leading to The Grinder's castle did the murmuring abruptly cease. Major General Kuk's neck was stretched nearly a foot long, and his once substantial greasy-haired ears were missing. Also gone were the medals and ribbons of honor that once proudly decorated his chest. In their place was now pinned his severed tongue. The major general's swollen lips were crudely sewn together and tattooed across his forehead were the words *BIG MOUTH.*

· · · · · · ·

Drawn out of his reverie back into the present moment, The Grinder sniffed the air. "Something is different," mused The Grinder. "I don't know what it is, but I know it *is.*"

Standing alone on a high bluff at the far westernmost point of Athulian, the Gootz leader stared out across the vast Sea of Valion to a place where streaks of cement-colored clouds sailed along the water's edge. Lightning flashed across the down side of a gloomy day, stabbing randomly into the dark sea. The Grinder nervously fingered the rings that decorated each of his fingers.

"I smells it!" The Grinder roared, shaking his fist into a cold wind that pushed against his snarling face. "I smells it, it's coming this way and it smells like dinner."

The Kenga were The Grinder's first line of defense. Beyond Athulian, they were his ears and eyes on the territories. Living in nests in the uppermost branches of dead trees, the mutated birds had distinct advantages over what they referred to as the "feet folk." Looking more like flying serpents than birds, the Kenga were without legs so they had no feet to stumble over. Kenga's webbed wings averaged more than six feet in span when in flight. They also had no feathers; rather, their silky, fur-covered skin resembled that of a bat's. When in flight, they glided more than flapped, unless of course in a rush to bring a snippet of juicy news to their patron.

Another advantage the Kenga enjoyed over "feet folk" was that the stealthy gatherers of information came equipped with a pouch under their tongues containing an endless supply of deadly poisonous saliva. The flying spies could project spit some twenty feet when necessary, paralyzing the nervous system of a victim in less than a minute. The resulting incapacitation prevented breathing, which guaranteed the recipient of the Kenga's spitball a painful but mercifully quick death.

Long ago The Grinder had determined the Kenga, whose brains were not much larger than a gumball and therefore of limited storage capacity, would be used sparingly as an offensive weapon. Because of the Kenga's tendency to be slow breeders, he decided to conserve their numbers and make them serve his needs as spies. This arrangement was perfectly fine with the Gootz army, who were not keen on the idea of competing for gory glory with The Grinder's own personal intelligence-gathering force.

How is it, you might ask, that those with the least intelligence are often those that wind up holding positions requiring the most intelligence? Perhaps you might want to ask someone in government that question. Oh, now where was I?

· · · · · · ·

Bumbreth, who was better known by his nickname Twitch, was the half-brother of The Grinder and was the general in charge of The Grinder's air force that consisted exclusively of the Kenga. The flying Kenga spies had been aware of the small group of travelers since first observing them gathered at the tulk tree just two days earlier. Twitch concluded there was no great hurry in alerting his grumpy brother on the sighting of a small ragtag group of hikers. He wanted to be thorough and prepare a detailed report for The Grinder, including the exact number of hikers, their strength in weapons if they carried any, and any possible threat they might pose to the security of Athulian Island.

"We're protecting the interests of our homeland," he reasoned. "If a confrontation is required with another territory, better to fight them over there than here on Athulian." Twitch was great at pep talks to motivate his troops. He would always end his motivational cheerleading sessions with his standard shout, "Let's git 'er dunnn!"

The Kenga did not gather much information from their initial sighting of the young hikers, but Twitch did conclude these were most likely Wiggwoggs. This made sense since the first observence of the band of backpackers was made while flying over Wiggonwoggen. Even after the Wiggwoggs crossed the border into Dweeg Territory, no alarms went off in Commander Twitch's head.

The Wiggwoggs in general were of little concern to the brother of The Grinder, who considered them rather dull-witted and unmotivated. Twitch had written off his old stomping grounds of Wiggonwoggen as hardly worthy of a good plundering. After all, reasoned Twitch, it was The Grinder who now possessed the Circle of Power. The Wiggwoggs had no hope of going up against the great Gootz army to regain the Circle of Power, and certainly not with a tiny group of children he imagined armed at best with slingshots and rocks. It had been many ages since anyone foreign to Athulian with aggression on their minds had dared set foot on the island.

Twitch's half-brother had a murderous reputation. The Gootz leader prided himself on the mountain of bones stacked behind a great wall of barbeque pits at the far lower end of the castle's grounds. The gruesome bone yard was The Grinder's personal playground where many enjoyable hours were spent playing with his "tinker toys." Stripped bones were all that remained of an enemy after being marinated overnight in The Grinder's private reserve of tangy barbeque sauce before the unfortunate victim was roasted alive at a castle potluck. The resulting abstract sculpture of bones was the centerpiece of a ragged park where, at The Grinder's invitation, Gootz soldiers and their families would gather to picnic.

A simple appearance of The Grinder on the roads of Bludenbonz caused even the boldest of Athulian's soldiers to lower their eyes when he passed. The Gootz feared that with even the briefest eye contact they risked being pulled into their leader's awareness. If The Grinder was in one of his typically bad moods, the results could have disastrous consequences for a citizen's health. It was as if simple eye contact alone would somehow place the offending individual one step closer to showing up on The Grinder's dinner plate.

"You over there!" The Grinder had shouted at one of the castle's gardeners. "Did I just see your eyes? If I see anyone's eyes, I will personally take pleasure in removing them. Look at me!" The Grinder commanded. The poor gardener was confused. Should he do as ordered and risk losing his sight? The gardener remained with his eyes downcast.

"Good job, gardener," The Grinder said, patting his servant's head. "OK now," he continued, smiling down at the unnerved Gootz, "Simon says: 'Look at me.'" This time the gardener took a chance and looked at The Grinder.

Big mistake.

The gardener arrived home for dinner that night later than usual. Sometime during the day, he had misplaced his sunhat—and lost his eyes as well. As you might imagine, the incidence of blindness on Athulian was considerably higher than in the surrounding territories.

The Grinder's body of considerable girth was covered with a coarse tangle of matted hair. Even the now-blind gardener knew when he was in the presence of his leader. The awful stench exuded by The Grinder's body was enjoyed only by the nasty horseflies that must have suffered from the same weirditude as those who enjoy the smell of stinky cigars. Odor-loving "buzzers," as The Grinder fondly referred to the flies, circled in a consistent flight pattern around his foul-smelling head. The Gootz leader's tacky noggin appeared to some as if purchased out of a mail order catalog selling cheap but scary Halloween masks. Among the several sheaths that hung from The Grinder's sword belt holstering his creative instruments of death, one loop was designed specifically for a flyswatter. The Grinder and the flies shared a symbiotic relationship. For the flies, his juicy head was the tree of life, and for The Grinder, the unluckiest of the flies, probably the old and the feeble, represented a tasty afternoon's snack on a cracker as well as an excellent source of protein and fiber.

· · · · · · ·

"What a joke my brother is," chuckled Twitch, whose bad breath could make a weasel weep. The terrible smell made even him gag. "When I get back to Athulian, I've got to see my toothworker," he promised himself.

Of course Twitch's intention was nothing more than a big fat lie. Twitch didn't have a toothworker. As a matter of fact, there was not a single licensed toothworker left on the island of Athulian, thanks to The Grinder.

Long ago, before The Grinder's meteoric rise to supreme commander of everything and everyone on Athulian, his given birth name from the territory of Wiggonwoggen was Harvey Putzer. It was a name he never much cared for. Too ethnic, he thought, certainly not a name befitting a leader of his great stature. So he dropped Harvey and although not thrilled with his last name, in deference to his loving mother, he kept the name Putzer.

I digress here to tell you a short story about The Grinder. I share this tale not to shock or offend you, and I apologize for the following assault on your sensibilities. That being said, I feel it important you have additional insight as to The Grinder's depraved character so you will not be overcome with remorse upon learning of his inevitable fate. I can understand how some might develop a sense of misplaced compassion for the leader of the Gootz, but in his case it is totally undeserved. Most all creatures of one kind or another have some redeeming quality. Not so The Grinder. Totally lacking a conscience, he is simply mean to the bone and, in the following example of his disposition, especially mean to the jawbone.

One day some time ago, Putzer, his name at the time, went to his tooth-worker to replace one of his many fillings. When it came time to pay for services rendered, Putzer, with an air of entitlement, walked out without paying. The next time Putzer returned to the oral technician with another cavity, he was told this one was really deep, and to avoid significant pain, he would need a strong dose of gas to put him to sleep during the procedure. When Putzer eventually awoke, the toothworker advised him that because of additionally discovered cavities, he had taken the liberty, even without a signed release form, to make an executive decision. Rather than having to bill him for future follow-up visits, he made sure that Putzer would never again have to worry about cavities, replacing fillings or paying the oral technician's "reasonable" charges.

"Today's visit is on the house," the toothworker told his patient. Putzer was thrilled with the news. That is, until he noticed his broad smile in the mirror and observed he no longer had any teeth. Understandably upset, Putzer killed the toothworker on the spot.

Years later, after becoming a big shot, dropping the name Putzer, and getting a spanking new set of high-end silvery metal choppers, The Grinder ordered all but a handful of toothworkers on Athulian rounded up. One by one, each of them received a free ride on The Grinder's brand spanking new toothworker's chair, accessorized with leather straps for wrists and ankles.

"Welcome and a good day to you, sir," The Grinder would say politely to his patient who was forcibly dragged by Gootz soldiers to an appoint-ment with the masquerading toothworker.

"Won't you step up and have a seat in my specially equipped chair? Careful now, we don't want you to hurt yourself. I promise this won't take too long and we'll have you out of here in no time. I regret to inform you that we are unfortunately fresh out of gas today. If the discomfort becomes unbearable, we do have an alternative to the gas." He would then point to the dental tray alongside the chair that held a few scary instruments and one *really* large mallet.

The wide-eyed patients always rejected The Grinder's alternative to anesthesia. Using the leather straps to secure his patient, the Gootz leader might say something like, "Why don't you sit back, relax, and enjoy the experience. I know I will."

Using an old pair of rusty pliers and without benefit of the gas that had been so problematical in his own past experience, The Grinder, wearing a freshly laundered white gown, proceeded to remove each tooth from nearly every tooth technician on Athulian. This took great patience as well as eye-hand coordination due to the chair's rapid up and down movement caused by the agitated patient. A little twist here, a little yank there. He responded to each practitioner's agony with squeals of delirious laughter every time a terrorized toothworker screamed.

Most toothworkers died in the customized chair from the sheer horror of their ordeal.

"Scaredy-cat! Crybaby! Loser!" The Grinder taunted. For those whose misfortune found them still breathing past their final extraction, The Grinder feigned a toothworker with a bad memory. He might "accidentally" drop an instrument such as a mirror or a scraper down the open clamped mouth of his tortured victim. Then with dramatic exaggeration while pretending to check his pockets and floor for the missing instrument, he would say something like, "I seem to have misplaced my widget thingy. Have you seen it? I'm sorry I can't understand what you're trying to say. Why don't you try clearing your throat?"

Oh, how he loved that line. He would rehearse his question in front of the mirror endlessly. If the victim didn't get the joke—and not surprisingly none did—he would happily play the scene all over again, just for the opportunity of delivering the practiced punch line a second time. *"Why don't you try clearing your throat? Get it?"* The hysterical Grinder would then collapse onto the floor rolling around in a maniacal fit of tearful laughter.

Unfortunately for The Grinder, there was a limited supply of Gootz toothworkers. As word spread amongst the dental practitioners of their dwindling number of co-workers' untimely demises, those remaining quickly chose other professions. In the end, although no one heard them, the dearly departed toothworkers had the last laugh from the safety of their graves.

First, a few dingy yellow teeth started showing up amongst the citizens of Athulian, who were not known to embrace the best dental hygiene practices anyway. Soon the yellow degraded to green, then gray before finally turning black. Gum disease became rampant and then a few citizens began to lose a tooth or two. Before long, rotten Gootz teeth began collecting along the roadsides of Athulian like dirty snow.

Only the high mucky-mucks of Athulian hierarchy could afford a full set of snazzy metallic teeth. A blinding smile, such as The Grinder's, became a sought after status symbol among the Gootz, to be flashed while attending some nose-in-the-air snooty party or other upscale Gootz social event. For those with lesser disposable income, wood was the only available alternative for the common Gootz. However, in a land of excessive humidity or the opposite, near total absence of moisture in the summer, there were serious complications with wooden teeth. The swelling or shrinking of the discount choppers caused the lips of those wearing the "falsies" to appear either grossly bloated or prune puckered. And as if all that wasn't problem enough, there was also the inevitable, down-the-road issue of irreversible oral dry rot.

Those Gootz who chose neither of the two alternatives, wishing to remain toothless for personal or financial reasons, were snobbishly looked down upon by their peers. These low-end Gootz were commonly referred to as "gummers."

At some point, as you have probably already surmised, it is in The Grinder's destiny that he crosses paths with Carter Nicholsworth, whose grandfather, interestingly enough, had been a dentist.

But that comes later, and I have much to tell you before then.

· · · · · · ·

Off in the distance, Ushi made out the faint silhouette of Mourners Mountains. Like a spilled bowl of pea soup, the Valley of Dread poured out, spreading dull green to the mountains. Along the raised edges confining the valley, the landscape was designed with pockets of clumpy brush and an occasional tree. Some of the trees appeared thin and sickly with curled leaves barely holding onto life while a lesser number stood brazenly bare-naked, having already given up the fight.

Sniffing the late morning air, Ushi shook his head. "I don't like it. I smell an unfamiliar odor. My sense is that whatever is out there is not friendly."

"If that is true," Serene said, "then we will have to deal with it. We must go through Dweeg Territory and that means past the Valley of Dread and over Mourners Mountains."

The day, which had opened bright, was now moving quickly into a patch of still air and foreboding gloom. This was also true of the mood settling over the explorers on their journey through the Valley of Dread. Serene had great respect for the accuracy of Ushi's nose and was on full alert for any signs of danger. Aside from the strangely sculptured images carved from rock outcroppings growing from the valley's floor, everything seemed perfectly normal.

After pausing for a quick meal of alagwa, a smooth-skinned crescent-shaped fruit, and a quick, refreshing bath in a secluded pool fed by two lethargic streams, Carter, Nevermore, Imalima, and the Wiggwoggs were once again on the move.

By mid-afternoon the promise of continued good weather had broken its word. A gang of sooty clouds, as if on a hunt for mischief, came churning up over the top of Mourners Mountains, chasing the still air with a chilling wind. Turning from bleak to near black then changing back again to bleak, the threatening sky tumbled down the mountains toward the adventurers.

Nevermore kicked and scratched, trying to hunker down in his nest of red hair. Raising his face upward, Ushi saw the first flakes of snow dancing grace-fully out of the sky. Scenting the air once again, Ushi's grim expression as he turned toward Serene and Carter told them more than they wanted to know.

"Bad news! We have to hurry," Ushi urged, appraising the landscape. He spoke in an even, controlled voice, but his words were all the alarm Carter, Imalima, and the Wiggwoggs needed. Ushi loped off in the direction of a high bank that ran parallel to the trail with the others following in quick pursuit.

When they were little more than halfway, the sky lost its patience. Hail the size of tennis balls rained down, snapping tree branches on the way and sending them crashing to the ground. Shards of ice chiseled the landscape, stripping bark and leaves from trees. The frozen missiles ricocheted wildly in a deafening performance of nature's power.

"Faster!" Ushi shouted. Racing toward the bank, Carter's progress was slowed by the awkwardness of running while holding his hands to his ears. Wiggwoggs and Imalima flashed past him. Nearing the bank, a sudden sharp knife of pain cut into the back of his thigh. Almost immediately Carter felt a burning sensation in his leg. Luckily it was not a direct hit but rather a glancing blow of ice, and while it did not stop him, he now ran with a noticeable limp. Boulders, unconcerned with the weather, rested between Carter and the bank, creating an obstacle course. Those in the group who had run past Carter disappeared behind them.

It was just about then that Carter noticed an opening in the bank. Sitting on an improvised stool in front of a small table just inside the opening and blocking the entrance was Imalima. Outside the opening stood Imalima's cart and a beat-up old umbrella stand overflowing with garishly decorated umbrellas. Don't ask where the umbrellas came from. Imalima has his ways. Hanging from the umbrella stand was another of Imalima's creative signs. *Umbrellas and Tickets to The Lost Cave for Sale* read the sign. A chaotic assortment of mangled umbrellas lay scattered on the ground next to the stand. A second sign stuck up from the ground: *Slightly defective umbrellas 50% off.* The umbrella fabrics stretched over wire stays had once protected the user from bad weather but now sported several recently acquired holes.

Diving for the entrance while tucking into a tight roll, Carter completed two perfect forward somersaults. Coming up into a sitting position, Carter found his face pressed tight against Imalima's. "So how's business?" he asked the surprised creature.

Ignoring the question, Imalima said, "No room. We're sold out of both umbrellas and tour tickets. Move on down the road."

Carter was getting a better sense of the quirky creature. If at one time he might have been intimidated by Imalima's squirrelly behavior, this was no longer the case. As a matter of fact, his overall confidence was growing because of the sincere respect he had experienced from Elderwiser, Serene, and the other Wiggwoggs. For the first time in Carter Nicholsworth's young life, he felt genuinely needed.

"Nonsense," Carter responded. "Make room or I'll have to throw you out." Aside from his growing comfort with his newly discovered self-confidence, Carter's leg hurt and he was not in the mood for what had the makings of a generous serving of Imalima's famous cattywhampus pie.

One of the larger incoming ice bombs whistled just outside the cave's opening, scoring a direct hit on Imalima's fledgling umbrella business. Carter looked first at the wrecked umbrella stand with its now twisted, unusable merchandise scattered about the landscape, joining the other dead umbrellas. He next turned his attention to the fresh crop of new divots scarring the ground, and then to Imalima. "Well," said Carter, trying hard to hold a straight face, "that should lighten your load. Besides, the weather is sure to change shortly and then you would have to deal with a bazillion grumpy customers in the 'returns' line."

Looking out onto the jumbled remains of his most recent failed enterprise, Imalima sighed and, without looking directly at Carter, said stoically, "I suppose my misfortune is a source of amusement to you. Personally I see adversity as opportunity in disguise. Each apparent failure is just another lesson to be learned on the path to enlightenment. I may be out of the bumbershoot business, but I feel something good is just around the corner." Imalima struck a pose of someone deep in thought, tapping his bearded chin with one of his floppy webbed feet.

"Great gobs of slick sticky skunk snot!" Imalima shouted into the storm. "Sorry to interrupt my impressive train of thoughts hurtling down the tracks, but I just had a fabumagnificus idea. You know how all of us are soaked to the bone from the storm? Well, I figure we could gather up all those broken umbrellas, bend up their stays, and make wire things that we could attach our wet clothes onto. They could hold the clothes while they dried. I even have a name for my invention: holders. Yes, that's it. Holders!"

"Might I suggest an alternative to the name 'holders?'" Carter asked. "How about hangers?"

The broad smile faded from the goat creature's elongated face as he carefully pondered Carter's suggestion. He paced thoughtfully back and forth in front of the cave's entrance. Slowly, like the suns' reappearance from behind a cloud, the smile returned.

"Oh, aren't you the mister smarty-pants, Carter Nicholsworth? There is good reason I chose you for my partner." Imalima thrust one of his floppy feet in Carter's direction, inviting a formal handshake cementing their partnership. "Let's shake on it." Carter looked down at the webbed foot, cautiously considering the offering.

WHOOOOP echoed loudly from the depths of the cave, startling both Carter and Imalima. "What was that?" asked Carter, looking over his shoulder.

Imalima's eyes were as wide as saucers. "Sounded like a high pitched WHOOOOP," he answered, imitating the sound perfectly. His imitation was so good, in fact, that a second responding WHOOOOP was heard from the bowels of the cave.

"Where is everyone?" Carter asked Imalima, all of a sudden feeling anxious. For the moment, Imalima's new enterprise was on the back burner.

"In there." Imalima gestured with his head in the direction of the darkness that waited breathlessly beyond the cave's opening. "Want to buy a ticket?"

Ignoring Imalima's question, Carter asked, "How come you didn't go with them? Afraid of wild creatures in the dark grabbing and eating you?"

"What's it to you anyway?" nervously responded the shaggy-haired creature. A shiver began at his tail and worked its way up the entire length of his body. The shudder terminated at his head and shook Imalima so violently that his eyes momentarily uncrossed. "Ow!" cried the Wimzical. "That hurt!" He cradled his heavy head between two flappers. Carter tried to hide a smile by covering his mouth with his hand in a feigned attempt at a yawn.

"As a matter of fact, I do have some issues with the dark," Imalima confessed. "Nightmares about Athulian and The Grinder frequent my dreams and never with an invitation. In one such bad dream, I am snared in a camouflaged trap laid by The Grinder. The first thing he does is shave my entire body right down to the skin. Now there is nothing wrong with my ego, mind you, and I do have a pretty good body. But if you ask me—which, by the way, no one does—I must say, as a total baldy, I was . . . how shall I say this without hurting my feelings . . . grotesque. Anyway, the next thing he does is ties up all my feet and then with a gaffing pole under the ropes, he secures my feet on a swiveling crane and winchjamadingy. I am next dipped into a thickly mixed batter of flour and beer then swung over to a deep fryer where I am slowly dunked into hot, bubbling oil."

The small grin that had been working its way onto Carter's face quickly faded as he remembered his own frightening episode with the cartoon crabs.

"That is scary, Imalima, but surely you understand your nightmare is nothing more than a bad dream."

"I tell myself that, but it seems so real. I keep having the same dream over and over. Even though I know how it always ends, I am still horrified. It always ends with me being served at The Grinder's banquet table, not as a guest, mind you, but on a platter with an apple in my mouth as the main course.

"No matter how hard I try, I don't seem able to awaken myself. The Grinder starts carving me up and the young-uns begin yanking off my legs, garnished down around the ankles with a brightly colored assortment of curly ribbon. So there I am flailing around in my bed screaming desperately—and unsuccessfully, I might add—for me dear old pappy to come and rescue me, when I am finally and mercifully able to wake myself up. And that's why I always sleep with one eye open, so no one can sneak up and do me in."

"Interesting enough," said Carter, "but once again, not pertinent to the situation at hand. Right now we need to find the others, so gather up your courage and follow me."

Upon entering the cave, the first thing Carter noticed was a "One Way" street sign affixed to the cave's wall pointing in the opposite direction of the entrance. Down into the dark cave they walked, Imalima following Carter so closely the boy could feel his warm breath on the back of his neck. When he turned, Imalima was standing on his hind legs walking upright and frontwards.

"I didn't know you could that," Carter said.

"Nor I. However, there is much about me we don't know," Imalima responded. "I hope to prove myself worthy and of value on this journey. I may be genetically predisposed to appear a bit wack-a-doo to outsiders, but in *reality*, which is not a familiar word in the territory of Wimzi, I am not as cuckoo as I may appear."

Carter had his doubts about the reliability of Imalima's statement, but he had at the moment bigger fish to fry. The stuffy cave that smelled of rotting food led downward then sharply to the left into total darkness. It was as if someone had instantly turned off the lights.

Carter shouted Serene's name into the void. There was no response. He could see nothing as he slowly inched along with one hand against one side of the cave's wall and the other hand held out straight in front of him in an attempt to avoid bumping into anything. The texture of the cave's wall was a surprise to Carter and, for that matter, so was the floor. Instead of the expected hard rock, the cave's interior surface was soft and fibrous. After walking a distance then carefully rounding another corner, Carter's concentration was broken by Imalima's voice.

"It sure is dark in here. If I were a goblin or some other kind of scary creature, this cave would make an ideal clubhouse."

"A candle sure would come in handy," responded Carter.

"A candle, you say, why didn't you mention that earlier? It just so happens . . . I don't have a candle."

Raising Carter's hopes then pulling the rug out from under him was great sport for Imalima. Purposely he left an intentional distance between his last words and his next. "But I do have something even better, a lifetime supply of Imalima's Exclusive Five-star Earwax. These long, floppy ears of mine are good for something besides wrapping round my neck on a chilly day. I also have a roll of twine, and I believe you have some matches. That should be all the materials we need to do the job."

Within moments, the Imalima Candle and Floor Wax Factory was in full operation. Supplied with a half-dozen brownish-yellow candle tapers, the two once again set off, going ever deeper into the cave but now moving more rapidly and with more confidence. Carter held three lit candles in each hand. "That's much better," said Carter, looking at Imalima whose crossed eyes stared at each other.

After a while, the cave began to slightly narrow, twisting back and forth like a curl of smoke.

"Do you hear that?" asked Imalima, his hairy head cocked to one side.

Carter's drifting mind was pulled back to the present by Imalima's question. "No, I don't hear anything, but if ear size makes a difference, your hearing is probably much better than mine." Standing absolutely still, Carter strained to hear the origin of Imalima's question. "What did it sound like?"

Imalima thought for a moment. "Can't rightly say, but it surely sounded familiar. Wait a minute. No, that's just too strange."

"What is it? What's too strange?" Carter asked uneasily.

"Well, I know this is kind of weird, but it sounded something like the sound of my stomach grumbling when I'm hungry or if I have eaten too much or too fast. I told you it's weird. What do you think?"

"I don't know what to think. I sure wish we could find the others. I'm not feeling good about this cave. Are you sure they came in here?" Carter tried to take a few steps back in the direction they had just come, but the floor of the cave was so slippery that for all his effort, he could not gain traction. He then remembered the "One Way" sign at the cave's entrance.

Imalima did not have a chance to answer Carter's question. Without warning, a powerful undulating wave of energy rolled through the cave. The two were instantly thrown from their feet. Downward they tumbled. The candles blew out and Carter lost his grip on them while deeper into the tunnel they slid. The walls stretched then contracted while the cave's floor heaved in violent convulsion.

"EARTHQUAKE!!!" shouted Carter.

"I have absolutely no idea what that means," responded Imalima as he cart-wheeled past Carter. "But I have a feeling it is not a good thing."

"Carter! Imalima! Is that you?" Serene's familiar voice came echoing from out of the darkness just up ahead.

"Yes, it's us. Where are you?" answered Carter, his anxious voice betraying his concern.

"A better question is," interrupted Imalima, "where are we?" In less time than it would take to say "Jack Black lacks the knack to stack train track," the tumbling Imalima crashed with full force into Zebenuza, who was known as a bit of a hothead.

"BIRDBRAIN!" yelled Zebenuza, who was knocked off his feet. Nevermore took Zebenuza's offensive comment personally and concluded the Wiggwogg was a bird bigot. Zebenuza was preoccupied with a bloody nose and not impressed with Imalima's grand entrance. "Why me, you lunatic hairball?"

"Wool," reminded Imalima.

Carter, on the other hand, gently came to rest at the shoulder of Serene. The remaining Wiggwoggs sat huddled just beyond. In a moment, Carter's eyes adjusted to the dark, and with some effort he could identify each of them.

"While I am happy to see you," greeted Serene, "I would have preferred other circumstances and location for a reunion. To best answer your question, Imalima," she said, disregarding the creature's explosive confrontation with Zebenuza, "I believe we have unfortunately wandered into the intestinal track of a giant morphodorph. Elderwiser warned me about them. Most of a morphodorph's time is spent either napping or lying still as death, anticipating it won't be long before their next meal literally drops in. They appear as just another hill, but that's hardly the case. They're never without their mouths open, and they can go for long periods, even weeks, without eating. Morphodorph don't have teeth or need them since they don't chew their food. Rather, an unsuspecting animal becomes dinner upon being deposited in the pool of acid waiting in the monster's belly. A group our size would probably be considered an excellent day's catch."

"You mean we're dinner???" Imalima cried.

"And if I had my way, you would be the first one into the pool," Zebenuza grumbled.

"Oh, Mommy!" Imalima wailed. "It can't end this way. I am destined for great things. What about my bus stop franchises? What about my invention of the holders?"

"Hangers," reminded Carter.

"What's a hanger?" Iat asked.

"NEVER MIND!" Retann shouted. "What is wrong with all of you? We have been swallowed alive by a huge monster. We are on the brink of death with our mission failed, and all you can do is blabber about holders and hangers. We need to think of a way out of here, and I mean fast, before the monster burps and drops us into its stomach."

Carter nervously played with the book of matches in his pocket, a keepsake from his treasure chest in Wickedwood. He turned the book over and over again with his fingers, his eyes fixed on Imalima, who he knew had exhausted his immediate supply of earwax.

Serene was watching Carter. "What are you thinking?" she asked. Carter did not immediately respond, but he removed the matches from his pocket so that Serene could see them. His eyes were still fixed on Imalima.

Imalima couldn't make out what was going on but figured it might have something to do with him. "Am I missing something here?" he asked, his voice noticeably more nervous and an octave higher than usual.

Slowly removing the long knife sheathed at his waist while intuitively picking up the silent communication between Carter and Serene, Ushi took a small step in Imalima's direction. Imalima was now on heightened alert, seeing everyone staring at him. In an instant his many legs were on the move but, unfortunately for him, all in different directions.

"How could you?" he sobbed. "You're going to roast me, aren't you? My nightmare has come true, but it's not The Grinder or the morphodorph who does me in, it's all of you. I thought you were my friends. Why can't you roast that dumb bird on Carter's head or cranky old Zebenuza? Why me?" Imalima's teary eyes darted pleadingly around his fellow prisoners.

"Settle down, Imalima," Carter said. "No one is going to roast you, at least none of us. I figure our only chance of escape is to build a hot, smoky fire in the bowels of this beast and just maybe, if we're lucky, the morphodorph will throw us up and out. At least it's worth a try. We need your woolly coat."

"You're not going to kill me? You only need my wool?"

"That's it. No murder, just wool," Carter responded.

"Well, why didn't you say so?"

Imalima couldn't help himself. He was a relentless entrepreneur. "I would be remiss not to remind you, my wool is a highly sought after product and has a value on the open commodities market. What say we open our financial negotiations at, let's say . . ."

"Excuse me, Imalima," said Serene, growing impatient. "We don't have time for negotiations."

"Give it up now, and I mean right now," Zebenuza cut in, "or we will just do it the hard way. You're not going to like that one bit. If you are not cooperative, Ushi's knife might just slip. There is the distinct possibility you could accidentally get punctured, letting out some of that hot air."

"Not altogether a bad idea," grumbled Ferbert. "Better yet, since time is an issue, how 'bout we just pass on the haircut and light up the wool while he's still in it. That would be the quickest solution."

Zebenuza concurred.

Recognizing his poor bargaining position and the immediacy of the situation, Imalima cut to the chase. "OK, it's a deal. Perhaps at a later date, when you all are in a better mood, we can discuss reasonable compensation."

"Right," Ushi said, approaching Imalima.

"Please be gentle and do a good job," Imalima implored. "I'm thinking of something like maybe a quarter- to a half-inch off the top, but leave the sides kind of long so as at least to partially cover my ears. And while you are at it, would it be asking too much to trim up my eyebrows?"

Imalima was accustomed to being ignored and tightly shut his eyes as Ushi set about the task of removing enough wool to do the job. In a matter of moments, Ushi was finished. As evidenced by Imalima's disheveled appearance, the goal was obviously quantity not quality, and time was critical.

Disappointment would be an understatement for the description of Imalima's reaction to his new 'do. In short, it was not pretty. The Wiggwoggs and Carter had all they could do to restrain their laughter. Imalima looked as if he had been violently attacked by a half-starved wild beast. Large chunks of his matted coat appeared ripped from his body and now lay stacked in several random piles all around him.

Glancing down at Imalima, Nevermore thought, *Rather ratty* into Carter's mind. *Nasty batch of potholes along that stretch of road,* he continued. *That poor critter looks like the leftover remains in an old maid's hope chest after an infestation of voracious moths.* The little black bird was on a roll.

"Sorry," Ushi said to Imalima, standing back and examining his shoddy work. "It was dark and I was in a hurry."

"Is it really that bad?" Imalima was trying desperately to make eye contact with Ushi, but the Wiggwogg was not cooperating. There was, of course, no mirror for Imalima to make a more thorough inspection, which was a good thing since it helped minimize his trauma.

Upon gathering several piles of the woolly material into one great pile, Carter squatted, preparing to light a match.

"WAIT!" Lohden yelled. "What if we all catch fire in here and burn to a crisp or simply die from breathing in too much smoke?"

"Both of those are certainly possibilities," Serene answered. "However, the next digestive wave can't be far off. That one will most likely send us all into the belly of the beast where we will simply melt like butter in a hot broth. Have you a better plan, Lohden? Has anyone a better plan?"

Lohden fell into silence. None of the others spoke up either. "All right then," Serene said softly, nodding her head at Carter, who then proceeded to light the match.

At first the damp, oily wool simply smoldered and smelled just awful. There was growing concern after the third match failed that the wool was simply too wet and would not burn. Carter found a small pile of nearly dry wool and separated it from the larger stack. Getting down on his hands and knees, he lit the fourth match and gently blew into the glowing promise of fire. A very small flame grew into a bit larger one as he added fuel and more breath to the small stack of wool. Before long, there was fire, a smoky affair that drifted upward in curls toward the mouth of the morphodorph.

Carter, Serene, and the other Wiggwoggs stayed as low as they could get, which meant lying prone directly behind the fire. They joined hands to ensure that they would not again be separated. One way or another, they were all in this together, and their fate would be jointly shared. Of course, Imalima had no hands to join with the others, but still he managed to position his shabby body so as to be in the center of the huddled circle.

It was becoming increasingly difficult to see or breathe as the odorous smoke filled the space. Carter's lungs felt like they too were on fire, and he thought that at any moment they would burst. He heard more than one of the Wiggwoggs coughing but couldn't make out which of them it was.

At the cave's entrance, the gathering smoke began first to seep then billow up from the interior of the beast. A long, loud burp was followed by the sucking sound of the monster trying desperately to gasp a breath of fresh air. That didn't work out well for the giant, only adding oxygen to the now raging fire. The morphodorph opened and closed its mouth rapidly several times, while its great body was thrown into a series of heaving, convulsive spasms.

Uh oh, Nevermore said anxiously to Carter's mind. *I feel a sneeze coming on. A sneeze from someone my size won't do much damage, but what if this morphodorph sneezes or something even worse?*

A low moan came from the cave's opening in the form of a plaintive message of distress for anyone listening. The cry for help came from deep in the throat of the morphodorph and rolled out onto the valley floor below.

The full length of the giant's body constricted as it rose in anger on its hind legs, belching thick black smoke from its mouth.

Thar she blows! Nevermore shouted from his crow's nest atop Carter's head.

Then came the retching sound of a massive, smoking projectile being shot from the monster's mouth, closely followed by the exit of Carter, Serene, the ten other Wiggwoggs, and one screaming Imalima. Like cannonballs, they were fired into the night sky, barely missing a low-flying red-feathered owl. All this in the moments just before the flailing morphodorph exploded in an amazing show of pyrotechnics.

One by one the adventurers landed in a farmer's field of stacked hay, amazingly none the worse for wear. All except Imalima, that is, who, true to his character of needing to be the center of attention, managed to land in the only tree in the field.

"Well, this is a first!" he shouted to the others who were busy pulling straw from their clothes. "I have never been in a tree before. How do I get down?"

Carter stood staring up at Imalima in the tree. He gingerly patted his arms and legs to make sure he had not lost any body parts in the morphodorph's explosion. Imalima was sitting with all legs dangling in the crook of a lower tree limb about fifteen feet from the ground. Looking at the long donkey-faced, terribly tattered, miserable mish-mashed body of a woolly goat-thing with the webbed feet of several ducks now stuck in the tree, Carter shook his head in disbelief.

"What a piece of work he is," Carter said under his breath to Nevermore.

"Hello, down there. Is anyone listening? I need help getting down. Hellooooo." Imalima's raised voice communicated his growing annoyance.

"Perhaps bringing Imalima along was not such a good idea," continued Carter to Nevermore. "If there is a problem, you can count on Imalima to be involved in it. We certainly don't need to look for more unwelcome situations than those probably out there waiting for us."

What would we have done without him inside the morphodorph? volunteered Nevermore to Carter's mind. *About this time, we would all be turning into glue.*

"You make a good point. He may be a few screws short of a full set, but I guess he did save our lives. Not that he willingly volunteered."

Carter's conversation with Nevermore was cut short by a loud cracking sound from the limb Imalima was sitting on.

"FORE!" shouted the Wimzical as he suddenly came tumbling down out of the tree, just missing Zebenuza.

The Wiggwogg glared at Imalima, who lay stunned on his back, the wind knocked out of him.

"You aimed for me, didn't you?" Zebenuza accused. "Strike two!"

"I did no such thing," Imalima responded in a breathless whisper. "Anyway, I missed, didn't I?" Painfully getting to all his feet, Imalima knocked the dust from his sore and splotchy body. "When I get back to wherever it is I was going, I shall file a formal complaint with the proper authorities. My body has been criminally abused, and a simple request for help getting down out of a tree was ignored. As a matter of fact," he said, turning to Ushi, "you shall hear from my attorney. I believe what we have here is an open-and-shut case of assault with a deadly weapon. What have you to say for yourself?"

Nothing, apparently. Ushi along with the others stood in silence staring at Imalima. The little goat-like creature simply stared back, not blinking an eye. It was as if someone had taken a picture of the moment and time had stopped. Finally Serene cleared her throat, breaking the tension.

"First things first," she said. "We are behind schedule on a critical mission that we cannot afford to fail. Far too much is at stake." Turning to Imalima, she continued. "Yes, indeed, we are most grateful to you, Imalima, for your generous personal contribution to that end. I fear more sacrifice lies ahead, and with this unscheduled delay, we have no time to lose. Surely the sound of an exploding morphodorph didn't go unnoticed. We are not safe here and should leave immediately."

Serene's acknowledgement of Imalima's sacrifice was enough to pacify and soothe the feelings of the Wimzical, who now trotted with renewed pride to his position at the caboose end of those on the journey.

With the group quickly formed up, they were once again on the move and none too soon. After all, where there is one morphodorph, there are bound to be others. If there was such a thing as revenge among the morphodorph, the loss of a family member, a friend, or just simply one of their own could send them hunting for those responsible.

Several times during the night's walk, the loud sound of something or things was heard crashing through the tangle of underbrush growing alongside the road. One time, a passing juvenile morphodorph the size of a freight container came within a road's width of the crouched adventurers.

"That was too close for comfort," Carter whispered to Serene.

For his part, Imalima was busy rubbing into submission an outrageous case of goose bumps that had blossomed from his recently acquired patches of raw skin. "I'm cold," Imalima whispered self-consciously to Abogamento, who he noticed watching him intently. In truth, he was attempting to deflect attention away from the increasingly bizarre quality of his physical appearance.

"Looks like you're scared to me," responded a smiling Abogamento.

"Which just goes to prove looks can be deceptive," Imalima replied defensively.

"It's nothing to be ashamed of," injected Iat. "We are all tired as well as scared. That was a close call, and we are far from out of danger. Stay alert, keep walking, and keep the talking down to a minimum is my advice."

And that is exactly what they did. For Carter and the chilled Wiggwoggs, morning couldn't come soon enough, and the eventual warm arrival of Suva and Ahneese would be greatly welcomed. They had not seen nor heard a morphodorph for hours now, and with the passing of time, the travelers grew more confident that the immediate danger had passed.

· · · · · · ·

It was still early morning and overcast when Serene signaled for an assembly. She removed from the inner pocket of her tunic the old folded map of Aeiea that Elderwiser had long ago drawn and taught her to read. Everyone gathered around as she opened the map and laid it flat on the ground. Based on identified landmarks and the position of the sister suns, Serene estimated they had three to five hard days walk to reach the border of Wimzi.

After a quick breakfast, they were once again on the march. The day proved uneventful, which was just as well for the exhausted explorers. Clearing weather had actually turned hot, giving soggy clothing a chance to dry. They were making good time. For now, they felt reasonably safe from the threat of an unexpected meeting with another morphodorph. In any event, they would not be so easily taken by surprise if there were to be a next time.

Not a single Dweeg was encountered all day, or even a small sign of their recent presence. Serene wondered aloud if perhaps those few Dweeg farmers who had remained in the valley after the Gootz plundering had the misfortune to wind up in the stomach of a morphodorph. Ushi, with the help of Serene's map reading, set a course for Oxbuk Pass, which according to the map was one of only two known routes up and over Mourners Mountains. The pass would eventually lead into Stanelhooven.

Somewhere on the heights of the western side of the mountains was rumored to be the little village of Millililli, home of the dwarf-sized Minnininni. Practically nothing was known of the Minnininni, as they were a secretive tribe. There were plenty of stories, such as the one about the buckles on the Minnininni shoes being fashioned of precious jewels mined from tunnels under their homes. But that's about all there was, only stories.

Elderwiser had warned Serene that the Minnininni could be a problem and that they might prove an obstacle on their quest. Many years ago, he had by chance briefly met the leader of the Minnininni, who was hunting for game in the lower elevations of Mourners Mountains. The old wizard found him to be of strong character and very independent, somewhat impatient, and not one whose trust could easily be won.

More concerning to Elderwiser was the sense that the little king of the Minnininni was a master of deception and could himself not be trusted. That was about all he had told Serene, for at the time of telling, the hour was late and the old wizard was weary. Serene, whose own eyelids had been heavy, appreciated the story for what it was and chose not press her father for more information.

On several occasions the Gootz had unsuccessfully searched the treacherous mountains for the mysterious Millililli village. There were stories of treasure chests laden with precious jewels that needed to be confirmed. Not even their Kenga sky spies had any luck locating the whereabouts of the elusive Minnininni or their hidden village. Every attempt to find and pillage Millililli resulted in failure, leading to The Grinder's bouts of outrage and thunderous frustration. Excuses were not acceptable. The Grinder had made it a priority to conquer the Minnininni, but first he had to find them, and he was drawing up plans to do just that.

What the wretched leader of the Gootz did not know was, there would indeed one day be a meeting between the Gootz and Minnininni, but the results would not be to his liking.

Chapter 11
The Minnininni of Millililli

Well rested and in good spirits would be the best description of the seekers of the Circle of Power on their second day in Dweeg Territory. Their narrow but clever escape from the slippery interior of the morphodorph had increased their confidence. Making good time, Serene led the group in singing an ancient Wiggwogg folk song passed down from one generation to the next. For most of the remaining day, they walked the narrow, tree-lined road that intersected smaller roads, splitting abandoned farmland as it twisted toward the mountains.

Carter was becoming increasingly comfortable with his role as a trusted member of the Wiggwogg fellowship in their quest for the Circle of Power. He whistled the simple melody heard earlier while tracing Serene's steps. Smiling, he wished the moment would last forever.

Daylight was slipping away as the single file of adventurers arrived at the foothills of Mourners Mountains. They decided to make camp before attempting the steep climb looming just ahead of them. Still, not a single Dweeg had been seen. Serene thought perhaps tomorrow they would uncover the mystery of the hidden caves where the Dweeg were rumored to have retreated. That night, with evening's dinner still heavy in their bellies, embellished stories of individual past heroic adventures were shared around the campfire as, one by one, the tired explorers drifted off into a well-deserved easy sleep.

The small team of travelers rose fully rested early the next morning. After breakfast, they broke camp and set off through the rolling elevations of the mountains' foothills. By their ever-increasing efforts, there was no doubt they were climbing.

"I thought I was in pretty good shape," said Carter, who was walking just behind Serene. He was attempting to keep from sounding winded but not doing a particularly good job of it. "Don't worry about me," he continued. "I promise I will not hold us up."

Serene turned to him with her permanent smile. Words were not required. An hour's walk brought them to the more challenging inclines of the mountains. Roots of shrubs grew from chinks in the rock, providing the adventurers footholds leading upward. They were now beginning their steep ascent of Mourners Mountains.

Good weather was enjoyed for most of the day as the group continued to climb. Ferbert was overheard mumbling his displeasure with the difficulty of the ascent. As he was attempting to cross a particularly large boulder, the Wiggwogg lost his footing. He slid backwards across the crumpled face of the boulder, tearing skin from his knees, elbows, and hands. Small patches of blood stained the hem of his tunic as well as the knees of his leggings as he sat at the bottom of the boulder patting his body to make sure everything was where it should be and that nothing was broken.

Coming to Ferbert's aid, Fermond helped his brother up and saw to his superficial wounds. Just then Fermond noticed a small opening between the boulder and another great slab of rock resting up against it.

"Come see what I found," he called to the others, who quickly came to have a look. Further inspection concluded it was indeed a cave, but was it occupied?

"What do you suppose we would find in there?" Fermond queried to no one in particular. The group was definitely not looking forward to another morphodorph experience.

"Hello," Serene called tenuously into the cave's opening. "Is there anyone home? We are friendly and mean you no harm. I am Serene, daughter of Elderwiser, from the territory of Wiggonwoggen."

After a moment a frightened voice called back, "What is it you want with us?"

"If you are Dweeg," Serene continued, "please come out and show yourselves. We are on an important mission that you may find of interest. We just want to talk to you."

Agitated whispers were heard from within the cave and then all was quiet. Before long a thin, elderly, silver-haired female dressed in rags came from the dark interior of the cave to its sunlit entrance. She was small, the top of her head came midway between Carter's waist and shoulders. Her loose skin was pale and marked with age. She looked gaunt and worn down.

"I am Salise, grandmother of the Dweeg," she offered timidly, standing curled over in front of Serene and Carter. "I apologize for the lack of hospitality and my appearance, but we Dweeg have fallen upon hard times. If indeed you truly are Serene, then I have heard tales of both you and your father. What I know of the Wiggwoggs is honorable."

"Then perhaps you know we have had our treasure stolen by The Grinder," responded Serene.

"We know of it and have personally experienced the painful devastation resulting from that theft," said Salise, lowering her eyes to hide a swell of tears. "Once we were a proud and thriving territory. We were peaceful and happy to be working our farms in the valley. But now, all that is gone. Our fields lie fallow, and we have been reduced to a few miserable souls, cringing in caves."

"I am sorry," Serene said sympathetically. "We are on a quest organized by Elderwiser," she explained, conscious of not saying too much yet wanting to lift the old Dweeg's spirits. "I am limited in what I can reveal at this time, but if we accomplish our goal, you will no longer have to live hiding in fear."

"What, if anything, can I do to help?" Salise inquired.

"What do you know of the Gootz?" asked Serene. "Have you ever seen their leader? Do you have some knowledge of The Great Sea Valion or Athulian? Any information could be helpful."

"I can tell you on good word," responded Salise, "that the prize you seek is not in The Grinder's castle at Bludenbonz but rather hidden in a crypt under a remote Gootz castle. This secret, obscure castle is said to be located somewhere on the opposite side of the island of Athulian, deep behind a forbidding forest.

"The Grinder is a vicious foe," she continued. "We know this from personal experience. Blood excites him, and he shows no mercy on the battlefield. He has either killed or enslaved most of the Dweeg. There are now more Dweeg on Athulian than there are here at home. Those left are mostly old like me and too frail to fight. I can say with reasonably good authority, any attempt to defeat The Grinder will most assuredly be met with failure. He is personally under the continuous protection of a large force of heavily armed loyal Gootz soldiers. If by some miracle an army would get past them, they would then face an elite guard, hand-picked and sworn to protect The Grinder and his treasure at the cost of their own lives. Waiting at Bludenbonz Castle, thirsty for blood and just behind the Gootz Elite Guard is The Grinder himself.

"As if all that wasn't enough to discourage any attempted invasion, rumor has it that the island of Athulian is guarded by flesh-eating sea serpents that troll The Great Sea Valion. I don't know of your intent, but I would venture to say anyone foolish enough to try attacking The Grinder on his home ground is most surely doomed."

The mere thought of a possible invasion of the island of Athulian, the resulting devastation caused by the Gootz army, and the inevitable defeat of the well-intentioned had left the old Dweeg exhausted. She excused herself and sat on a nearby rock. Deep in thought, the old woman scratched the matted hair on her head. "If you are an advance scouting party for the fools I speak of, how many loyal soldiers will fight for you? Where is your great army anyway?"

"This is it," Serene said proudly, waving her arm in the direction of the small band of seekers of the Circle of Power. "A large army would be easily spotted and give an advantage to The Grinder. Besides, we can't match the weapons of the Gootz, nor do we share their thirst for blood. War would be foolish and play right into their hands."

"Then what *is* your plan?" asked Salise.

"If I could say, I would, but I can't, so I won't. Besides, at the moment I have little more than faith," Serene answered.

The adventurers shifted uneasily, and Imalima poked Carter. "If I didn't know better, I would think she is me. Is she making fun of me?" he asked in a whisper.

There was no response. Carter's mind was elsewhere. He had been hoping that between Elderwiser and Serene there was a carefully laid plan, and he had trusted that when the time was right, Serene would share it with him and the others. The news that there was no organized plan was an unwelcome surprise and very disturbing.

"I know our cause is just. I have faith that when the time comes for decisions, we will have the wisdom for good choices," Serene said confidently, directing her words as much to her friends as to Salise. "Don't give up hope, Salise. All we ask from you is to send us on our way with positive thoughts for our success. If the information you have shared is true, then you have been most helpful and we are grateful. The hour is late and we have a long journey ahead of us." Serene hugged the old Dweeg, and after the usual awkwardness of good-byes, the band of Wiggwoggs and Carter Nicholsworth once again set off on their climb.

Dusk was having its way with daylight. The earlier breeze had been replaced by a steadily growing wind that howled its way between the curling canyon walls of Mourners Mountains. The wind's woeful wail grieved the approaching loss of sister suns Suva and Ahneese, who were fast sinking behind the mountains.

Carter was overtaken with despair and longing. Walking with his head lowered, his fists thrust deep into his pockets, he felt like weeping. Lost, he thought, barely restraining a flood of tears. For some reason known only to those who have experienced true friendship, Serene intuitively looked over her shoulder and saw the cloak of distress heavy on the shoulders of her friend. She dropped back and slid her arm between Carter's arm and his body, gently hooking him closer to her. They continued walking that way quietly for a while before Serene finally spoke.

"Now you should know why the wind howls," she said in a slow, deliberate voice. "Mourners Mountains cries out for all lost souls. If you are with inner peace, no matter where you happen to be, you are never lost. When you try to find the path back to where you have been, you will fail, finding it overgrown with regrets. You can only visit the past in the fleeting memories stored in your mind. If you try and hold too tightly onto what was, like water through a sieve, it will surely slip through your fingers, leaving your hands empty and your heart broken."

Carter let Serene's words settle in his mind. In his brief life he had never personally experienced a broken heart, but he had seen enough movies to know there is a kind of suffering beyond physical pain.

Where did she learn all this? he wondered. *Serene doesn't seem old enough to have gathered her depth of understanding.*

In case you've forgotten, reminded Nevermore, *this is Aeiea, not Earth. Things are different here, and if you doubt it, you have to look no further than your friend Imalima over there.*

Carter's conversation with Nevermore was interrupted by Serene, who had not quite completed her thoughts on the subject of a life well lived.

"When the memories are pleasant, visit, but do not linger. You need to be where you are. If, on the other hand, the memories are unpleasant, embrace the lesson and release the pain to the wind.

"On occasion we may become confused and appear to wander from our path, but we are actually visiting important lessons that call out for our attention. If we don't learn from experience then the lesson is held in limbo, kept stored in a classroom for a future revisit until we finally do learn. But know this, my friend, always we continue on."

Carter raised his head. "Always?" he asked.

"Always," she said.

"Do you mean, even aft—"

"Always," she said forcefully. "In Wiggonwoggen we have a saying:

Open it up.
Set it free.
Light follows darkness.
The rest is yet to be."

Removing her entwined arm from Carter's before rejoining the rest of their group, Serene cocked her head while looking sideways into Carter's eyes. "Trust," she said before leaving Carter alone with his swirl of thoughts.

Finding strength in Serene's comforting words of wisdom, Carter allowed himself the luxury of a small smile. He had not given much thought to the strength of their relationship, but now as he considered his friendship with Serene, he realized the importance of trust. He concluded that he would trust Serene with his life. What he didn't know was that in the days that lay ahead, this is exactly what he would have to do.

· · · · · · ·

Smoke curled from the green wood fire Zebenuza had built hastily as Serene joined her traveling companions around the campfire. A fickle wind kept changing direction, blowing the smoke this way and that.

Moving his seating location four times, Ferbert grumbled, "Has anyone else noticed how the smoke seems to follow me wherever I go?"

Carter overheard the comment and recalled a character in the Sunday newspaper comic strips that was constantly followed by a dark cloud. The cloud represented bad luck that the character, by his poor attitude, attracted like a magnet. Ferbert, he thought, reminded him of that character. Carter was also keenly aware that home was feeling more distant with each passing day.

Changing his location for a fifth time, Ferbert didn't bother to sit. This time, he remained standing, anticipating his move to another location as soon as the smoke found him. Pulling his bandana from around his neck, he closely wound it over his nose and mouth. His bloodshot eyes peered from above the mask, fishing the circle of friends for sympathy. None was forthcoming. He began to cough as once again the smoke searched him out. Fermond came to the rescue of his twin who was now coughing so hard that he could barely catch his breath.

"Hands up, Ferbert!" yelled Fermond while pounding his masked brother's back.

Imalima, who was relieved to have the attention focused on someone other than himself, said, "Look's like the sheriff's got his man." Indeed, with his arms raised high over his head and the scarf covering most of his face, all Ferbert needed was a cowboy hat and a pair of six-shooters to look like an outlaw surrendering to the posse.

Larger pieces of dry wood were added to the fire, and soon the smoke, along with Ferbert's hacking cough, began to fade.

Refusing to cook the evening meal, Ferbert retreated into a deep sulk. Wild bitter greens, hard crusts of bread, and fruit were endured by all except Ferbert who, even with his brother's coaxing, refused to eat. After dinner, the Wiggwoggs shared stories with each other and Carter, while Imalima snored quietly as he napped.

Herkifer's was a scary tale involving a Valion sea serpent that hungered for the tender flesh of children. The stealthy serpent slithered from the sea at night and searched the small villages tucked along the coastal shadows to snatch an unsuspecting child from its sleep. He would take his catch back to the sea, then to a small, isolated island behind Athulian where he had imprisoned an endless supply of the tasty, tender treats. The serpent was never captured and, according to Herkifer's story, for all anyone knows still prowls the murky waters of The Great Sea Valion.

This was just a story, of course, assured Herkifer, but the Wiggwogg told it so convincingly that in the minds of the huddled listeners fiction had slipped unnoticed into the realm of possibility.

Not only did the band of explorers have to tolerate a skimpy dinner, they suffered a light sleep that night as well. Tossing and turning over a bed of unforgiving rock, they fought their way through nightmares of sea serpents that brought them grumbling into the new day. Ferbert had a good deal of practice in the specialized art of grousing, but inexperience among the other adventurers did not seem to hamper the number of complaints that appeared contagious this morning. They scratched annoyingly at countless insect bites received during the long night. Breaking camp, experiencing the effects of sleeplessness, they marched off in silence.

After climbing for most of the day, they came upon a fairly level rock plateau that jutted out and over a hazy valley. Swarms of large, hairy-legged black spiders, busy with their secret plans, scuttled across the flat surface only to disappear over its far edge. Suva and Ahneese were nowhere to be found. The sky had bled out most of its color, smudging into a dark shroud worn casually over the shoulders of Mourners Mountains.

Serene called for a break. The group of exhausted climbers stood on the high, level ground leaning into the incessant wind that pushed up against their bodies. Looking at his fellow travelers, Carter saw something that made him uncomfortable. Their energy seemed drained as they sat down close together in small knots. For all it mattered, they might as well have been sitting miles apart. No one spoke, and weariness was worn on their faces. Ushi, who never seemed to tire, went from his sitting position to lying prone on the hard surface. Before long, the others joined him. It is not clear who was first to close their eyes, but with the wind wailing in the background, one by one, each fell into a deep yet restless sleep.

Most of the next day was already behind them when they finally awoke from their slumber. With tightly clenched fists, it was Carter's familiar habit to rub the sleep from his eyes upon awakening. The impossibility of this simplest of tasks abruptly shortened his transition. His experiences in Wimzi came flooding back into his mind.

"Hey, what's going on here?" he yelled, attempting unsuccessfully to sit up. The others were now awake as well and found themselves in the same predicament as Carter. Each of the friends, while deep in their sleep, had been neatly wrapped in a sticky, thread-like substance. Only their heads and legs from the knees down had not been bound. Carter looked over at Imalima, who was lying closest to him. The goat creature's elongated face was twisted in terror as the army of spiders clambered over his struggling body, completing their expert job of packaging. Because of his many legs, Imalima's wrapping proved the most challenging of all the adventurers for the hard-working spiders.

"Oh, Momma," Imalima moaned. "I hate spiders. They give me the woolies, which, by the way, are first cousins of the willies. In my case, the woolies are more animal-appropriate than the willies. On the subject of woolies, has anyone noticed how slowly my wool has been growing back?"

"No," Carter said, "I have not noticed how slowly your wool is re-growing. At the moment I am busy trying to figure out a way that we don't wind up as some spider's dinner. Do you think for a little while you could give it a rest?"

"Well!" said the creature, taking offense at Carter's tone. "Look who woke up on the wrong side of the bed."

With their bundling work now completed, the horde of spiders scampered off across the rocks. "Does their departure mean we are not on the spiders' dinner menu tonight?" asked Imalima.

"Based on my observations of spider behavior, your optimism, Imalima, seems a bit misplaced. I don't believe we've seen the last of them," Carter said.

Carter didn't know what to make of the spiders' exit. Would they return later? Were they operating at the direction of another party? Could he and his friends escape? He had lots of questions but no answers. Rolling onto his other side, Carter tried to locate the whereabouts of Serene and the others. He found them not far away, tied up tightly like himself and Imalima.

• • • • • • •

Barely three feet tall and sitting atop a large boulder with his legs crossed, Graggasnaxx looked down on the captives from his vantage point with amusement. His white beard, falling almost to his toes, was stained a brownish-yellow around his mouth. A pipe, not quite half the length of his height, dangled loosely from his teeth. Small puffs of smoke punctuated his laughter. By the expressions on the detainees' faces, there was little appreciation for his sense of humor. Removing the pipe, he spat the sour taste of tobacco juice before wiping his lips with the sleeve of his tunic.

Graggasnaxx stood then shouted to the captives below him. "I would like to ask you folks to join us for dinner as my guests," he said curtly, his bushy eyebrows dancing on his words, "but it looks like you're all tied up." He chuckled at his little joke. He was the only one amused. Jumping from the rock to the ground, Graggasnaxx moved in closer for a better look at his prisoners wrapped in their cocoons. Mockingly, he shook his head while strolling among the helpless lot. It was not often that Graggasnaxx had the opportunity to stand over anything, and he was thoroughly enjoying the horizontal intruders having to look up to see him.

"Did you folks mistakenly make a wrong turn while out for a walk?" he asked.

No answer.

"Tell me the purpose of your being here," he continued.

Same response.

Impatiently he circled the disabled trespassers while pulling at his long beard as he considered his captives' lack of cooperation. Turning quickly on his heels, then squatting directly in front of Serene's face, he asked, "Are you stone deaf or just unfriendly?"

He had reason to believe these wayward travelers were mostly Wiggwoggs, although never previously having seen one, he could not be sure. But he had heard rumors. Graggasnaxx had no idea about the who or what of the odd-looking, red-haired stranger, or, for that matter, the multi-legged creature lying next to him. With the exception of the Gootz, most inhabitants living in the various territories stayed pretty much to themselves, living out their lives peacefully within their borders. For Graggasnaxx, an elder Minnininni, this group's presence begged the question, what were these strangers doing here so close to Millililli?

So far his interrogation was not going well.

"Tell you what I'm going to do," he said, standing up. "Won't be long now before someone blows out the final candle on this day. That means soon it will be dinnertime for spiders. You don't have to be too smart to figure out what's on their menu for tonight's main course, if you catch my drift."

Imalima's chattering teeth gave him away.

"You there! Graggasnaxx yelled, wheeling around to face the bug-eyed creature. "Get up!"

Imalima looked like an encased sausage sprouting legs, lots of legs. Three attempts to follow Graggasnaxx's order met with failure. Finally on his fourth try, Imalima succeeded.

How sad Imalima looked in his confining wrapper. His eyes welled with tears and his head drooped barely inches from his two closest webbed feet. One of his many back legs was now one of his more frontal legs and his severely tweaked rear-end was considerably lower to the ground than it was accustomed to. Imalima was twisted uncomfortably like a pretzel, making it a real challenge for him to simply stand. For a creature that was never particularly well-balanced to begin with, either physically or mentally, at least he was still mostly upright and not embarrassing himself by bawling.

Approaching Imalima, Graggasnaxx removed a long, jewel-handled knife from his belt that also housed a curled whip. Holding it just inches from Imalima's face he said, "Cat got your tongue? If it does not presently, it soon shall if you don't start talking." With his free hand, Graggasnaxx reached deep into his tunic, quickly producing a long-haired cat that exercised its claws in the air. Held by the scruff of its neck, the feline flashed razor-sharp teeth behind its smile.

Rusty gears in the goat creature's mind rewound and played back the scary scene in the giant morphodorph's interior when Ushi had pulled a knife on him. Not again, he thought, fearing the possible outcome much worse this time than previously. Releasing the cat that quickly disappeared up a nearby tree, Graggasnaxx slid the knife back and forth from one hand to the other while staring mischievously at the pitiful creature. Imalima squeezed his eyes shut in an attempt to deny reality, but amazingly, he remained uncharacteristically quiet.

"Well," said an amused Graggasnaxx, "you have proven braver than I thought you might. I must admit, I am impressed. It is obvious you need a bit more persuasion."

Instead of cutting off Imalima's tongue as threatened or slitting his throat, Graggasnaxx cut the tight bindings of spun thread, freeing two of Imalima's legs. That was a surprise and a small sense of relief, but still there was no way to escape. Positioning himself so that Imalima couldn't topple over and fall on top of him, Graggasnaxx tilted his head while cupping his hand to his ear.

"Is that the spider's dinner bell I hear ringing?" he asked, pretending to hear what he did not. "Why, I do believe it is," said the bad actor, continuing his little skit. "Would anyone care to join us for dinner? Oh, silly me, I almost forgot . . . you are dinner. Sorry, my memory is not what it used to be.

"Not speaking from personal experience, of course, but I would imagine being eaten alive is probably as bad as it gets when it comes to discomfort. I'm pretty sure that after one or two of you have been munched on, someone will speak up. So who volunteers to be eaten first? How about you?" he asked, pointing at Ferbert, who mumbled something under his breath about the nature of his luck. "Maybe you?" he said, turning to Abogamento. "Or you?" pointing at Zebenuza.

As Graggasnaxx focused separately on each of the adventurers, they in turn glanced over at Serene, waiting for direction.

"Well, I guess I will be going now. I get a queasy stomach at the sight of bloodshed," said Graggasnaxx, calmly pulling his pipe from his mouth and tamping it against the palm of his hand. He dusted the pipe's contents from his hands and stuck it in his belt next to the knife.

"Remember, you had an invitation to be guests at dinner rather than to *be* dinner. Eat or be eaten. Seems like a simple decision to me."

"You have had us drugged and tied up by spiders. Now you threaten our lives. Why should we trust you?" asked Serene, finally speaking.

"Mostly 'cause you have little choice," Graggasnaxx answered nonchalantly. "If our manners are a bit rough, it's because we're not accustomed to visitors. We don't know you, and we don't welcome strangers up here. Not any. Frankly I'm surprised at my generous invitation to join my fellow Minnininni in Millililli for dinner, but if lying around waiting for hungry spiders to feast is what you want, then I'll be going."

Graggasnaxx turned and began to walk away. The band of travelers glanced from one to another, finally settling on Serene. Not bothering to look back, Graggasnaxx said to no one in particular, "It's one thing to find your way up Mourners Mountains. It is quite another to find your way over the top and down the other side. If you plan to reach Stanelhooven, there is only one way, and I assure you the going will be hazardous to your health. I suggest, in the interest of seeing another day, you follow me."

"And just how do you suppose we do that with our legs bound?" Serene inquired. "Cut us free," she demanded.

"You are obviously in no position to be giving me orders. Can't do it anyway, too risky. Besides, I don't have the authority," responded Graggasnaxx.

"Then who does? What do you want from us anyway?" Serene asked impatiently.

"I wanted little more than information, but you have proven most uncooperative. So I will turn you over to Pappasnaxx, who no doubt will have his own plans for you. I have already said more than I should. No more questions."

Up to this point, the Minnininni's bluff had not produced the results he was looking for. Graggasnaxx was now resigned to returning to Millililli on this day just as he had earlier left, empty handed. His plan of a hero's welcome as he led his captives into the village, dashed.

He was about to give up on squeezing cooperation from the adventurers when a shaft of light broke through the clouds.

"Can you at least untie our legs so that we can walk?" asked Serene, trying to soften her tone. "I don't know how else you expect us to follow you."

The giant had a good point, reasoned Graggasnaxx. Perhaps his celebrity status was not in jeopardy after all. It sure would look a lot better on his resume if he personally marched at the head of his line of prisoners when returning to Millililli rather than sending for carts to bring them in. Someone else was sure to take the credit in that scenario or at least claim partial credit. Graggasnaxx was not big on sharing.

"Tell you what," he said after giving Serene's request some consideration. "I will untie your legs, if you promise not to run away. Let me look into the palm of your hand to see if you can be trusted." Serene managed to wiggle free one of her hands, which Graggasnaxx promptly grasped and pulled up roughly toward him. Serene was surprised at his strength. With her hand just inches from his face, he spat into her palm, which she immediately tried to withdraw.

"Now, now," he muttered, holding tight while not taking his eyes from her hand. "No need to get uppity with me, stranger. I just needed to clean you up a bit so I could better read the signs." After a moment of rubbing her palm with his thumb, he released her hand. "Well, I guess you're honest enough," he said, looking slightly disappointed.

Once again withdrawing his long knife, which for his size was probably more like a sword, he sliced through the thread binding Serene's legs.

"No funny stuff," he ordered, holding his knife close to the Wiggwogg's throat, "or you won't see the light of tomorrow."

"Would you please free the legs of the others so that we may do as you wish and follow you to wherever it is you are taking us?" Serene asked, ignoring the Minnininni's threat.

Seeing no better alternative, one by one he cut the web that wrapped the legs of Carter and the other Wiggwoggs. He then took the rope that hung from the side of Lyke and secured each of them one to the other at the waist. "OK, now everyone get in a single line and follow me," he said, pointing his knife threateningly at them.

This was indeed a rare opportunity for a low-ranking Minnininni to be in charge of anything, and Graggasnaxx was thoroughly enjoying his moment of power. It would especially look good if he came marching into Millililli at the head of the invasive giants who were more than twice his size.

"And where is it we are following you to, dear sir?" Serene asked while trying to keep up with her captor.

Graggasnaxx took pleasure in the respectful tone of Serene's question, especially the "dear sir" part. He couldn't remember if anyone had ever referred to him as "sir." Feeling confident in spite of his size, and very much in control of the situation, he responded, "We are going to where I am taking you. I said no more questions!"

They had walked in silence for some time when Graggasnaxx veered from the trail. Up, around, down, and then back up again they went several times before coming to a series of tall berry bushes that were clumped tightly together. "Follow me," said Graggasnaxx once again as he disappeared into the bushes. Carter's eyes followed Serene as she also disappeared into the undergrowth, and the others quickly followed. Like artificial shrubbery on a stage, the bushes turned out to be little more than a theater prop.

The entrance to a tunnel lay just ahead of them. Graggasnaxx lit a candle and led them in.

"This feels way too familiar," Imalima said. "Been there, done that, and I don't much care to do it again," he complained.

"Well, I don't think you get that choice, Imalima," said Carter.

Several somewhat smaller tunnels fed off the main one they were traveling along, and still others led away from those. Their captor didn't hesitate, moving deftly from one tunnel to another then to another, climbing the entire time. The adventurers were totally turned around and completely lost. On they went. Finally up ahead appeared a small circle of light. As they continued walking, the intensity and size of the light grew.

When at last they all stood at the tunnel's end, they looked down into the hollowed scoop of a great valley. The beautiful landscape was completely encircled by the tall, sharp peaks that outlined Mourners Mountains. After catching his breath, Graggasnaxx was once again on the move, descending a steep slope cut tightly into the side of the mountain.

"Surely this must be the only way down into the valley," whispered Serene to Carter. After some time and many switchbacks that took them about halfway down to the valley's floor, they stopped for a much-needed rest before continuing on.

Night had just begun to close around the straggling cord of tired travelers when they rounded a bend and came upon the edge of a village tucked into the overgrown crevice of a hillside. The community was built entirely on the right side of the narrow road. Trees grew over the structures, hiding them from both above and below. Unless you knew where you were going, thought Carter, this village would be impossible to find.

The first building was different than the others: long in length and fitted with bars in the windows. The smattering of homes that followed on the inside of the road were small and square with steeply pitched thatched roofs. Freestanding walls, built from timbers and mountain stone, framed the buildings. An arched door, made from straight, thin willow branches woven together with strands of bright, colorful fabrics, served as the entrance. Each home had four small, round windows, one on each side of the door fronting the road and one on each side of the house. Hushed voices and inviting candlelight flickered warmly from behind the curtained windows of several dwellings, and a fine wisp of smoke curled from several stone chimneys.

There were also a few buildings that looked like inns. They were larger than the other structures and were two stories tall.

Interesting, thought Carter. Why would there be inns in Millililli when visitors were unwelcome? And why were all the structures almost the size of normal buildings when the Minnininni were so small? He did notice the door latches were lower than they would have been in Lake Mohegan.

At one particular curve on the thin road, Carter looked over the embankment to the valley floor below. There a series of simple structures, much like the ones on the road they traveled, made up a second sprawling village complete with a town square. Carter thought it odd that there was no light coming from any of the homes, no sign of activity from the lower village's inhabitants or, for that matter, no smoke coming from any of the chimneys although it was quite cold.

They closely followed their captor along the narrow cobbled road that wound through the upper village. A string of stocky miniature horses stood at the road's edge in front of an inn without benefit of saddle, bridle, or reins. A rope hung from below the head of each horse securing it to a hitching post. Long, coarse hair growing along their thick necks was neatly braided and tied with colorful ribbon. Fresh hay lay strewn at the horses' front hoofs. Their heads bobbed in a disjointed dance as they enjoyed their evening's meal. Just beyond the horses and the last home on the road stood the largest building in the village. Like the others, the building was constructed of stone and thatch, but stood two stories tall and ten houses long with a bell tower on its steep roof. Above the door, a simple hand-scrawled sign read *EAT.*

Several individuals were gathered in a heated discussion on a second-floor balcony that overhung the building's entrance. Their voices quieted and their eyes shifted to Graggasnaxx below who was shouting orders. More of the curious came out from their homes and the village inns to watch Graggasnaxx dispensing commands.

"Step lively, you sorry excuse for whatever it is you are!" He snapped his whip above his head while leading a parade of tall strangers whose arms were bound behind them. The sorry lot, were obviously his prisoners.

Ushi was particularly unhappy. He was embarrassed to be entering the village as a prisoner of the likes of Graggasnaxx. On the other hand,

Graggasnaxx was quite enjoying the moment and the attention from above, his small barrel chest puffed fat as a pigeon's.

"What a mess," said Carter quietly to Serene. "If this is the best we can do," he continued, "what hope is there that we can complete our mission?"

Serene had no response. What could she say? As the mission's leader, she felt the burden of responsibility for their predicament heavy on her shoulders. She saw their capture as her fault, and she felt the weight of her decisions like never before.

If Ushi was embarrassed, she was angry and frustrated, but not without hope. She understood this mission was not going to be easy and, at best, a long shot. In addition, she had no idea of the intent of her captors. All this might have caused someone of lesser character to consider giving up. But this was no ordinary Wiggwogg. This was Serene, daughter of Elderwiser. Giving up was simply not an option. Serene had power unknown even to her.

Graggasnaxx herded his string of captives toward the structure with the bell tower and through the building's entrance into a vast hall. Suspended from the high ceiling, a series of heavy chains connected to candelabras coated thick with candle wax. The light fixtures hung low over rows of long tables. Placed end to end, the tables, laden with bowls of fruit and dinnerware, ran almost the full length of the rectangular hall. Benches were neatly tucked under the long tables. The room was windowless, and much of the partially white plastered walls were draped with a decorative scarlet velvet material. Like the structure's exterior walls, the floor was also cobbled stone.

There was no sign of activity in the room, but there was now the distinct aroma of unfamiliar food cooking. The bell in the tower echoed loudly three times then fell silent. From outside the dining hall, a growing din grew from the anteroom at the entrance of the building. The doors flung open and a noisy crowd rushed the tables. Serene guessed that, based on their size, they were probably Minnininni. She had heard stories of the secretive little ones from her father.

The adult males were dressed much like Graggasnaxx with untucked loose-fitting blouses over their trousers. All sported beards of various lengths. There seemed to be some sort of order, as those with the longest beards stood behind tables closest to the front of the hall.

The females, like the males, were small in size and seemed without humor. They appeared gruff and angrily aggressive toward each other. From the general tone of their conversations, you could say these Minnininni were a cranky lot.

If possible, thought Carter, the females would, if they could, have also grown beards. Three-quarter-length knickers covered most of the hair that grew from their muscular legs, and several blew smoke from long-stemmed pipes such as the one Graggasnaxx had earlier been smoking.

At the head of the room, a single long table was centered on a raised platform so that any occupants sitting on the elegant, hand-carved chairs behind that table could look out over the audience below.

The prisoners were led in by Graggasnaxx and lined tightly against the far wall at the opposite end of the room from the stage. From a doorway closest to the head table, a single small individual whose face was etched with age entered the great room. The hall became hushed. Soon two more official-looking individuals also came through the doorway, joining the apparent leader on the stage while standing just behind and to each side of him.

The first onto the raised platform took his seat on a chair that was considerably fancier and taller than the other unoccupied chairs and positioned prominently at the center of the table. Without looking up, the seated individual, who appeared to be in charge, raised one arm above his head and brought his hand down hard on the table. An ear-piercing screech of benches being dragged from under the neat lines of tables flooded the hall. When all were finally seated and the room once again quieted, the leader spoke.

"Really, Graggasnaxx, whatever has become of your manners?" he asked across the hall in a soft but reproachful tone. "Let me introduce myself to our guests. I am king of the Minnininni, more fondly known to all as Pappy Pappasnaxx, or more informally to my grandchildren as Grampy Pappasnaxx. My adoring wife simply refers to me as The Big Ninni."

Carter clapped his hand quickly over his mouth to stifle a laugh that threatened to ruin the moment.

"We welcome you to Millililli and our dinner table," continued the king. His mouth turned up at the corners in a rather cheesy smile that boasted insincerity. The king's counterfeit grin floated off in the direction of the uncomfortable adventurers.

"Untie our honored guests immediately, Graggasnaxx," reprimanded the king, "and seat them at my table. They shall dine with me and be our overnight guests. I insist," he said, as if his offer carried the weight of generosity or the possibility of choice.

With great effort, Graggasnaxx returned the king's forced smile. He bowed deeply before turning to his captives and muttering his displeasure under his breath. Removing their bonds, Graggasnaxx, still wearing his pained smile, led the group onto the stage and sat them at the king's table.

King Pappasnaxx was dressed in a wine-colored cape with a dark fur collar flecked with white. The clawed foot of what must have come from a large animal hung from a leather cord tied around his neck. Removing his helmet that was adorned with a small set of antlers, the king placed it prominently on the table. Raising a goblet above his head, he offered a simple toast, but one that sent a chill down Serene's back. "To our guests and to the success of their mission."

The king's words caught the adventurers by surprise. How did Pappasnaxx know about their mission? This was a disaster. If Pappasnaxx knew, then who else knew? If the element of surprise was no longer viable, their quest was most likely doomed. Advance knowledge by The Grinder of their mission would ensure them of walking right into a trap. It would be a slaughter. They wouldn't stand a chance.

It was at that precise moment that Serene had another thought. What if the king of the Minnininni was just bluffing? She was sure that visitors to the higher elevations of Mourners Mountains were infrequent and anyone attempting to cross the treacherous mountains was obviously doing so for reasons other than exercise. Serene took a deep breath, determined to find out precisely what the king knew.

Platters of hot meats and assorted vegetables along with cauldrons of soup were placed at the king's table. After he began eating, the servers brought more food for those seated below the stage at the long tables. The Minnininni, who had been noticeably quiet prior to the king's toast, were now engaged in a graduating volume of conversations while occasionally stealing a peek at their king and his guests.

The king was sitting next to Serene, dabbing at his beard with the oversized napkin that had been tied around his neck. Recognizing her as the group's leader, he addressed his question directly to her.

"So," said Pappy Pappasnaxx, who in a few short moments had managed to devour most of his dinner, "what news do you bring me?"

Serene inhaled deeply and then let out a long sigh. The makings of a frown knitted its way onto her brow. While lying was not an option, determining just how much information to share was. The king had not said or done anything to win over her confidence or trust.

"This one," she said, pointing to Carter who was seated on the other side of her, "has traveled through time and dimension to be here. We are in search of his destiny."

There was no deceit in what she said without being overly revealing. Her frown seemed contagious, as it now appeared to have infected the brow of Pappy Pappasnaxx as well.

"So let me see if I understand you correctly," said the king, twirling the wispy hairs of his beard around his index finger while contemplating his next chess move. "This one over here," he said, gesturing with his thumb at Carter, "is from somewhere other than Aeiea. He has traveled here, I would presume, for some special purpose. How am I doing?" Without waiting for a response, the king continued. "What makes you think you are going in the right direction?"

"My fellow traveling companion Herkifer is capable of charting the stars. We trust his expertise." The muscled Wiggwogg smiled at Serene's compliment. "Since you know where we are and you know the direction from where we came, you obviously know where we are going."

The king's smile faded and his face darkened. He was tiring of the joust and losing patience with Serene's clever but evasive responses to his probes.

"I am not amused!" he shouted angrily. "Enough of this game!" The garbled din of chatter at the tables of the Minnininni came to an abrupt end with the raised voice of their king.

"Since you are obviously withholding information, let me tell you what I know. You are no doubt familiar with the Gootz and their leader. Just two days ago, we had the good fortune to capture a Kenga, one of The Grinder's flying spies. They are quite a tasty bird, but their spit is poisonous. It kills within minutes after coming in contact with the skin. We lost two Minnininni before squeezing some information from the neck of your dinner."

Carter looked down at the small remainder of the unappetizing gray meat on his plate. Unable to finish his meal, he placed his knife and fork across the Kenga's remains.

Imalima, who was sitting next to Carter and not known to be one to miss an opportunity when presented, glanced into Carter's plate while licking his lips and whispered to him, "If you're not going to eat that . . ."

With conflicted feelings of amusement and disgust, Carter stared at Imalima. Not waiting for a response, Imalima picked up Carter's plate and, with his knife, noisily scraped the remaining Kenga meat and assorted who-knows-what onto his own plate.

His sizeable head hanging just an inch or two above the table, Imalima, much like a vacuum cleaner, sucked food noisily into his mouth. He ate everything except for a blue-colored vegetable that he didn't much care for and another item that he now recognized as a bird's beak. Looking up and down the table and thinking no one watching, he slid the vegetable and beak under the table. When finished, he proceeded to lift up his plate and, with his long tongue, licked it clean.

"Now that's my idea of good old-fashioned home-style cooking," Imalima said loudly while returning Carter's plate. "Sumptuous fare, good sir. Compliments to the chef." He smacked his lips at the king. "Quite the nosh." He finished his words with a quick double cluck of his tongue, a wink, and a smile of thanks directed at Carter. Accompanying his expression of gratitude was a low, rumbling burp brought up slowly from a dark corner of his gut. The blistering belch grew in intensity as it traveled. The impolite indiscretion was heard throughout the great hall.

Choosing to ignore his guest's poor table manners, Pappasnaxx continued his conversation with Serene. "The Gootz spy was aware of your journey and identified you as Wiggwoggs of Wiggonwoggen. I know of you through tales of an ancient Wiggwogg wizard known as Elderwiser. According to legend, the wizard lost a treasure long ago to The Grinder, leader of the plundering Gootz. By your numbers and lack of weapons, the spy considered you to be an insignificant distraction and not a meaningful threat. I can understand now that I have a close-up picture why he might have come to that conclusion. No insult intended.

"That still leaves the unanswered question of your intentions. You are quite a distance from home to be simply on a camping trip wandering aimlessly hither and yon across dangerous valleys and mountains with no purpose. In all confidence, however, I can tell you this: every step you take in the direction you were heading takes you one step closer to never returning home."

The old king's words were met with silence.

"Surely you wouldn't be foolish enough to be considering a run at the island of Athulian, would you? You wouldn't delude yourselves into believing that it is possible to locate that which was once yours and is now theirs and miraculously steal it back, would you?"

Pappasnaxx stared up at the timbered ceiling, his slow and deliberate question directed at no one in particular. Not waiting for an answer, the king quickly made his move. With his head snapping in Serene's direction, his face barely inches from hers, he stared intently into her eyes, his aggressiveness catching her totally off guard. "Well, would you?" The small but clever king had slowly been laying his trap and now, by Serene's horrified expression, he saw that he had snared his prey.

"Ah ha—why don't all of you just throw yourselves off the mountain? It would be a quicker death and, I assure you, a lot less painful than the fate that awaits you at the hands of The Grinder." The king pushed back from the table, shaking his head in disbelief that anyone in their right mind would consider undertaking a mission whose outcome was guaranteed failure. He had wasted a good meal on a bunch of lunatics who would soon be dead and didn't even know it. Removing his oversized napkin from around his neck, the king threw it down on his plate in disgust.

In truth, this was all show. The fact that the Minnininni had never in their long history been conquered by any invaders was directly related to their remote location, their animal-like familiarity with the steep mountains they inhabited, and the single narrow canyon leading to and from their village. The secret entrances to Millililli from both the east and west were the key to the Minnininni's security.

Citizens of Millililli were not by nature aggressive, but they were stealthy hunters and fiercely protective of their secluded village. The king knew that, based on the happenings in the surrounding territories, an attempted Gootz invasion of Millilili, difficult as it might be, was just a matter of time. In fact, he expected it and had planned for it.

"You are indeed fools," continued Pappy Pappasnaxx. "If—and that is a big if—you made it into Wimzi still alive, there would be little hope of any of you making it through still wearing your skin, hair side out. Let's just say for argument's sake you pulled off a miracle, escaping your most certain fate at the hands of the Wimzicals, then you somehow managed to cross The Great Sea Valion overrun with sea monsters. You would exhaustedly arrive on Athulian's shores with your luck run out and flat out of miracles. The absolute best you could hope for from The Grinder and the Gootz would be a quick death."

Not known for diplomacy, the old king looked at his guests and saw fear beginning to infect their faces. At that moment, he thought it better not to burden the visitors with the bad news that none of his scenario mattered anyway. Pappasnaxx was just toying with his company. When it came right down to it, the successful departure of the adventurers from Millilili was just not going to happen. Oh well, for the time being the mercurial king of the Minnininni was thoroughly enjoying the play's inevitable ending.

After a short time of awkward silence, Serene cleared her throat and spoke up. She was beginning to feel a sense of discomfort. Things were not as they seemed. Their host was not the benevolent soul he was pretending to be.

"Well," said Serene, taking her napkin from her lap and placing it on the table, "this was indeed a delicious meal, for which we are most grateful." The others took their cue from Serene and nodded their heads in agreement. "You have been a most gracious host, but we don't want to overstay our welcome. If it's all the same to you, we shall be on our way."

"Yes," piped up Imalima, patting his bulging stomach, "the food was quite yummy. Might you happen to have a couple more of those tender spy birds lying around somewhere in the kitchen that you might toss into a doggy bag? You know, kind of like a going away present."

Carter, attempting not to be obvious to their host, poked the creature with his elbow hard to the ribs. The last thing he wanted was to insult the leader of the Minnininni. Like Serene, he too was feeling increasingly uncomfortable with their situation.

The king was growing weary of the charade, and Imalima was not showing the Minnininni king the proper respect he was accustomed to. His face reddened with impatience and he shouted at Imalima while banging both fists on the table.

"There will be no going away presents for the simple reason that you are not going away, you moth-eaten excuse for a . . . for . . . a . . . whatever it is you are!"

You could have heard a pin drop in the silent hall. It was as if the past and the future had been erased and all that was left was this precise moment. Saliva was beginning to form at the corners of Pappasnaxx's angry mouth.

Like a New Year's Eve paper noisemaker, Imalima unfurled his very long tongue in the direction of King Pappasnaxx. Carter simply closed his eyes, as if that might somehow protect him from the freight train he saw hurtling toward them.

"Sticks and stones will—" That was about all Imalima could get out of his mouth before the tiny king drew his sword and jumped up onto the long table, scattering dishes every which way. He held the blade so that its tip was pressed against Imalima's neck.

"Say another word and it will be your last."

That was too bad because Imalima had thought of a really good "gotcha" and had his mouth open, ready to insert a foot or hoof or whatever.

"Don't even think about it," whispered Carter to Imalima through his tightly clenched teeth.

"My deepest apologies, good king," intervened Serene. "I'm afraid our little friend here has undoubtedly suffered severe head injuries. Obviously the creature is not quite right. He cannot be held responsible for his behavior. I assure you, he meant no harm."

Pappasnaxx was not totally convinced but slowly lowered both his sword and temper.

"My cook likes to experiment with food. He enjoys creating exotic dishes. Why, just the other day he asked me if I had anything in particular I might enjoy for this night's dinner. As luck would have it, along comes a volunteer Kenga and drops straight into the cook's pot."

That, of course, was not all true. The king failed to include the part about the painful stripping of fur endured by the spy prior to the shivering, bald bird's "dropping straight into the cook's pot." The spy bird did require some wing twisting along with more than a bit of "friendly" encouragement to spill the beans on the purpose of its mission.

The Big Ninni continued. "An idea is beginning to take form in my mind of what tomorrow night's dinner menu might look like." Pappasnaxx shifted his eyes from Serene and focused directly on Imalima while slowly running his tongue along his upper lip.

"Now hold on," Imalima said nervously, taking two cautious steps backward. "Let's not be too hasty here. There is the distinct possibility I may have overstepped my authority and misinterpreted myself."

"What does that mean?" the confused king asked, turning back to Serene.

"Hard to tell," Serene responded, attempting to appeal to the king's good graces.

"As I suggested earlier, the poor creature is no longer capable of operating at full speed. I believe his problem can be traced to an irreversible condition of chronic brain sludge. Regretfully, his time may be short, as I see certain signs of his fading. Sort of like a flickering candle struggling to hold onto the light just before it . . . burns out." Serene looked over at Imalima, squinting her eyes while daring him to say another word.

Not sure she was convincing the king to soften his feelings toward Imalima, she reached deep in defense of the Wimzical and threw out a card she would shortly regret.

"He is functioning with something considerably less than a full deck, if you catch my drift." A big tear filled one of Imalima's eyes.

"More like a deck of cards without numbers, if you ask my opinion," said Ferbert under his breath to his twin brother with whom he was sitting at the far end of the raised platform.

"Generous," said the king, overhearing Ferbert's malicious observation.

Breaking free of Serene's glare, Imalima yelled, "Think I'm deaf? I heard that, and I don't recall anyone asking your opinion, FURBUTT, so button it up!" The exiled Wimzical was on a roll and out of control. There was no stopping him now. "These beautimus ears of mine are more than decorative accessories, I'll have you know. I hear all, and much of it I simply overlook in the interest of not appearing overly sensitive. That being said, I draw the line at slanderous remarks."

Now directing his words at the king, Imalima continued. "I personally have never had a problem with my intelligence. I am way more than half as smart as I need to be and at a minimum, three times less than most others. My IQ is somewhere in the high thirties, which I have been assured by my psychiatrist is, I believe he used the term *incredible*. I don't like to blow my own horn," he said, unscrewing the curly protuberance jutting from just above his nose. Placing the instrument to his lips, he blew a piercing sour blast that bounced off the walls of the dining hall. "However, sometimes it is necessary. For example," he said, re-screwing his horn, "to my credit, I am the famous inventor of the holder—"

"Hanger," reminded Carter in a whisper.

"Whatever!" continued an annoyed Imalima, who didn't appreciate Carter's interruption of his resume. "I also invented the bus stop and accompanying fast food franchises known as Fatso's with all-you-can-eat lemon meringue pie. I don't know exactly what a franchise is, but it sounds like a good idea, don't you agree? How would you like to get in on the ground floor and be my partner or first investor?"

Not waiting for a response from the king, Imalima plowed ahead. "The remarkable thing about the bus stops is I don't even know what a bus looks like since I haven't invented them yet. Doesn't that make me some kind of genius?" Imalima's crossed eyes bulged and he cupped one of his flappers to his ear, tilting his head as if trying hard to hear a response.

"Helloooooo, I can't hear you," he said, looking directly at the king. "And you have the nerve to question my intelligence. By the way, what's for dessert?"

No one had ever talked to the great leader of the Minnininni in the outrageously disrespectful tone used by Imalima. Carter and the Wiggwoggs simply hung their heads in despair, attempting to avert the eyes of their host. Serene, who was sitting next to Pappy Pappasnaxx could actually feel the wave of red heat coming off the king's face.

Gesturing at a uniformed guard standing in the doorway, the king, stuffing down his anger, said to Imalima, "There will be no dessert for you tonight as you have been quite naughty and insolent. You have offended your gracious host the king, Pappy Pappasnaxx, Grampy Pappasnaxx, The Big Ninni, and more importantly, me, who are all one and the same. As a matter of record, do you recall your last dessert? I certainly hope you do, and I also hope you really enjoyed it, because you shall never have another."

· · · · · · ·

The following morning, the would-be heroes woke stiff and cold from an uncomfortable night spent on straw mattresses scattered atop a dirt floor. They were prisoners in a cell located in the large building with barred windows they had passed the day before. There was just a single window high on one of the four solid walls opposite the cell's heavy wooden door, which included a square barred opening. The only light in the cell came through the small window. Two rats scurried across the hard-packed dirt floor checking out their new neighbors before disappearing into a dark corner.

Sitting upright in a lotus position with his eyes closed, Imalima was deep in a state of meditation. He had arranged his sitting location directly in the center of the crowded cell so anyone moving from here to there would have to walk around him.

An overweight Minnininni guard, with a heavy ring of keys dangling from his belt, waddled down several stone steps to the cell holding the adventurers. In one hand he held a lit lantern, in the other, a bucket of foul-smelling gruel that sloshed over the rim, spilling onto his shoes. As the guard approached the door, from inside the cell Ushi sniffed the air. He interrupted Imalima's solitude with a solid knock on the creature's head.

"Hello, anyone home? I think I smell the dessert you ordered last night and I believe it's about to be served."

From outside the cell, the guard poured the gelatinous mix from the bucket into wooden bowls. With an expression of disgust, he slid the slop under a gap at the bottom of the door. Imalima examined his breakfast then peered at the guard through the cell's barred opening.

"Didn't you forget something?" he asked. The guard stared blankly at Imalima. "Surely you don't expect us to eat this porridge without brown sugar and cinnamon. And while you are at it, would you heat this stuff up and fetch some golden raisins? That's always a nice touch and a good source of fiber, I might add."

Ignoring Imalima, the guard turned and began walking away.

"Oh, and if it would not be too much of a bother," called Imalima after the retreating guard, "a few pats of butter would be much appreciated." The guard rounded a corner and was now well beyond earshot of Imalima's growing wish list.

It was sometime around midday when the Minnininni guard finally returned. He did so without the requested raisins, sugar, cinnamon, or butter. Six more armed thugs accompanied the original guard. In addition, one more Minnininni, dressed in a stiff white high-buttoned jacket with matching pants and a tall chef's hat, joined the guards in the cell. When the Minnininni left the dungeon a few moments later the number of prisoners remaining in the cell had been reduced by one. Imalima was taken down the hall, his head covered by a black hood.

"We must do something," Serene said, "and soon, or the Minnininni will eliminate us one by one. Imalima may be a bit whackadoo, but he is one of us. Although he angered the king, I don't believe for a moment that we would have been allowed to peacefully leave Millililli. Does anyone have any ideas how we might escape this dungeon and rescue Imalima?"

Carter was way ahead of the Wiggwoggs and had already been thinking of an exit strategy.

Nevermore, you're going to get us out of here.

Chapter 12
Twitch

Twitch, who you may recall as the half-brother of The Grinder, witnessed his birth name, Bumbreth, pretty much disappear from use in the seventh year of his life. It happened one unusually hot summer day while he was exploring a field of wild flowers. With his face just inches away while attempting to discern the unique fragrances between the varied flowers, a bothered pollinating bee decided to take a work break. The bee considered the cool, dark, inviting interior of young Bumbreth's nose, a good place to rest in the shade.

Less than a gracious host was Bumbreth to his uninvited guest. He first attempted to pick then blow the exploring bee from his nose. It was impossible to know whether the bee was angry or scared with Bumbreth's rude attempt at eviction. I guess it really doesn't matter since the bee made Bumbreth well aware of its displeasure by painfully inserting a barbed stinger deep into the fleshy interior wall of Bumbreth's left nostril. Howling in agony, the stung youngster pounded madly with both fists at his rapidly swelling red nose.

The poor bee died, of course, unmercifully pummeled to death. Bumbreth's nose took such a beating that the physical, not to mention psychological, damage caused by the traumatic experience left the young Gootz with a severely tweaked sniffer. Bad enough that his nose now resembled a deformed potato, the irreversible nose spasm resulting from the trauma lasted until the final moments of his life, as did his unwelcomed new nickname, Twitch.

The nasal tone infecting the speech of The Grinder's half-brother was possibly the result of his nose beating. His voice also had a whining quality that grated on most listeners, especially the supreme leader of the Gootz, who was not known as a wellspring of tolerance anyway.

Although The Grinder had little use for his dull-witted sibling, he had promised his mother on her deathbed that he would look after his younger half-brother. He had assured Mother Putzer that Bumbreth would have an important position in his administration.

"Bumbreth has issues," Mother Putzer had told her elder son. "That shouldn't be held against him. He means well," she reminded him.

"He's a loser," said The Grinder. "If it weren't for you, I wouldn't have him polish my boots."

"I'm an old Putzer," said The Grinder's mom. "I don't know how much time I have left, and I'm worried what will become of Bumbreth after I'm gone. Promise me you will take care of him."

The Grinder sighed. "All right, Mom, I promise." He was not very happy with the commitment he had just made, but he loved Mother Putzer in his own twisted way and she didn't ask much of him.

Even though Twitch was not held in high regard by his big brother, his military position entitled him to a small castle complete with a staff of Dweeg slaves who saw to his every need. Materially he was not wanting. Strange as it may seem, the inept half-brother of The Grinder was the second most powerful individual on all of Athulian. He actually harbored illusions of one day replacing The Grinder as supreme leader of the Gootz. Twitch had dreamt of capturing every one of Aeiea's territories and enslaving all their inhabitants. He envisioned himself with untold wealth while sitting at the height of power.

The Grinder is good, Twitch said to himself, *but I would be an even better leader. After all,* he reasoned, *aren't I the absolute master of deception?* And with the exception of his disfigured sniffer, he felt he was much cuter than his hairy-eared, pimple-faced brother.

Unfortunately for the sly Twitch, his unrealistic fantasy was never to be realized. While it was true that Twitch was a far more practiced sneak than his closest competitor, he had little else going for himself that would qualify him for The Grinder's position. Groveling seemed his expertise and a natural by-product of the hunchbacked sniveling manner required in

Twitch's dealings with The Grinder. He was severely insecure, preferring to remain close to his castle where he would spend most days in his hidden vault obsessively counting his looted fortune.

It was also a fact that Twitch was a devout coward, which went well with his mewling, high-pitched voice. If an opportunity came along for Twitch to exhibit some small degree of courage, he would somehow always manage to find a reason to make himself scarce. "I have a splitting headache," or "I feel a severe nosebleed coming on," were just two examples that would send him scurrying to the rear of a battle formation for medical treatment. Swollen feet or hands or glands, or any other part of his anatomy capable of swelling, were a few more excuses on his lengthy list to keep from harm's way.

In the privacy of a personal underground dungeon located beneath his small castle, Twitch obsessively practiced his sword fighting skills. An odd collection of elderly, half-starved prisoners were kept barely alive for just such purposes in cramped, rodent-ridden cells. The Gootz Director of Spies used the miserable unfortunates to hone his limited fencing skills, which due to his commitment to cowardice, had never been tested in actual combat. Twitch's carefully handpicked sparring mates were so old or infirm they could hardly unsheathe their swords let alone lift them in self-defense.

Barely budging the needle on the smartness scale, Twitch's snobby pretensions of being "Mr. Know It All" were simply a mask worn to disguise his blundering ways. His public appearance brought hushed snickers of disrespect from the otherwise humorless Gootz. Perhaps if stripped of his family connections and military title, what would remain would be a highly qualified candidate for membership in the Athulian Who's Who of Losers Club. By even the most fundamental and forgiving standards of measuring intelligence, Twitch was stupider than spit.

· · · · · · ·

When the Kenga spies who were assigned to monitor any unusual happenings on the mainland failed to return to Athulian on schedule, The Grinder summoned his director of spies to appear at his castle offices for a closed-door briefing.

Growling at Twitch, The Grinder said, "What do you mean 'disappeared'? No one just disappears. Perhaps the Department of Spies needs an updated training manual or, better yet, a new director. I don't want excuses, I want answers!" With each word, the volume of his voice increased. "I want to know what happened to those Kenga, and I want to know now! If you can't do a better job, I'll find someone who can. Do I make myself clear?" The purpling color under The Grinder's face deepened as he pounded his desk so hard that all the maps stacked neatly on its surface flew into the air before scattering across the floor.

"Now see what you've done!" he yelled at Twitch.

When you get to be the boss of everything, you get to yell at anyone, about anything. That was one of The Grinder's favorite perks of his job.

"Dear brother," Twitch said in his whining voice, not daring to look into his brother's angry eyes, "I am as equally frustrated as you. I can tell you the Kenga's disappearance and their recovery is of the highest priority for my department. I am doing all in my power to find answers."

"Do more and do it quickly. Now get out while you still have legs to carry you!" yelled The Grinder.

"Of course, Your Most Gracious Greatness." Twitch's well-rehearsed quick, deep bow was probably responsible for the heavy paperweight thrown by The Grinder missing its intended target by inches as he backed rapidly out of the high double doors.

"Not bad," Twitch said to an unresponsive guard standing close by. "I'm still wearing my skin right side out."

Years of abuse at the hands of The Grinder had taught Twitch some valuable life-extending lessons. Reminding his brother of their family connection along with his promise of protection made to their dearly departed mother was Twitch's often-punched first-class ticket to survival. Existing in the perpetual state of an apologetic worm, Twitch's expertise at creating excuses for his ineptness was a skill in which he held no pride. In the company of his older brother, Twitch had learned to keep his comments as short as a sawed-off Kenga's beak, not volunteering anything but absolute support for the opinions or decisions of the supreme commander.

· · · · · · ·

Deep down in his bones The Grinder felt it. Something was definitely up and he was going to find out what it was. Had he not earlier smelled danger blowing across the sea from the mainland? He was convinced his snake of a brother knew more about the missing Kenga patrol than he was letting on. When the time was right he would enjoy punishing his baby brother for his deception. Creative ideas for new means of torture danced through his head, but there was no rush in putting them into practice. He felt he could no longer trust his little brother, but he decided Twitch wasn't going anywhere.

The Grinder was wrong.

· · · · · · ·

One of the Kenga spies, although badly wounded, had managed to elude the full wrath of the Minnininni archers. All of his fellow Kenga now lay dead. Severely injured, the bird had the good sense to take cover in a dense thicket, the splintered end of a broken arrow sticking painfully from his chest.

The proud Minnininni bowmen gathered their war trophies, stretching and tying the deceased Kenga between long wooden poles in preparation for their triumphant march home to Millililli. They practiced the telling of their successful encounter amongst themselves. With each telling, the story grew larger.

When at last the lone surviving Kenga was sure the Minnininni were gone, it emerged from its hiding place. Summoning all its remaining strength, and with great effort, it took flight. Flying with a strong tail-wind, the injured spy coasted much of the way across The Great Sea Valion on its journey home to Athulian.

Twitch was called by his trusted lieutenant to the death scene of the mortally wounded Kenga. The purpose of Twitch's visit was to interrogate his spy. No one except The Grinder's brother and his aide knew of this secret meeting.

The lieutenant standing near Twitch was ordered to take down the information pertinent to the circumstances of the Kenga's failed mission, but he had nothing to write with. Besides, the Kenga was so weak it could barely be heard. The spy's mission was supposed to be simply observational. The Kenga were to locate and report back to Twitch any activity in the territories that had the potential to threaten Athulian. To date, it had been quite the boring job.

The dying Kenga, lying stretched out on the lieutenant's desk, motioned for Twitch to come closer. The Grinder's brother bent to hear the bird's final words. In Twitch's opinion, the bird told a trivial, mostly uninteresting story involving the ongoing journey of the small, harmless group from what he believed was the territory of Wiggonwoggen. If the spy's information was accurate, the Wiggwoggs were little more than children and their apparent leader also a child. The Kenga had no new information shedding light on the purpose of their journey. The spy bird reported that most recently the young Wiggwoggs last seen in Dweeg Territory were now attempting to cross Mourners Mountains. Since they had recently dropped out of sight, the spy could not report on the Wiggwoggs' present location.

As Twitch was about to walk away, the Kenga pulled at his sleeve, drawing him closer. The lieutenant, sensing a secret about to be revealed, also leaned in. The Kenga's last whispered words told of a windstorm that blew the spy birds off course into an uncharted region of Mourners Mountains where they sited the legendary village of Millililli. The howling gale had swept aside rope netting woven into the surrounding trees that camouflaged the hidden kingdom. Numerous small structures were exposed along with what looked like a castle higher up on the mountain.

Finally the mystery of the Minnininni was solved. Now, thought Twitch, this was a great discovery and information worthy of being kept secret. If the rumors of precious gems buried under the houses in Millililli were true, he was about to become a very rich Gootz. Before the bird could speak another word, death snatched its last breath.

Twitch stared emotionlessly at the scrawny, lifeless bird that had fallen from the desk and was now lying at his feet. While scratching at his greasy beard he gave the spy bird a tentative nudge with his foot to ensure the bird was really dead.

The dying Kenga's last words left more questions unanswered than answered, but at least Twitch knew Millililli existed and now he knew how to get there. He shifted uneasily on his legs mulling over the incomplete information from his spy. More details, including the possible location of rumored treasure, had died with the bird. His second, this time more forceful, kick to the bird was made in anger and sent the limp body of the Kenga flying across the room, where it smacked hard against the wall before sliding heavily to the floor.

Twitch always carried a vial of deadly Kenga spit in the pocket of his tunic "just in case." This moment presented one of those special cases.

During a private lunch with his aide that afternoon, Twitch slipped a little Kenga juice from his vial into the lieutenant's drink, ensuring no one but he would know the secret divulged by the spy who had spilled the beans.

"Good job with that bird, Lieutenant. Let's have a little toast. To your health! Bottoms up!"

The two Gootz soldiers drained their drinks, and wiping his mouth with his sleeve, the lieutenant said, "Guess I had you wrong, Twitch. I'm really getting to like you!"

That was a moment before the lieutenant keeled over dead.

Upon further assessment, it did not seem reasonable to Twitch that the little band of Wiggwoggs were simply out roaming the territories with no intention. He sensed something was up but at the same time didn't feel threatened by a ragtag band of children. Still, his curiosity tickled at the burnt edges of his mind. Were they an advance group of scouts? They didn't seem to simply be wandering without purpose, but the nature of that purpose puzzled The Grinder's brother. The small band of Wiggwoggs was traveling in a mostly northern direction. If they managed to traverse the challenges of Mourners Mountains and didn't change course, their path would likely lead to a dead end at the border of Wimzi. Twitch knew the Wiggwoggs were by nature not aggressive. They didn't even have a small army. Something must have happened to cause the Wiggwoggs, who normally chose isolation from their neighbors, to breach their homeland borders. Confused, The Grinder's puzzled brother rubbed his chin.

What Twitch did know was that the Kenga had encountered hostile Minnininni archers and that the Gootz spies had had the worst of their meeting. This did not sit well with the Gootz Director of Spies, but far more concerning for Twitch was the explosive temper he knew he would have to face when news of the slaughtered spies reached The Grinder.

In one of Twitch's rare thoughtful moments, a spreading smile revealed a mouthful of rotting teeth. The wrath of The Grinder could be avoided if he acted quickly. He would take a number of Kenga and a special force of his most highly trained Gootz soldiers. Together they would sneak up and catch the Minnininni unaware. He would capture the leader of the elfish mountain dwellers as well as a few of his commanders. Perhaps if he got lucky, he might even find and bring back a few Wiggwoggs for The

Grinder's pleasure. The fortune of gems would make him a hero. Of course, unbeknownst to The Grinder, Twitch would reserve a healthy percentage of the treasure for himself.

Yes, thought The Grinder's simple-minded half-brother, rubbing his hands together in glee, this would put the clever Twitch in great favor with his king.

Twitch's mind drifted to a daydream of a large crowd of cheering Gootz gathered alongside the wide road leading through Bludenbonz and up to The Grinder's castle. He was at the head of a colorful parade of returning victorious Gootz soldiers. Twitch would be riding in an ornate chariot, cracking a long whip above the huddled Minnininni and, if lucky, perhaps a few Wiggwogg children thrown in to make it even more interesting. The defeated leader of the Minnininni would be cowering just in front of him, begging for his life. Oh yes, he thought, what a celebrated homecoming that would be.

Without plans or provisions, Twitch swiftly gathered his hand-picked soldiers. That very night the Gootz, riding atop the saddled backs of their swiftest flying spies, set out to inflict an incisive surprise attack on the mountain stronghold of Millililli. The elite Gootz soldiers were not enthused about this loosely planned adventure, but as all good soldiers must, they simply followed the orders of their commander.

"This will be a rout," Twitch had reasoned with his fellow attackers. "We may be small in numbers, but the Minnininni are reported to be small in size. What's the worst damage they can do? Stick us in the knee? Their blades can't be much more than useless toothpicks against our swords. Like disgusting bugs, we shall squash them underfoot."

Twitch needed to pump himself up even if he felt it would hardly be a contest. As the ultimate coward, he had to feel entirely assured of victory and that no physical harm would come to him before he would risk involvement in any conflict.

On through the dark, moonless night they flew. The lead Kenga was the acknowledged best navigator in Twitch's fleet of flying spies. He was somewhat older than the other Kenga flying this mission, but his years as a spy gave him the required experience for this type of secret operation. Twitch took up his familiar position in the tight formation of single-file raiders at the rear.

"So far, so good," said Twitch into the ear of the bird beneath him. They had just taken off. On his head he wore a tight-fitting aviator's cap with a pair of large round goggles covering his eyes. "There is still a good deal of night left, which works in our favor for the surprise party we are about to spring on the Minnininni. I figure by late afternoon we'll be back on Athulian, welcomed home as heroes. Of course, naturally, I as your commanding officer will be recognized as the head hero."

The bored bird had no comment.

· · · · · · ·

Long ago, when the Gootz were in the process of settling into their new home of Athulian, and while they were still in the adolescent period of their rise to power, a sizeable but ill-prepared invasion force was sent across The Great Sea Valion to conquer the Wimzicals of Wimzi. Their intelligence reports were woefully inadequate, lacking the depth of information that would have informed the invading Gootz that the Wimzicals were more than worthy opponents and weren't to be trifled with.

Initially the invasion of Wimzi was uneventful. Proceeding on schedule, the Gootz had as of their third day in Wimzi yet to encounter any opposition or, for that matter, a single Wimzical. It was late on the fourth day of the invasion that all communication to Athulian from the Gootz in Wimzi was terminated. From that point forward, not one Gootz soldier who was in that invasion force was ever heard from or seen again.

The final communication from the territory of Wimzi came to Athulian as the advancing army of Gootz had entered a gorge so narrow the invaders had to march in single file. Towering rock walls rose perpendicularly hundreds of feet from the ground. The gorge twisted and turned so sharply that at times it was impossible for a soldier to see anyone directly in front or behind him. The last routine news was received at a listening post on Athulian by a daydreaming clerk: "No enemy seen as of 1700 hours on the fourth day of invasion."

And so it was, on a day that began much the same as most, that each of the Gootz soldiers, right down to the last, took a single step at a ninety-degree turn to the right and, without a single word, stepped off the narrow pathway into a bottomless abyss.

Such are the ways of Wimzi. One moment you are; the next, you are not.

· · · · · · ·

Having learned the hard way long ago, the Gootz of today were not about to try any funny stuff on the tricky Wimzicals.

The Gootz may have had the Circle of Power, but in fact were limited in its use by the rather puny size of their brains as well as a lack of a service manual for the proper care and handling of their prize.

In addition, the Gootz were lacking in the IQ department. To best give perspective as to the degree of intelligence and appearance of the average Gootz brain, picture the crown on a large-sized stalk of broccoli. As if this wasn't bad enough news for the Gootz in regard to their future contin- ued dominance of Aeiea, they had a far larger problem. A long history of inbreeding was having serious consequences on their evolutionary process and actually reducing the size of a Gootz brain to what would soon be roughly the size of a walnut, a very small walnut. Whether broccoli or wal- nut, if you're a Gootz, the news is not good.

· · · · · · ·

On this moonless night of departure from Athulian for the surprise raid on Millilili, about the last things on Twitch's mind were vegetables or nuts. He had never seen a Minnininni. Twitch was looking forward to cutting into one with his razor-sharp, jewel-handled sword that he had cleverly named "Sticker." Somehow the elegant sword that dragged the ground while hanging loosely from the sloppy air force general's belt never looked very dangerous. Twitch's rumpled appearance was his signature on Athulian. Not only was his uniform too large, it always appeared slept in and stained as well.

The Kenga had made the flight over the strait of The Great Sea Valion many times before. They were always careful to avoid the possibility of a dangerous over-flight of Wimzi. The frightening reputation of Wimzi was only magnified by the secretive territory's complete isolation from its neighbors. Over the years, stories of Wimzi were exaggerated beyond rec- ognition as they were passed down from one generation to the next. Scary became scarier as time distorted reality.

Separating fact from fiction was not Twitch's job. Not that he would have been very good at it anyway, even if it were. The Gootz Air Force Commander and Director of Spies was such a proficient liar it was hard for him to keep straight his own bottomless well of fabrications. He was sometimes asked the origin of his lumpy nose. When snared in one of his surplus of deceits, he would refer to his nasal embellishment as simply a mark of character and superior intelligence. Once, caught in a lie when telling a subordinate about one of his many great fishing expeditions, he explained, "Well, it could have been that big a fish, if only it were longer."

He blamed his fibberosity on an overly active imagination and a rare, self-diagnosed personality disorder, the result of a chronic sinus infection that had leached down into some underperforming gland. This of course was also a lie. It was ultimately Mother Putzer who Twitch accused of responsibility for his complicated and challenging relationship with honesty. He told of horrific bloody bedtime stories read to him by his mother as candlelight danced recklessly on his bedroom walls and ceiling. All this at a most emotionally critical developmental stage during the time he was just beginning to talk. More lies.

Diagnosed in his teen years with an extremely rare disorder of mega-mendaciousness by Bumpi Scugglesnitch, the famous Gootz fire juggler as well as a part-time psychotherapist, Twitch's future looked rather bleak.

"Perhaps you might want to consider a rather simple brain transplant," was one of Scugglesnitch's suggestions. "Surely with the relatively small size of your existing thinker," Bumpi reasoned, "the operation would pose little danger. I have a friend who has two heads. One is a tattooed sword-swallower while the other head is that of a brain surgeon. Be sure to make the appointment with the brain surgeon. He works in the sideshow of the circus and said he would do it for you at a real good price if you paid cash."

"Would it hurt?" Twitch asked.

"Are you referring to hurt me or you? I guess I would be mildly upset if you went through with it, but I believe under the right circumstances and given the proper pain medication, I could deal with it. I don't know if *hurt* would necessarily be my experience of your operation. But enough about me, let's talk about you and your relationship with your father."

Were it not for his family connections, Twitch's fate most likely would have seen him skinned, chopped into small pieces, and baked into a tasty meatloaf.

· · · · · · ·

In the cramped, depressing cell in Millililli, Nevermore flew from his familiar nest in Carter's hair toward the back wall of the dungeon. The little black bird landed on the window ledge high above the prisoners and, after a brief wing-flapping dance, flew through the bars to his freedom.

"Who can blame him? I would probably do the same thing if I were in his place," Zebenuza said. "What's the point in sticking around here, watching us one by one disappear, most likely to reappear in a stew pot cooked up and soon to be served on a Minnininni dinner platter. Poor Imalima. I hope he doesn't suffer before the end."

"Well, personally I think the bird's a coward. I mean, talk about a rat deserting a sinking ship," said Ferbert, in one of his dark moods.

There wasn't a moment's doubt in Carter's mind that Nevermore had not abandoned them and would soon return. Sure enough, within the hour Nevermore was back, and he had brought company. A dozen "peckers," as Zebenuza referred to the woodpeckers, crowded onto the window ledge. The birds immediately began to drill at the wood bars. When they had whittled away most of the bars, they flew into the cell, circling three times before the cheering adventurers then out through the window.

Lyke, the rope master, had managed to conceal under his tunic a length of cord. He quickly fashioned a lasso at one end and on his second try managed to loop it over one of the short remains of a window bar. Up the rope scrambled Lyke and out through the window where he dropped to the ground below. One by one the others followed with Carter then Serene the last to escape.

Serene's eyes revisited the village of Millililli. She saw the outline of Minnininni homes lining the wall of the ravine. The prison stood like a bookend at the beginning row of houses. Down at the other side of the village was the dining hall. She motioned to the others to quietly follow her in the direction of the houses. One after another, the little dwellings were examined, but all were found empty.

"It is dinnertime and everyone must be in the dining hall," Serene said. For Carter and the Wiggwoggs, it was time to think of their next move and keep on looking. There were just not that many places Imalima could possibly be.

Chapter 13
Twitch Gets Stuck

Flying low, just above the surface of The Great Sea Valion, the Kenga spies skirted the coast of Athulian before heading out over the open water toward the eastern coast of Wimzi. When finally he saw landfall just up ahead, Twitch sucked in a mouthful of air and held it. Clutching so tight to the long neck of his Kenga that he was in danger of choking the poor beast to death, Twitch dug his spurs deep into the soft under-flanks of the bird, urging it full speed ahead. "Giddy up!" he shouted. They were now just clipping the corner of Wimzi, and the Gootz commander of the Department of Spies had no desire to spend one moment more than necessary over the home of the Wimzicals.

In the blink of an eye, all the Gootz were flying upside down. "How did that happen?" questioned the panicked Gootz commander. Twitch's face lost all its color. He worried he would fall and thought he was going to be sick and throw up on himself. "Wait," he muttered to himself. "If I do get sick, do I throw up or down?" It was of no matter since happily he did neither. In a moment it was over. The upside down ride was simply an illusion. It never happened except in the mind of the trespasser flying over Wimzi.

"So much for shortcuts," Twitch said. "Next time, leave a bit more room. Attempting to cut corners could be hazardous to my health." He filed his instruction in his memory box.

Over the squirming River Sme they flew, then straight on toward Mourners Mountains and the remote village of Millililli.

"This is kind of exciting, don't you agree, Kenga?" Twitch asked.

"To tell the truth," replied the bird, "I would say I am somewhat less excited than you. The last Kenga patrol never returned, not a single one of them. I guess that dampens my enthusiasm a bit."

Twitch wasn't thrilled with the attitude of his Kenga, but he understood that, unlike him, the bird had nothing to gain from this raid and was just doing as ordered. The rest of the night wore on silently save for the slow-motion rhythmic whoosh of flapping wings.

Finally, with the first hint of dawn, the long, silhouetted outline of Mourners Mountains loomed directly ahead. With the sighting, Twitch's heart picked up its pace. He understood from intelligence gathered by the now-deceased Kenga spy that a full-grown Minnininni was not much taller than a three-year-old Gootzling, a Gootz child. He also recalled that the unarmed hikers suspected to be Wiggwoggs were not soldiers at all and appeared to be little more than children themselves. This was Twitch's idea of a perfect fight. Surprising the Minnininni and Wiggwoggs while under the cover of darkness seemed a good and simple plan. They would catch the old king while he was still in his pajamas.

Any resistance from the defenders of Millililli would be dealt with swiftly and crushed like a stinkbug, thought Twitch. The king's generals and advisors along with the Wiggwoggs would be captured, bundled into large burlap sacks, and delivered back to Athulian and The Grinder.

That was the extent of the plan. Not a lot of details, but in Twitch's opinion, details were unnecessary and only complicated that which would otherwise be simple. While still a student, he had slept straight through the planning and strategy classes in military school, snoring loudly. He most assuredly would have flunked out of school had it not been for his brother's intervention. As to their present situation, the Gootz had superior weapons, Twitch reasoned, including a fancy crossbow that could hold and accurately fire five arrows within a second of each other.

Sister suns Suva and Ahneese were indifferent to the plans of the Gootz commander. They were already busy with the business of pulling up the new day from behind Mourners Mountains. Twitch cursed under his bad breath, which only made his foul language more pungent. They were behind schedule. He blamed the Kenga for slothful flying, rather than taking responsibility for his own miscalculations of flight departure and arrival times. Blaming others for his own sloppy thinking was not untypical of Twitch.

When we get back to Athulian, he said to himself, *these good for nothing birds are going straight to the soup pot. That way they can be right there with me at the banquet table to help celebrate my victory. How considerate of me.*

Regrettably for Twitch, his surprise party for the Minnininni was not off to a particularly good start. Upon landing at the edge of a wood, several Gootz immediately got into a loud shouting match about which of them had landed first. The verbal altercation threatened to escalate to a nose-punching fight.

The arguing soldiers were overheard by a local Minnininni youth who had observed the Gootz approaching and was hiding in a nearby tree. To make matters even worse for Twitch, the Minnininni were already on heightened alert because of their present Wiggwogg experience as well as their recent capture of the Gootz spy birds.

· · · · · · ·

The King of Millililli was not in his pajamas as Twitch expected, but rather dressed in full battle armor. The invasion force had been spotted, and the Minnininni leader, who had not enjoyed the privilege of attending military school, was, however, smart. He respected an intelligent plan of defense. The Minnininni had a strategy and were well rehearsed. When King Pappasnaxx received word of the invasion, his plan based on precision timing was set in motion.

"Get Blabbasnaxx in here immediately," ordered the king to his assistant. Blabbasnaxx was the king's most trusted advisor and an expert at military tactics.

"Is all ready as planned?" asked the king.

"Yes, my good king, we are as prepared as we can be. Now we will see if all that work and training has been worth the effort," responded the usually long-winded Blabbasnaxx.

It was estimated the invaders were a small force of perhaps two companies. The soldiers were identified as Gootz, and the king was well aware of their reputation for cruel brutality.

The small number of invaders was good news for the Minnininni. Of equal good news was the report that none other than Commander Twitch himself was leading the assault. As you might expect, Twitch had a reputation.

In the distance, a structure resembling a castle stood at the edge of a deep, clear lake that served as a reservoir providing year-round fresh water to the citizens of Millililli. The reservoir was also used as a source for irrigating the fertile terraced farmlands of the Minnininni, hidden amongst the steep mountains.

A town square for a duplicate village was situated down the mountain from the castle at the bottom of a bowl-shaped valley. The neatly staged village was lacking any inhabitants, and the small dwellings were actually a series of cleverly disguised and fabricated stage props whose interiors were empty of furnishings.

The real populated community of Millililli, home to the Minnininni, lay well hidden, as we already know, tucked higher up from the counterfeit town on an adjoining mountain slope. It was only accessible by the same winding, obscure road taken by Graggasnaxx when delivering the Wiggwoggs to his king. The only visible road leading to the apparent castle of King Pappasnaxx ran between two high stone walls, straight up the mountain's face from the center of the empty village. It was this very same road the sneaky Gootz were watching as they lay hidden high above the fake hamlet at the opposite end of the ridge from the king's ornate, although not very tall, "castle."

· · · · · · ·

Twitch called over his second-in-command, whose name at the moment he had misplaced. "Major Frmg . . ." he said, mumbling something under his breath that he hoped the major would interpret as his name.

"Krebs," the major reminded. "Major Krebs."

"Whatever. Here's the plan. Our forces sweep down into the valley in two pincher columns and surround the sleeping village of Millililli. We will then locate and capture any Wiggwogg or other important Minnininni officials while killing the rest. After regrouping, we will charge up the road to the castle where we will triumphantly march in and capture the king. Curtain down, end of show. We will finish our plunder in just enough time for a celebration lunch at the Minnininni king's castle. What do you think?"

Before the major could answer, Twitch said, "Never mind, I really don't care what you think. Brief the soldiers and make sure they understand my plan and are ready to go."

The Gootz commander twiddled absently at his sparse, wispy attempt at a beard. "Good plan," he reassured himself. "Keeping it simple works for me. We will probably catch the Minnininni still asleep in their tiny beds of straw. I wonder," he said while sliding his tongue over dry, chapped lips, his hand fidgeting on the hilt of his sword, "how many of the Minnininni I can shish kebab before the end of the day?"

· · · · · · ·

After escaping the Minnininni's dungeon, Carter and the Wiggwoggs had a restless night's sleep. At the first morning's light, they renewed their search for Imalima. The adventurers found the village, including the dining hall, entirely deserted. Once again working their way silently from house to house in the filtered light, they could find neither hide nor hair of the banished Wimzical.

"What do you make of this?" whispered Serene to Carter. "Everyone is gone, but I wonder for how long? The Wiggwogg leader was more thinking aloud than actually asking questions and expecting a response. "As to where they are and why they left," she continued, "your guess is as good as mine."

· · · · · · ·

The king of the Minnininni was concealed up in the bell tower that straddled the roof of the dining hall. Together with a secret code and reflecting mirror, he directed the Minnininni who were hidden in the hills above the phony village. He had a perfect bird's eye view of the three separate but related stories that were unfolding on the stage below him. Pappasnaxx watched with amusement as the escaped adventurers tiptoed around the Minnininni village. One or two at a time, they darted under the cover of shadows from one home to another.

Switching his attention to the town square in the center of the phony village, Pappasnaxx looked down at the delirious Imalima tethered to a post attempting to free himself from his bindings. The nuisance from last night's dinner was little more than Gootz bait.

Finally turning to face the hills above the action below, the king observed the outline of Gootz soldiers picking their way down the steep slopes of the mountain. They were heading in two separate columns toward the edges of the fake village. Rubbing his small hands together in eager anticipation, the king was pleased with most of what he saw.

"Blabbasnax," the king said, "everything is coming together. There have been minor glitches here and there but nothing to ruin our plans. The escape of the prisoners from the dungeon is unfortunate and certainly not something I would have preferred. Still, I don't see it as a major obstacle to victory. If the Gootz don't terminate the Wiggwoggs shortly, I will."

· · · · · · ·

Imalima saw slivers of morning light reflecting off metal and looked to its source. From the foothills at the far edge of the village, he saw two columns of Gootz soldiers approaching.

"UH-OH!" he shouted in a panic as loudly as he could, "THAR'S TROUBLE IN THEM THAR HILLS!" His voice echoed off the walls of the surrounding mountains, but from where he stood, it didn't seem there was anyone around to hear him.

He was wrong.

From their position in the hills, the Gootz heard the alarm being shouted from the village below. They knew they had been discovered. So much for Twitch's surprise party. Now their modified plan was simply to get down into the village as quickly as possible and still catch the Minnininni before they had a chance to organize and defend themselves.

Pappasnaxx also heard Imalima, as did all the other Minnininni, who were still hiding behind the raised sod rim of the "castle" moat high above. Frustrated, the old king slammed his fist hard on the watchtower's railing. He was concerned that his genius of a plan might have been compromised by Imalima's warning.

"Wait a minute," Pappasnaxx said aloud. "Maybe, on second thought, this may even be better. Why not kill two birds with one stone?"

The king of the Minnininni pictured all the Gootz invaders together in the center of the fake Millililli village surrounding Imalima at exactly the same time the Wiggwogg adventurers would be attempting his rescue. "No stragglers left on the mountain to find," he mumbled to himself. "On the other hand, two separate Gootz columns in a pincher maneuver could be a problem. And what if the timing is off and the two trespassing forces don't come together at the same time as I am hoping?" Doubt had planted seeds, and the old king simply shook his head.

If Pappasnaxx thought he might have problems, they were nothing as compared to Twitch's mounting troubles, which were about to become far worse. The strategically nearsighted Gootz commander hadn't prepared for alternatives in case his loose plan began to unravel. His lack of creativity and basic common sense left him with a military logistics vision that couldn't see much farther than beyond his deformed nose.

· · · · · · ·

Meanwhile, in the town square of the imitation village, an already nervous Imalima was becoming increasingly worried. He believed his friends were locked away in a dungeon and the Gootz were now coming in his direction down the mountain like a rolling avalanche.

"Oh, Momma, this could be it for your hero, the late, great Imalima," he said sadly.

Imalima had gone from one disastrous situation to another. Being chained tightly to a prep table in the Great Hall's kitchen after being taken from the cell he had shared with his friends was not Imalima's idea of a fun day at camp. When one of the waiters had inquired of the chef, "What's for dinner?" Imalima had caught the head chef giving him the once over while he slowly and deliberately sharpened one of his long carving knives.

"I suspect," Imalima had said with a sigh of despair to a fat rat scurrying across the kitchen floor, "my presence at this evening's dinner table might be something of a different experience from last night's banquet."

The rat was far too busy determining the safest path to a crumb of cheese lying under a kitchen chair to stop for a friendly chat.

"That's gratitude," Imalima said in an annoyed voice to the rat's passing tail. "How often does one of my superior stature take the time to talk to a nasty little bug-eyed scrambler such as yourself? May you encounter a ravenous, long-whiskered kitty on your day's journey," he cursed after the fast-disappearing rodent. Although Imalima felt better after giving the rat a piece of his untidy mind (he had precious few pieces left to give away), it did little to improve his dire situation.

When the king's trusted aide came into the kitchen and ordered Imalima released into his custody, Imalima's spirits were momentarily lifted. The surprised chef, on the other hand, looked sincerely disappointed.

Led from the kitchen of the dining hall down the mountain into the town square of the faux village, Imalima was chained to a stake in the ground and left alone without knowing the purpose of his latest confinement.

· · · · · · ·

"I want the first company to sweep along the eastern flank of the village and the second company to do the same along the west," Twitch said. "When you get to the northern edge of the village, swing around so that you meet up and encircle the enemy."

Twitch was standing on a low knoll near the base of the mountain trying to catch his breath. From his vantage point he could see the village just below as well as the town square and some kind of odd animal sitting on the ground, slumped over.

The Gootz, who had surrounded the Millililli village, were just beginning to tighten the noose by closing in on the gazebo in the town square. They were becoming concerned by the lack of opposition from the Minnininni. Then, all at once, the wheels on the Gootz invasion wagon seemed to come off.

The two pincher columns of Gootz soldiers realized there was no one around in Millililli to pinch. The little homes and other structures in the village were not real at all. They were just empty shells intentionally disguised from the outside to appear real.

"What's up with that?" said Twitch, scratching his bug-infested hair. The creature he had observed earlier, whose shouting had probably warned the Minnininni, thereby ruining Twitch's surprise party, was now gone. Standing in the center of the village, the Gootz commander took off his helmet, threw it angrily to the ground then tugged at his perpetually wiggling nose.

"When I catch up to that, that . . . whatever *that* is, I am going to barbeque and eat him on the spot."

· · · · · · ·

Imalima had soaked his chained leg with his tears and with considerable effort had managed to slip free. Off he ran back up the path he had recently taken when led from the dungeon down to the fake village. He planned to rescue his friends, who he thought were still imprisoned. Together they would figure a quick way to escape from the Gootz and the nasty little Minnininni.

When he had climbed—backwards, of course—all the way up to the single main road running the length of the real Millililli village, much to his surprise he was jumped from behind. The ambushers had been well-hidden in the tall grasses lining the path that intersected the village road.

Carter and the Wiggwoggs couldn't see beyond the brush that hid them and thought that whoever was approaching, either Gootz or Minnininni, needed to be dealt with. After a good deal of thumping and flailing around in the roadside brush, there was finally recognition and the beating quickly turned to hugging.

"I thought you all were in prison," said a moist-eyed Imalima, rubbing one of his many newly bruised legs.

"We thought we heard you down in the lower village and were on our way down to rescue you," said a relieved Carter.

"Quick, while the Minnininni are still gone and before the Gootz spot us," Serene said anxiously, "we need to make our way out of here and get down the other side of the mountain into Stanelhooven. We must go now, and there will be no time to rest until we are down from Mourners Mountains."

Shifting her backpack, the Wiggwogg leader set off at a quick pace in the opposite direction they had traveled when first arriving as prisoners in Millililli.

· · · · · · ·

Up on the mountain above the fake village, the Minnininni worked feverishly sliding back the heavy timbers that secured the front gate of the apparent castle of their king. I say "apparent" because appearances can be deceptive. In this case, they most certainly were. The gate was indeed a gate all right; however, the castle was hardly a castle. A rock-hardened front wall of the imposing structure was merely a clever mask worn on the face of a dam that hid a deep cold-water lake behind it.

The road leading down from the "castle" to the center of the fake Millililli village was also a counterfeit. With vertical walls on each side of the roadway, the "road" became a sluiceway intended to direct the channeled torrent of death that was about to be unleashed. Upon release, the lead edge of whitewater would make a wild sprint down the mountain to the valley floor below where it would smash anything in its path. Continuing on its deadly path, the water would next fill then overflow the bowl that made up the low point of the valley, drowning the fake village and anyone in it.

Just moments before the gates were opened, Twitch did what was for him an unusual thing and totally out of character. In little more time than it takes to grow a good sneeze, the Gootz commander moved from his safe observation position far to the rear of his soldiers to stand directly in front of them. Twitch was pretending to be interested in the architecture of the town square. He was actually quite angry that his surprise party had been ruined. As The Grinder's brother, he wanted to appear as a fearless leader to his soldiers, and a close-up view of the scene where the creature had made good his escape might present some clues as to his present whereabouts. The Gootz commander desperately wanted to find and torture the shaggy-haired little animal that he believed responsible for tipping off the Minnininni to their ill-fated invasion. He was, however, uncomfortable at his new position and not accustomed to being on the front lines.

"Krebs," called out Twitch to his second-in-command who, like all wannabe leaders, groveled just behind the Athulian Director of Spies and Air Force Commander. "Something is not right here, but I can't quite put my finger on it."

"I agree sir." (Second-in-commands are trained to say that.) "But I can't quite put my finger on it."

"Yes, thanks for your always valuable input, Krebs. What would I do without you?" Twitch said sarcastically.

The Gootz commander just happened to glance up at the apparent castle high above. He saw what appeared to be a swarm of Minnininni running toward the castle's main entrance. Something bad was happening, thought Twitch perceptively. In panic, the assortment of stripped screws that held his mind together came undone and his voice froze.

Not so his nose. Almost immediately his nasal protuberance began to spasm uncontrollably. It wiggled at such a furious pace that for Twitch to look directly at it would most likely have caused him to become permanently Imalima cross-eyed.

Instead of watching the lively contortions taking place on their leader's face, the uncomfortable Gootz looked down and away from Twitch, shuffling their feet uneasily. It was most likely for this reason the Gootz soldiers didn't see what Twitch saw: the Minnininni working feverishly to unlock the "castle's" gates.

Twitch's eyes glistened then blurred. His right hand was fully occupied just trying to hold onto his squirming nose that was now gyrating with ever increasing momentum as if trying to escape his face. His left hand flailed the air while he tried to keep his fishtailing body from falling over.

The Grinder's incompetent sibling resembled a rookie cowboy in a bull-riding event at the rodeo. One hand waved frantically for balance while with the other, the cowboy usually held on for dear life to a bucking bull's leather grab-strap.

Twitch would have taken off running but his mind was not communicating with his legs. Escape would have been impossible anyway. There is just no way to avoid the unavoidable.

In the distance, the deep-throated rumble of rolling thunder broke the silence. Strange, thought several Gootz, to have thunder on such a perfectly clear day. Twitch, who had been focused on trying to bring his nose under control, looked up at the "castle" once again just in time to see its gates ripped from their hinges. A wall of water exploded from the interior of the masquerading castle above the fake Millililli village, cascading down the "road" toward them.

"Very clever," acknowledged a fascinated Gootz soldier standing close to Twitch. "That's quite a piece of engineering."

It was at that precise moment that Twitch, the underperforming half-brother of The Grinder and most incompetent commander of the Gootz Air Force, spoke his final word.

"Yikes!" Twitch said.

Not a very moving or profound sentiment on such a momentous occasion, especially for an individual of his importance given his family of origin, title, and such. But for Twitch, who would best be remembered for a brief resume of underperformance and was not known for flowery eloquence, his feeble expression of alarm was most understandable.

The soldier standing directly behind Twitch immediately saw what his commander saw. Unfortunately—not that it would have altered the inevitable—the soldier did not notice poking from the ground the wedge of rock he clumsily stumbled over while attempting a reflexive step backward. As the soldier fell, his frightened commander standing directly in front of him instinctively stepped backward and, tripping over the same rock, also fell.

The full length of the prone soldier's drawn sword, which had been awkwardly angled upward toward the back of The Grinder's half-brother, pierced Twitch's armor. The tip entered his back smoothly just below the left inside corner of his shoulder blade like a sharp knife slicing through tofu. The sword continued its deadly journey without obstruction, finally exiting Twitch's throat just below his chin.

"Sorry, sir," said the bewildered soldier beneath him. "That was quite clumsy of me. I'll try to be more careful next time."

Unfortunately for The Grinder's brother, there would not be a next time.

When the Gootz commander looked down to see if he had injured himself in his fall, Twitch noticed with a great sense of relief that for the first time in so many years, his wiggler of a nose had given up the struggle and was now still. He was also momentarily grateful for the soft landing provided by the apologetic soldier who had cushioned his fall. Smiling appreciatively for the termination of his nasal vibration, Twitch looked curiously beyond his now tranquil nose to the pointed length of metal protruding from below his chin as if to say, "What the heck is that doing there?"

The Athulian Director of Gootz Spies and cowardly half-brother of The Grinder peacefully closed his eyes then slipped away to the netherworld just before the water struck, his question lost in irrelevance.

Chapter 14
Imalima Goes Home

Losing no time, Carter, the Wiggwoggs, and Imalima scrambled down the backside of Mourners Mountains, focused on getting as much distance as possible between themselves and those who would put an early end to their mission. They had not been long out of Millililli when a ground-shaking roar was heard from above and behind them. The deafening explosion of colliding energy echoed with authority, bouncing off the cold, indifferent surfaces of the mountains surrounding them.

Carter remembered a shiny chrome pinball bouncing off the rubber bumpers in a bell-ringing, lights-blinking pinball machine. His mind spun back to Moody's Grocery in Lake Mohegan—a small mom and pop store with an uneven wood floor that squeaked underfoot. The freestanding building tilted downhill, with its snapping neon RC Cola sign in the window, flashing an open invitation to people and flies. From inside the store, yellow flypaper curled from several locations along the ceiling, boasting Mr. Moody's unappetizing "Fresh Catch of the Day." Half-empty dusty shelves smelled sweetly of stale cupcakes and overripe fruit.

Mr. Moody had installed against the back wall of his grocery store two abused pinball machines. The gluttonous machines eagerly ate Carter's supply of nickels long before they became too comfortable in his pockets.

"Hey, boy," Mr. Moody would holler after Carter, who was on his way out of the store. "I really wouldn't mind if once in awhile you bought some groceries. How do you expect me to run a business with customers like you?"

The building stood across the road from a community of tightly fit, loosely built summer bungalows. At Formica kitchen tables and out on the rickety porches of the modest homes, the popular Chinese game of mahjongg was a blood sport played by gossiping, flabby-armed women. Some of these women wore scarves on their heads covering super-sized pink plastic rollers that tightly wound their freshly washed hair.

"I sure do miss cupcakes," Carter said to Serene just in front of him.

"You miss what?" asked Serene, glancing over her shoulder.

"Never mind. Do you have any idea what that explosion was about?"

"Not really, but I know it wasn't thunder. If I were to guess," Serene continued, "I would say it came from the direction of Millililli. Either the Minnininni or Gootz are most likely up to no good. Let's just hope they are so preoccupied with each other that they haven't noticed we are no longer hanging out in the neighborhood."

It was a cool, crisp day high in the mountains, but the adventurers were perspiring heavily in their anxious rush to get down into the valley below them.

"That would be Stanelhooven," said Serene, pointing at the green expanse that flowed to the horizon.

When at last they reached the base of the mountain they were exhausted and starved. They had been on the run since morning, and now the door was beginning to close on the day.

As they neared the line of trees separating a forest from the open valley, Serene eased up and raised her arm to slow those behind her.

"We will rest here under the trees and spend the night," she said, wearily removing her backpack. "I do not think the Gootz knew we were in Millililli. It seems reasonable to assume they were simply attempting a sneak attack on the Minnininni. If they did know we were in Millililli, they would be curious as to the purpose of our visit. I am hoping that if we were spotted by the Gootz, they would simply dismiss our presence as coincidental. I don't think at this point they would see us as a significant threat either to them or to the Circle of Power."

"That's a big 'if,'" said Carter. "At a minimum, the Gootz would be curious as to what you Wiggwoggs were up to so far from home."

"We will have to be even more careful in the future to not cross paths with the Gootz. The closer we get to Athulian, the more threatening we will appear to them," Serene said. "I wonder what that loud noise was awhile ago and if the Gootz and Minnininni fought with each other."

"I wouldn't underestimate that Pappasnaxx character," said Carter. "He and the Minnininni may be small in size, but I got the feeling that they have a trick or two up their sleeves when it comes to protecting the interests of Millililli."

After dinner, the Wiggwoggs, Carter, and Imalima sat relaxing around a campfire discussing their recent experience in Millililli.

Carter asked Serene, "What should we expect in Stanelhooven, and how much farther will we have to travel before we arrive at the border with Wimzi?"

"Stanelhooven should not be a problem, but the territory of Wimzi is going to be a serious challenge. We will need to be well-rested before attempting a crossing of the homeland of the Wimzicals. There will not be a moment to spare, and we will have to move quickly. Once we have breached its borders, there will be no turning back."

"What about me?" Imalima asked. "I'm not allowed back in Wimzi, and if they catch me, my punishment will be death. I think I'll just lie out under a tree on the Stanelhooven side of the border, catch up on my reading, and wait for you to return with the prize."

"I'm afraid it's not as simple as that, Imalima," said Serene. "If any of us are captured, our fate would likely be no better than yours. We are depending on you to help navigate through Wimzi. Your knowledge of the territory and the Wimzicals is critical for our safe passage."

Imalima felt torn. The Wiggwoggs and Carter were his friends. They needed his help. The Gootz were never a serious problem for him or, for that matter, Wimzi, but he could see how their aggressive, deadly behavior was a problem for his friends and could in the future be a problem even for the Wimzicals. There was also the issue of Carter. His presence was an interesting bewilderment to Imalima, who knew the stranger was not from anywhere in his reality. On the other hand, due to extenuating circumstances, the entering of his former home territory was *not* something he looked forward to. The image of Wimzi held too many bad memories, and his re-entry would most likely put an end to his happy-go-lucky wanderings beyond Wimzi's borders.

"OK, I guess I'm in," said Imalima. "Don't ask me why, it makes no sense. I guess for me, 'no sense' or nonsense makes sense. Perfect for an old Wimzical such as myself. I guess it also just sounds like the right thing to do. Doing the right thing feels strange to me. Not only is it a great offense in Wimzi, it also is a high crime, carrying the severest of punishments. I can't tell you why I'm choosing to do the right thing. Very un-Wimzish, I'll have you know. Something must be happening to me that I can't explain, but if I can be of help, that's what I want to do."

Imalima's touching words were met with gratitude and hugs from his appreciative friends. Even Ferbert. Under all his matted hair, Imalima's face blushed beyond the awareness of his friends. A broad smile unrolled across his face, revealing two upper front teeth that stood out at an odd angle from his mouth.

The next morning, the well-rested adventurers woke early to the music of songbirds swooping in the tall green grass that stretched from the tree line into the valley for as far as the eye could see. They watched birds harvest their breakfast from among the grasses then fly back to the treetops to do their dining. After their own all-too-familiar breakfast of the hard-cake staple of the Wiggwogg diet, the fellowship packed up and set off to cross the open, rolling territory of Stanelhooven.

Carter's mind remained with breakfast. His thoughts went first to the kitchen of the house in Lake Mohegan. He remembered the delicious cooking smells of his favorite breakfast that his mother sometimes made him. In his mind's eye, her back was to him as if she was unaware of his presence. Cynthia Nicholsworth faced the stove where she made blueberry pancakes in one heavy cast iron frying pan and scrambled eggs with cheese in another.

Memories of Lake Mohegan or even Wickedwood had not been frequent visitors in his mind of late. It was as if the past was a distant dream and only the present was reality. When he was in Lake Mohegan, his reality had been filled with fantasy. Now, that which would have been his fantasy in Lake Mohegan had become his reality. It didn't bother him that he didn't miss Lake Mohegan or his family. He felt comfortable with his friends and the buzz of excitement in the adventure he was now living.

So preoccupied in his thoughts was Carter that he walked up on the heels of Serene, causing her to trip forward before catching her balance. "Sorry," he said smiling. "Hope you had a nice trip." This was a bad joke that would have been better off forgotten and, judging by Serene's annoyed expression, was a cleverness she didn't appreciate. "I was lost in a day-dream," he explained.

"Where do the locals live in Stanelhooven and what are they like?" Carter asked, changing subjects.

"Friendly enough, I guess," Serene answered thoughtfully. She was now walking alongside Carter. "There are few who live in Stanelhooven, and I don't know why. The land seems reasonably good for farming and there are no wild beasts, but for some reason, the local population prefers the Gushkin Territory to the west.

"I have heard," she continued, "that the Gushkin have a treaty with Wimzi. They have built guard towers and regularly patrol a mutual border that follows the River Sme and includes the territories of Stanelhooven as well as Bunnicloven. The purpose of their watchfulness is to prevent way-ward trespassers from entering Wimzi. In exchange for the vigilant border patrols, Wimzi protects the Gushkins from the Gootz. I don't know for sure that any of this is true, but it might explain why hardly any 'Hoovens' are left living in Stanelhooven and why so many have made their home in the Gushkin Territory."

Up ahead, a hardened bank of low-flying clouds travelled confidently along the horizon. By mid-afternoon, the ominous dark clouds had filled up most of the sky. When the rain finally did arrive, it swept in out of the northwest, across the valley, and toward the travelers. It wasn't long before the rain intensified into a heavy downfall that quickly drenched the valley and those crossing it. The land turned to pools, and the going was slow as they sloshed through slippery mud that clung to their feet.

Normally Carter loved the rain. He had enjoyed the experience of walk-ing for much of the day through Wickedwood while soaking wet. He was in awe of how the eventual return of sunlight brought the freshly washed forest to an eye-squinting brilliance. There was always the promise of a hot shower at the end of the day when he returned home. No hot shower today, he thought.

The rain kept up its hammering rhythm all through the day and into the night. Carter and friends put up a type of canvas lean-to and squeezed under it to get some relief. There they slept, one against another, trying to preserve some heat. Serene was on her side facing Carter's back.

Directly in front and facing Carter, sleeping with his crossed eyes wide open, was Imalima. His matted wet hair smelled something awful, but Carter was more aware of the warmth of Serene's breath on the back of his neck. He slept fitfully in short bursts that night and woke in the morning feeling even more tired than he did before he had first fallen asleep.

That day was more of the same. It wasn't as if the rain would start and stop or, for that matter, even slow. The consistent intensity of the torrential rain was something Carter had never experienced. In the distance, he watched a small pond grow to become a small lake in a matter of a few hours.

It seemed the only ones enjoying the deluge were Nevermore and Imalima. The small bird would stretch upward, flapping his wings in his nest of hair as if in a birdbath, while the Wimzical splashed like a duck in the water with his assortment of webbed feet.

Before arriving at the border of Wimzi, aside from slipping and sliding in the mud, "uneventful" is probably the word that best describes the nearly two days it took to cross Stanelhooven. There was no threat of danger or, for that matter, no sign of anyone's awareness of their crossing. Prior to the monsoon rain, Serene had been somewhat concerned that because of the wide openness of Stanelhooven and the possibility of traveling under a clear sky, they might easily be spotted. With the enlisted help of Nevermore, she made it a point to steer clear of the guard towers and avoid any likely contact with a Gushkin patrol.

"Perhaps the rain has been a good thing after all," she said to Carter.

In the hours that followed, the skies finally began to clear. Dark, swollen clouds that had been their constant traveling companions moved past them on their eastern journey into Mourners Mountains. Upon the rain's arrival in Millililli, the empty reservoir above the destroyed fake village would begin to refill.

Finally the band of explorers stood before a steep berm stretching from left to right for as far as the eye could see. Road signs littered the hill warning of dire consequences to anyone who might consider entering. They had arrived at the border of Wimzi.

"Been there, done that," Carter said aloud. "Seems I'm pushing my luck to attempt a return."

"Look," Serene said confidently, "you were without benefit of a guide on your first visit, and you still managed to escape unharmed. You didn't know the reputation of Wimzi. My guess is you were simply lucky. Now that Imalima has bravely agreed to step forward and act as our guide, our chances of success are much improved. Why, he knows Wimzi like the back of his flapping feet. Besides, there is no Plan B. Imalima!" Serene shouted sharply. "Where are you?"

Imalima peeked out slowly from behind a gathering of Wiggwoggs. The Wimzical was standing as far as possible from the Wiggwogg leader while still being part of the group. He had felt a lot braver earlier when he first made his offer to help traverse Wimzi. The mere sight of the territory's forbidden border made his multiple legs feel as if they were stuffed with jelly.

"We need you up in front to lead," she said. "You are in charge from now until we have safely passed through Wimzi."

"*If* we safely pass through Wimzi," Imalima whispered under his breath. The Wiggwoggs who had stood in front of Imalima had melted away now, leaving the once long-haired creature totally exposed. "All right, all right. I'm coming. Hold your water."

Slowly Imalima walked to his lead position at the top of the berm. Below, a gathering of boulders bridged the River Sme. An abundance of small waterfalls made their way down and around the rocks, making for what would be an easy crossing.

"It appears the River Sme has had a change of heart and extended its hand in a gesture of apology for past bad behavior," observed Serene.

Imalima turned his attention, limited as it was, to the tree-crowded forest on the other side of the river that was the gateway to Wimzi. He slowly counted out loud to fifty.

"OK—you in there, ready or not, here I come!" Imalima's eyes searched for any movement in Wimzi. "Anyone around my base is it!"

Carter remembered with Imalima's words the game of "hide and seek" that he had often played with his second cousins, Dennis and Lewis, in Lake Mohegan.

Imalima looked in Carter's direction and found the boy staring back at him. The creature didn't know where his own words came from or why he was looking at the stranger who was from a place beyond Aeiea. His mind slipped backward to a game of "find me if you can" that he had often played with his second cousins, A. Dip and A. Louza, in Wimzi.

· · · · · · ·

Upon entering Wimzi, the adventurers immediately found themselves in the thick of a mixed forest. At first notice, the forest was dark and dank. Deciduous trees mingled without prejudice with sweet-smelling evergreens whose flexing branches were weighted down with pinecones. Hump-backed boulders wore coats of neatly trimmed moss to keep warm, while under the shade of the forest's awning a community of sword fern grew wild from the mulch of a spongy wet carpet.

A cold breeze leaned up against the fern, and the accommodating fern bowed politely in a gesture of welcome, then gracefully waved farewell to the backs of the travelers. A relatively short distance from the well-mannered fern, they found themselves walking under a stone arch that had a double gate bolted to it. The gate was wide open. Normally you would expect to find some sort of fence or wall on each side of a gate to keep an assortment of creatures in or out, but there was none here.

At this point, the forest that favored the cool hand of winter gave way to a tropical jungle. The tall, dignified tree trunks that had towered over them only a moment ago exchanged their rough, rutted bark for a graceful, more fluid trunk that curved smoothly toward a crown of serrated palm fronds.

Sinuous vines, with their hairy centipede legs, relentlessly climbed the palms, and for that matter, anything vertical. Immense leaves ventured from the vines' stems, their shiny paddle-shaped faces reflecting sunlight into the adventurers' squinting eyes. The uninvited guests were now completely engulfed by the sweltering tangle.

None of this was very surprising to Carter. He easily remembered his short, but not short enough, recent visit to Wimzi.

"Can we move a little faster please?" Carter anxiously shouted up the line to Imalima.

"No one wants to get this over with faster than me," came the response from Imalima. "It has been a long time since I have been in this part of Wimzi. If I go any faster, I could get lost. As a matter of fact, now that you bring up the subject, I'm afraid I'm already lost."

"What???" shouted Carter. "That can't possibly be true! We've only been in Wimzi a few moments. You're supposed to be the expert navigator."

"Only joshin' ya," said Imalima. "Can't ya take a joke? Besides, remember I have my horn bell for just such occasions. I can always ring the bell if I need to know where to find me."

Imalima was, in fact, not kidding. He was as lost as Hansel and Gretel were in the forest after the birds had gobbled the breadcrumbs they had intentionally dropped to find their way home. His pride and genetics prevented him from telling the simple truth, so deeper into the jungle they all went.

The day dragged on, as did the weary walkers. They perspired heavily in the heat, and their clothes that had finally dried were once again soaked through. Words became an effort, so talking was held to a minimum. It seemed best to conserve their energy for whatever uncertainty lay ahead.

Imalima searched for familiar landmarks, but there were none he recognized. On their second day in Wimzi, just as he was about to fess up and accept the consequences, he stopped dead in his tracks.

"Does anyone smell what I smell?"

"It smells like a plumbing problem, Imalima, in one of your fancy bus stops," Ferbert grumbled. Everyone had a good laugh at Imalima's expense.

Ignoring Ferbert, Imalima continued. "If my memory serves me correctly, we are in the vicinity of the Gagmi Swamp. I must admit, I have never been to the swamp, so I don't know what to expect. There are a number of stories I heard as a child from Granny A. Harrumpt. Good old Granny could tell a story, fine tuning it so you couldn't tell what was from what wasn't." Now Imalima had a turn at laughing. "My old granny could lie and cheat with the best of 'em. Why, she could knock a flea out of the air at twenty paces with a fat juicy goober of beetle juice spit."

"Impressive," Retann acknowledged. "And just where did your grandmother do her training for her specialized skill?"

"Probably the Academy for Hopeless and Useless Grannies," volunteered "Ferbert the miserable."

Imalima's smile was replaced with a frown. "Granny would whup your bottom if she were here. She didn't take kindly to no smart-alecky sassing. It would be wise of you, Ferbert, to show a little respect since as long as we're in Wimzi I'm your leader. Without me, you're nothing and would be lost."

"Which opens the discussion to another subject. Imalima," said Serene, "it feels a bit to me as if we have been wandering about of late. Am I wrong?"

Thinking fast on his feet was just one more challenge since he was so unsure on them, but Imalima said, "Yes, you are wrong. Wrong as a sweet slice of peanut butter pie. Wrong as hot-buttered cauliflower on the cob or a glazed mushroom donut or—"

"OK, enough, I think we get it," Carter interrupted.

As they kept walking in the direction of the swamp, the smell got worse.

"You will either get used to it or toss your cookies. Take your choice," said Imalima. They paused to tie the bandanas they had been wearing around their necks around their faces. It didn't help that much, but it was better than nothing. Carter thought they looked like a gang of outlaws. He heard one of the adventurers "tossing some cookies" and wondered if he had remembered to first remove his bandana.

The ground had become boggy underfoot, leaving a telling message for anyone interested, as the overgrown tropical jungle backed off and made room for the Gagmi Swamp. Breaking free through a tangle of vines, the trespassers found themselves standing at the perimeter of a clearing. Holding court over a sizeable brackish pool, an ancient, decomposing, gray-bearded tree stood on gnarled feet that were slowly rotting into the stagnant water.

Bulbous mosquitoes, nearly the size of a small hummingbird, eagerly swarmed the fresh new offerings. Their whining greeting overwhelmed the weary walkers as the bloodsuckers rose en masse from their hidden nest tucked under the tree's twisted roots. The vampire mosquitoes of the Gagmi raced in a feeding frenzy to sample the newly arrived buffet. Nasty welts as big as marbles gave evidence to the assault and blossomed itchy red on the skin of the newcomers.

As quickly as their legs could carry them, the trekkers turned and ran in the direction they had just come, all the while beating at the stubborn, buzzing bugs. When the emergency evacuation was over, there was a period of intense glaring in Imalima's direction.

"Alright, I made a mistake. I got my internal compass turned around. Everyone is entitled to make a mistake once in a while. No biggie."

"No biggie??? These *are* biggies!!!" yelled Ferbert into Imalima's wide-eyed face. He was pointing to a lumpy landscape of fresh bumps that were now occupying the greater portion of his head.

"I told you I had never been to Gagmi Swamp before," said Imalima. "I also told you all I knew of the swamp came from stories told to me by Granny Harrumpt. My granny said, 'If you put a foot in the wrong place while exploring the Gagmi, quicksand will suck you down in a matter of minutes. Once you are in, there's no getting out. The more you fight, the faster you go under.' That's what my Granny told me. Is any of it true? Not likely. That would be against the law. As you probably have figured out, like all good and decent, upstanding Wimzicals, Granny had credibility issues."

"Enough about your granny, Imalima," said an impatient Serene, scratching at the fresh crop of itchy welts rising hot on her arms. "We need to keep moving in the right direction. Right now, all we are doing is backtracking."

"I suggest we slide along the western edge of the Gagmi. I believe that would be the safest way to go," informed Imalima. "That route will eventually take us straight to The Great Sea Valion."

Following Imalima's latest directions with understandable reservations, the group set off on its new course.

Imalima was once again in the lead position. Walking backwards gave him the pleasure of a continuous view of his friends. He was enjoying his new role as head of the pack, although Ushi, with his wolf-like instincts and appearance, was always close by in case Imalima ran into trouble.

Imagine that.

They were soon back among the delicate palms that grew along the margins of wetlands and the deadly Gagmi. After several hours, the jungle opened into a yawning basin of red-flowered trees. The fragrant blossoms appeared wet, as if just painted in brilliant high-gloss enamel. Upon closer examination, it was discovered that there were no flowers growing from the trees at all. Instead, blooming vines snaked their way up the tree trunks, wrapping their limbs in bouquets of flowers. A variation of the climbing vines, heavier with curly tendrils and clusters of crimson-streaked bell-shaped yellow flowers, crawled along the ground having little enthusiasm to join their tree-climbing relatives. Fallen sprays of the delicate red and yellow flowers lined the swale.

When Carter took a step for a closer look at the intriguing trees, Ushi yanked him back with a word of caution.

"Something's not right here. I can sense it, but I can't see it."

In another moment, the possible cause of Ushi's concern came swinging out of the tree's branches.

"Look over there," Ushi said, pointing. He drew the boy's attention to the tallest tree in the valley where several creatures resembling chimpanzees swung noisily from branches. They seemed in concentrated pursuit of another smaller monkey.

"Looks like fun to me. Maybe a game of tag," Carter commented to Ushi. Carter, Imalima, and the Wiggwoggs watched the show from a distance. In a moment, the monkeys melted into the shadows of crowded foliage. The tree branches shook fiercely. Flowers, leaves, and the little monkey all fell to the ground at once. The monkey howled with horror. He tried unsuccessfully several times to jump back into the tree. It seemed one of its legs was caught in something.

"Look at that!" Ushi said. A tendril from one of the vines had begun to twist around the monkey's foot. As Carter watched, the struggling little monkey managed to break free, disappearing into the ground cover. Not twenty feet from where it had originally landed on the ground, the monkey briefly reappeared, its round eyes reflecting terror. The monkeys were apparently tree dwellers and never ventured to the ground—for good reason.

A second tendril had now wound around one of the monkey's arms, while at the same time another began to tightly wrap both legs. The panicked monkey shrieked in desperation.

"Someone has to help him!" shouted Carter.

Ushi raised his hand. "No!"

"If no one else will help, then I will." Carter took one step forward and for a second time was immediately pulled back, this time by both Ushi and Serene.

"You cannot do anything here but lose your own life," Ushi said forcefully. "This is nature at work, cruel as it may seem. Let it be."

The monkey tried desperately to escape and, in doing so, brushed up against one of the oversized yellow flowers. The sweet-smelling seducer shuddered with excitement then leaned over the ensnared little monkey. Hypnotic beauty, intended to captivate its victims, was now transformed into something hideous.

Like the sultry blues music flowing out the open end of a saxophone, from the mouth of the bloom oozed a syrupy substance down onto the monkey, which instantly stopped fighting, surrendering to its fate. The beautiful blossom began to transform in shape and color into a flat-faced flower, not unlike a sunflower. As it swiveled toward the adventurers, smiling in their direction, it revealed multiple rows of pointed sharp teeth.

Silent and still, the monkey's playmates watched helplessly from the safe distance of the tree's high branches. The flower's teeth made a sickly gnashing sound in anticipation of its meal. In one quick gulp, it was over. A loud burp violently shook the flower, sending fur flying in all directions from the opening where the monkey had just disappeared.

Profound expressions of both horror and compassion were exchanged between the primates in the trees and the travelers on the ground.

"Elderwiser mentioned this place in one of his many stories," Serene said. "He called it the Garden of Illusion. Now I know how it got its name. It is indeed beautiful, and I can see where someone could easily be lulled into carelessness. This is Wimzi. We must not, even for a moment, forget where we are."

· · · · · · ·

It was Ushi who first sensed a new impending disaster.

"I smell fire," he said, sniffing the air. Within a few short moments, smoke started to billow over the tops of distant trees and the wind picked up.

"Quick, follow me! We are not that far from the shore of Valion," said Imalima, who proceeded to duck under a low-hanging tree limb before disappearing into the dense overgrowth that skirted the Garden of Illusion. Ushi and the others were not far behind Imalima. Although they could not see him, they could easily hear him crashing through the jungle, leaving a freshly cleared path.

They went on like that for some distance. Ushi was aware that the irritating fragrance of fire was, if anything, getting stronger. His throat was beginning to burn. Finally he caught sight of the Wimzical.

"Stop!" Ushi called out to Imalima. "You are leading us directly into the fire!"

With those dire words, Nevermore instinctively did what any smart bird would do under those circumstances. He flew away.

"The problem is," said the Wimzical to Ushi, "you're right, but unfortunately this is the only way I know to The Great Sea Valion. I'm afraid the fire is dead ahead of us and blocking our path. The flames from the fire are behind us as well and raging on both sides of us. In other words, we're surrounded. It's all over. We are trapped, doomed, finished, incinerated, burnt toast, kaputski." Imalima flung himself to the ground and wailed loudly, "Why me?"

"It doesn't have to end this way if you will follow me."

From just beyond Imalima stepped a second Imalima. Then to the left a third Imalima appeared.

"Totally bogus," the third Imalima said of the second Imalima. "Follow him, and you will wind up a bunch of crispy critters. The Imalima you have been following since leaving the scene of the terrible monkey munching is also a fraud. When you weren't looking, he grabbed me from behind, then gagged and dragged me into the bushes. He tied me up then left me there to die. He has intentionally lured you into a trap."

"Liar, liar, leggings on fire . . . or they soon will be. Don't believe them. It's me, your old friend Imalima," said the crybaby Imalima. "They are hoaxters obviously on the payroll of the Gootz and will lead you directly into the fire."

The adventurers were growing increasingly confused as to which of the three was actually the original.

"Oh boy," a bewildered Carter moaned. "What a mess. As I see it, they are all Wimzicals, which means they are all well-practiced fibbers, even our friend Imalima, whichever one he is."

By now, the heat coming off the fierce flames was making the fire's approach unmistakable. Following the lead of Serene, they each wetted their bandanas with water from the shallow creek and then tied them around their noses and mouths.

"I have an idea," Carter whispered to Serene.

"Whatever it is, make it quick."

"Imalima!" Carter yelled, addressing none of the three in particular, "what was the name of the fast food franchise at your bus stops?"

The two imposters looked with puzzlement at each other while the authentic Imalima said proudly, "Fatso's." With that single word, the Imalima wannabees began to fade until, a moment later, they had both completely vanished.

"No time to waste," said the authentic Imalima. "We have to travel along the creek to the deeper water, which should not be too far ahead."

Carter sure hoped so. The growing heat made his eyes sting and his vision blur. Solid objects began to soften, looking as if someone was slowly letting the air out of them. He glanced up at the decorative green headdress worn atop the jungle's tall trees. Busy palm fronds undulated anxiously, trying to shoo away a billowing black sky smeared with angry flecks of burning embers.

In what seemed but little time, Imalima had found the section of creek he had been looking for. Around a bend, the sound of surging water had become much louder. Imalima huddled Carter and the Wiggwoggs together and said excitedly, "This is it! I remember playing here as a young Wimzical." He shouted over the din of a waterfall that cascaded from high above them into a deep basin of water. "We will escape the fire by hiding safely behind the waterfall. Follow me!" he yelled while pinching his nose closed with two of his flappers.

"Geronimo!" Rolling all his legs up tightly against himself, the enthusiastic creature did a massive cannonball into the deep pond.

Following Imalima's lead, the others quickly followed suit. Yelling "Geronimo!" they each proceeded to cannonball into the pool. The cold water instantly took the searing heat of the fire right out of them. They swam to the falls and felt the sting of pounding water hard against their bodies.

"We will be safe here behind the falls. See you on the other side," said Imalima.

Taking a deep breath, Imalima disappeared under the water. Once again the others followed, coming up on the other side of the falls where there was a shoulder-high shelf jutting from the rock wall. The roar of the falls was, for unknown reasons, greatly reduced on this side. Pulling themselves up onto the ledge, they sat worn out and quiet for a time.

"That's strange," Carter said to Serene. "There is no such thing as sitting quietly with Imalima around." He glanced quickly down the line of seated friends, but there was no sign of the Wimzical.

"Where's Imalima?" Carter shouted to the others.

When there was no response, he plunged into the water. The Wiggwoggs immediately joined the search, scouring the bottom of the pond. Nothing was found; the Wimzical was gone.

The hunt continued for the rest of the afternoon without changing the results. The fire on the other side of the pond continued to rage, allowing only for quick gulps of air before having to dive back under the water. Finally, giving up all hope, Carter and the Wiggwoggs retreated to the safety of the shelf behind the waterfall.

Disappeared was the word that rattled around in Carter's head. That word was becoming increasingly comfortable and quite familiar to the boy from Lake Mohegan. What he had learned in his brief life was that disappearing only meant leaving one place to eventually show up in another. He was also learning not to be afraid of disappearing.

The skin on the tips of Carter's fingers was shriveled and nearly translucent from spending so much time in the water. He wondered if, somehow, the Wimzicals had managed to capture Imalima and were making good on their threat to torture and kill his friend. He had understood from Imalima that if the Wimzicals ever again found him in Wimzi, the future of the goat-like creature would most likely be painful and brief. Carter and the others sat quietly without speaking, until one by one, they fell from exhaustion into a troubled sleep. With two of his friends now missing, the last thoughts on Carter's mind before his eyes closed were of Nevermore. He hoped his little feathered friend was safe.

Waking slowly at the beginning of the new day, Carter watched sunshine filter through the waterfalls, throwing flashes of reflected light against the wall behind them. Under different conditions, the beautiful light show would have been something to be enjoyed. But the circumstances of Imalima's disappearance wore heavy on his mind. When he and his friends slipped back into the water to see if it was safe on the other side of the falls, nothing could have prepared them for what they were about to experience.

They resurfaced in the pond on the other side of the waterfall then climbed out to sit with their backs to the water. What they saw challenged their sanity.

Shift.

The fire was gone all right, but more interesting, the landscape appeared as if the fire had never happened. There was no smell of lingering smoke, and the dense jungle that had surrounded them yesterday was also gone. Carter shuddered at the sudden and radical transformation. As if all that wasn't strange enough, when he turned to look back, the waterfalls and pond were gone as well.

All this felt a bit overwhelming and far too familiar to Carter.

"Wimzi is a place drawn on Serene's map," Carter mumbled to himself, "but it really doesn't exist. There is nothing solid about it. There is no there, there. Wimzi is simply a figment of imagination, an illusion, a mirage." The words kept looping through Carter's mind.

· · · · · · ·

The seekers of the Circle of Power stood on a high, grassy knoll overlooking a great body of water.

"The Great Sea Valion!" Serene announced. "You have done the impossible, Carter. You have beaten the magic of Wimzi and you've done it twice. Perhaps there is something more going on here than just plain luck."

"We're not yet out of this crazy place, and getting this far has come at a heavy price," Carter replied. "We've lost Imalima, and I don't know where Nevermore is. Let's not forget, it was our friend Imalima who got us most of the way through Wimzi."

Serene turned and put her hands squarely on Carter's shoulders. "When we began this mission," she said, looking deeply into her friend's eyes, "we understood the likelihood of success was uncertain and, if achieved, was not going to come without sacrifice. No one expected that we would all return safely to Wiggonwoggen, but our undertaking is for the greater good of Aeiea. The most dangerous part of our operation still lies ahead. The successful completion of our assignment hangs like an acrobat high on a trapeze without a safety net. We still have a distance to go before we get to the sea. We had better move quickly before Wimzi changes its mind about releasing us."

From a palm tree growing nearby, Nevermore flew to Carter's shoulder. *Miss me?* Carter heard the bird ask.

With a great sense of relief, and a surprised Serene looking on, Carter said, "Of course I missed you. One thing I'm learning to trust is that when the time is right, you always manage to find your way home. Imalima is the only one missing now. We have no idea where he is or what happened to him. If the Wimzicals have him, he could be in big trouble—that is, if he's still alive."

Imalima has his ways, Nevermore responded. *If he is still alive, I imagine he is trying to sell buses to the Wimzicals.*

Carter turned to face Serene. "Something is strange here. Outside of the two Imalima impersonators, we haven't seen a single Wimzical. From what you've told me, this is out of character for the citizens of Wimzi. What do you make of it?"

"I am as confused as you, but we are not out of here yet. That can't happen too quickly for my preference, though I am glad we've been here long enough for Nevermore to return to us. Let's go before any more time is spent on questions that may not be answered to our liking."

For the short remainder of daylight, the weary and wary band of explorers jogged the headlands of Wimzi. They finally arrived down at the coastal beach just in time to see the curtain begin to close on the day. Looking past Carter to where the sky and water met, Serene watched as sister suns Suva and Ahneese slowly slipped into The Great Sea Valion.

"But how will we get to the island of Athulian?" Carter inquired.

It was a question that caught the attention of all the Wiggwoggs whose eyes were riveted on their leader. It was a question that if Serene had an answer to, she wasn't sharing.

"We cannot waste another moment," she said over her shoulder as she began quickly walking the beach littered with driftwood and boulders. The others followed, close at her heels.

· · · · · · ·

Night arrived riding hard on the back of a punishing gale. The wind bucked and whistled its way through wild thistle that stubbornly held onto life while growing along the banks of the narrow beach. Distorted trees, whose bare and twisted limbs suffered the stingy nutritional offerings of sand, tilted with willful determination into the storm's unforgiving rage. Tumbling across the night, a great army of leaves invaded a corner of the sky, their flight recorded on a shaft of lightning.

At the same time, three Wimzicals who had led simple lives as fisher folks but hadn't the pleasure of knowing each other, were about to have something else in common: As of this night, all of them would be out of the fishing business. Their battered fishing boats had escaped their moorings, pushed by the front edge of a savage squall.

"I have never seen such a storm," Carter shouted over the eruption of bedlam. Uncontrollable shivers racked his body. He dug his knuckles into his eyes, trying unsuccessfully to clear the rain that blew horizontally across the beach from The Great Sea Valion.

The three empty boats dipped and heaved in a rowdy dance as they celebrated their newly won freedom. Having lost anchor, they were being rudely forced from behind by pounding waves breaking toward the cove's steeply banked shore. The small fleet jostled in a foamy brew, trying to survive impressive rock formations growing from the sea.

Serene, who had been huddled in a short meeting with several of her fellow Wiggwoggs, approached Carter, who was standing with his back to her staring out to sea. She watched the play unfolding before them. Her cold hands were thrust deep into her tunic side pockets.

"Perfect," she said. "Our transportation has arrived right on time. I'll bet these boats have Elderwiser's fingerprints all over them." Her broad smile and comment seemed a strange contradiction to the angry weather. Up in his wet nest, Nevermore scratched around trying unsuccessfully to get comfortable.

"I would imagine in messy weather like this," Serene continued, "The Grinder will be hunkered down close to a warm fireplace. It is the best possible situation for an unannounced arrival on Athulian. The sea serpents, however, are quite another story. I have no idea what the effect if any this storm will have on them. Beyond the certainty of their existence, we know very little about them. Mostly rumors and scary hand-me-down stories. The sea route, however, is our only choice. Carter, will you join me in the lead boat?"

"Yes, of course," Carter responded. "But if we happen to make it across The Great Sea Valion onto Athulian . . . what then?"

Serene pulled from her tunic the worn, folded map she had first shown Carter upon his arrival in Wiggonwoggen.

"You remember this map entrusted to me by Elderwiser? It shows the way from Bludenbonz Castle to a remote, well-hidden castle. If you recall, I believe this is what Salise the old Dweeg was referring to when we found her hiding in the cave at Mourners Mountains. Because so little is known of this fortress, the route to the castle is unfortunately not very detailed. I believe this is the only map on which this castle even appears, and I also believe this is most likely where we will find the Circle of Power."

"Then the Circle of Power is not at The Grinder's castle? Carter asked.

"I think not. Based on information Elderwiser has shared with me, as well as what Salise told us, I think it is more than likely that the Circle of Power is being hidden in a vault somewhere under this obscure and uncharted castle."

"Can we be absolutely sure this is where we will find the medallion?" Carter asked.

"No, not absolutely. It is possible the whispered secret is a mere diversion. Elderwiser said to me that perhaps what he had learned was intentionally disclosed to throw off any pretender to the sacred trust."

"That means if it's not in that castle, it could be anywhere," Carter stated.

"True," Serene answered. "Nothing is certain or guaranteed. We will just have to see, when and if we get to Athulian. Meanwhile, let's not get too far ahead of ourselves. We may have more than we can handle just trying to get off this beach. The only thing I am reasonably confident of is that you and I are here in this moment and that there exists the eternal struggle between the forces of good and evil. We have placed our faith and trust on the side of good. We are in the hands of a power far greater than anything we are able to identify or fully understand. So I have no answers. I am only certain of uncertainty."

Carter deeply inhaled Serene's wisdom. These were not the reassuring words he would have preferred to hear, but somehow her straightforward honesty calmed his racing mind.

Serene looked at Carter with an expression of urgency. She hooked her arm into his and, taking a last look at Wimzi over her shoulder, whispered in his ear, "Time to go."

Chapter 15
The Great Sea Valion

Down at the wide mouth of the beach, the busy Wiggwoggs were waist deep in water trying to corral the uncooperative fishing boats. The bow of one boat nearly smashed down on the head of Zebenuza, missing him by inches. It was Lyke who saw the impending disaster and at the last moment was able to push Zebenuza out of the way as a wave that had thrown the skiff up in the air suddenly collapsed within itself.

"I owe you one!" shouted Zebenuza over the fury of the storm.

Lyke, the rope master, had lassoed together one of the oarlocks sitting on each of the boat's gunwales. The Wiggwoggs had all they could do to keep the boats from filling and sinking in the churning sea. Luckily, prior to the storm, the single sail on each one had been pulled and stored. A pair of oars had also been tightly secured to a grab ring on the sides of each of boat.

Quickly tossing all their wet gear in, the friends one by one and four to a sailboat climbed or were hauled aboard. As they freed the oars, the three pitching boats threatened to ride up on each other before Carter and the Wiggwoggs gained control. Summoning all their strength, they pushed off against the many outcroppings of rock into the furious surf that seemed intent on testing their swimming skills.

In the lead boat, Serene was in charge of navigation at the bow. She busily relayed hand signals to Carter, who tightly held the tiller at the stern. He actually enjoyed being at the helm, steering the sturdy boat. Carter had earlier shared with Serene his sailing experiences on Lake Mohegan.

Abogamento was seated next to his cousin Zebenuza at mid-boat, each pulling with all their might to forge through the relentless assault of waves.

In the second vessel Lyke was in the bow, Lohden and Retann at the oars, with Ushi at the helm. The three brothers, although quite different in nature, worked quite well together when necessity called. This was precisely one of those situations. Grim determination was written on their faces.

Bouncing in the last boat, Ferbert and Fermond were on the oars and having a hard time keeping up with the other two boats. They bickered back and forth.

"You are not," said Ferbert.

"Putting your oar deep enough into the water," finished Fermond. "You are getting on your oar," responded Fermond.

"More air than water," complained Ferbert.

Paying no attention to the quarreling twins, Iat was at the bow while Herkifer was in the stern arm-wrestling the tiller.

Iat, who could run like the wind, and Herkifer who had the strength and determination of a hungry bear, had become inseparable friends. Their individual skills complemented each other and would prove invaluable to the mission in the days that lay ahead. Iat's wiry, athletic body was extremely well coordinated and he was snappy of mind as well. Aside from being a bit of a tease with a quirky sense of humor, he was a most generous and loyal friend.

"No time to lose!" shouted Serene, looking back over her shoulder. "So as not to be seen, we must be ashore on the island of Athulian before sunrise." She gave a signal for the boats to raise their sails even though she understood this was a dangerous risk in the ferocious, wind-tossed sea.

"But there are no stars. I can't see much beyond our boat. How can you be sure we're going in the right direction?" yelled Carter back at Serene. Fear and doubt were whispering into his ear in an attempt to undermine his courage.

There was no reply. Concentrating, Serene just stared straight ahead into the dark night. Carter took a deep hitching breath and exhaled slowly. Their boat was being tossed like a rubber ducky in a splashing baby's bathtub. He felt his stomach rise and fall with the rolling sea.

Row, row, row your boat gently down the stream, Nevermore sang happily into Carter's mind. *Merrily, merrily, merrily, merrily, **life is but a dream . . .***

Perhaps he was too preoccupied with his rapidly deteriorating intestinal problems to grasp the full implication of the small bird's profound message. In any event, Carter was in no mood for bird songs. He was busy dealing with a strong case of the queasies, moving up unchallenged from the depths of his stomach to his throat. He gave serious consideration to being sick. Sailing the flat waters of Lake Mohegan was never like this.

The Great Sea Valion smelled as you might expect a dark-pitched sea would, pungent and raw. It was a bit too much for Carter's overwhelmed stomach. Serene saw the color drain from Carter's face. She noticed his limp arm draped loosely over the tiller. He had lost focus, and their runaway boat was now sliding sideways through the choppy water. Serene moved quickly, stepping carefully between Abogamento and Zebenuza to Carter's side at the stern. Gently she placed her two cupped hands over Carter's ears and held his attention for a few moments with her hands and eyes.

"Take deep breaths in through your nose and out through your mouth," Serene instructed. "Imagine you can see land just ahead on the horizon and focus on that image."

To Carter's surprise and relief, the emergency ebbed then passed. He was soon back at his job, attempting to re-establish control over the erratic tiller, which stubbornly seemed to have a different agenda than his. Pulling with strength he didn't know he had, Carter convinced the protesting tiller to surrender its independence, and the boat slowly came about. Once again they were tacking back on course.

"Did you see it?" shouted wide-eyed Herkifer, pointing into the night, his round face alive with excitement. They had been at sea now for more than an hour.

"Quiet," hushed Serene. "See what?"

"I don't know. Maybe eyes, red eyes in the water not five or six boat-lengths ahead on the starboard side, burning like hot coals." Herkifer no sooner finished his words when, from behind the three boats, the sea erupted.

A long, curved form with undulating spikes running along the upper edge burst from the depths of The Great Sea Valion. Several javelin-like spears splitting off at the end of a whipping tail broke the water's surface and thrashed the turbulent sea. The enormous monster's jaws were gaping wide and trailed long lengths of rubbery seaweed that dripped seawater from several rows of triangular teeth. Appearing more like a reptile than a mammal or fish, a section of the creature's curved back rose up from the sea, giving some idea as to the size of the massive monster. An iridescent coat of shingled green algae wrapped its entire body. Aggressively swinging its huge head back and forth, it sent sprays of water from the dangling seaweed flying across the sea, splashing the terrified group.

The sea monster seemed to be looking directly at Carter, or at least that's how it felt to him. So frightened was Carter that he totally lost his ability to speak. Instead of words, small, quick gasps of air were all that he could push from his mouth. He stood stiffly next to Serene, unable to move. The Wiggwoggs were also frozen in a snapshot of fear. Finally able to shift his eyes from the main attraction, Carter saw the heads of more than a half dozen other sea serpents floating quietly in the water surrounding the three boats, their fiery red eyes staring in quiet anticipation.

And then, with the explorers expecting disaster, the strangest thing happened.

The sea serpent that had been the first to appear smiled. Or if sea serpents don't smile, the monster's face definitely wore an amused expression. The upturned mouth revealed more teeth in one head than Carter believed possible. Each tooth looked razor sharp, able to slice through meat and bone in a single bite.

The serpent cleared his throat and said in a deep voice that travelled across the sea like the rumble of distant thunder, "Have you any idea how long you have kept us waiting? Of course not," he said, answering his own question. "Why would I expect you to know? Is this it? Is this all of you? Surely not, and where are your weapons, foolish children?"

He looked with disappointment past the waterlogged group to his fellow sea serpents.

"Hardly worth the effort, wouldn't you say? The lot of them would barely make for a light bedtime snack. Ah well—it is as it is. You down there in the boats," he said dismissively, "follow us."

Carter's newly found voice surprised the Wiggwoggs, but most of all, it surprised himself.

"Where do you intend to take us? Do you serve The Grinder? And what exactly do you plan to do with us when we get to wherever it is we're going?" he shouted up to the monster.

"Hmmmmmmmm," mumbled the amused sea serpent calmly. "Too many questions," he said, putting some distance between his words. "Let me make this as simple and as clear as I can. It appears you have but two choices. The first is to do as I have ordered, and do it immediately. The second option, and the one I personally prefer, is for you to refuse my order and for me and the boys here to have some hors d'oeuvres right now. So, what'll it be?"

"Never mind any more questions," Serene advised in a whisper. "Just tell him to lead the way."

"But—"

"Never mind, Carter. Just tell him."

Do it! thought Nevermore to Carter.

Carter did as told.

So the sea serpent and "the boys," as he referred to his gang of bullies, led, while Carter and the Wiggwoggs followed. Through much of the long and miserable rainy night, with their backs and sails to the wind, they switched off, taking turns pulling the heavy oars. Their arms ached and their weary shoulders, along with their spirits, sagged. Their clothing was drenched, and they were chilled to the bone.

Warm pajamas, smelling of heat and fresh out of the basement dryer, tickled at the fringes of Carter's memory. Things were turning. Life on Earth felt distant, like a fading dream. He reasoned that perhaps time was simply an illusion, constantly slipping past him like fine sand through a strainer. It was only the present that you could touch, that seemed real with form and substance. But that too was temporary, only to fall away, joining the past in a container of all that had been.

Impermanence, Nevermore reminded Carter.

Just then Serene excitedly grabbed Carter's arm. "Look, Carter, over there!" she exclaimed, pointing at the horizon through the gray mist of first morning light. "Do you see it?"

Carter squinted into the wet haze that had finally begun to replace the rainstorm. Peering off in the direction Serene was pointing, he saw a soft silhouette rise up directly ahead at the sea's edge.

"Athulian," the leader of the Wiggwoggs said, her tenuous voice a restrained mixture of anticipation and uncertainty.

The sea serpents had formed a protective wedge formation out in front of the three boats.

"The big smiling serpent must be their leader," offered Carter to Serene. He was positioned at the head of the fleet of sea serpents and boats. Every once in a while the lead sea serpent would turn and look back, his mouth fixed in his frightening grin. "By the look of things, it's reasonable to assume we are once again prisoners. Do we have a plan, and if so, when are you going to share it?" asked Carter anxiously.

"Whatever the case," Serene responded, "it seems the serpents have a plan, and I'm waiting to see what it might be before coming up with a plan of my own."

"Aren't you surprised they can talk?" Carter questioned.

"Why would I be?"

Reflecting on the absurdity of his question, Carter concluded that reality was just a matter of perception. How you saw things. It was all in the eye of the beholder. If he were to base his reality simply on his earthly experience, all that was Aeiea would cause him to go out of his mind. He thought about the expression "out of his mind," which was used loosely on Earth to negatively describe someone whose actions or words did not conform. He considered how his own mind could terrorize him, hold him captive to his fears and play tricks on him. Being out of your mind could be a good thing. Nothing wrong, he reasoned, with the freedom of occasionally escaping your mind.

If those furry creatures in Wimzi that hung from a tree branch by their tails could talk, if a three-toed toad could talk, if his own friend Nevermore could speak into his mind, why should he be surprised that there was such a thing as a talking sea serpent? Carter's daydream went to an image of Imalima attempting to convince him of the wisdom of partnering up in one of the creature's several loopy financial ventures. The fact that he would never see his friend again was painful beyond words.

Carter's wanderings were reeled back to the present situation, where he found his and the other two boats no longer advancing toward the island of Athulian. Like last night's pounding storm, their forward progress had come to a dead stop. The three vessels bobbed up and down like apples floating in a metal tub at a Halloween party.

The sea serpents had maneuvered into a circle surrounding Carter and the Wiggwoggs.

"School time," grinned the ever-smiling leader of the sea serpents, "and class is in session. I am the professor who will attempt to offer you foolish juveniles an education that may possibly make the difference as to whether or not any of you live long enough to witness tonight's sunset. Do you catch my drift or am I moving too fast for you? If 'too fast' is your thoughtful answer, then perhaps you dullards would be so kind as to consider sparing me the labor of this teaching exercise. If indeed that is the case, you might as well jump overboard right now and swallow the sea. Any jumpers?" Seeing that no one was taking him up on his offer, he continued.

"All right then, let's get to it. Time is of the essence, so listen up. 'Things are not always as they appear,' is your first lesson. My name is Arni. Me and the boys here have frequented the sea long before The Grinder discovered Athulian. We ancients are beyond time. The first misconception I would like to clear up is about our dietary preferences. Contrary to popular opinion and slanderous bad press that we sea serpents are mythological monsters that prowl the sea in search of two-legged creatures to consume, I can tell you that is a gross exaggeration and we stand falsely accused. We do appreciate that our size and fearsome appearance has some distinct advantages in certain situations, but . . ."

At this point, Arni stopped speaking. He carefully looked around to determine whether ears of the uninvited were in the neighborhood to hear tidbits of revealing information intended only for a select few.

Feeling reasonably assured of their privacy, Arni bent his long neck low and close to the trio of boats. Continuing in little more than a whisper, "we are actually wussy vegetarians," disclosed the serpent sheepishly.

Carter hung his head and with a wide grin that threatened to spill over into laughter breathed a sigh of relief.

What next? thought a distrustful Nevermore. *Maybe he has a bridge in Brooklyn he would like to sell at a real good price.*

Quiet, bird, thought Carter back to Nevermore.

"Excuse me, Professor Arni." Carter's raised arm was waving for attention. "I have a question."

"Well, of course you do. Get on with it. Say, is that a bird in your hair?"

"Nevermore," Carter informed.

"Never mind," Arni responded. "What is your question?"

Wiggwogg eyes were all focused on Carter. "You never answered my earlier question as to whether or not The Grinder is your master. If you are taking us to Athulian to be handed over to the Gootz, at least allow us the opportunity of knowing our fate. You must have some plan. Athulian is directly in front of us. If we continue in the direction you have been leading us, surely it is just a matter of time before we are seen by those on the island."

There was an awkward moment of silence as Arni, appearing mildly irritated and glancing at his fellow sea serpents for their reaction, considered Carter's questions. Finally he looked down at Carter and began to speak.

"Alright then, you shall have your answers."

Carter's confidence swelled as Serene patted his back. He also felt a sense of approval and respect coming from the other Wiggwoggs. Carter had stood up to the sea serpent. Although there was yet to be a response, there was no doubt the boy from Earth was learning lessons Arni was not qualified to teach.

"I have heard from a usually reliable source," continued Arni, "to be on the look out for visitors with the power to go unnoticed and who are on their way for a secret visit to Athulian. Actually I was hoping for a sizeable, well-armed invasion force, not a small band of children with little more than sticks and stones for weapons. Adjustments will be necessary."

Arni hesitated. "As to who is my master, whom we sea serpents serve, and what is our plan—" Once again, the suspicious serpent carefully scanned the empty sea for possible eavesdroppers. He gestured his students to come closer and tighten their circle around him.

Chapter 16
Athulian

The Grinder was in a particularly foul mood. He had not slept well since receiving word of Twitch's ill-fated venture and subsequent life-terminating event. Make no mistake: the death of his half-brother had nothing to do with his loss of sleep. The Gootz leader had considered Twitch a bothersome bumbler as well as an incompetent oaf.

"Good riddance," The Grinder said aloud, standing alone high in the north tower of his castle. The Grinder was depressed. He peered from his bedchamber window into the moonlit night and out across the sea.

"What more could I want?" he pondered aloud. "I have all that I could possibly ever use or need. The Circle of Power has given me dominion over all life on Aeiea. I am the ruler of everything, yet the enjoyer of nothing." With all that he had, he was experiencing the emptiness of a meaningless existence.

Beside his depression, The Grinder was bored. He hadn't the pleasure of a bloody battle for some time, and he so missed the tortured screams of his victims, their life flowing crimson into the ground.

"That's it!" shouted The Grinder. "I just need some sticky red juice on my blade then I'll feel better. It's always worked before."

He slowly drew his long sword from its scabbard. Light from an overhead candled sconce bounced from the ornate jeweled handle, splashing against the dimly lit walls. Out of the shadows, a myriad of reflections jumped up for a fast dash across the high ceiling.

The Grinder looked longingly at the sword. "You are my life, my one true love," he said in a soft voice. "I have always been able to count on you.

It is you, and only you, that nurtures my soul." As he studied his reflection staring back at him from the blade, the Gootz leader slowly moved his large head this way and that, examining his fleshy, pimpled face. Tightly curled hair corkscrewed randomly in tufts from several weeping sores festering on his blotchy, reddish-blue skin. Like a series of rivulets on a map, dark veins snaked along the surface of his large, gnarled nose, spreading out across his face above bloated and scabbed lips.

"Looking good," said The Grinder, admiring his distinctive reflection. "Real good!"

It was more than discontent The Grinder was feeling this night, but he was unable to understand exactly what he was experiencing or identify its source. Holstering his sword, he returned his distant gaze to the sea.

"Tomorrow I will meet with my generals in a war council," he said aloud. "Surely there must be some territory in need of a really thorough plundering. I don't even care if it's a ratty old 'do over.' My doctor says I need some serious exercise."

His mind traveled a well-worn path leading from one territory to another, finally settling on the heights of Mourners Mountains and the village of Millililli.

"It doesn't feel right that the little ones have not been properly thanked for dispatching my half-wit brother. Yes, indeedy, a little personal visit from yours truly showing my gratitude would be the right thing to do, and as we all know, I'm all about the right thing to do."

A noise behind him turned his attention away from his thoughts. An unfortunate brown-haired mouse, making a disastrous navigational miscalculation, scurried across the floor in the direction of the motionless Gootz leader. The mouse abruptly stopped directly in front of The Grinder. Looking this way and that in an attempt to get its bearings, the little rodent prepared to continue its journey.

Strictly on impulse, The Grinder swiftly raised his thick leg then brought his boot down heavily, shaking the floor as well as the large picture of Mother Putzer that now hung askew on the wall above his bed.

"Gotcha!"

The mouse instantly disappeared under The Grinder's heavy boot with hardly a complaint. "Not the same as the proper sticking of a Minnininni," he reasoned aloud, "but for an unexpected quickie, not bad."

He unbuckled his heavy belt and placed his sheathed sword upright at the foot of his bed. "Now I may be able to get a decent night's sleep," he said, once again studying his sword. "I shall have sweet dreams of cracking little heads and sitting down to feast on Minnininni shish kebab." The pleased Grinder, standing with both arms extended from his sides, fell belly flop-fashion face down across his bed. The flattened deceased mouse remained still affixed to the bottom of his boot.

But sweet dreams were cancelled, replaced by foreboding nightmares. Awakened in the morning by raised voices, the grumpy, sleep-deprived Grinder, who had tossed and turned his way through a restless night, sat up in bed, his hands covering his ears.

"What is going on? Who dares interrupt my sleep?" he cried out.

Peggi, The Grinder's most trusted advisor and second-in-command after the King of Everything, barged uninvited into The Grinder's bedchambers.

Peggi wasn't his real name. His real name was Bob, but he came to his nickname through a most unfortunate accident and his nickname had stuck. He was tall by Gootz standards, being only an inch shorter than His HIGHness. No Gootz was allowed to be taller than The Grinder. If someone had the misfortune to grow taller than the Gootz leader, they were required to immediately report to the Gootz Chief Surgeon General's laboratory. There they would be officially measured before being strapped securely onto a cold, uncovered metal gurney. Their legs were then scrubbed, shaved, and precisely marked with a dotted line before undergoing a personal height reduction surgery—or a "leg modifying alteration," as the Gootz Chief Surgeon General liked to call it.

Rejected insurance claims referred to the operation as "ineligible elective surgery." Because the operation was not covered by insurance, it of course did not apply to the insured's deductible. The Grinder was, in addition to his many other titles, CEO of Athulian's only insurance company.

Fondly, the Gootz leader referred to the surgical procedure as a painless (at least for him) "whittling down process." I would imagine The Grinder's preferred term for describing the gruesome reduction procedure was used because the outpatient operation was often repeated on multiple occasions, until the unlucky individual mercifully reached full height.

Standing alongside The Grinder's bed, Peggi struck a contradictory presence. His jaw was unpronounced, lost somewhere in the flabby skin of a walrus neck. His other facial features, with the exception of his nose, seemed also somewhat soft if not sloppy. He had small, beady round eyes placed ever so closely to the bridge of a broad nose that bumped its way down his face to a flared, upturned ending that revealed two nostrils overflowing with hair.

From the waist up, strands of muscle bulged from under his sleeveless tunic. From the waist down was quite another matter. His left leg conformed well to his upper torso, but from his right side a wood peg notched with a stroke for each victim he had slain ran from mid-thigh to the floor.

"Lost me kicker," he would concisely reply to the insensitive queries concerning his physical challenge. If pressed for details, he would defer to his standard response, "Accident."

He was, in fact, a Gootz of few words, but in truth couldn't remember the specifics of his traumatizing limb lopping. On rare occasion when a more detailed explanation seemed unavoidable, he would simply tell the listener that a long time ago while in the throes of a pitched battle, "the lousy thing just fell off."

Of course, we who know better understand that legs and other assorted body parts don't just "fall off." Once, when attempting to share the details of his tragic dismemberment with his wife, he told her that he did have some memory of the clash of swords, the sharp ring of metal against metal, the sound of distant voices, some screaming in anger, others in pain. And then, just like that, the leg was gone. The whacked limb was lying less than ten feet away from the rest of him, looking more like a log than a leg.

For a split second Peggi had been focused on the idea of retrieving the amputated leg and, with the tape from his first-aid kit, somehow reattaching it. He quickly changed his priorities when he saw the guilty leg-lopper standing rather sheepishly close by, looking first at his bloody sword, then at the disconnected leg lying on the ground. The soldier's face was pale, drained of blood. He appeared in a state of shock. Peggi, who was in a rather foul mood, hopped over to the leg and, picking it up, hopped back over to the lopper. Then in a state of rage, Peggi, with his whacked limb firmly in hand, proceeded to mercilessly club to death the unfortunate individual who had hacked it from him.

· · · · · · ·

"There has been a landing on Bludenbonz Beach just below the castle," Peggi said. "At this time, sir, the details are still quite sketchy, but a few boats have been spotted on the beach. We don't know who, nor the size of—"

Before Peggi had completed his sentence, The Grinder had sprung into action. "Perfect!" he shouted, leaping from his bed and throwing a fist in the air.

"At dinner tonight we shall drink a toast to our victory with their still-warm blood! Assemble the Gootz Elite Guard and alert the army." The Grinder smiled and winked confidently at Peggi. "Put the reserves on standby alert until we have further information as to the enemy's strength in number. While you're at it, launch the long boats."

It was a dream come true. The Grinder wouldn't have to wait to get back into action. The battle had come to him. He rubbed his hairy hands together in glee and did a little jig around Peggi, losing the squashed mouse from the sole of his boot in the process.

Strapping on his personal armor made his heart quicken with excitement. He drew his jewel-handled sword and carefully wiped it clean before bringing it to his blistered lips for a kiss.

"It has been a long time, far too long, since we have had some fun around here, don't you think, my beloved?" he said to his mirrored image reflected in the sword's blade. "I can hardly wait to meet the fools and show them my personal version of Bludenbonz hospitality."

Sheathing his weapon, The Grinder then pulled on his battle helmet, pinched his cheeks to bring up the color, and, turning to Peggi, asked with a dazzling metallic toothy grin, "How do I look, ha cha-cha?"

· · · · · · ·

The origin of the invaders held little interest for The Grinder. He was simply grateful for the opportunity to get in a little needed exercise. Believing his forces far superior in arms and training to anything the territories offered, thanks to the Circle of Power, he had little concern as to the outcome of any battle. On second thought, he wondered who would be so ignorant as to intentionally make the journey all the way to Athulian, only to wind up on the wrong end of a sword.

The Grinder's mind skipped to the hidden Circle of Power, protected by a small but fiercely loyal number of the Gootz Elite Guard. The name of the castle where The Grinder had hidden his stolen treasure had been a closely held secret known only to a handful of The Grinder's most trusted soldiers. Even the castle's location was confidential.

"Inform those at Thorn Castle that we have uninvited guests," The Grinder commanded Peggi. "And while you're at it, double the security down in the vault. Imagine the gall," The Grinder continued, now on a rampage. "We must make the enemy who dares an unwelcome visit pay for their arrogance. Those responsible must be made to suffer unmercifully, allowing only one or two of them to return home from wherever it is they came, to tell of their miserably failed mission.

"Those individuals who might be entertaining a future fun-filled vacation on the island of Athulian must be made to have second thoughts. The bearers of bad news will tell how helpless they were as they watched their brother soldiers dismembered, slowly taken apart piece by piece, starting at the toes and working all the way up to their noses before the fatal blow was delivered. To entertain those fortunate enough to have been chosen messengers, we will have them watch a friendly, civilized game of lawn bowling. For a ball we shall use their leader's head and for bowling pins we will use the legs of their fellow soldiers. What d'ya think?"

The Grinder shivered with delight as the colorful images of his plan skipped though his twisted mind.

Dressed in his favorite suit of armor along with his heavy sword, The Grinder checked himself out in the full-length mirror. Satisfied with what he saw, he turned then clanged and banged out of his bedchamber. With considerable effort the Gootz king made his way noisily through the winding hallways of Bludenbonz Castle with loyal Peggi at his side.

"Time to get down to business," The Grinder said to Peggi. "There will be no lying around sunbathing on the beach this day, except for our slain enemies, of course, who I imagine by nightfall will have quite the sunburn."

"That will be the least of their problems," snickered Peggi.

"I wonder how they managed to get past the sea serpents?" pondered The Grinder. "Perhaps a meeting with the leader of the serpents might be in order. I would hate to accuse them of negligence or, worse, betrayal without hearing how something like this might have happened."

"Before this," Peggi asked, "has there ever been an attempted landing on Athulian from anyone besides us?"

"No, not to my knowledge. Peggi, are you questioning the sea serpents' loyalty? Might you be suggesting that perhaps the sea serpents have never favored us and that we were wrong in assuming they were part of our defense system?"

"I am implying nothing, sir, merely curious. In any event there remain several unresolved concerns. I think after a proper investigation we shall have all these loose ends sorted out fairly quickly."

Cracking the knuckles of his dirty fingers, The Grinder was growing increasingly impatient. He could hardly wait to break the bones of whomever it was that waited down at the beach. "I want you to alert the Coast Guard to blockade the outlet to the sea. Take a contingent of our best soldiers, Peggi, then head to Thorn Castle and reinforce the Elite Guard. Leave as soon as you can."

· · · · · · ·

The climb down from the castle to the small beach on a good day was treacherous and not for the inexperienced rock climber. For this reason, the beach seldom had Gootz visitors from Bludenbonz. Those Gootz who came to the secluded location did so by boat. The shoreline curled from one end of the bay to the other. Driftwood, bleached to a smooth chalk gray, lay scattered among boulders that backed up to the bluff. Small glass-like stones littered the coarse sand. The glistening beach stretched to the steep climb that led to Bludenbonz Castle.

Between the physical challenges of strong winds and slippery wet rock, remnants from last night's storm, The Grinder and the castle guard had all they could do not to lose their footing and fall to the beach hundreds of feet below. Slowly they snaked their way single file down along a narrow ledge, hugging the inside wall as they went.

On one particularly perilous section, nearly a score of Gootz defenders, who for safety reasons were tied together at the waist, were caught in a sudden gust and blown from their tenuous foothold to the beach below. Paying the losses no never mind, The Grinder and castle guard pushed ahead.

The deaths of his soldiers was seen by The Grinder as merely an unfortunate consequence of their occupation but definitely nothing to get overly excited about. Certainly not when measured against the thrill of gazing across a bloodied, body-littered battleground. To know that he was not only a participant in the spirited sporting event, but that he was personally responsible for all that pain and suffering gave the master of the Gootz a raging case of the goose bumps.

"Who better than me deserves the joy of a lively day of carnage? After all," The Grinder reasoned to himself, "aren't I the Great Initiator and Director in Chief of the Gootz Office of Mayhem?"

· · · · · · ·

Peggi was by Gootz standards mildly clever, which is not saying much. His impulses led him to be a bit reckless on occasion and he didn't always think things through very well, but he was not a complete fool. He could have tried to convince the Gootz leader that he should join him in his descent to the beach, but The Grinder's trusted lieutenant had a little secret. He was deathly afraid of heights. His fear would have limited his rise in the Gootz military, so he simply concealed his phobia. The thought of having to walk the wet, narrow path leading from Bludenbonz Castle to the beach in this wind made Peggi's stomach queasy.

The Grinder had made it easy for him. Strangely, Peggi was fearless on the battlefield, but put him at the edge of a cliff and he would squeeze shut his eyes and cry like a baby. Attempting to climb down that wall would have been certain unintended suicide.

"Grateful," followed by "relieved," would be the best words to describe Peggi's feelings on being ordered by The Grinder to Thorn Castle. There was nothing more important than ensuring the safekeeping of the crown jewel in The Grinder's extensive treasure. With no idea of just how substantial a threat was unfolding on the Athulian beach, Peggi was resolved to take no chances with protecting the Circle of Power. Riding hard on the back of his prized black horse with its flowing, brightly dyed purple mane flying like a flag, Peggi and a contingent of his most skilled soldiers headed overland toward Thorn Castle.

It was by no accident that this relatively small castle, protected by obscurity and the impenetrable bramble of Thorn Forest, was chosen as the hiding place for The Grinder's most valuable possession. Approximately two miles back from Thorn Castle and on all four sides the forest had been carefully pruned into an elaborate maze of tall hedge complete with razor-sharp thorns.

The extensive puzzle of twisting passageways was just another example of The Grinder's mean-spirited sense of humor. All the thorn-lined paths were designed to confuse an unsuspecting traveler, leading to one of a series of depressing dead ends. Upon entering the maze, the victim would panic and immediately be lost, eventually going mad in a failed attempt to find his way out the other end, or back to the entrance. And to make the journey even more interesting, directional arrows were cut into the hedge along with the words "THIS WAY OUT" at various locations, giving a wayward trespasser an extra dose of confusion. Of course, the unhelpful directions only led deeper into the maze. For good measure, The Grinder had placed several long mirrors at strategic locations intended to finally push what remained of a rational mind over the edge.

Just one passageway among hundreds of possibilities led ultimately to Thorn Castle. There, only a few of The Grinder's most trusted confidants such as his Elite Guard shared his secret. Not even the talented creator of the maze, who was kept under lock and key while he designed the topiary, survived The Grinder's paranoia.

With final completion of the complicated project and upon The Grinder's orders, the doomed landscape architect was blindfolded and taken deep into the maze by a soldier from the Elite Guard. Once the soldier was convinced The Grinder's contractor was thoroughly lost, he was left to try to find his way out. This was the ultimate test of his work's effectiveness. A successful escape for the landscaper would have meant his plan was flawed. He held no illusions as to his eventual fate even if he somehow managed to escape. On the other hand, if his design worked, he would die in the maze. For the unfortunate landscaper, it was a lose-lose proposition.

"Good luck," one of the Elite Guard had said before departing, "and here's a cookie in case you get hungry." The soldier placed the cookie in the landscaper's hands, which were tied tightly behind his back.

More than a week after the labyrinth's completion date, the landscaper was found deep in the maze. He had lost not only his way, but, not surprisingly, his mind as well. The crazed gardener, running at full speed, had launched himself onto the hedge of thorns. His tongue was now so swollen it permanently protruded from his mouth, and his delirious words were difficult to understand.

"Merthy," whispered the dehydrated horticulturist.

"Good job, very good indeed," said the upbeat and appreciative Grinder, ignoring both the landscaper's recently acquired speech impediment and his request. He had made it a point to make a guest appearance at the maze so he could personally thank the architect for his craftsmanship. Showing his genuine appreciation, he kept repeating, "Good job," while vigorously slapping the landscaper on the back, further embedding the thorns that fortunately soon killed the tortured contractor.

The ingenious design of the maze was recognized and actually appreciated by The Grinder; however, his concerns for security took precedence over his admiration of the landscaper's work. A possible security breach at Thorn Castle was simply unacceptable. The topiary experiment was pronounced an enormous success and cause for celebration.

At the site of the impaled architect, with military music blaring in the background, a fancy plaque was posthumously awarded the deceased. In gratitude for his work, with several of Thorn Castle's Elite Guard looking on, a small ceremony was held with the stuck gardener permanently affixed to the thorn hedge. The Grinder thought it rude of the landscaper to have his back to his audience and tried unsuccessfully several times to twist his head one hundred and eighty degrees around so that his dead eyes could be looking out at the appreciative audience.

After a predictably boring speech, the Gootz leader attempted to place the plaque and a single red flower in the contractor's limp hands, which remained tied behind his back. The guests politely applauded then feasted. On the dearly departed, flashbulbs flashed, and on his body, ravenous flies feasted.

However, the plaque and flower kept falling to the ground. The embarrassed Grinder attempted fruitlessly to prop up the sagging landscaper who hung limply from the thorn hedge like so much wet laundry pinned on a barbed-wire clothesline. Finally giving up, The Grinder cursed the uncooperative corpse, picked up the plaque for the last time, and, in disgust, tossed it into the bramble.

"That's what you get for trying to be nice," he grumbled, kicking an unfortunate distracted cat high into the air. The cat had had the misfortune of picking a most inopportune time to cross The Grinder's path and screamed at him its displeasure of mistreatment. The Gootz commander, ignoring the protest, walked the short distance to his horse and, upon mounting, rode back in the direction of Bludenbonz Castle.

· · · · · · ·

Charging through the familiar maze with his cadre of Elite Guard in close pursuit, Peggi spurred on his sweating horse. For quite some time they traveled the erratic path of the labyrinth. Eventually they arrived at an opening. The Grinder's most trusted had reached the center of the maze. A vast, empty stretch of land bordered on all four sides by a tall thicket of thorns spread out before them. Located in the center of the manicured open space, an immense rock column rose majestically up from the acreage, only to disappear into a bank of clouds. From atop the clouds, Thorn Castle appeared to grow. At the base of the calcified column, camouflaged from curious eyes, was the castle's secret entrance. Inside, a long circular staircase wound its way up into the fortress.

The Grinder's stronghold was positioned on a large plateau, encircled by a shallow moat. Small flesh-eating fish, whose protruding teeth were nearly as big as their bodies, swarmed the water. More than two dozen half-starved wolves, most with mange-thinned coats and ripped ears earned while fighting over scraps of food, roamed a large penned area.

Peggi hurriedly entered Thorn Castle and quickly briefed the Elite Guard that had been awaiting his arrival on what he knew about the invasion. He then went directly to his private quarters located in a tower at the far end of the castle. Just how substantial a threat was unfolding on the beach below Bludenbonz Castle was anyone's guess, but he needed to prepare for the worst. Peggi would take no chances in making sure the Circle of Power was not at risk. He stood for what seemed an eternity in front of the large mirror propped against the wall in The Grinder's private dressing room.

"Protect the Circle of Power at all costs, including your life," came The Grinder's distant voice. Slowly Peggi's eyes, reflecting back from the mirror, began to change shape, followed by the other features that distinguished his face. In the next moment, it was as if Peggi was standing at a window looking through at The Grinder.

"We are on the beach, but the beach is empty," The Grinder continued. "I might think you had sounded a false alarm, Peggi, if not for all the many fresh footprints on the beach. There are two curious things. The footprints are small, child size, and the 'children' seem to have disappeared into the sea."

"But sir, that seems unlikely. What would be the point? There is only one way to get from the beach to any other part of the island and that is up the trail you just came down. I don't understand, unless they got back in their boats and returned to sea looking for a different landing site."

"Well, Peggi, don't you think I'm smart enough to have thought of that? The fact is, neither of the two options is possible since their boats are still here at the beach and we passed no one on our way down from the castle," The Grinder said calmly. "I would be more alarmed if not for the fact that there are only three boats here, and like the trespassers' footprints, they are also small. Still, I have hope of exercising my sword before day's end, even if only against puny children. Somehow they must have hidden as we were coming down from the castle and we passed them by, but that seems im—"

The Grinder's face paled. "I just thought of something. What if this is a trick? What if somehow Wimzi is involved?"

Peggi, in all his years at The Grinder's side, had never experienced the unmistakable sound of fear he now heard in his leader's voice. Give The Grinder a foe he could see, and there were none more fierce in battle on all of Aeiea. But the unpredictable deceptions of Wimzi, hidden just beyond the mind's ability to reason, struck a deep note of dread into the Gootz leader's heart. If The Grinder had an Achilles' heel, it was the bizarre power of the Wimzicals. Any territory on Aeiea was his for the taking, except one. Wimzi was forever off limits. And then The Grinder's mind shifted.

"Elderwiser!" he said aloud. "I think there's a good chance the wizard of the Wiggwoggs is involved in all this. Oh, how I hates him . . . running around the territories in his crummy old bathrobe stirring up trouble. If I catch him with his hands dirty and somehow mixed up in this invasion, I personally will chop them off."

Back in The Grinder's dressing room at Thorn Castle, Peggi watched as the image of The Grinder's face faded in the mirror until it was finally gone. Now he was once again staring into his own eyes. Peggi partially pulled a book from a large bookcase, and the mirror began to move. It slid to the left and receded into a slotted wall. The opening revealed a long hallway of stone lit by candle sconces on each side. The drooling candles dripped down onto the capped peaks of newly formed mountains of wax below. Along both walls, two Elite Guards were stationed under each sconce. At the far end of the hall, a stone staircase without railing curled downward. As Peggi entered the secret hall, the mirrored wall silently rolled closed behind him. He walked swiftly past the guards toward the staircase leading to the keep and the Circle of Power.

· · · · · · ·

Serene sat silently in her boat listening to Arni, leader of the sea serpents. The hinges of her jaw appeared to have come undone. Her mouth gaped open. The legend of the sea serpents inhabiting The Great Sea Valion was ancient Aeiean history. Stories and sightings had been passed down faithfully from one generation to the next. What Arni now revealed challenged her reality.

I don't know if sea serpents can get embarrassed, but Arni's expression, at minimum, communicated his obvious discomfort.

"Well," he said, clearing his throat, "it goes something like this. Me and the boys here are . . . how shall I say it . . . hmmm . . . figments of someone else's imagination. In other words, here one minute, gone the next. Get it? If you put us in front of a mirror, you would not see our reflection. Am I getting through to you?"

Serene scratched her colorful head. "Are you trying to tell me that all those stories, for all these years—"

The sea serpent simply nodded his head.

Arni was not real. None of the sea serpents were real. What she was seeing was created by someone else's imagination deep in the territory of Wimzi. The sea serpents were merely an illusion.

"Why?" Serene looked at Arni in disbelief. "This cannot be true. Why?" she repeated, dazed by the serpent's revelation. "What about all the stories?"

The sea monster flashed a knowing smile. "In due time, brave little leader of the Wiggwoggs, you shall have most of your questions answered. For now, the important thing is that you survive and successfully complete your mission.

"I must inform you that without me and the boys here, your mission is doomed because your plan is ill-conceived and far too loose. As a matter of fact, we have reason to believe that a Gootz fishing boat spotted you not long after you set to sea. Failure of your mission will have serious consequences for both your red-haired friend next to you as well as the territory of Wimzi, whose long lease on insanity is sadly coming to an end. I am aware from my sources that you also have the ability to become invisible. I suggest this may be the right time to use that power."

The sea serpent's revelation caught Carter and the Wiggwoggs by surprise, but this was not the time for more discussion. It was time for action.

Arni maneuvered himself carefully so the adventurers could step directly from their boats onto the sea serpent's back. "For short periods of time," the sea serpent said to Serene, "we have the power to give ourselves form. It takes great energy of which we have less and less these days, so we can't waste time. Quickly, climb aboard."

His thick scales were layered, much like coarse roofing tiles, giving the climbers an easy foothold. Once sitting astride the long backbone of the monster, each took firm hold of a single triangular scale that jutted perpendicular from the serpent's curved spine. For balance, they dug their knees into their host's backbone.

Arni's head rested atop a long, twisting neck. He turned to ensure all were safely aboard and smiled with amusement watching them squirm to get comfortable. When all were securely seated, he and the flotilla of other sea serpents began to fade from sight.

"Low battery," Arni said.

While the band of friends could see each other, the sea serpents were fast disappearing from view beneath them. What a bizarre image they would have presented to an innocent passerby, suspended high above the water's surface while tethered by some invisible wire attached to a passing cloud.

The sea serpents locked in on their objective, heading with great haste toward Athulian. Arni had told Carter, Serene, and the other Wiggwoggs that they had to trust him. Besides, what other choice did they have?

Serene took Carter's hand and spoke softly to him for a few moments, sharing Elderwiser's secret. She took a small amulet from around her neck and, opening it, first placed a few drops of its contents to her lips. She then handed the vial to Carter and instructed him to do the same.

"Pass it along to the others," she told him.

In a matter of moments, the Wiggwoggs and Carter had also become invisible except to one another and the sea serpents.

"I can still see you and the others," Carter said.

"Yes," Serene replied, "but no one else can. I know that you as well are also invisible."

"How do you know for sure?"

Serene's answer came in one word. "Elderwiser."

The sea serpents came as close to the shore as they dared. Three abandoned boats bobbed aimlessly in the salty water somewhere behind them, gently encouraged by fluttering scarves of waves toward the island. In their final moments together, Arni instructed the adventurers on what they were to do upon landing on Athulian. After reaching the beach, if they encountered a Gootz welcoming party they were to create some kind of diversion through confusion.

"You will use your invisibility to throw the Gootz off your trail," said Arni, "then you will get to the big rocks at the far west corner of the cove by using the shallows of the sea and wait there."

"Wait for what?" Carter asked.

"Wait and see," Arni answered. "If your quest for the Circle of Power is successful, you will need to give us a sign that you need our help for your escape from Athulian. We'll be watching and waiting. Now off you go," he said, carefully tipping to one side.

Carter and the Wiggwoggs slid into the cold water and, without looking back, struggled in the foamy breakers while swimming as fast as they could for shore. As they swam, they heard in the distance a sorrowful lament from Arni as he sang:

> *"I once knew a flea who swallowed a bee*
> *The bee who stung the flea on the knee . . ."*

Chapter 17
The Beach Party

The beach was long and carved in the shape of a crescent moon. Steep rock walls running down from Bludenbonz Mountain kept the beach tightly confined. From high above, an ominous castle anchored to the sliced-off top of the mountain bluff kept a silent watch over the interesting performance beginning to unfold below.

Wading in the shallow water, the exhausted travelers observed a half-dozen large sailing vessels come up on the horizon far out at sea.

"Are those Gootz ships?" Zebenuza wondered aloud.

There was no response to his question, as any answer would only have been a guess anyway.

It was Ushi who first heard the excited voices coming from the Gootz soldiers who were midway down the mountain. He signaled to Serene who then motioned her group to quickly get up on the beach. Once there, she instructed Carter and the Wiggwoggs to run around in circles leaving lots of footprints to confuse the beach-bound Gootz. Serene was sticking to Arni the sea serpent's plan. After a while she gestured for all of them to follow her. She ran to the sea and walked knee deep in the surf toward the tall, rock-lined western corner of the beach. They climbed a dozen or so feet to a vantage point that oversaw the entire length of the beach as well as the trailhead leading up to Bludenbonz Castle.

· · · · · · ·

The Grinder's conversation with Peggi had been disturbing, yet he concluded the possibility of Wimzi's involvement was at best remote. *I must deal with what I know, not what I fear,* he said to himself.

Upon further investigation of the beach, the only thing that made sense to The Grinder was that the invading force must be more in number than the three boats had indicated. If he hadn't been so focused on the beach, he would have noticed the appearance of the six sailing ships balancing on the line that separated sea from sky.

"Perhaps the invaders on the beach saw us coming down from Bludenbonz," he said aloud. "When the cowards became aware of our presence they beat a hasty retreat back to the water. For whatever reason, they must have simply abandoned three of their dinky boats on the beach. Maybe the boats just carried their scouts, yet why so many footprints?"

As if trying to send an intentional signal to the unaware Gootz leader, light cast from a metal object on the largest of the "sailing ships" out at sea finally caught The Grinder's eye.

"To the long boats!" he shouted. "Where are the Kenga? Why didn't we have some warning from our spies in the sky? And where are the sea serpents?"

The Grinder, who had a history of acute seasickness, had decided not to join the attack at sea. Rather it was determined a more prudent use of resources would be for himself and several of his commanding officers to return to the castle and draw up contingency plans to deal with a substantial invasion if that should become necessary.

Just coming into the bay from around the far corner of the inlet, a dozen or so long boats surfed their way toward the beach. Each vessel was manned by a good number of Gootz sitting side by side along built-in benches. The rowers bent to their task of pulling their heavy oars through the waves.

Seated by himself in the bow of the lead boat, a heavily muscled Gootz with metal bands at his ankles and wrists pounded a large drum held securely between his legs. He wore the small bleached skull of a child with straight ponytail hair affixed atop his helmet. The drummer, using the leg bones of a Gootz victim, gave the sweat-drenched rowers a rhythm for the strokes of their oars.

"Put yer backs into it, ya bunch of slugs!" he shouted above the din to the laboring rowers. Behind them, the armada of anonymous sailing vessels sat motionless, as if on a stretcher frame of blue-painted canvas. Moments later, those "ships" began to move toward the bay.

When the long boats came aground on the beach, a number of the Elite Guard waiting in the shallows flooded onto them, nearly capsizing one.

Once the Elite Guard were settled aboard, each of the boats were pushed off the beach using a quantity of skinned logs that had been placed under the vessels to act as rollers. They quickly headed out toward the sailing ships where they believed they would confront the little ones who had soiled Bludenbonz Beach by their uninvited presence.

The flat monotone din of a horn being blown from Bludenbonz Castle was heard floating above the beach. It was a call for the Gootz reserves to mobilize. Although not a drop of blood had yet been spilled, or for that matter an enemy seen, The Grinder was taking no chances. He didn't like surprises unless he was the initiator, and he was growing increasingly uncomfortable with the possibility of Wimzi's involvement.

There had not been a single invasion of Athulian since The Grinder and the Gootz had made the unpopulated island their home. There would be no mercy for those unfortunate enough to be taken prisoner. Upon further reflection, The Grinder was hard pressed to recall a single occasion when mercy had ever been a consideration.

A repetitive mantra looped The Grinder's mind: rip, gouge, smash, and slash. It nearly put him in a trance. He unconsciously swallowed the thick saliva threatening to escape the corners of his mouth.

· · · · · · ·

Serene nudged Carter with a sharp elbow. "The big one calling out orders, I believe that is The Grinder. I have not seen him before, but from the descriptions in the stories handed down in Wiggonwoggen, I imagine that is likely him."

Carter focused on the large, animated Gootz who was shouting while waving his arms and pointing out to sea. With one hand he grabbed one of the smaller Gootz who was standing in his way and flung him hard to the sand. The Grinder was definitely large and no doubt in charge.

"So you think that maybe the big one down there is the keeper of the Circle of Power? If you're in doubt," Carter added, "why don't we just go up to him and ask? While we're at it, we might also ask him if he would be a good sport and wouldn't mind returning it? That seems about as good a plan as any I've heard so far." Carter was smiling through his sarcastic remark. Serene was not.

By her expression, it was clear Serene was not at all amused by Carter's quirky sense of humor. On other occasions, Carter had said something to Serene he felt was really funny, but she rarely seemed to get it. Her reaction was usually flat, as if she hadn't heard him, as if he was speaking a foreign language.

Now that's interesting, he thought. You could live anywhere on Earth just over the border from another country. You could walk just down the road, cross over the border into that country, and they would be speaking a different language. Now here he was, who knows where, and he spoke the same language as everyone he had met. Weird.

Very weird, indeed, came Nevermore's response to his mind. *And something else that's strange. Do you notice how Serene and her father talk? They sound kind of old fashioned or stuffy. I guess Elderwiser is so ancient that he grew up speaking that way and passed it down to his daughter or maybe that's just the way wizards and their kin speak.*

Serene, choosing to ignore Carter's earlier comment, said, "Arni told us to wait. I can see the Gootz looking directly at where we stand, but they make no movement toward us. It should be as easy for them to see us as it is for us to see them, yet they do not."

"We're invisible. That magic potion of yours really does work," Carter said. *All these Gootz against us,* Carter thought to himself, sighing. *I sure am uncomfortable with all this uncertainty.* He lowered his head. It all seemed so impossible, so overwhelming.

If he had as much confidence in Elderwiser as Serene did, then there would have been no doubt that spells created by the Wiggwogg wizard really worked. But that kind of confidence takes trust, and trust takes time. For someone new to the concept of friendship and trust, Carter was coming to understand his survival required him to adjust and be on a fast learning curve. Still, it was his nature to question.

And what if we by some miracle manage to find and capture the Circle of Power, what then? In that moment, he remembered an earlier conversation between himself and Serene. Her words were comforting and reassuring. The goal was not to live a safe, predictable life but rather to live fully, as if this day might be your last.

Courage, Nevermore said.

"Thank you," Carter replied.

"For what?" Serene asked.

"Oh, nothing really, I was just thinking how lucky I am to have you as a friend."

"Best friends."

Returning her smile, Carter repeated, "Best friends."

"As you reminded me a moment ago, we are invisible, but that doesn't mean we can't be heard. Keep your voice low," she said in barely a whisper. "Right now we are far enough away that I don't believe they can hear us, but we should take no chances."

Carter pointed out to Serene The Grinder, along with several of his high-ranking aides, moving quickly up the mountain.

Now, with the exception of Carter and the Wiggwoggs, the beach initially appeared empty and quiet. It was Lyke who first spotted what he believed was a Gootz soldier clambering over the rocks at the other end of the beach. He alerted his friends. Soon many more joined the first figure on the beach. They were making a loud commotion and seemed to be looking in the general direction of the adventurers.

Perhaps our invisibility is wearing off, thought Carter. "I believe they see us," he said to Serene.

"And worse than that," Serene added, "they now appear to be coming toward us."

"Should we make a run for it?" Carter asked. He could feel the fight or flight response of adrenalin pumping into his quickening heart.

"Run for what? There is nowhere to run to. We are trapped."

"But Arni said—"

"I know what Arni said," interrupted Serene, "and I say, never trust a smiling sea serpent. The Gootz seem to be picking up speed. I think it must be a battle charge. In a few moments, they will be upon us."

"Can't you do something?"

"I am open to suggestions . . . What is that?" Serene asked.

"What is what?"

"Hard to say," she answered, "but from here it looks like there is a shaggy pony out in front. I can't quite . . ." Serene squinted while holding her hand against her brow to shield her eyes from the intense morning light. She was trying to bring the pony into focus.

"I don't believe it," she said slowly. "It can't—look closely, Carter. Does that little pony seem to be running . . . backwards?"

Carter stared in disbelief. "No. It can't be," he repeated Serene's words in little more than a whisper. He rubbed the knuckles of both hands deep into his eyes. The red scarf around the creature's neck left no doubt. "If that's a pony, it's in terrible need of a plastic surgeon," laughed Carter.

"What did you say?"

"I said if that's—oh, never mind. Imalima!" Carter shouted past Serene. "Where have you been? And what are you doing here?"

The odd collection of creatures that were following closely behind Imalima proved not to be Gootz after all. Instead the eclectic assortment of the most absurd animals, some dressed in unusual masquerade costumes, were actually fellow Wimzicals. Eyes and ears, arms, legs, and tails grew from the strangest places.

"Imalima!" Carter cried out a second time. He couldn't remember ever being so happy to see anyone.

Upon hearing his name, Imalima abruptly halted, causing those who were following at his heels or, in his case, flippers, to run over him. Slowly gathering up his inflated ego and dusting himself off, the Wimzical said, "They admire and can't get close enough to me. That appears to be just one of the many pitfalls of exemplary leadership. To whom do I owe my gratitude for this unscheduled meeting?"

"Imalima . . ." began Carter.

"You already said that. Do you think I have forgotten my name? Why not tell me something I don't already know. To whom do I owe my displeasure of their company?"

"Oh please," Carter pleaded, "we're not going to have to go through this every time we meet, are we?"

"You imply we've met; however, I do not recall your red-headedness nor the feathered flapper grubbing in your hair . . . apparently scratching for worms."

Imalima glared with an expression of disgust at Nevermore who returned the favor with his own look of disdain.

Rather than giving in to his initial impulse of annoyance, Carter found himself with warm feelings of compassion for Imalima. It was now apparent that among the creature's obvious challenges, Imalima had serious memory issues.

"My name is Carter, Carter Nicholsworth, and this here is Nevermore," he said, pointing to the top of his head.

"Not *the* Carter Nicholsworth? Well, why didn't you say so in the first place? I have a mind like a steel trap, you know. Never forget a thing. What goes in stays in, locked in forever. What was it again we were talking about? Don't tell me. Let me guess. I love puzzles, how about you? Do you do the crosswords?"

No doubt about it . . . Imalima was back.

"What are you doing here, and who are your friends?" Carter questioned.

"I might ask the same of you, sir, except that puzzle is far too easy to figure out."

"That may be, but you have not answered my question. Why are you here and while I'm thinking about it, how did you get here?"

Imalima pulled the red scarf from around his neck and threw it forcefully to the ground. He then blew a shrill blast from a whistle that hung around his neck.

"PENALTY!" he yelled. "After asking your first question, you repeated it without giving me ample opportunity to respond. Then you asked a second question within the first question before I had a chance to answer the initial question. That, sir, verges on a forfeiture of the game. Need I remind you, sir, you are not dealing with some common country bumpkin who just bounced off the melon truck. I can honestly say I am flummoxed by your blatant disregard of the rules. Your behavior is at best totally unforgivable and at worst even more so. Did I just say what I thought I said? Anyway, as any serious student of the game understands, a double infraction of the 'unforgivable' clause in any officially written contract carries with it the maximum unsportsmanlike conduct penalty of fifteen yards."

"OK," said Carter. "Fifteen yard penalty against me. Now can you please answer my first question? What are you doing here?"

"Why didn't you ask me that in the first place?" Not waiting for a response, Imalima continued. "It is a rather long and complicated tale. We don't have much time, so in the interest of keeping it simple, which would probably work best for you, if you catch my drift, I will give you the 'preferred customer' condensed version. Listen up because it has been radically abbreviated and you could easily miss subtle clues critical to the story line. Are you ready?"

Imalima could see by Carter's anxious expression that he was more than ready. He reached into his cart and pulled out a large, heavy book and a pair of round wire eyeglasses missing their lenses. Carefully putting on the glasses so as not to stick himself in the eye or smudge the absent lenses, he opened the book. The goat-like creature cleared his throat, repeating several times, "testing, testing, check, check, check, one, two, three . . . test, test. OK, here goes . . .

"It all began in the beginning, as all things do, that once upon a time, long, long ago . . ." Imalima then riffled quickly through the pages until he reached the very last one. He ran a flipper down the page until he came to the final sentence. ". . . And through her tears of joy, the beautiful young princess couldn't have imagined a more perfect gift. The end."

He slammed the book closed, removed his eyeglasses, and looked up.

"Whoa," said Carter. "I think you skipped a few pages. Somewhere between the beginning and the end, there must be a middle part. You can't just have a beginning and an end. There has to be a middle of a book. Ask anyone."

Imalima stubbornly folded his uppermost legs across his chest. You may recall that Imalima had the physical appearance of a goat. In addition, he had the disposition to match and could be just as ornery.

"No middle," Imalima said dismissively, his twirly horned snout pointed up and away from Carter.

"OK, no middle." Carter knew the futility of getting into a debate on matters of common sense with Imalima. "Is it possible there is more to the beginning or, for that matter, the end than you have shared?"

"Now you're onto something," smiled Imalima. "Can you figure it out? It's a twiddler of a twister, you know. My Granny Harrumpt would call this kind of puzzle a real brain buster. I think I remember one time Grandpa Harrumpt getting really angry at Granny Harrumpt. He called her a real 'brain buster' or something nasty like that."

"I'll play."

"All right then," nodded Imalima. "Let the games begin."

What am I doing? thought Carter up to Nevermore.

The response was immediate. *Don't think about it. Just say what comes to your mind. Trust your intuition.*

"You're in some way connected to Arni and the sea serpents," Carter ventured timidly.

"Bingo!" Imalima shouted, surprised at Carter's response.

"Wimzi is somehow involved," continued Carter. The words seemed to just fall from his mouth. "Arni and the other sea serpents were like you, created in Wimzi." Carter tried to fit the pieces of the puzzle together, remembering Arni's recent and surprising confession.

"Oh, you're good, right again. Now if you can finish the rest of the mystery, you will have filled in the middle and we already know the end. If you can do that, I'll tell you all and more."

Carter closed his eyes. His mind seemed empty. Nothing was coming to him. *Help, Nevermore,* he pleaded. Then a familiar voice was whispering into his mind.

"Time is just about up," said Imalima, checking the face of his over-sized pocket watch. "It's too bad. You were doing so well, but you should know there are no losers on our show. We do have a booby-prize for the defeated." Imalima was digging deep into his cart of stuff looking for a consolation gift that would be appropriate for the occasion.

As if someone had just turned on a light in a dark room, a big smile spread across Carter's face. "You made a deal. The Wimzicals are concerned about the growing power and aggressiveness of the Gootz. You were ordered here to help us defeat The Grinder and see the Circle of Power returned to Elderwiser and the Wiggwoggs for safekeeping. If successful, there is the possibility you would be welcomed back to Wimzi as a full citizen and a national hero. Like my friends here, you are also temporarily invisible to all except us."

There was an awkward moment of silence. Imalima made the first move by once again rummaging through his cart of stuff. Finally finding what he had been searching for, Imalima pulled a noisemaker from the depths of the cart. Putting the party favor to his lips, he blew hard, and a long, pink paper unfurled as it filled with his breath. A high-pitched squeak came from the fully extended instrument.

As if on cue, the creatures to the rear of Imalima began what appeared to be some sort of ritualistic celebration dance. Extending their arms and or legs up and down rapidly into the air, the Wimzicals began poking their heads rapidly back and forth while wildly wiggling their most unconventional bodies.

Lohden said to Retann, "How weird is that? These Wimzicals look like an odd collection of squirming caterpillars that have been tossed into a boiling pot of water." The Wimzicals made low guttural sounds as if they were going to be sick right there on the beach.

"Are they going to throw up?" Carter asked Serene.

"By the sound of it, I would say that is a strong possibility," Serene responded.

As it turned out, the Wimzicals were not about to be sick but merely exercising their First Amendment right under their constitution, which protected each citizen of Wimzi's lawful birthright to get down and boogie. Imalima turned to face the wildly undulating crowd of creatures, drawing one of his floppy feet across his neck.

"Cut!" he shouted.

The celebration came to an abrupt halt. He was obviously in charge. Turning to face Carter and the Wiggwoggs, he continued, "The Grand Wimzard of Wimzi has wisely given yours truly the opportunity to redeem himself by assisting you in your attempt to recapture the Circle of Power and return it to its rightful caretaker, Elderwiser, the wizard of Wiggonwoggen. Word has reached my most abundant ears that The Grinder and his murderous army of butchers and thieves are hungry to cut into fresh flesh. Our Inferior Department of Intelligence, a bunch of losers, if you ask me, which no one has, places Wimzi on The Grinder's short list of territories for possible plunder. Therefore, His Wonderful Wonderfulness, the Grand Wimzard of all wacky and wobbly Wimzicals, has called for a pre-emptive strike."

"I got it right!" Carter exclaimed to Serene in amazement.

We got it right, Nevermore reminded him.

"It appears you have. However, trusting anything connected to Wimzi must carry with it an element of doubt," responded Serene. "Stories of fantasy originating from the 'land of lies' are legendary throughout the territories of Aeiea."

"They are just that, baseless stories for the consumption of gullible children," injected Imalima dismissively. "Here's the real deal. Hoo-Ha, the Grand Wimzard of Wimzi, is first and foremost before anything else a well-respected scientist. He uses specific instruments of science rooted in nature to accomplish a state of altered imagery. Let me give you an example. During the daylight hours and in partnership with Suva and Ahneese, refracted light, which is simply bent light, is harnessed and used for creating a mirage. You know, something that looks like it is, but really is not. At night a collection of fireflies could be used to create a wide variety of illusions such as an invasion of extra-terrestrial spacecraft. Now, when you combine the qualities of illusion with those of imagination, the results can appear magical.

"Oh, I almost neglected to mention the component of genetics as it relates to the subject at hand. As you may have already gathered, we Wimzicals are rather unique or as some insensitive yahoo might say, 'physiologically challenged and psychologically disturbed.' You get my point, which brings me to my next subject.

"In case you are not already aware, Arni and the other sea serpents are a creation of His Wonderfulness, the Grand Wimzard of Wimzi. You know he is quite the genius, as he would readily tell you upon a chance meeting. In truth they do not actually exist except in the form of hardened illusion. They appear then disappear where and when the Wimzard chooses. The Gootz think they protect Athulian when, in truth, oh how I hate that word, the sea serpents were created as an early warning system for Wimzi. Their patrolling of the sea would serve to alert the Grand Wimzard of any impending Gootz attack. The joke is on The Grinder, who thinks the sea serpents are working for him."

Just for the following few moments, Imalima's eyes came uncrossed. It was unheard of for the creature from Wimzi to have said something associated with an element of reason. Yet there it was. His fellow Wimzicals looked on, concerned and puzzled that Imalima may have broken yet another law and actually said something that may have made sense.

Even though Arni had alluded to what Imalima was sharing, it was a difficult concept for Carter to grasp. "Illusion? How can that be? We rode on Arni's back," said Carter, whose human mind still struggled with the difficult abstraction of "hardened illusion."

"You experienced only what the Grand Wimzard intended for you to integrate into your reality. You look puzzled," Imalima said to Carter.

"Have I lost you? Although pure illusion, Arni and the other sea serpents have been given the ability to take actual form, but only for brief periods of time. During this period, they cross over the threshold from illusion to reality, but they cannot stay. This is no easy feat, even for someone with the skills of the Grand Wimzard of Wimzi. Arni and the other sea serpents were your guides to ensure a safe voyage to the shores of Athulian. With the first stage of their mission completed, they disappeared under the sea's surface. Up came the 'sailing ships.' If you are making the connection between the sea serpents and the 'sailing ships,' you are beginning to catch on."

"But what is the point of the sailing ships?" Carter asked, still rather confused that Imalima was sounding logical.

"A mere diversion to draw The Grinder's attention away from his first thoughts after seeing your footprints. More than likely, The Grinder would have been preoccupied with questions of how to find and destroy you. The ships gave The Grinder pause to reflect on a much larger invasion than he first believed, which distracted his attention away from you. Concluding you were nothing more than a scouting party, he became focused on the ships and saw them as the imminent and real threat. By the time the Gootz arrive where they believe the ships are located, the ships will have vanished. Isn't this fun?"

Nevermore hopped from Carter's head to his shoulder.

Just when I was thinking Mr. Woolly over there is out of his mind insane . . .

"Shhhhhhhhh."

"Does the bird have an opinion he would like to share?" Imalima's crossed eyes uncrossed as he glared at Nevermore. "If not, may I suggest he keep his big beak shut!"

A bucktoothed smile rolled across Imalima's face and his eyes returned to their normal crossed position. Then a most peculiar thing happened. Imalima's head faded then disappeared. The head of the cross-eyed Wimzical was immediately replaced by Arni's head, but the toothy smile was still Imalima's. The Arni head said just one word:

"Illusion."

Carter rubbed the knuckles of his fists deep into his eyes. When he again was able to focus on Imalima, the goat-like creature was once again wearing his own head.

"Nevermore, did you see what I just think I saw?"

I don't know what you saw. I was focused on a wee worm down below begging to become breakfast so I didn't notice anything unusual. What are you referring to?

"His head! Didn't you see . . . Oh never mind."

Serene, who had to this point remained an amused silent observer to the one-way conversation between Carter and Nevermore, spoke up. "Well, Imalima, it seems you have some special insight as to what happens next."

"Indeed I do, and it's not a pretty picture I am about to paint." Imalima wiped a single fat tear that had collected at the corner of his eye. "This is the sad part, especially if you happen to be an unfortunate Gootz aboard one of those long boats or a friend or family member waiting for dinner tonight. Arni and company will surround those boats from below the surface of the water then rise up out of Valion, fire shooting from their mouths. The Great Sea Valion will boil with bedlam and sea serpents. The confused Gootz in their long boats will be overturned in a panicked attempt to escape the trap."

As if a fish on a hook, Carter's mind hung on the words of Imalima's riveting tale. "What happens next?"

"Glub, glub, glub . . ." Imalima said, wiping a second tear. He removed his bandana from around his neck and blew his nose, sending a long and loud wet burst into the scarf. Checking the scarf's contents, his face contorted in an expression of disgust. Retying the neckerchief around his neck, Imalima was careful to keep the sticky part toward the back where he wouldn't have to see it.

"Glub, glub, glub as in drowning?"

"Oh, you're the smart one, aren't you, Mr. Nicholsworth," responded Imalima.

"How did you become the chosen one to lead this expedition of Wimzicals?" Serene inquired of Imalima.

"I assure you, it was an innocent enough accident. I was minding my own business, peacefully sleeping under a sweet potato tree when I felt someone kicking at one of my flappers. To my great surprise, it was none other than Hoo-Ha. I had never seen the Grand Wimzard before, but I knew it was he by the silver stars on his black pajamas. Also, the hat was a dead giveaway. Tall and pointy, the hat had a series of multi-colored ribbons flowing from the peak, with a wide band at the base imprinted with the single word 'Wimzard.' I was quite familiar with the hat as my dear old

Granny Harrumpt had a large picture of the Grand Wimzard hung prominently over the toilet in her kitchen."

"Disgusting," Carter said, looking mildly annoyed.

"I totally agree," concurred Imalima. "It is disrespectful to have the Grand Wimzard's picture in the kitchen. His picture belongs prominently exhibited above the mantle and fireplace in the living room."

"No, Imalima, I mean it's disgusting to have a toilet in the kitchen," explained Carter.

"Where else would you put it?"

"Let me think, hmmmmmmm." Carter tapped his chin, pretending to be deep in thought. "I have it. How about the bathroom?"

Imalima looked puzzled. "We don't have bathrooms in Wimzi. It sounds like a bathroom would be used for taking a bath, which in Wimzi is legally illegal. Anyway, you have some problem with a kitchen potty?"

"Never mind."

"Excuse me, you two," Serene interrupted, "I don't mean to be a party pooper . . ."

Imalima fell to the ground, rolling around hysterically. "That's a good one. You didn't mean to be a potty pooper." The other Wimzicals joined Imalima on the ground in a fit of mass hysteria.

"I think we need to change the subject," said an unamused Serene, "or did you forget where we are and what we are here for?"

Imalima regained both his feet and composure. "Well," he said indignantly, "aren't we testy today? Lighten up, Wiggwogg." He reached into his cart and, after a bit of rummaging around, pulled out a folded map.

"I never got to finish my story on how I got picked to lead this expedition, so due to an obvious lack of interest, I will postpone my narrative to a later date," he said in a huff. He was convinced that Wiggwoggs were far too serious and, sadly, born lacking a funny bone.

"I don't know if this map is reliable," Imalima continued while unfolding the paper. "Information squeezed from the throat of a Kenga spy by the Minnininni and used to create this map identifies the location of the Circle of Power in Thorn Castle. The remote castle about two or three days' journey across Athulian is surrounded by a wicked thicket of thorns protecting the golden medallion from anyone not on the guest list. That would be us."

Carter and Serene looked at each other. It was Serene who first spoke. "So it is looking more and more like the old Dweeg Salise was right. The Circle of Power is not at Bludenbonz Castle but rather hidden in a forest castle on the opposite side of Athulian, just as she said."

"How can we be sure Imalima's information is correct?" Carter asked.

"We cannot be totally sure, but Salise's story, my map, and Imalima's map fit together. In any event, we cannot stay here. Good job, Imalima! It looks like that's our best hope. Since you are the one with the most detailed map, how would you like to take the lead? You are, for now, our guide."

Imalima's face grew stern with the acceptance of his new responsibility. He was standing on his most rear legs to maximize his height. Beginning to pace back and forth in front of his army, he slapped a riding crop rhythmically against the side of his leg. He reached into and pulled from an interior pocket of his shabby wool coat a large pocket watch, a treasured gift given to him by his late grandfather. The unusual pocket watch had no second hand and, like Imalima himself, ran backwards. His grandfather, who had been a hoarder and a collector of everything, bought the inoperative second-hand watch minus the second hand on sale from A. Dummi, who had never learned to tell time anyway.

"Time's a wasting," Imalima said, loudly shaking the pocket watch and holding it to one of his super-sized ears. His eyes narrowed as he scanned his army of wacky Wimzicals, Wiggwogg children, and a red-haired boy with a black bird living on his head. Perfect, thought Imalima. If ever there was a military force destined for a chapter in the great history book of Aeiea, this most certainly *wasn't* it.

"Ready, soldiers?" Imalima asked, uninterested in an answer. "OK . . . forward . . . go," he said in a voice that attempted some degree of confidence.

Carter stifled a smile. He looked directly at Imalima and what he saw was an obviously deformed goat-like animal whose electrical mind connectors were either faulty, installed incorrectly, or, through lack of use, gummed up with sludge. He was briefly willing to follow Imalima's orders, but only up to a point. Too much was at stake. In everyone's best interest, the creature from Wimzi needed to be kept on a short leash. At the first sign of problems initiated by Imalima, his abbreviated role of leadership would come screeching to an abrupt halt.

The beach was eerily quiet. The small ragtag army of invaders readied and stowed their gear. Within minutes, two single columns were following Imalima, whose head was buried deep in his map. They walked along a narrow spine of rock that was moderately steep on both sides. The path connected to the trail used earlier by The Grinder and his soldiers.

The Grinder and his aides were just entering the castle's grounds while the Elite Guard was preoccupied with Arni and the sea serpents. The trail was empty of Gootz. Near the top of the bluff, the trail split. One path led toward, and the other away from, Bludenbonz Castle.

The scenery gradually transformed from hard gray to a soft green, from rock to a textured carpet of rain-swollen hills. It was now approaching midday, and the effects of invisibility were wearing off. Serene was growing increasingly uncomfortable with their wide open exposure that could provide the perfect setting for an enemy ambush. Her concerns were justified.

Carter and the Wiggwoggs had last eaten the day before, and that had only been a light breakfast at sea. Serene's stomach complained noisily of neglect. In grumbling sympathy, Carter's stomach responded.

"General, sir," said Carter, playing along with the charade while walking directly behind and therefore facing Imalima. "Do you think we might stop shortly for some lunch? We are really quite hungry as we haven't eaten in quite some time." Carter snapped off a crisp salute to Imalima, who appeared to be thoroughly enjoying the privilege of rank.

"What'sa matter, son?" drawled Imalima. His weak impersonation of a western film actor caused memories of Carter's second meeting with Imalima at the creature's bus stop to come flooding back. "Can't handle a little discomfort? Next thing ya know you'll want a half-hour coffee break with assorted pastries. Where does it end, pilgrim? Before ya know it, you'll be wanting to organize and form a union."

Imalima had pushed too far. First what began as a small amount of low-volume grousing from a few Wiggwoggs grew into a storm of protests. Some angrily threw their backpacks to the ground.

At best, Imalima had been walking a thin line of authority. Now, the continuation of his leadership was at risk. Smelling mutiny, Imalima took a step back from the brink. Clearing his throat, he said, "At ease, troops. I have decided this is a perfect place to break for lunch. Those few still wearing a backpack can remove them. Those not wearing a backpack don't have to remove them."

"Thank you, General Imalima," Carter said, working hard to hold a straight face.

Carter felt Serene's eyes on him. Her expression was serious and at the same time distant.

"What are you thinking? You're looking at me so strangely."

"Sorry, Carter. I am thinking our time together may shortly be coming to a transition. I don't know where that comes from or how all this plays out, but when I was looking at you, I was feeling a real sense of change."

Serene's words felt deeply disorienting and uncomfortable to Carter. Like a punch to the stomach, they forced the energy right out of him.

"I sure don't like the way that sounds," Carter said, his tight voice betraying his unease with her words. "My future is uncertain enough, and now what you're saying makes me feel really nervous."

"There is nothing to fear. The perfection of the Universe is at work," Serene replied, trying to reassure her friend. "What I am saying here is, it seems like we are much closer to that side than this," she continued. "My sense is the Circle of Power knows we are coming. This is absolutely no assurance of our eventual success. If we are fortunate enough to regain that which we were sworn to protect, it will not come easily. The Gootz have created a partnership with the evil forces of power and will not let the medallion go without a fight. The temptation to control and hoard is the dark side of the Circle of Power. This is what the Gootz are all about. Power in the wrong hands has the ability to create great suffering. There is also the other side that projects light. This is the gift of natural abundance. What I mean by natural abundance is bounty without the necessity of form or material value."

Carter looked at his friend with an expression of confusion, but it was not unusual for Serene to talk in riddles. "I think you lost me," he said.

"Well, let me see if I can make it simple. Stuff has form. A new toy, for example, has form. Love, gratitude, and inner peace are examples of bounty without form or material value. Get it? To experience the feeling of infinite bliss, you must open your heart to the innocence and awe of the Universe in its natural state of perfection. It is what we Wiggwoggs refer to as achieving harmony with natural abundance.

"If we are successful in our mission, it is this gift of abundance we want to share with all. We must remain ever vigilant to try and contain the dark side of the Circle of Power, for as long as there is one side, there is always the other. Does any of this make sense to you, Carter?"

"I guess. I really haven't given the subject much thought. Where I come from, knowledge gets you good grades in school. With good grades, you can someday go to a university where you get more knowledge. As I think about it, there seems to be a connection between knowledge and power.

"In my world," he continued, "most measure a successful life based on a scale of personal wealth. What I mean is, how much money and stuff you have managed to collect over the course of your life. Now that I think about it, that doesn't make a lot of sense. I mean, the more stuff people have, the more they want. Then they live in fear and worry someone will steal it or that they will somehow lose it.

"Living with you, Serene, and the other Wiggwoggs has been a great lesson for me about how to live with different values; how to be a trusted friend and at the same time be OK with who I am. I can see how power can be used for good purposes and also how it can be terrible in the wrong hands. Thank you, Serene, for your friendship."

Carter reached out to shake Serene's hand.

Taking Carter's hand, Serene in a surprise move pulled him toward her in what was, for the boy from Earth, a most disorienting and awkward embrace.

Chapter 18
Waiter, There's a Fly in My Soup

Imalima was vigorously ringing the bell tethered to the end of his spiraled nose bone. "I guess that means lunch break is over," Carter said.

"Fall into formation! Double-time, you slobs!" shouted Imalima in an attempt to give the impression of authority. "We are about to move out."

He stood on his hind legs glaring his disappointment at his troops while moving among the Wiggwoggs and Wimzicals who were not snapping to his command. Every now and then he stopped and wheeled around, his serious face just inches from another Wimzical's face who always just happened to be smaller than him.

"What do you think?" Carter asked Serene.

"Could be our little friend is losing it," Serene whispered.

"Seems to me first you must have it in order to lose it," laughed Carter.

With lunch still heavy in their stomachs, the adventurers were once again on the move. The pace of their march quickened with Imalima in the lead position. Continuing their brisk advance for most of the rest of the day, the beginnings of an unhappy grumble amongst the ranks began to take shape. A hot, muggy stillness had settled over the would-be heroes, and their clothing was soaked through with perspiration. Herkifer stumbled, tripping over a downed branch as he struggled with exhaustion. The others were not in much better shape.

And then it happened.

Without warning as they rounded a bend, the two banks that ran parallel to each other on both sides of the trail and each less than fifty yards from the surprised hikers, rose up. Steel weapons blindingly reflected the piercing glare of the sister suns, Suva and Ahneese. The seekers of the Circle were greatly outnumbered. A well-armed company of Gootz soldiers lying quietly in anticipation of ambush now came screaming, red eyes wild, down the hills toward Carter, the Wiggwoggs, and the Wimzicals. The outnumbered invaders stood frozen in place where on this day there was sure to be a massacre.

To everyone's surprise, it was Imalima who first swung into action.

"Fly!" he commanded loudly. "Fly!" Imalima was standing on his hindmost legs frantically flapping his other legs as if they were wings.

Without knowing what Imalima was up to and with no better plan of their own, the others followed the activity of the Wimzical and feverishly flapped their own arms or legs or whatever limbs they had.

Nevermore had no problem with Imalima's order and took off immediately from Carter's head. The others were not having near the success of the small black bird. The murderous Gootz were quickly closing in.

With the enemy almost upon them, a single fly, which initially Carter thought was Nevermore and was almost the size of the bird, came buzzing up from behind the opposite bank. Revealing a full set of razor-sharp, silver-plated teeth, the horsefly swooped in over the band of friends and Wimzicals and headed straight toward the advancing Gootz.

Now if you recall, The Grinder, along with all Gootz, barely tolerated the bothersome flying flies that are most annoyingly attracted to their stinky body odor. They preferred their flies deceased and de-winged. The Gootz consumed huge quantities either as a deep-fried finger snack or mashed into a paste to be spread on a cracker. Their favorite, however, was flies boiled up in a spicy, flavorful soup.

Of course, this doesn't sit well with the large toads just across the sea. In Wimzi, where the filthy flitterers are the toads' main source of protein, flies had become in short supply thanks to the Gootz's gastronomical fondness for the dirty delicacy.

But this particular horsefly was not your ordinary run of the mill fly. Quite the contrary. Oh yes, this beastie was big and nasty. He was like the Clydesdale of horseflies. And he had friends, lots of friends, who swarmed up and over the bank to join their leader in a gluttonous attack of revenge. They charged into the company of Gootz soldiers in a vengeful fury.

Swords were swung furiously to ward off the carnivorous insects. Unfortunately for the Gootz, most blades missed their intended targets, coming to rest in the body of a fellow soldier, or simply cleaving off an important body part.

"Sorry," said a beleaguered soldier, looking down at the ground into the surprised eyes of a comrade whose head he had just lopped off. He was confused . . . unsure whether he should be apologizing to the head or the body that had slumped over but still remained standing. The apology, as thoughtful as it was, didn't matter much. In another moment, the voracious flies had discovered the dead Gootz. After polishing him off, the flies eyed his slayer before going to work systematically removing the poor apologetic soldier's skin.

As you might imagine, at this moment the Gootz were experiencing a good deal of horror and pain. It was quite the mess. Hard to know who was the more fortunate—a Gootz that had been hacked to death or one simply eaten alive by the horseflies.

Carter's eyes were frozen big as a Minnininni's Frisbee. In spite of the hysteria surrounding him, there was very little actual bloodshed. The small amount of Gootz blood seeping into the ground was the color of pumpkin juice. When it was over, a great assortment of body parts lay strewn about like so much driftwood washed onto a beach.

Imalima had saved the day—or at least the moment—though the circumstances of his successful defense against the Gootz attack were a bit suspect.

Shaken, the adventurers, who just moments ago had been ambushed by the Gootz, sat huddled closely together quietly considering their recent brush with death.

"Fly?" questioned a skeptical Carter, looking directly into Imalima's eyes. "It isn't that I'm not grateful. I am grateful, indeed, most grateful. But were killer flies really what you had in mind?"

Imalima stared back at Carter with a look of disdain.

"Do you question my tactics, pilgrim?" It was the cowboy character again, back for an encore performance. "Where I come from, a soldier who questions his commanding officer is not given the opportunity to do it twice." His bushy right eyebrow was raised an inch for theatrical effect. A piece of straw dangled loosely from his mouth. Imalima tilted his head while squinting an eye shut in a failed attempt to convince his audience of his acting talent. He slowly reached for his six-shooter holstered at his side. Of course there was no six-shooter or, for that matter, a holster. Imalima glanced down at his side with an expression of surprise and disappointment.

"Darn thing must have come undone in the heat of battle."

Fruitcake, came word from Nevermore who had returned to his nest. *This guy's noodles were obviously left boiling too long.* At the same time, Nevermore was relieved that Carter was safe and, as hard as it was to admit, grudgingly grateful to the creature from Wimzi.

"Time's a wastin'," Imalima drawled, wiping nonexistent tobacco juice from the corners of his mouth with his most convenient leg. "Let's mount up and head out." He pointed down the trail to where it narrowed before disappearing into a dark thicket of thorn bush.

Almost immediately upon entering the thorn forest, Serene and company came to the realization they were lost. "Didn't we just pass here?" asked Abogamento, barely into the forest.

"Ouch, that really hurt," Lohden cried out. A trickle of blood slid from just above his elbow down his forearm. Lyke, Retann, and Iat came over to Lohden to see the extent of his wound and to give first aid.

"Be more careful to stay away from the edges of the trail," Serene instructed. "Those thorns look like they could do some serious damage."

It was no more than an hour of turning first this way then that before the foot soldiers came to an abrupt halt.

"Dead end," said Imalima, facing his army. "The trail just stops at a wall of thorns."

"Well, most great and wise leader," Ferbert said, "we can see that. The question is what next? We passed several intersections that you chose to ignore. I thought you knew where you were going."

"Someone has fiddled with this path. I know the way to the center of this maze and the castle."

"Well, let us not debate the worthiness of your navigational skills," Serene said, coming to Imalima's defense. "I was not aware you had ever been on Athulian before."

"I never said I had. I could have been referring to the map I shared with you earlier showing a direct route to the castle, or perhaps I have inside information."

"You make a good point," Serene acknowledged. "So you were referring to either the map you showed us or some kind of secret knowledge. Correct?"

"Incorrect."

"Well then . . . Oh, never mind," Serene said in frustration. "No doubt the Gootz guarding the castle know we are on our way. We are easy targets while we are not moving and bogged down in disagreement. It's obvious we can't go forward, and it's my guess we have stumbled into an intentionally set trap. There are probably many roads to take with all but one leading us to just another dead end. The question is how do we find the one true path to the castle?"

"How about a Ouija board?" Imalima suggested. "I think I have one in my cart. Oh," he reconsidered, "I forgot and left my cart on the beach."

"Better idea," Carter said. "How about we request the assistance of a real navigator?" Carter pointed to Nevermore, who had been sitting comfortably in his nest watching the scene unfolding below. "My friend will fly above this maze and get the lay of the land."

The suggestion was met with overwhelming approval from all except Imalima, who preferred his idea of the Ouija board and even volunteered Ferbert as the perfect one to go retrieve it from his abandoned cart on the beach.

Ferbert had a one-word response to Imalima's suggestion: "Pass."

It didn't matter much anyway as no one was giving Imalima's suggestion any serious consideration.

Always sensitive to Imalima's insecurity, Carter patted the creature on the back reassuringly. "I know in another minute you would've thought of using Nevermore as a scout, but with all of your responsibility as supreme leader, you have far bigger fish to fry."

Imalima thought for a moment about Carter's kind words. "Why would anyone want to fry a fish? It is simply not very heart healthy, you know. Poached would be a much better choice. Perhaps with a little white wine, garlic, olive oil, and a squeeze of lemon, suggests my cardiologist. That is my absolute favorite, you know. I think you meant to say I have far bigger fish to poach. I don't mean to put words in your—"

"Stop, Imalima!" shouted Serene, whose volume and tone surprised even her.

"OK, I have an idea," Imalima declared. "How about we use that little birdie on your friend's head as a scout?"

"Now you're thinking," Serene said in a much calmer voice. She began to clap her hands, and soon everyone was applauding the cross-eyed creature. Imalima took a deep and appreciative bow.

· · · · · · ·

Wiggwoggs, Wimzicals, and Carter sat without speaking in the middle of the road, waiting for Nevermore's return. Hours passed and Nevermore was gone long enough for Carter to become concerned. The thorn forest was growing darker by the minute, casting a series of unnerving shadows across their faces, and still there was no sign of Nevermore. Carter knew his little friend would not fly at night. His fearful imagination was following the day into darkness.

This time he's not coming back, Carter said to himself. *He's been captured or, worse, killed. I will never see Nevermore alive again.* Fear had infected his mind, and his body shivered at the thought of life without Nevermore.

There was nothing anyone could do but wait. They would spend the night where they sat and with first light of day begin their search for the little bird. One by one, the seekers of the Circle of Power drifted off into an uneasy sleep . . . all but Carter, who could not sleep at all.

In the total darkness, Carter had lost track of time. Was it closer to sunset or to sunrise? For that matter, what season was it? How long had he been on Aeiea? Maybe he had left his sunglasses in the Hunters Hut. Everything all at once seemed to blur and run together. How do you know if you've gone cuckoo?

Off in the distance, he heard a muted cry of pain that pulled him back from his reverie. This was not his imagination; he was sure of what he heard. Immediately the forest returned to a breathless silence. Carter reasoned that somebody behind them on the trail just had an unscheduled meeting with the wall of thorns, someone who sounded close by.

End of game, thought Carter. They were trapped. He woke Serene with his index finger to his lips and whispered what he had just heard. She sat straight up and motioned for Carter to wake the others.

"There is not a moment to lose," she said. All were now up and huddled around Serene. Imalima was not happy with his sudden loss of authority but, for the time being, went along with the evolving developments. In another moment, they could hear the Gootz who were obviously not far off and heading in their direction. Wrapped by a thorn forest, the only way out for the adventurers was back down the trail they had earlier traveled. That choice would have taken them headlong into the Gootz swords.

"Can you get the flies back?" Carter quietly asked Imalima.

"No can do," he replied. "Totally against the rules of military engagement as set forth in the Wimzical Fair Fighting Act. That would be article three, paragraph eleven in sub-section nine. I could get sentenced to hang for doing that which you request or, worse, lose my fishing license."

"Ridiculous," Carter said. "You are not even a citizen of Wimzi. What does the article say anyway?"

"Thou shall not use the same illusion twice within the same quadrant of time, unless given special, officially documented, notarized, and cauterized permission by the Grand Wimzard of Wimzi, the great Hoo-Ha himself."

"All right, Imalima, we're running out of time," Carter said. "We need to do something now. What else do you have?"

"I'm drawing a blank," Imalima responded. "I've got nothing."

"Nothing?" Carter asked.

"Nada," Imalima answered.

"Well, the way I see it," Carter said, turning to address Serene, "if we sit here and wait much longer, we're most certainly doomed. The Gootz are sure to be upon us any moment. Our other choice is to take the offense. We could surprise the Gootz by charging right into the center of their forces. Hopefully we can push them off the road and into the thorns. It's a long shot, I admit. Maybe some of us will get through. Does anyone else have a better idea? If so, better speak up now."

Serene stood alone in the center of the path, her arms stretched out perpendicular to her body. The distance between her fingertips and the wall of thorns was just a few feet on either side. Her eyes were closed, her face soft and relaxed. She mumbled something repeatedly that Carter couldn't quite make out. Deadly branches of thorns, anxious to take a bite of anyone venturing too close, leaned toward Serene as if trying to hear her words. The sharp spikes of bramble reached from each side of the trail toward each other. In a moment, the hedge had completely joined together.

In the time it would take to say, "No way, Cousin Ray," the trail they had traveled completely disappeared behind the realigned thorn wall. The adventurers now stood safely, for the moment at least, on the other side of the hedge.

· · · · · · ·

"Where can they be?" questioned Rager, a captain in The Grinder's Elite Guard and first cousin to Peggi. "I know they couldn't have been far ahead of us." His body was drenched in sweat, and his eyes narrowed as they fell upon one of his soldiers.

"You there, Gummer, how did you manage to get us lost? You were in the lead and somehow chose to take a wrong turn. Now we are upside down, turned around, and at a dead end."

Gummer was an older, more experienced soldier than most of the others. He had come to his name through possessing a dark, toothless opening under his nose. Gummer's lack of teeth was the result of the poor dental hygiene we know to be quite common among the Gootz.

"Perhaps," offered Gummer, "what we mistook for the sounds of the invaders was nothing more than the scuttle of animals in the briar, you know, like birds. If it was the invaders we heard, maybe they were disguised and hid along the briar's edge. It's possible we just passed them by."

"Yeah, right, or perhaps they simply made their escape on the backs of a flock of low-flying oomaduma," Rager mocked sarcastically, offering his own unreasonable possibility.

Ignoring the obvious insult, Gummer suggested, "I think we need to go back a ways and search the briar's edge for any sign of the enemy."

"And *I* think that you need to shut up and remember who's in charge here! I give the orders!" raged Rager. "Actually, I am beyond tired of your mewling voice. Don't you think, Gummer, there should be some small punishment for your insubordination and losing the enemy? Any suggestions?"

When none were immediately offered, Rager took matters into his own hands. The Gootz captain drew his sword and, in one swift move, ran it straight through Gummer's chest.

"Ow!" Gummer cried out while frowning at Rager. "That was really mean." Then he fell over dead.

Rager removed his sword from Gummer's lifeless body and wiped it clean on the toothless soldier's tunic before replacing it in its scabbard.

"Let that be a lesson to you, Gummer," sneered the Gootz officer. "All right, soldiers, about face. Forward, march."

Leaving the scene of the murder, Rager smiled broadly at Gummer, who did not return the favor.

"We need to go back a ways and search along the briar's edge for any sign of the enemy," Rager ordered. "Check carefully. They may be disguised."

In a moment, all the soldiers were gone, except for Gummer, of course, who had already begun to hang out with the flies.

· · · · · · ·

Not twenty feet away Carter, who was so nervous he had barely been breathing, exhaled a breath of relief. He was so close to the enemy a moment ago he could smell the rank odor of the Gootz who were now in quick retreat. After a few more moments of silence, it was Imalima who first spoke.

"Nice trick, Wiggwogg." He looked directly at Serene, who was standing at Carter's shoulder. "Now get us out of here."

Serene moved so that her back was to the newly grown hedge, once again spreading open her arms. Moments passed and nothing happened.

"Need to charge up the ol' battery?" Imalima queried. He shook his heavy head wearily. "Amateurs," he scoffed. "Step aside, Wiggwogg, and observe the master at work."

Imalima stood on his hindmost legs and positioned himself next to Serene. Smiling to the assembled audience, he gave the Wiggwogg leader a hard hip bump, causing her to stumble and nearly fall against the thorn hedge. "Sorry," said the hairy creature, who really was not sorry at all. Imalima didn't look at Serene but rather continued to face the others, still wearing his toothy grin.

It was obvious Imalima felt his short stint at leadership slipping away. The woolly Wimzical was attempting with desperate humor and some untested razzle-dazzle magic to regain his position of authority. "Pardon me," he continued, still not making eye contact with Serene. "An obvious accident. How uncharacteristically clumsy of me."

The creature tightly closed his eyes and stretched all his legs at just the right angle from his body so that he looked like a furry pinwheel. Seeming to have placed himself in some type of trance, Imalima squeezed his muscles—or what should have been muscles—tighter and tighter so that the color of his face first reddened, then darkened to a deep purple.

A high-pitched squeak escaped down a corridor and out the posterior vent of the creature's body. For the sake of the reader's sensibilities, I shall not go into further detail.

"Pardon me again." Imalima's face immediately morphed from purple back to a lovely shade of red. "Well," he stammered, "now that *is* embarrassing. I must have gotten into a bad batch of tofu."

Imalima's eyes searched the odd assortment of adventurers for a reaction. Most simply stared blankly back at him. A few held their noses and Ferbert, who was highly sensitive to odors, threw up all over his leggings and bare feet.

"All right, soldier!" Imalima yelled at Ferbert. "Do you really think that was necessary? That was insulting and rude. Drop and give me fifty push-ups."

The sick, green-faced Ferbert wiped his mouth on the sleeve of his tunic and responded, "I don't think so."

"Are you challenging me, son?" shot back Imalima.

From somewhere in the thick assembly of the travelers came a voice, "If he's not, then I am." Zebenuza pushed his way to the front of the group. The usually quiet but intense Wiggwogg glared at Imalima. "I've had it with you!" He threw his hat hard to the ground and kicked it, just missing Imalima's face. Some of the other Wiggwoggs verbally joined in on the mounting hostility.

Sensing mutiny, Imalima took a few steps backwards, his eyes wide.

The Wimzicals were noticeably upset. Imalima, although banned from their homeland, was nevertheless still a Wimzical. They felt a sense of loyalty to one of their own and felt Imalima was being disrespected. Separating themselves from the Wiggwoggs, they spoke harsh words and gestured angrily in the direction of the Wiggwoggs.

Serene saw what was happening and knew she had to do something at once. Her calming voice came up like the mellow strings of a harp. With her arms raised over her head she repeated, "Friends, friends," several times until finally there was quiet. "We should not forget why we are here and the importance of our journey. If we are to be defeated in our quest, it should not be for petty reasons of dissension and ego. Let us not forget who the enemy is and what the failure of our mission would mean for all the territories of Aeiea. Do not be distracted from the urgency of our operation. If we are unsuccessful, there will be no one behind us to challenge the Gootz. Having now been invaded, the Gootz would only further fortify their defense of Athulian and the Circle of Power. Our world would grow increasingly dark."

Serene continued. "The smell of death would be everywhere and a great cloud of despair would rain misery over all of Aeiea. We need to find our way out of here and continue our search. There really is no other choice. We must prevail. If there is a chance of success, it will have to come from all of us working in harmony, all of us working together doing our separate parts yet singing the same song."

It was so quiet you could hear a black bird burp. Serene's face was turned skyward, her eyes closed, arms outstretched from her sides. She turned ever so slowly in a circle. "Come to me," she whispered over and over, her lips barely moving.

Time seemed to stand still. Carter shuffled the weight of his discomfort from one leg to the other. They had been very lucky to come this far on their journey, but it seemed neither the power of Serene nor the use of illusion by the Wimzicals could free them from the oppressive walled prison of the thorn maze.

Beginning as barely a noticeable breeze, the wind gathered strength out of the south from the direction of Wiggonwoggen. Flexing its muscles, the gale hurled spears of lightning across a darkening sky that filled with nature's passion. The lightning slashed through clouds that threatened those below with a storm while a shattering volley of thunder shook the ground.

Carter raised his hands to his head and cupped his ears. After all he had experienced on his incredible journey, Carter was nonetheless filled with a renewed sense of wonder and respect as one of the bolts of blinding light buried itself in the hardpan of the trail. The strike hit not five feet from where Serene stood. If Carter's eyes had not been fastened into his head, surely what happened next might have caused them to fall out.

The place on the trail next to Serene where the lightning had hit was now scorched black. From that spot, a leftover plume of smoke drifted slowly upward. As it did so, the smoke began to gather form. The process reminded Carter of a movie he had seen in a school science class. The film detailed the wondrous process of metamorphosis in the transition from caterpillar to butterfly.

On this occasion, there were neither caterpillars nor butterflies.

Out of the smoke stepped Elderwiser. The red-haired wizard stood facing Serene and spoke directly to her as if the two of them were completely alone.

"Congratulations, you have done a remarkably good job to have made it this far, yet much still remains to be done. The hour grows late and the moment of truth is close at hand. We will need all that we have, but that alone may not be enough. I call upon the great light of all that is good and just to gather from the far corners of the Universe and join us on this honorable quest."

Elderwiser's words hung motionless in the air and then were picked up by a passing breeze to be carried to a destination existing only in the minds of those with faith.

I don't imagine it's easy being a wizard. From what I have learned, the job can be quite demanding, having to constantly be on the go while flying around from here to there. Seeming exhausted, the ancient wizard sat in silence with his eyes closed and his legs neatly folded in front of him. In little time he drifted off to sleep. The others felt the weight of sleepiness heavy on their eyes as well and followed the old sage off to the land of dreams.

· · · · · · ·

How long they slept is hard to tell. Minutes, hours, maybe even days— it really doesn't matter. They most likely would have slept even longer if not for the ground that shook them awake. The deep voice of what sounded like rolling thunder rumbled toward them.

"What is it?" questioned Carter, rubbing the sleep from his eyes.

Ushi stood quickly. Cocking his head to one side he said, "They're coming."

"Who?" Carter asked anxiously.

"The Gootz, of course, and from the sound of it, there are many and they are not that far off. This time they are coming from the opposite direction of the maze."

Carter's face paled. He swallowed hard as if a crust of bread was stuck in his throat.

In a moment, all were awake and on their feet. Serene moved to Carter's side.

"I trust Elderwiser with all my heart," she said. "He has power beyond your understanding. For all time, he was entrusted with the responsibility of caretaking the Circle of Power. From the beginning of days known, he protected the treasure until the forces of greed stole it from his safekeeping. I know him as my father and as the enlightened leader of the Wiggwoggs. Watch, listen, and be ready to move quickly. The Gootz could be close, but they still will have to deal with another dead end. We may be trapped in, but they are locked out. If anyone can escape this maze, it is Elderwiser."

The wizard quickly walked the four rectangular walls of confinement. As he did so, he held his hand as close to the bramble as he dared. Finally he stopped and stood in front of the impenetrable curtain of thorns that imprisoned his integrated army. Raising an arm, he pointed at the barrier and a stream of fire shot from his finger. The barbed wall crumpled then soaked into the ground.

"Amazing," Carter said to Serene. "The melted wall was an outer wall of the maze and thanks to Elderwiser, we are now free."

Elderwiser had done more than release The Grinder's prisoners. What the adventurers could not see was that at both ends of the maze now stood in place of an entrance or an exit a new wall of thorns. No way in, no way out. The appearance of the fresh hedge that effectively sealed off the maze also sealed the fate of anyone trapped within. Specifically, that would be Rager and his company of Elite Guard as well as the reinforcements of Gootz who had entered the maze from the opposite end hoping to close the vise on the adventurers.

Carter's overworked mind wavered then steadied while adjusting to the new landscape outside the maze. At this point, a narrow overgrown trail ran parallel to the outer wall of thorns, and behind it, a thin forest acted as a backdrop.

"The Gootz may be close," Serene whispered to Carter, "but the joke is on them. They have just been dosey-doed and they are now the prisoners. The good news is we are out of the maze. The bad news is we are out of the maze."

Another of Serene's riddles, thought Carter.

Serene explained, "If we are to win back the Circle of Power, we are eventually going to have to find our way back into the maze so we can get to Thorn Castle."

"What are we going to do about that?" Carter inquired.

"I don't have an answer for you. Perhaps there is another way into the maze. I just don't know. In any event, we have to continue pressing forward."

The small army was attempting to orient themselves to their new environment. Way off in the misty distance, a tall column of rock that disappeared into a cloud stood out against a magenta backdrop.

"That could be it—Thorn Castle!" exclaimed Carter. "What now?" he anxiously asked Serene.

Overhearing the question, Elderwiser turned to the two friends.

"It is not what you see that should concern you. That which you cannot see is where the real danger awaits. Somewhere between here and the castle, death warms her hands in eager anticipation of our arrival. You do not know of the communal grave she is working so hard to prepare in our honor. The burial site lies hidden in a deep gorge beyond both the maze and the great tower of rock that stretches to touch the sky."

Carter felt a prickle of fear tingle up his spine.

"The castle crouches like a cat about to pounce," continued the wizard. "It sits atop a wide table perched on this tower you see off in the distance. It is here that I believe the Gootz are busy preparing a surprise party in our honor. Concentrate and perhaps you will be able to see in more detail the mysterious castle shimmering in the light of Suva and Ahneese."

Elderwiser's words had the effect of turning up the volume on Carter's chattering teeth. He stood by helplessly watching an aggressive invasion of goose bumps swarm his arms.

Serene, who always seemed courageous and self-assured, was having a moment of doubt herself. She did not look at Carter. Rather, as if hypnotized by what she saw, the young Wiggwogg stared straight ahead at the outline of Thorn Castle. Closing the distance between them, Carter draped his arm over her shoulder. No words were spoken or needed to be. Once again, the power of trust calmed a gathering storm that threatened all in its path.

Even Imalima was uncharacteristically silent. The other Wiggwoggs and Wimzicals had also heard Elderwiser's words and were quietly considering their meaning. If they somehow managed to survive the wrath of The Grinder's sword and were captured by his Gootz soldiers, surely they would spend the rest of their pitiful lives as slaves in the most wretched and filthy conditions. There would be no hope of escape, and misery would be their constant companion, never farther away than their shadow.

Imalima asked Carter if he could have a private word with him and so the two drifted off from the others who were resting in the shade while considering the wizard's message. With head bowed low, Imalima confided to Carter, "I'm depressed." His wispy chin hairs had become a massive tangle of burs from dragging the ground. "One day I am supreme commander of everything, then the next," for dramatic effect, Imalima drew one of his upper floppy feet across his neck, "I'm dead meat. I'm just a washed up Wimzical has-been." He widened his already large crossed eyes and blinked back a tear. "I am done, dismissed, dispatched, disrespected, distained . . . disrespected—"

You could almost hear the dry and rusty grinding wheels of Imalima's taxed brain slip out of gear as he unsuccessfully searched the vast wasteland of his mind for his personal inner dictionary and more "dis" words.

"You know, you used 'disrespected' twice, Imalima."

Based on past experience, Carter should have known better and been more sensitive to how his friend would react to this bit of unnecessary information.

"Why don't you just stick your thumb in my eye and be done with it?" lamented Imalima. "Nothing like kicking your best friend and *almost business partner* when he is down. I know, I know. I am such a loser."

Now Carter felt terrible. Imalima was just being Imalima and he should have been more understanding of the insecure creature's probable reaction to the slightest hint of criticism.

"You're no loser, Imalima. You're right, I did not need to correct you on something that really doesn't matter one way or the other. I'm sorry. Will you forgive me?"

"If your bird ever shows up again, give him to me to keep, and then I will consider your request for forgiveness." Imalima squinted at Carter, waiting for a response to his offer.

"You're kidding . . . right?"

"I'm kidding . . . wrong."

Thoughts of Carter's missing friend weighed heavily on his slumped shoulders.

"There is no way under any circumstances I would consider giving Nevermore to you. Just for the sake of curiosity, exactly what would you do with him if I did?"

"I would do right by him and sell the little fella to the circus where he would have a proper and safe home. I hear there is big money in sideshow attractions. Why, he could comfortably move into the Bearded Lady's beard and live the high life with all the premium birdseed he could possibly eat." Clearing his throat, the Wimzical continued. "Because I have strong business ethics, I could perhaps be convinced to offer you a small commission—very small, of course. You could visit him on weekends, if he isn't working. Whata ya say???"

"Nevermore is not for sale, not now, not ever! Do you understand? I can't believe just a moment ago I was feeling sorry for you. I should have known better."

"OK, just forget what I said about your bird. Let's get back to the good part where you were feeling badly for me. I believe you were begging my forgiveness and about to heap praise upon me. I really liked that part."

"Well, I was going to tell you that you had done a really good job in getting us this far. You called in the flies and saved us from the Gootz. You deserve a lot of credit for that. There is no shame in your leadership."

"Do you mean it?" Imalima straightened his back and lifted his large head.

"Of course I mean it," Carter reassured. "Why, without you, we might still be standing on Bludenbonz Beach scratching our heads and wondering what to do next. Worse than that, the Gootz might have captured us, cut us up into small pieces, and fed us to the fish."

Carter thought that was enough praise. If he continued, who knows, Imalima might seriously consider an attempt to reestablish his leadership and that, reasoned Carter, would undoubtedly not be a good thing.

"Nevermore is back!" shouted Lohden, who was farther up the trail with the others.

As if on cue hearing his name, Nevermore appeared, coming over the hill toward them. He wasn't flying, but was walking slowly and with an obvious limp. Elderwiser, who was closest and second to see him, went to the small bird and scooped him up into his hands.

"Where have you been, little friend, and what has happened to you?" inquired the ancient Wiggwogg. The question about Nevermore's condition was barely out of his mouth when he had his answer. Nevermore was missing some claws on both his tiny feet and, worse, his wings were also gone.

Upon seeing this, Lohden, who was standing closest to Elderwiser, screamed in horror. He had a thing about blood and altered body parts.

"I do not know a spell to repair your feet nor to grow you new wings," Elderwiser said sadly staring at the broken bird. "But I do know a thing or two I could try." The wizard began speaking in a strange tongue that none of the adventurers could understand. After a few moments with nothing happening, Elderwiser said, "Let's try something else." He raised the small bird up so that its beak was just an inch or two from his mouth. "Open wide," he said.

Nevermore did as told. Elderwiser inhaled deeply and blew his breath into the open beak. The little bird breathed in the powerful life spirit of the great Elderwiser of Wiggonwoggen.

After a few sputtering coughs, Nevermore asked, "Where is Carter?" He looked around, shocked that his thoughts came out as words.

"He spoke!" said a disbelieving Serene. "Did anyone else hear him? I believe Nevermore spoke."

All the adventurers were amazed. They had indeed heard him and crowded in closer so they could get a better view. Wiggwoggs and Wimzicals were milling about excitedly discussing Nevermore's newly found voice. Unbeknown to all, including Elderwiser, the wizard's magic was still at work attempting to fix the damaged bird.

"Nevermore!" Carter called out excitedly. "I'm way over here with Imalima."

Serene quickly filled Carter in on the reappearance of the injured bird.

There was a bonus to the blessing of Nevermore's ability to speak aloud, and no one was more pleased than Carter, of course, when the little bird flew with his newly restored wings and claws from Elderwiser's hands to the comfort of his familiar red nest atop the boy's head.

"I was flying just above the maze searching for an exit when the Gootz caught me with a snare, but I was brave," explained the little bird, who was so excited he now seemed unable to stop talking.

"When I wouldn't tell them where you were or give them any other information they wanted, I mean, how could I with no voice, the Gootz quickly lost patience and began to torture me. First they plucked a few feathers. When that didn't produce the results they were looking for, they cut off a couple of claws on both of my feet. Then when that didn't work either, they clipped off my wings. A little snip here, a little snip there, and they were gone. I thought surely I was going to faint, but I didn't. I don't know why, but for some reason I felt no pain. Perhaps I was in shock.

"There was a brief moment of confusion. They thought I might be a Wimzical and had some magic power since I didn't react to the pruning. I saw my opportunity, and in that instant, I attacked my torturer. I know this sounds disgusting, but instinctively I pecked out his eyes.

"The Gootz soldier wasn't nearly so brave," Nevermore continued. "Screaming in pain while slapping his hands to where his eyes had been, the soldier dropped me to the ground. Landing on my back, which knocked the wind out of me, I fought to regain what was left of my feet. Quickly hobbling toward the wall of thorns, which hurt a lot, I hid at the base of the hedge. When the Gootz finally gave up their search, I managed to make my way through the thicket, and eventually out of the maze."

"As we can all see," said Elderwiser, "size is no measure of bravery. Soon you will need all the courage you have, perhaps even more than I have the right to expect of you. That is what it will take, and that holds true for all of you who stand before me. The Grinder will not easily surrender his beloved treasure. He has never before been challenged in his own back-yard, and he probably thought by this time of day, they would be well into their victory celebration. I am sure he is angry. That might make him react illogically, which could make him even more unpredictable and dangerous.

"We know our cause is just," Elderwiser continued. "While build-ing his dark and cruel empire of gluttonous greed, The Grinder has abused the responsibility of power, using weapons of death and destruction to crush and enslave the peaceful citizens of Aeiea. This behavior is incompatible with the harmony of all that is good and the perfection of the Universe. It is an evil assault on the fundamental laws of nature and has caused an unsustainable imbalance in the natural order of all things. We shall finally put right all that The Grinder has wronged here on Aeiea."

Carter wasn't sure he had followed all that, but there was no doubt he felt a powerful energy of confidence coming from Elderwiser.

Like an anxious cat in a cage, the wizard paced back and forth in front of his unlikely army. Then pausing, he vigorously rubbed his thumb into the palm of his other hand until his thumb glowed with soft green light. He walked quickly amongst his army, gently pressing the illuminated digit onto the forehead of each. With eyes closed, his lips moved, but no words were heard. Finally, opening his eyes, the great wizard of the Wiggwoggs again spoke.

"Some of you already have the ability to become invisible, others to create illusion. You each had one of the two capabilities, but not the other. By my touch, all of you now have both. And this," he said, holding up a vial of liquid for all to see, "will set the process in motion. This includes you as well, young Carter Nicholsworth. In the days ahead, you will need both powers. But remember, those of you not from the territory of Wimzi, your use of illusion is only possible for brief periods of time. And so it is also for you Wimzicals with your borrowed use of invisibility. You may access the power only through intense conscious concentration. Use this expertise wisely, for it is temporary and has its roots in the unexplored Downunderworld. Beware. These powers have the potential to be dangerous. The possibility exists that you could become trapped in the downunder, never to see or be seen in the light again."

Not exactly the encouraging words Carter would have preferred to hear. In one moment he had been filled with increased self-assurance, only to have that moment taken from him as if it never existed. Would these special powers really help them succeed in their mission or would they be their undoing?

Elderwiser turned and began walking toward the distant castle. The adventurers followed.

It wasn't long before dusk snuck up on the hand-picked militia, and like a starved beast, night quickly devoured the day. Keeping company with the moonless night was a sad, melodic theme that rolled cold over the hills, chilling the spirit of Carter Nicholsworth. Heavy with a quality of profound sorrow, the haunting music, ushered in by a fickle wind, whistled through the skinless bones of dead trees whose bark had been stripped bare. It was not unlike a funeral dirge.

Is it my funeral? Carter wondered. He thought he heard the sound of a woman way off in the distance, sobbing.

As was all too often the case lately, that evening there was little sleep to be had.

When morning did finally arrive, it seemed as if sister suns Suva and Ahneese had decided to sleep in. The lifeless weight of the low gray sky hung barely above the barren trees. Without prejudice, collected drops of moisture fell on the group from boughs that leaves once hid. Tears, thought Carter, remembering last night's misery. The early morning gloom seeped into the spirit of the weary travelers, who quietly went about the business of gathering and storing their gear without exchanging words. A cold meal of sweet hardcakes with lungberry jam was nourishment taken but hardly enjoyed.

Soon after, they were once again on their march toward the castle. For much of the morning the Wiggwoggs, Wimzicals, and Carter pressed ahead, their angled bodies leaning into a gale that pushed up hard against their determination. Progress was slow and only made with great effort. Already exhausted from a lack of sleep and the labors of their march, they were unaware of the many watchful eyes hidden by foliage growing along both sides of the road.

The seemingly uneventful day wore on, and with night once again approaching, Elderwiser's army stopped to make camp. The dark mood that had infected all of them earlier was much like the recent weather— unchanged. What had changed was they were now fewer in number than they had been when they set out earlier that morning. Someone or something was snatching them from the rear of their single file formation, and no one had noticed.

Serene counted the Wiggwoggs and Imalima counted the Wimzicals. When the count was in, four Wimzicals were missing.

Chapter 19
Checking Out

Elderwiser ordered everyone into a circle, appointing several, including Imalima, with the responsibility of guarding the perimeter of the camp. They would work in shifts so as not to tire and risk falling asleep. A second restless night for Carter only added to his growing anxiety.

First morning light was greeted with the panicked screams of Imalima, which instantly woke the others.

"What is it, Imalima?" Carter shouted, his trembling voice reflecting Imalima's alarm. Imalima was speaking rapidly in the ancient language of Wimzi that only some of the older Wimzicals understood. He ran back and forth several times between a rise not far from the camp's edge and the huddled group.

It was Elderwiser who first made it to the knoll. There, in a ditch just to the side of the road, lay the remains of the four missing Wimzicals. The bodies seemed to have been intentionally placed in the positions they were found, with all their heads pointing in a southwesterly direction. Two were laid out in a straight line, the second with his head to the feet of the first. The other two were positioned on each side of the first Wimzical so that their heads rested against his neck and they were situated at a forty-five-degree angle from his body.

"What does it mean, Father?"

Elderwiser looked deep into the anxious eyes of his daughter.

"It is a warning," he said. His flat voice was barely audible to his army, who leaned in toward the wizard, trying to seize his every word. "The bodies have been carefully positioned to form an arrow, and the arrow is pointing in the direction we have come from. Someone wants us to go back, and they are willing to kill so that we will have no doubt of their intent if we ignore their message."

Of course, retreat was not an option. They were well past the point of no return without so much as a glimpse of the Circle of Power or even the assurance of its location.

"I have an idea," Carter said. "To avoid being snatched one at a time, how about we take a length of rope and tie it one to another around our waists?"

"Good idea, Carter," Lohden responded, "except there is a problem. If one of us should happen to fall off a cliff, he would pull the rest with him. I think it would also limit our ability to act independently if we had to."

"Good point, Lohden," Carter replied. "What if we use Imalima at the rear position as we did when he first joined us? Running backwards will make it difficult for anyone attempting to sneak up on us again."

There was agreement from all.

The Wimzicals had their own rituals around death. After a private ceremony honoring the loss of one of their own, to which neither Carter nor the Wiggwoggs were invited, the four Wimzicals were buried.

Without a better plan, the group slogged on with Imalima bringing up the rear. The outline of the castle came slowly into focus as they went. The day wore on wearily, and as evening approached, a sweet, familiar fragrance accompanied it.

"Chocolate," said Carter aloud. His fertile young mind did a gymnastic back flip to his kitchen sink in Lake Mohegan. He was standing with a wooden stirring spoon in hand, coated thick with the last of hot chocolate pudding scraped from the cooling pot on the stovetop.

The image was forwarded to Carter's empty stomach that had been complaining noisily of neglect. They had been walking all day since an early breakfast and had not stopped to eat. He quickly realized the source of the chocolate aroma was coming from small purple berries growing in thick clusters and hanging from branches of trees lining the road. When the fallen berries peppering the road were stepped on, they emitted the sweet scent of warm chocolate. Carter wondered if the others were as hungry as he, and just as he was about to reach for a handful of those sweet-smelling berries, the march came to an abrupt halt. Dinner time, he thought.

Just up ahead, some members of the group were quickly encircling something lying at the road's edge. Pushing his way in, Carter found Elderwiser, Zebenuza, and Serene kneeling at the side of Abogamento. The young Wiggwogg was lying pale as the rising moon except for his lips that were now permanently stained purple. His body lay motionless. Fear flashed from Carter's eyes to Elderwiser's and then to the faces of the others who stood by helplessly, surrounding their friend.

"What can we do, Elderwiser?" Carter pleaded.

"There is nothing that can be done. I have heard tales of the moniferberry, not to be confused with the harmless lungberry. To my knowledge, the moniferberry tree only grows on Athulian and its deadly fruit kills in a matter of moments. There is no antidote or magic to reverse the effects of this poisonous fruit. Thankfully, death is supposedly painless. One simply goes to sleep." As the wizard finished his words, Abogamento managed a weak smile for his friends.

"You must go on," he said. "Failure of our mission will only make those who abuse power stronger."

Finishing his final words, which were spoken with difficulty, Abogamento closed his eyes for the last time and his spirit drifted off to a secret, unknown place.

For the boy from Earth, it was hard enough losing the four Wimzicals. The loss of Abogamento was far too personal, and he had nowhere to go with his grief.

Being a relative newcomer to the emotional requirements of authentic friendship, Carter Nicholsworth was unprepared for the tidal wave of emotions that washed over him. Burying his face in his hands, he sobbed until his swollen eyes ached. Carter could taste the salt that ran to his lips. He felt like sitting down where he was and not moving. Not now, not ever.

For Carter, death had always been a distant, impersonal thing, something old people did privately in a place far removed from his innocent mind. The unique relationship between himself and the Wiggwoggs had become more than he could comprehend. What he did understand was Abogamento was gone. Carter was there for his friend's last breath, and no amount of tears or magic would bring him back.

There was little consoling Carter as he sat in the company of his misery, grieving the loss of a friend. Elderwiser tried, as did Serene and the other Wiggwoggs, even Zebenuza, who all in their own ways were also trying to deal with the sorrow of a lost friend. Finally, with no more tears left to shed, Carter took a hitching breath and stood. While the loss of Abogamento had shaken him to the core, it had also grabbed hold of him and painfully dragged him toward a deeper level of awareness.

Carter thought about Lake Mohegan and Earth. He thought about his parents and the kids at school. Instead of feeling homesick, there was the sense that he was now where he belonged. Before Aeiea, he had never felt connected to anything besides Nevermore and Wickedwood. Aside from a life created by his imagination, as far as he was concerned, he had been born in the wrong place at the wrong time. Now he had friends. His life had purpose and meaning. He was beginning to internally stretch and get comfortable with himself and impermanence.

"Why, amazing as it may seem, I believe you have just gotten taller, Mr. Nicholsworth," Nevermore said, but Carter's mind had already moved on.

Standing at Serene's shoulder, Carter gazed absently into a pulsing yellow haze that enclosed the castle. He drew another deep breath, this time with more assurance. As he slowly exhaled, he also let go of his fear. He fully understood the dangers of their mission, yet until now the risks had felt impersonal and distant. He realized how close he had been to swallowing a mouthful of the poisonous moniferberries himself.

The burial ceremony for Abogamento was brief but not without emotion. His cousin, Zebenuza, took the loss of Abogamento particularly hard. But there was no time to linger. Danger had smelled their presence, and a new urgency was upon them. It was time to go.

They had to keep moving. This was no time to reconsider their mission. The forces of Athulian were gathering to defend their treasure.

"We will continue to follow the perimeter of the maze," Elderwiser said to Serene and Carter. "Danger increases as we move closer to our quest, so we must be on heightened alert."

"How do you expect to get to the castle with this impenetrable maze standing in our way?" Carter asked.

"I am not sure. I have what may be some helpful information, but it is not necessarily dependable. I want you and the others to continue to focus on a possible break in the hedge."

The seekers of the Circle of Power were as alert as they could possibly be. The castle now seemed little more than a mile or so away, its ominous presence growing in intensity with each footstep closer. It was Ushi with the instincts of a wild animal who first heard the deep bass drum beating out the staccato rhythm of a heartbeat.

As they continued their advance, the volume of the drum increased. Carter felt the vibration deep in his chest, or was that the beating of his own heart? He was confused, but one thing felt fairly certain. The drum was a signal to the Gootz, informing those in the castle to prepare for possible attack. Carter also heard the drum's throbbing, monotonous message as a warning, "turn back, turn back, turn back."

It was too late. There would be no turning back now. As they marched, the bass sound of the drum grew ever louder until finally the ground began to tremble.

The heavy thump of a drum is one thing, the threatening growl of wild beasts quite another. Ushi, who was now in the lead, abruptly held up his hand and the others quickly halted. With the slow deliberateness of a wary animal sensing danger, Ushi first scented left then right. He turned to face the group and said just one word.

"Wolves."

In spite of Ushi's warning, they continued to push forward. Without notice, the weather turned bitterly cold, biting at the exposed skin of Elderwiser's small army. When they had reached the top ledge of a ravine, they stood together shivering in a long row looking down into the valley below. There Thorn Castle stood within the maze, tall and menacing on its pedestal of stone.

From Carter's view, what made this particular castle most intriguing was that rather than having a traditional foundation, it seemed to sit precariously atop a cloud. Propping up this most unusual image, from below the cloud stood an enormous vertical column of rock growing out of the ground like an exaggerated stalagmite.

Day was done. The exhausted adventurers had a quick meal, and with the monotony of the drum in the background, they curled into their sleeping bags and fell quickly to sleep.

· · · · · · ·

Early the next morning, Elderwiser discovered one of the Wiggwoggs missing. Ushi's sleeping bag was empty and he was nowhere to be found. Also of note, the sound of the drum and baying wolves had ceased. Neither Carter and the Wiggwoggs nor the Wimzicals knew what to make of it, but they were too preoccupied with trying to find Ushi and their mission at hand to give it much thought.

"They are continuing to pick us off one by one," Carter said to Nevermore. "I don't see how we can do this without Ushi. Who will be next? How can we possibly—"

"I believe we will see Ushi again," Nevermore said. "My sense is that he is safe and has not come to harm. But I am just a bird, what do I know?"

"You are of the natural world, Nevermore, and have intuitive power. My sense is that you know a lot, but what if you're wrong? I feel so full of doubt. I'm not so much frightened as uncertain. I can feel a great transition coming, and with that . . . the possible end of my life."

"I think not. Besides, I have my own theories on life and death, but I'm just a bird, what do I know?"

"Please stop saying that you're just a bird. Anyway, I hope you're right."

"Are you afraid to die?" Nevermore gently asked.

". . . Well . . . I like life. I don't know that I fear death, but I'm uncomfortable with uncertainty. When I'm reading a book I really enjoy, I never want it to end. When it eventually does, I feel a sense of loss. All the characters I have come to know are gone with the final closing of the book."

"Actually . . . not gone," said Nevermore. "Those characters are simply waiting patiently for the next reader to come along and open the book. And what do you mean you are uncomfortable with uncertainty? What could be more uncertain than where we are, where we are going, and what lies beyond? I see you as far more brave than you give yourself credit for—how would you like to see the world as I do?" Nevermore asked, sliding into an unrelated topic.

"You mean how would I like to experience nature as you do? Hear what you hear and see what you see?"

"Exactly."

"Well, I should think that would be most interesting."

Turning his attention from his conversation with Nevermore to the ground, Carter distinctly heard a small twig snap beneath his foot. A strange calm settled over his mind. For a moment he stood staring at the magnified textures embossed on the bark of the broken twig. Just a short distance away, a platoon of ants struggled to carry a leaf many times their size into a hole at the base of a tree. Looking up from the action on the ground, he gazed out across the valley. Carter saw not only the outline of the castle balanced on a cloud, but a window high up where someone or something was moving back and forth in front of it.

"My eyes!" he shouted.

A wayward fly flew into Carter's slack mouth and, recognizing its navigational error, reversed course, making a hasty retreat. Returning his attention to the castle, Carter realized his vision was intensified beyond human capability. He could see what Nevermore could see, and he was in wonder at the breadth of all that filled his senses.

From where he stood, Carter could easily see the details of the castle. It didn't appear particularly impressive to him. There was no elaborate ornamentation or flags. The structure was obviously built in a simple, straightforward manner as a fortress with the intent to protect whatever treasure lay hidden inside.

At the castle's base, a ribbon of blue water reflected a timeless dance off the ramparts of the white fortress. Centered on the front wall was a raised drawbridge behind two pikes sticking from the ground and adorned with the heads of two unfortunates, who had obviously fallen into disfavor with those occupying the castle. The grotesque heads provided an unwelcoming greeting to all uninvited visitors.

Under a small circular tiled roof was a short tower sitting astride the castle's outer wall with its single window that Carter had already spotted. With the exception of this one small opening, there were no other windows he could see. Also, he noticed a lack of any activity along the entire length of the defensive battlements. The notched wall, after turning the corners at both ends of the fortification, died into the structure's shadows.

"How strange," Carter said to Nevermore. "I would have expected a lot more activity from the Gootz knowing that we can't be far off."

No matter what happens, Carter reminded himself, *I am trying to do something important here that, if successful, would be for the greater good of many. Few take that challenge in life, and I am grateful for this opportunity.*

That unselfish thought gave Carter a sense of confidence he had never previously experienced. It seemed an eternity since last he had felt relaxed, yet here he was, smiling as if he knew something amusing that no one else did. Something was happening to him that he couldn't explain.

Serene, who was searching a short distance ahead of Carter, felt a wave of energy from just behind her. She turned and immediately saw Carter's body softly outlined by light. She looked at the broad smile highlighting his face, then into his eyes.

In that sacred space, Serene thought she had never seen anything quite as beautiful in all her life. Hesitating for a moment, then closing the gap between them, she slowly put her arms around him. Carter remembered his confused feelings when last time he was hugged by Serene. This time he felt more at ease. Her touch, at first, was barely noticeable, but soon she was holding him close to her. Serene rested her head in the curve of his neck.

"I don't remember you being taller than me. I think you are growing, Carter. Yes, in many ways, I believe you are growing." Serene's soft voice was barely a whisper in his ear.

Placing his hands on Serene's shoulders, Carter gently pulled away. They stood there in perfect silence gazing into each other's eyes, and for a moment in the lives of Carter and Serene, time stood still.

Elderwiser came between them, and Carter blushed. Locking one of each of their arms separately into his own, he steered them in the direction of the others who were in the process of breaking camp, unaware of Carter and Serene's personal moment.

Soon, they were once again marching in the direction of the castle.

"We must move more quickly now," said the wizard who had taken the lead, "or we will—"

Elderwiser's words were interrupted by the sound of a dull thud, much the same sound you would hear if you took your open hand and thumped a ripe watermelon.

Herkifer, who had been walking at the heels of Elderwiser while talking to his good friend Iat next to him, also stopped in mid-sentence. He turned to look over his shoulder to see the feathered end of an arrow, probably meant for Elderwiser, sticking from the center of his back. His head dropped, his chin resting on his chest. Herkifer's strong legs buckled, and he slumped to the ground. Serene ran to him and, joining Iat, sank to her knees. Iat held his friend's face between his hands.

"Oh, Herkifer, don't go!" he cried. But it was too late. Herkifer had already left.

Carter, the Wiggwoggs, and the Wimzicals had no time to grieve. A volley of arrows flew through the air barely missing them as they were gathered around Herkifer's body. They had no choice but to leave. That was so hard for Iat. He bent and placed his lips to Herkifer's forehead. Then he stood silently for a moment, gazing down for a last look.

"Hurry," Carter said to Iat and Serene. "There is little time to spare."

Together, the three took off after the others running in the direction of the castle. Iat, who was by far the fastest, quickly disappeared into the forest. Carter and Serene ran after him. Tears blurred the vision of the daughter of Elderwiser and the going was difficult.

"This way," Carter called to her, moving deeper into the forest.

Feelings of personal responsibility for the loss of Herkifer weighted both her heart and legs. She stumbled on a tree root, falling heavily to the ground. Carter was instantly at her side, lifting her as if she were as light as a flower. She stared at him in amazement, wondering where his strength came from.

Carter looked at her wounds. Both her hands and knees were bleeding. "Serene, are you hurt badly? Can you still run?"

"Not too badly, and I think so."

"Then run as quickly as you can," he said. "We have to catch up with the others."

He placed her back down on the ground. At first Serene ran with a slight hobble, but soon she ran past her pain. She ran as if trying to distance herself from the raw, unprocessed grief of a recently lost friend. Carter tried to keep up. Urgency pushed at her so that her feet barely touched the ground. In spite of her injuries, Serene ran like the wind. Carter was moving faster than he had ever run before, but still the distance separating them grew.

Down a long, treeless bank he went. Carter could feel the sting of perspiration burning his eyes.

Deeper and darker, he thought, *deeper and darker.* The words repetitively coursed through his mind as he ran. Carter was concerned with the possibility of losing Serene. And then, that is exactly what happened. Serene had so stretched the distance between them that going around a curve in the overgrown forest, she had completely disappeared from sight. Putting on an extra burst of speed, Carter ran to the beginning of the curve where he had last seen her, but she was nowhere to be found. The others were gone as well. He stood quietly for a moment just where he was, trying to pick up any sound of his comrades.

"Too late," came a familiar voice from somewhere above him. Imalima was sitting with his multiple legs dangling in the crook of a leaning tree whose branches overhung the path.

"Where is Serene and everybody else?"

"Didn't you hear me? I said, too late. The more important question for me is what am I doing for a second time sitting in a tree? This is an especially reasonable question since I don't climb trees. I mean, if you had these flappers for feet, would you attempt to climb a tree? Besides, my acrophobia kicks in big time at anything above four feet, four inches, which coincidentally is my height when standing upright. Good thing I am no taller than I am."

"Barfsville. Pukeadocious, if you catch my drift," Imalima droned on. "Most likely at such a pungent moment, 'catching my drift' would not be much fun. I have not always been afraid of heights, just since my earliest memory. I believe I was fine before then, as far as I can remember."

"I don't have time for this, Imalima."

"Then make time! I am not in this tree by choice but rather because I have to be. Check it out, birdhead. At any moment you could wind up as the main course for dinner. If you will closely observe, we are surrounded by an army of bloated, warty beasts known in Wimzi as pufferups or toadsters. I am deathly afraid of the toadsters as well as cats. My mother told me you could get warts all over your body from coming in contact with a toadster and, worse, gagging hairballs caught in your throat if you licked a cat. Fact is you just can't trust a cat. They always tell lies and make up stories about you behind your back."

The amphibians were well camouflaged and blended easily within the layered textures of the forest. At first Carter had a hard time seeing any of them, then he noticed one that blinked an eye, then he saw another. They were as still as the large boulders some of them were sitting on. Three more appeared, and then they were everywhere. Indeed, the "warty beasts" surrounded them. Many were quite large and intimidating.

As if on cue, the assembly of toads parted. Coming toward Carter with an awkward jumping style was a large toad nearly his size. Carter recognized him at once as the mean, green, three-toed toad he had encountered at the bottom of the dry creek bed when he had first crossed over into Aeiea. The toad recognized him as well.

"Well, well, well, a deep subject, I might add," croaked the toad. "Who have we here? Didn't we figure thee for a teller of tales when first we laid eyes on thee? If I had trusted thee back then to bring wretched me, the poor starvering toad, a few skimpy flies to snack upon, then that wretched, poor, starvering toad would surely by now be one croaked Croaker. We are indeed deeply disappointed, boy, but as an astute judge of character, not really surprised."

The toad slowly swiveled his head in the direction of Imalima in the tree. He bulged his eyes and snapped out his long tongue. "Yummmmmmmm."

For informational purposes only, some of you may confuse toads with frogs. Even though they are close relatives, they are quite dissimilar creatures. Toads, for example are flatter, dry, bumpy beasts living mostly on land, and they are not equipped with the springs of cousin frog. In a beauty contest, the frog would have a distinct advantage, even if the toad was wearing lipstick.

In the case of the toads that call Wimzi home, these wartsters often grow to the size of large dogs or even larger, and as you know, they can talk. While some toads and frogs, depending on the species, can be poisonous, most are not, and if they are, they're usually not deadly.

The toads of Wimzi, however, are another case. These fellows secrete from glands atop their heads a highly toxic version of amphibian poison that can paralyze a victim's nervous system within seconds of the poison touching their skin. Once coming in contact with a Wimzi toad's sticky goo, the resulting paralysis of the soon-to-be deceased's central nervous system causes an inability for the lungs to take in oxygen. With an oxygen-deprived brain no longer able to communicate with the other assorted organs of the body, the entire symbiotic life support system comes to a grinding halt, killing the unfortunate victim within moments. Not a pretty picture.

Carter was startled at that moment to hear Elderwiser's familiar voice. When he turned, he saw the wizard and Serene standing just behind him. Elderwiser stepped between A. Croaker and Carter. The hem of his robe was draped over his left arm, and with his right hand, he shook his staff at the intimidating toad.

"Why are you on the island of Athulian, Croaker, and what are your intentions?"

The toad, recognizing the old wizard from a previous meeting, had an immediate change of attitude. "We mean no trouble, kind wizard," answered the cowering toad while avoiding the wizard's eyes and taking one hop backwards. Bet you never saw a toad do that.

"We are here for the flies, good sir," the toad said, deeply bowing. "It is a well-known fact Athulian is under siege with a plague of the delicious winged delicacies. Back home, the toads are in the middle of a drought, so we have had to branch out in search of greener pastures. Not a fly to be found anywhere in Wimzi, so, as I say, we are here for a sampling of the nasty tiny tasties." Croaker's tongue took another slow motion swipe across his rubbery lips. "Yummmmmmmmmm."

"Don't you know this is the home of the Gootz?" Serene asked. "Are you not fearful of The Grinder?"

"We know quite well where we are, and we also know the Gootz would like nothing better than to run a skewer through us then toast a few select toadies on the barbie. I am sad to report that, in truth, we are quite desperate. Look at me. I am a mere shadow of my former magnificent self."

Croaker stood to the side, revealing to the unimpressed Wiggwoggs his skimpy profile. Carter, of course, had no point of reference since prior to their first meeting at the dry creek bed he had never previously encountered a four-foot-tall talking toad.

"So, as I have now explained," the toad continued, "we have come to the party strictly for the food. Rather rude, but then again I have a reputation to protect. Might I ask what brings all of you to Athulian? I have a strong feeling your travel plans across The Great Sea Valion were not intended as a leisurely vacation cruise for a week of fun in the suns."

"Very insightful. We may need your help, Croaker," ventured the wizard. The toad blinked one eye closed then opened it. He looked suspiciously at Elderwiser.

"Help doing what?" the toad asked, haltingly putting space between each word. "We won't be involved in anything illegal. We have our principals and are completely on the up and up, aren't we, guys?" As if rehearsed and in total unison, the toads ballooned their necks and croaked their agreement.

"Liars, all of them," Serene whispered to Carter. "I would expect nothing less from a Wimzical."

"The Gootz have taken from us what is not rightfully theirs," Elderwiser said to A. Croaker. "We are here to take back to the territory of Wiggonwoggen that which long ago was entrusted to me for safekeeping. I am aware we are greatly outnumbered, but we have confidence in our just cause. We expect by this time tomorrow to have defeated the Gootz and be on our way home with our prize."

Carter scratched his head. He was without a clue as to how any of this was going to happen. At this point, trust was about the only choice he had. There simply was no other option.

"What's in it for the toads?" A. Croaker queried.

"How about enough flies to eat so you will never have to go to sleep hungry again?" Elderwiser answered.

"Yummmm," Croaker responded. "Now you have our attention. What do the toads have to do?"

· · · · · · ·

It had been hours since the drumming had ceased. Carter had been assigned to replace Elderwiser in the lead position because of his recent greatly improved vision and hearing. He could not decide if the silent drum was either a good or bad omen. In the next moment, Carter concluded he had far too much on his mind to waste time thinking about drums and pushed himself and the others ahead at a fast pace. They were making good progress when suddenly the trail vanished. All the recent rains had washed away this section of the trail that wound through the trees. The wall of thorns was still visible through the branches of light-filtering leaves.

"Follow me!" called out Carter. "We'll take a little detour and catch up with the trail on the other side of this pond."

It is possible Carter's distraction of being on the lookout for those responsible for Herkifer's death was reason for his failure to notice the freshly cut branches lying just in front of him. In full stride, Carter stepped squarely onto one of the downed limbs and promptly tumbled headfirst into a deep hole where a tight noose wrapped his ankle. Imalima, who had been walking backwards directly behind Carter, followed him into the hole, falling hard on top of him. One of Imalima's many ankles was also noosed. Retann, who was following close behind, was the next to follow his two fallen companions into the pit.

"Cozy," said Imalima, whose wet, running nose was just inches from Carter's.

"Get off me!" shouted Carter into the smiling face of Imalima.

"Get off us now," seconded Nevermore, "or I'll peck my name onto your forehead."

When several others came to the rescue, they set in motion a chain of traps, capturing most of them as well. Not Elderwiser or the toads, however. Croaker and the other toads, along with the wizard, had been bringing up the rear of the loose formation. The recently allied toads had been grumbling under their breath that there were no guarantees or a written contract ensuring Elderwiser would make good on his promise.

Carter felt a dull pain in the small of his back. Moving his hand to the area of discomfort, he removed from under him what he thought at first was a broken branch. The object turned out not to be a branch after all. Instead it was a bone, a rib bone, to be exact, much like one of his very own ribs. As his eyes adjusted to the dark, he saw more bones and that the pit they had tumbled into was more of a tunnel than a hole.

Skeletons stacked tall as a horse and in various stages of decomposition lay just a few feet from him. Feeling his last meal rising in his throat for a return visit to his mouth, he turned his head away. Carter stared into the hollowed eyes of a decaying skull, its distorted open mouth twisted in the grimace of a last painful scream.

On sheer instinct, Carter screamed back at the skull, awakening in him a long forgotten nightmare. The scream also awakened an assortment of crawly creatures that poured from the eyes, nose, and mouth of the skull. Their legs under their squirming bodies marched in a parade of precision. Some had pincher-like tails, some had stingers tightly curled up over their backs. Some had claws. Carter was frozen with fright. Over his arm and across his chest they traveled, advancing toward his head. He couldn't move.

Dead, Carter thought.

Dinner, thought the toads, happily leaping into the hole.

It's all a matter of perspective. Croaker and crew gobbled the insects until there were none left except for small leftover remains of claws and assorted other odds and ends the toads dismissed as unworthy of consumption. Following several moments of after-dinner, loud, stinky toad burps, the adventurers who had not fallen into the trap, led by Elderwiser, carefully joined the others down in the crowded hole. Carter and company now had a new sense of respect and appreciation for the toads.

"This may be it!" Elderwiser announced excitedly to his ragtag army.

"Be what, Father?" Serene asked anxiously.

"There is a good chance that this hole you have fallen into may actually be a nitravole tunnel. If it is, then it is quite possibly just one of many. I feel a cool draft coming from deep in this hole, which means air is coming from another opening. I had mentioned earlier there may be another way back into the maze and to Thorn Castle. If this is what I think it is, then we have stumbled into good fortune. The next time we see daylight, we may possibly be that much closer to the castle."

"What is a nitravole?" Carter asked the wizard.

"Later. There's no time to explain now." To no one in particular, he said, "We need light."

Carter looked around. Spotting a branch with an abandoned nest that had fallen into the hole along with him and Imalima, he asked Elderwiser, "Will this work?" The wizard nodded. Squatting in the dark, Carter struggled to light the nest on fire. Finally succeeding, he handed the torch up to Elderwiser.

"Quickly now," the wizard ordered. Off into the dark tunnel he ran, his robes flying, with Serene, Carter, and the others following closely behind.

It was not a particularly long tunnel as tunnels go, and it wasn't very much time before Carter saw a small spot of light coming from the other end of the underground passage. The illumination grew as they ran. The light turned out to be the other end of the tunnel. That was just fine with Carter, who smelled the presence of someone or something unfamiliar.

Upon exiting, Elderwiser gathered his forces into a circle. "The tunnel led us directly under the maze, and just ahead is Thorn Castle," Elderwiser said.

Carter, along with the Wiggwoggs and Wimzicals, stood looking across the large open lawn separating them from the base of the rock column. Rope ladders hung down from where the top edge of the stalagmite connected with the sky. The ladders dusted the ground while dancing gracefully to the rhythm of the wind.

Carter shaded his eyes from the glare of Suva and Ahneese. His gaze traveled the long distance from where he stood to the top of the column.

"Impossible." Carter heard his thought spoken aloud.

"Difficult," came the response from Serene standing next to him, "but not impossible."

A commotion caused them to turn in the direction of Elderwiser. Carter could hardly believe what he was seeing. The ancient wizard was actually growing, the edge of his billowing cape securely held in both hands of his extended arms. First he grew a few inches, then a few feet, and still he grew taller. Finally ending his growth spurt at a dozen feet or so, he folded his arms across his chest, completely wrapping himself in his cloak. Looking down on his small army, the ancient Wiggwogg's deep voice was heard speaking in a language unknown to Carter.

Elderwiser's eyes blazed blue as he flung open his arms. Immediately the sky began to darken. A great cloud of winged, flat-faced creatures resembling some type of rodents flew out from under his cape, filling the sky. Up they flew, tracing wide, oblique designs above their master. The creatures made several skimming passes overhead, then swooping up and over a ridgeline of trees stretching along the boundary of the valley's floor, they abruptly reversed themselves to perfectly repeat their flight pattern.

"What are those?" Carter asked in a whisper.

"Elderwiser calls them rawks," Serene answered. "I am not familiar with them and they are not from Aeiea. My father says the rawks were recently sent to him when he called out to the Universe for help."

Daylight was fast closing. The tired heroes had not advanced since Elderwiser had released the flying creatures. In tireless repetition, the membranous-winged animals circled the army below. Elderwiser watched in silence. Then, as if upon some secret cue from who knows where, the wizard pointed directly at the flyer in the lead and swept his arm up in the direction of the castle.

Changing course, the great mass of rawks swerved out of their flight pattern, their silhouetted bodies etched against a darkening sky. Up the sheer wall leading to the castle they flew, their webbed wings slicing through a tinted curtain of purple. The bat-faced creatures circled the castle then flew to a stand of trees fringing the castle. There the rawks disappeared into the dense foliage of the trees.

Carter was having a hard time holding his mind in the present. He watched the drama unfolding in front of him and it was if he were back home at the Grand Lakes movie theater in Peekskill.

Serene tugged at his sleeve. "Time to go," she said. The others had already begun to move off toward the rope ladders that hung from the intimidating tower of rock just ahead of them. Without another word and running shoulder to shoulder, the two friends raced across the dangerously exposed field toward destiny.

That night Elderwiser's army made camp at the base of the imposing stone column. Anxiously anticipating the next day, they forced down an unmemorable meal and drifted off into a shallow sleep.

They were awakened early the next morning by the impatient glare of the twin suns and, after breaking camp, began their long, silent climb up the ladders. The toads were ordered to stay behind, which the toads greatly appreciated since they were not particularly well-suited for ladder climbing.

Chapter 20
Thorn Castle

Ushi had an idea. It came upon him suddenly, and although he didn't have an opportunity to include any of the others in on it, he wasn't overly concerned. If it all worked out as he planned, he would be back by daylight before anyone discovered him missing.

Under the cover of darkness, he slipped out of camp and headed straight for Thorn Castle, running toward the drumbeats and baying wolves. The air was still and cool, filled with the sounds of creatures that worked the nightshift.

Wolves are better known for their long distance endurance rather than their breakneck speed, and so it was with Ushi. Racing through the night, the Wiggwogg's highly developed sense of smell led him into the rocky foothills behind the northernmost edge of the maze and the backside of Thorn Castle.

Picking up a familiar scent, he followed his nose to a deserted wolf's den buried under the base of a great tree at the edge of the thorn maze. On his hands and knees, he cautiously entered the empty burrow that immediately led into a dank tunnel. If his instincts were right, the tunnel would take him directly under the maze. His sense was that this was most likely just one of a network of underground passageways located in this part of Athulian.

Upon exiting the tunnel, he found himself in a very large courtyard surrounded on four sides by thorn bush. With cunning stealth, Ushi silently scouted the outer perimeter of the tall mesa that stretched up into the sky.

From a bird's eye view, the flat surface at the top of the mesa looked like a stage for a theater-in-the-round with Thorn Castle its principal prop.

Ushi observed the column was hung with a series of rope ladders, and with his animal instincts he sniffed out a hidden entranceway carved into the base of the pillar of rock. The disguised opening was concealed behind a dense thicket. Once inside, the Wiggwogg climbed a winding stairway up to an opening not too far behind the castle. Squatting in the shadows, Ushi inhaled the night air in search of the musky scent of wolves.

Of all the Wiggwoggs who had joined in on this adventure, there was no doubt that Ushi was the most independent. It was not just his wolf-like appearance that defined him but rather an intuitive animal-like perception of the natural world that made him unique from the other young Wiggwoggs. Elderwiser considered him invaluable in the quest for the Circle of Power.

· · · · · · ·

Ushi's nose led him directly to the wolves' penned enclosure behind Thorn Castle. The starving, bone-thin animals nervously paced the fenced perimeter of their prison. Cautiously from a distance, they sniffed the air, their ears pressed back against their heads and their eyes locked onto his every move. One or two excited wolves darted forward then just as quickly danced back. The largest, a muscular, silver-pelted wolf named Lapis who stood a good head taller than the others, approached, head low, hackles up. His wrinkled muzzle was pulled up and stretched tightly over sharp canine fangs that glistened in the intensity of moonlight.

Lapis growled a continuous flat note, warning of his irritation at the intruder's presence.

From somewhere long ago forgotten, Ushi recognized the wolf's instinctive behavior. He knew not to stare back into the wolf's piercing blue eyes but rather to lower his head and look away in a sign of submission. There was no way he would win in a struggle for domination with this animal, and he did not want to arouse the sleeping Gootz guard. The best he could do was try to persuade the wolf that his presence was not a threat, that he brought good news and wanted to befriend the wolves. If they would agree to his reasonable plan, he promised the large wolf food and freedom.

Lapis slowly approached the fence where he warily nosed Ushi's extended hand. The wolf's threatening posture soon began to relax, and his ears that had been lying flat and back on his head came upright. Ushi squatted directly in front of Lapis, and with the triangular head of the wolf scarcely inches from his own, Ushi blew a gentle breath from his mouth into the animal's wet nostrils. The wolf's posture abruptly changed. There was an ancient and primal recognition of Ushi, and Lapis wagged his tail. The two talked in growled whispers then Ushi stood and went toward the front of the enclosure.

"Bring your friends and meet me at the gate," he told Lapis.

Slipping past the snoring guard, Ushi silently undid the wire that locked the gate to the fenced compound. The wolves' release was based on terms Ushi had laid out and to which Lapis had agreed. More than anything, the big wolf wanted revenge for his pack's mistreatment at the hands of the Gootz. He was also very hungry.

By the time the disoriented Gootz guard, who also served as drummer, figured out what was happening, he was helpless to do anything about it. The reflexive scream never made it out of his throat. Tamu, a brindled female and mate of the alpha wolf, Lapis, moved with lightning speed. The blood-curdling sound of teeth crushing bone shattered the otherwise quiet night.

I will spare you the gory details, but hungry wolves do what hungry wolves do. Most of his drum, along with fragments of the guard's boots, his fur hat made from the skin of a cousin of Tamu, and a blood-splattered chair were about all that was left after the wolves were done with dinner.

Sated with their feast and with the drummer now digesting in their stomachs, the pack followed the big wolf and Ushi to the hidden staircase. Necessity and circumstances disclosed by Lapis had required Ushi to have a change of heart. He would not be rejoining his fellow Wiggwoggs before daylight as he had originally planned. Instead, once beyond the secret entrance to Thorn Castle and through the tunnel under the maze, Ushi, Lapis, and his pack of wolves would head off in the direction of the White Mountains that fringed the northern coast of Athulian. There were many familiar caves in these perpetually snow-capped mountains. Once in the mountains, the wolves would be safe to make their plans of revenge.

· · · · · · ·

Meanwhile, back at Thorn Castle, the trap for the invaders was laid. It was a rather simple plan, but one that Peggi was confident would work. He went over the plan with his field officers several times until he was comfortable that the strategy was understood. The Gootz were in a relaxed, good mood. They knew they ridiculously outnumbered the inexperienced, unarmed invaders. Their easy laughter spilled from the castle's lone window out across a green meadow and over the cliff's edge that encircled the castle. From there, the sounds of amusement tumbled down the taut rope ladders that strained and twisted under the collective weight of the climbers.

· · · · · · ·

A run of sweat trickled the length of Carter's spine. His tunic was soaked through, weighing him down. Zebenuza was at his heel and behind him were the twins, Ferbert and Fermond. The brothers were followed by many others who were climbing the swaying rope ladder. With each laborious step upward, Carter whispered the word "believe."

What if the ladder breaks? he thought.

"Believe," Nevermore encouraged.

What if the Gootz are hiding just out of sight, waiting for the first of us to almost reach the top before they cut all the rope ladders?

Now his active imagination was working overtime, painting a most terrifying image of his impending fall to his death.

Carter's mind was wracked with fear, and his legs trembled with exhaustion. He heard laughter coming from somewhere above. Glancing down at the large toads on the ground, who now appeared small and far below, he grew dizzy. For a disorienting moment he considered simply letting go of his grip on the ladder, but luckily the moment quickly passed.

Reaching instinctively for the next rung, Carter was surprised to find Serene's firm grip on his wrist from above. When he looked up at her, he saw her face etched in the determination necessary to help haul her friend up and over the top of the cliff.

Once on flat ground, they crouched low waiting for the others to arrive. Carter scanned the surrounding landscape that included the castle, but didn't see any movement.

"This seems strange. Where are they?" Carter wondered, looking for any signs of the Gootz. "And what possible misery do they have planned for us?"

"That's for them to know and for us to find out," said Nevermore. "I would assume we most likely will not have to wait long to have an answer to your question."

"Help the others up over the top," Serene instructed.

Elderwiser had been the first to arrive on the flat mesa. When the last remnants of the first wave had successfully navigated the sheer wall, he signaled below, and within moments the second group began scrambling up the ladders.

On orders from Elderwiser, the intrepid explorers took up positions along a wide section of the ridge. Before long the second group had joined the first on the plateau.

Standing before his eclectic army, the revered wizard of the Wiggwoggs reached into a sash at his waist and pulled from it a simple amulet. Taking the glass vial containing a purple liquid, Elderwiser raised it up above his head, then, bringing it slowly down, pressed it to his heart. The great Elderwiser's hand started to tremble and the contents began to softly glow. When he removed the wax seal, a small curl of smoke delicately rose from the amulet's opening. Taking a drop of the container's contents on a finger, he placed it to his lips. He then handed the amulet to Serene and told her to do the same then pass the vial to everyone until each had sampled its contents. There was no explanation for the purpose of this exercise, nor were there questions from the participants. They did as Elderwiser instructed.

· · · · · · ·

Peggi peered through his fancy jeweled spyglass feeling secure in his "safe house." He didn't quite know what to make of the odd flying creatures that had filled the sky the previous night, but after circling the castle several times, they seemed to have vanished. "Some kind of bat convention," he shrugged without giving it further thought.

The one window opening high on the castle wall was designed so that the view from inside looking out was unobstructed. Someone attempting to see in the window would not be able to do so because a reflective metallic curtain hung on the back wall of the viewing room.

"There they are," Peggi said, smiling, not taking his eye from the spyglass. He was speaking into a can with a thin flexible wire that ran out the window, down the castle's stone wall, and over the moat before terminating at a second can. Peggi's next in command, Troag, was holding the other end of the crude communication system to his ear. He, along with a contingent of Elite Guard, kneeled uncomfortably behind a low wall, camouflaging their hiding place just in front of the castle moat.

"It could not be sweeter," Peggi said into the open end of the can. "Sitting ducks in a shooting gallery. They don't have any armor and are not even lightly armed. Oh, if I were only capable of feeling guilty," he lamented to Troag. "I suppose I would be influenced by that emotion, then again, probably not.

"Just as The Grinder suspected—Wiggwoggs and Wimzicals. I imagine the tall one with the red hair and beard is Elderwiser. Let loose the wolves!" Peggi commanded.

Troag immediately sent a runner to release the kenneled wolves. Upon reaching the gate, the runner discovered most of a large drum, a pair of drumsticks, and scraps of clothing lying on the ground alongside an empty, bloodstained chair where a drummer once sat. He also found the gate to the pen wide open but not a wolf in sight.

· · · · · · ·

Although they could not see the Gootz, the wizard's army was all too familiar with their disgustingly foul smell. Based on information supplied by their noses, they knew those who served The Grinder couldn't be far off.

"Nasty," Carter said to Serene, fighting his urge to throw up.

Standing motionless directly in front of Thorn Castle and a contingent of The Grinder's Elite Guard were eight armored machines on wooden wheels joined like cars of a freight train. The weapons on wheels were each about twenty feet from left to right and ten feet tall. The wheels of the fighting machines were round, similar to oversized beach balls, so that the machines could travel in any direction, including downhill like a rolling barricade toward the Wiggwoggs and Wimzicals.

Cannons protruded from seven gaping holes on each war machine, aiming down at the adventurers, and one more cannon poked out from a single turret atop the far left side of each vehicle. Just above, a series of Gootz flags waved a menacing greeting to the trespassers in a stiff morning breeze. Each machine held fifty of The Grinder's well-armed soldiers.

Curving downward from the turrets on the front of each machine was a swooping staircase ending a few feet from the ground. A heavy rope connected each staircase to the rear of the vehicle in front.

"A string of elephants on parade," Carter said unconsciously.

"What's that?" questioned Serene.

"Oh nothing. I was just daydreaming."

Just then, the war machines began to roll toward Carter, the Wiggwoggs, and the Wimzicals.

· · · · · · ·

Peggi's crooked smile revealed a handful of ground-down, rotted teeth. "What are they up to?" he wondered aloud, watching Elderwiser's laughable army. All along the ridge they were pulling up brush, then stacking it in front of themselves about twenty or thirty feet from the cliff's edge. Peggi's mind went to a long ago battle in which the Gootz's enemy was so overconfident that they made one stupid tactical mistake after another. "Some are just dumb while others are even dumber," he said to himself.

The Grinder's second-in-command tried unsuccessfully to stifle a shrill giggle that slipped from his mouth. His bizarre laughter sounded like a child being unmercifully tickled. Suddenly aware of how he sounded, Peggi's smile quickly vanished. He looked around to see if any of his soldiers had reacted to his strange emotional outburst. None had, and none dared to look directly at Peggi. Instead the intimidated Gootz Elite Guard stared straight ahead stifling their own temptation to laugh.

"We won't even have to fire a shot," Peggi said to the Gootz officers sharing the view from the window of the castle's tower. "Imagine them thinking that low wall of brush is going to somehow protect them. Save your ammunition," he ordered into his end of the walkie-talkie can. "Just roll the machines toward the enemy standing behind the brush then push them over the edge of the cliff."

The Grinder's choice to lead the Elite Guard pulled a lever on a control panel just in front of him. Secured clamps that had anchored the rope ladders to the cliff opened and the ropes fell to the ground far below. "They won't need them anyway since they're taking the express elevator to the bottom," reasoned Peggi.

The Gootz commander imagined the helpless invaders forced over the edge. He swiped with the back of his hand at a tear that squeezed from the corner of his eye. Looking at his wet hand while examining the remains of his tear, he said, "What's with that? Was that from laughing so hard or am I depressed?"

Peggi had been so looking forward to the messy juiciness of war. This was going to be far too tidy. His face contorted with frustration over the bloody pleasure he was about to be denied. It just wasn't fair.

"Lousy losers!" he shouted in the direction of the ragtag intruders.

· · · · · · ·

"Slowly drag the brush back toward the cliff," Elderwiser ordered his army. He didn't want the Gootz to notice the tactical rearrangement of the barricade. "Now stand just behind the brush. I want to make sure the Gootz clearly see you."

The purple liquid would soon begin to take effect. Elderwiser's potion drawn from his amulet and shared earlier by each of them contained the supernatural chemistry of teleportation—the ability to appear to be in one place while you are actually in another. In other words, this phenomenon made it possible to be transported across the unlimited dimensions of time and space. The potion would also allow them to take the physical form of any natural object.

The war machines rumbled toward them, closing the gap.

"I don't get it," Carter said nervously to Serene. "Is this our plan, to just stand here and not try to defend ourselves? What kind of plan is that?" Serene remained silent. Carter turned his head to see the edge of the cliff just a few feet behind him. He considered running, but where to?

When he turned to look back at Serene, she had not budged. The machines continued to bear down on them. Carter could now make out the faces of Gootz soldiers staring back at him from the cannon openings on the front of the war machines. Reaching down for Serene's hand, Carter closed his eyes.

What happened next is hard to explain because it sounds so impossible.

Carter reached over to where Serene's hand should have been. Not finding it, he reopened his eyes. She was still standing next to him, but when he tried to touch her arm, his hand passed right through it. She was there, yet she wasn't. He looked up past the fast-approaching military machines, in the direction of Thorn Castle. Serene was standing with the other adventurers off to the side under the line of trees ringing the castle. Even more shocking, he was there at her side.

When he blinked, he was physically standing next to Serene and Elderwiser. All were focused on the war machines lumbering toward where he still seemed to be standing along with the unflinching Wiggwoggs and Wimzicals at the edge of the cliff. For a moment, his mind stumbled. Carter wondered, *Am I really here or am I there? How can I possibly be in two places at once? I guess since my mind appears to be here, the rest of me is probably here as well. I sure hope so.*

As luck would have it, this show was going to be a double feature. The other optical illusion, courtesy of Imalima and the Wimzicals, was a mirage to make the cliff's edge appear farther away than it actually was.

Carter, the Wiggwoggs, and the Wimzicals stood mesmerized. One after another of the great Gootz war machines, the pride of the Elite Guard and The Grinder, plowed straight through the gathered brush. With cheers from within that would soon change to screams of horror, the machines continued at full speed through the illusory images of the adventurers who were frozen in place before tumbling over the cliff's edge.

And now it was Peggi's turn to be frozen in place.

· · · · · · ·

Carter stood staring silently at the sudden inactivity all along the cliff. Did he really see what he thought he just saw? He turned to Serene, who was now standing directly behind him. The pupils of her eyes were a fluorescent sea green. Carter had never before seen anyone's eyes so intensely piercing.

"This mission you have agreed to join is like the unfolding of a flower," Serene said softly to Carter. "It is an opportunity for opening into awareness. Some flowers in full bloom stretch to touch the light of Suva and Ahneese. Others choosing to hold back are more timid, finding it less risky to keep a low profile while hiding in the shadows. These flowers are most comfortable spending their stunted lives where predictability and conformity promise the safety of an uneventful life. They are afraid to die, and so they are afraid to live.

"We Wiggwoggs believe there is no end. Energy is infinite. Its form may transition to an entirely different form, like a caterpillar to a butterfly, but energy is boundless."

Carter felt a sense of calmness. He thought about his own life on Earth and realized he had never trusted another person, not any of his peers, not any of the grown-ups, not his parents, not anyone. That's just the way it was . . . until now.

"How lucky I am to have you as a friend, Serene. I'm learning so much from you."

"Then know this. It is not power that is necessarily evil, it is the seduction of the dark side of power that enslaves minds. Power, when used for the greater good, can light the darkest night. It is really about staying present, balanced, and in alignment with the Universe. Have I lost you?"

Not waiting for an answer, Serene continued. "Let me give you an example. When you walk, you always have one foot in the future and one in the past. One foot in front, one behind, but the rest of your body, which is home to your heart, is centered between the past and the future. Your heart in its natural state is in the present. If you are not in alignment, your body may be leaning forward, pushing into the stressful uncertainty of the future.

"On the other hand, you also could be misaligned with your body's weight over your back foot, stuck in the pain of past regrets. Neither the past nor the future is a healthy place to dwell. Peace of mind can only be created in the present moment, and it is your choice whether or not you bring that peace with you into the next moment.

"Personally," Serene continued, "I believe the best thing you can be is to be in love. It really doesn't matter who you love, just that you love. The more you love, the more you are loved. If you know how to love, you know how to live. Do you know how to love?"

That was a tricky question for Carter Nicholsworth. Some emotions are rooted in words Carter had little experience with. Love, for example, as well as heartbreak and grief, were just words he had read in books and until recently had been concepts foreign to his reality.

"I have never been asked that before," Carter answered slowly while sorting through his mind for a response. "I suppose not. Perhaps in a way I love Nevermore. I don't know. I really have never thought much about it." He shifted his weight uneasily from one leg to the other with the discomfort of the subject.

"Well," offered Serene, "perhaps this is a conversation you are not yet ready to have." Backing away, she took hold of Carter's sleeve, pulling him in the direction of the others. "Hurry. We have to catch up or we will miss all the fun."

. . . .

Peggi had withdrawn what remained of his ground forces behind the fortified walls of Thorn Castle. His right hand fidgeted nervously with the ornamental handle of his sword. It was a new and uncomfortable experience for Peggi to be placed in a defensive position, one that did not come easily for the "slash and smash" commander of the Elite Guard.

"Oh, how I will make them pay for their trickery," Peggi growled, gnashing his teeth so hard that his sore, infected gums bled out the corners of his mouth.

The Gootz, in full battle armor, were positioned four deep along the castle's parapet, shielded by the solid sections of battlement that ran the length of the castle's face. The wall hid Gootz archers some thirty or so feet above the advancing adventurers. The anxious bowmen awaited a signal to shoot.

Guarding The Grinder's treasure below in the castle's bowels, a contingent of Elite Guard officers, hand-picked by The Grinder himself, were in close communication with Peggi on his simple can-and-line communication system. These soldiers were charged with the ultimate responsibility of defending the castle's keep with its priceless treasure at all costs. They had been born to this task. From early childhood, they were groomed to be the guardians of the Circle of Power, spending most of their lives in preparation for this day.

The Grinder and the bulk of his Gootz army remained at Bludenbonz to blockade the cove and ensure that no reinforcements could land on the beach. A long vertical drop from the sheer walls surrounding Athulian made Bludenbonz Beach the only feasible choice to either enter or escape from the island. At this point, it was unknown whether more invaders were on their way or what to expect with the possible involvement of Wimzi.

The last word from Peggi had not brought good news to The Grinder. The Supreme Leader of the Gootz was surprised and not the least bit amused that up to now Peggi and the forces under his command had been unsuccessful in punishing the small band of thieving misfits. "Who are they that would dare challenge my authority?" One thing he felt confident about was that no one was going to get past him and his army in an attempt to flee Athulian Island.

Elderwiser's reputation as the most highly regarded wizard in all of the territories on Aeiea had not been lost on The Grinder. Still, his inflated ego wouldn't allow him to consider the wizard a possible match for a great and all-powerful leader such as himself. After all, The Grinder reasoned, wasn't it thoughtful of him to have relieved Elderwiser long ago from the heavy burden of caretaking the Circle of Power?

Surely, after all this time of having been without the medallion, referred to affectionately by The Grinder as "my sweetness," the wizard would undoubtedly be weak and certainly not serious competition for the king of everything.

"Mirror!" he loudly demanded. A one-eyed Gootz soldier with a scar running the length of where his eye used to be down to the lobe of where the rest of his hairy ear should have been squirreled off in the direction of his leader's private tent searching for a reflecting glass.

· · · · · · ·

It is true that it had been a long time since the Circle of Power had been "liberated" (The Grinder's term) from Wiggonwoggen. For many years prior to its theft, the Circle of Power had been regarded by the Wiggwoggs as a sacred trust. Elderwiser had been chosen by The Source as its assigned caretaker. But power in and of itself is fickle and does not choose its master.

The Circle of Power's energy is indiscriminating. It serves its possessor, whomever that happens to be at that moment, in the continuous struggle between vice and virtue.

For his part, Elderwiser had profound wisdom. His heart was good and true, his words carrying the signature of his integrity. The wizard enjoyed a life lived in complete harmony with all things of a natural or mystical origin.

On the other hand, due to a severely inflamed case of self-importance, The Grinder, who presently held the Circle of Power, hadn't learned one of the basic lessons in the engagement of war: "Never underestimate your enemy." It was just such a tactical misjudgment that had now positioned Elderwiser's improbable army at the doorstep of The Grinder's stolen treasure.

· · · · · · ·

Elderwiser stopped abruptly in his tracks. His unsuspecting followers, walking closely together, bumped clumsily into those in front of them.

"They can see us," the wizard said to Serene and Carter. "We are no longer invisible to the Gootz. The potion has worn off, and if we continue our march on the castle, we will be slaughtered. For the moment at least, we are safe, barely out of range from the Gootz archers on the ramparts of Thorn Castle.

"Wait," he said, looking skyward. "Could that which I hear be what I think it is?" The Wiggwogg elder took his staff and, raising it up, pointed it directly at Suva then at Ahneese.

In the blink of an eye, time held its breath. The wind died. An oblivious cloud, minding its own business while sailing across the magenta sky, paused then hung motionless, held tightly in the grip of anticipation. For that moment on Athulian Island, and for that moment in Wimzi, and the Dwarf Forest of Sarwinnia and the Gushkin Territory, in Stanelhooven and Wiggonwoggen, in Dweeg Territory and the Esbolien Red Desert, and throughout all the territories of Aeiea . . . every living thing connected to the small planet just stopped.

Then the sister suns, Suva and Ahneese, turned off the lights.

· · · · · · ·

There is no measure to know just how long that moment of total darkness lasted. Carter couldn't see Serene's head just inches from his own. The silence was broken by the shrill cry of what sounded like a familiar bird of prey. A falcon, he thought as the image of the stealthy hunting bird formed in his mind. The screech grew louder, closer. Carter pressed his hands to his ears, but a single note pierced his mind, causing him to fall to his knees in pain. A shard of iridescent silver flashed across the darkness, moving in the direction of the castle. Many others followed.

"Nitravoles," Elderwiser said in barely a whisper.

Then someone came along and flipped the circuit breaker. The twin suns slowly began to reappear.

"Nitravoles," Elderwiser repeated, but louder this time. "I have never before seen one and am only aware of their existence through the tales of other wizards. It has been rumored that they live deep in the Downunderworld, rarely venturing out.

"Once, when I was much younger and the Esbolien Desert was a populated territory named Esbolia, I thought one night that I had seen the nitravoles. It was a ferocious storm with the skies flashing and rumbling. Later I concluded I had probably seen nothing more than an unusual cluster of lightning strikes chasing frightened birds. I was disappointed, but over the years I have on occasion wondered if perhaps one day I might not actually encounter a real nitravole. I can say for certain what we just witnessed was no lightning strike."

"Are the nitravoles good or bad?" Carter questioned.

"Wrong question," Elderwiser answered. "They are neither and both. What I have heard from wizards who claim to have special knowledge of these shy creatures is that they have been chosen to represent the combined essence of all life. As there is day and night in the cycle of time, there is also truth and deceit, love and fear. We are each all of this, including good and bad, as are the nitravoles, but there is a difference. The nitravoles have lived without light for so long in the Downunderworld that they have developed the ability to see what we cannot. I am not talking about seeing with their eyes. The nitravoles see with their intuition and with their souls.

"The story has been told how once, long ago, the nitravoles of Athulian lived a rather simple, uncomplicated life nesting in the mountainous north-facing cliffs high above The Great Sea Valion. One day, a great wildfire raged across the northern mountains of Athulian, consuming everything in its path. The nitravoles were driven from their sanctuary to seek shelter. The frightened creatures were desperate and struggled for survival. In their panic to flee the disaster, they happened upon the entrance of a cave where they pushed into its depths to escape the scorching heat. Down and down they went into the cave, not knowing where they were going, only that they finally felt safe from the fire.

"Once the temperature had finally become bearable, the nitravoles huddled together in a corner of one of the many rooms located in the dark caverns. In time, they began to move about in small groups slowly exploring the cave's multitude of passages. Tortured souls and several twisted trolls excitedly lay in wait for their arrival. At every opportunity, a group of grotesque wretches that lurked in the shadows would leap from the darkness onto the backs of unsuspecting nitravoles. The cave's small entrance was kept under constant guard, leaving little hope of escape for the dispirited refugees. Such was the ongoing miserable life experienced by the persecuted and enslaved in the Downunderworld.

"It has been told how for many years the nitravoles lived in a constant state of crippling fear until one day, in the dank depths of the Downunderworld, there was a shift in the order of how things worked. It was as if Suva and Ahneese had chosen a different path to travel on this day, and quite by accident the twin sisters stumbled into the entrance of the Downunderworld. Shards of light pierced the darkness, waking the nitravoles from their long, paralyzing stupor.

"A solitary nitravole decided this was no way to live. With long, iridescent silver feathers, the large, elegant animal stepped out from among the huddled masses. Standing directly in front of the others, he lifted and spread his wings, then slowly brought them back to his sides.

"'Is this it? Is this really the best we can do?' he asked the whimpering heaps of feathers cowering before him. 'Is it our destiny to live out our existence as slaves to our fear? I think not.'

"With those words, the silver nitravole turned and boldly walked straight up to the guard standing closest to him. With one swift move, the nitravole took him to the ground. He then proceeded to drag him up past his stunned comrades guarding an entrance to the Downunderworld and out into daylight.

"Standing over the loathsome creature, the emboldened nitravole sank its talons into its grimacing face. To everyone's surprise, a lifelike grotesque mask was torn away. All the gathered nitravoles stood dumbfounded in a circle staring down not at a monster, but into the eyes of an old and very frightened Dweeg who had long ago taken refuge in the Downunderworld to escape from the brutality of The Grinder.

"With the creature now unmasked and revealed, like awakening from a bad dream, the frightening monster behind the mask was gone.

"Irrational fear when brought to the light of truth disappears.

"Now armed with a new sense of confidence, the nitravoles returned to the caves of the Downunderworld inspired with courage. It was time to clean a very messy house. Dressed in their newly found bravery, the nitravoles drove the miserable, abusive creatures from the Downunderworld out into the light of the sister suns. Today, most previously deranged dwellers of the dark caverns have moved on, settling in the highlands located in the Dwarf Forest of Sarwinnia."

"Will the nitravoles help us against the Gootz?" Carter asked Elderwiser.

"That remains to be seen," responded the wizard. "If what I have heard is true, these animals owe no loyalty or allegiance to any territory. They are free spirits who answer to no one. There is the possibility that the Gootz are not even aware of their existence. If the nitravoles were to help us, I believe they would do so because of their opposition to those who use the weapon of fear to dominate and control. They have a personal history with the abuse of power."

· · · · · · ·

The noise of impending battle was beginning to build along the castle's ramparts. Down on the ground, chaos was having its way throughout the front lines of the invaders. Wimzicals hiding behind trees taunted the Gootz forces.

The characters from Wimzi made unfriendly gestures at the Gootz, placing their thumbs (if they had them) in their ears and wiggling an assortment of hands, hoofs, and flippers in the direction of their enemy. To further frustrate and anger the castle's defenders, the undisciplined Wimzicals blew loud, wet raspberries in the direction of the Gootz, which in Wimzi is the highest form of insult. Some of the Gootz were so outraged by the loudly jeering Wimzicals that in mad frustration to get at their enemy they leaned a bit too far out over the parapets and, before they could taste the thrill of battle, fell to their deaths.

The Gootz were as prepared for battle as they could possibly be. They were, after all, armed with the latest and finest weapons available on all of Aeiea. The Elite Guard's personal armor was a head-to-toe light suit of chain mail made of woven rings of metal, giving their bodies greater protection and flexibility in battle.

Arrows in their quivers were fashioned of a unique hardwood found only on Athulian. The yap tree that grew in dense groves and was prolific along the mountainous northern coast of the island was the source of the arrows.

The sap of the yap is highly poisonous, rendering anyone receiving even the most superficial wound from one of these arrows soon dead. Depending on body weight and heart rate, the average time remaining in the life of a yap arrow recipient is fifteen seconds.

From the standpoint of armor and weapons, the well-intended invaders of Athulian were ill-prepared to take on the Gootz. Each of the Wiggwoggs was dressed as usual in their standard tunics worn over a tucked blouse and leggings, and of course, they wore no shoes. Carter was wearing the same simple clothing he had been given by Serene while they were in Wiggonwoggen. As to weapons . . . they had none.

On the other hand, the Wimzicals were dressed as if they had broken into a theater's backstage wardrobe room. They appeared to have picked the most outrageous costumes they could possibly find. Someone must have discovered a drawer of monocles because just about every Wimzical sported one. The single glass was worn to impress, I imagine, and also gave them a personal sense of upscale nobility. Glitzy shoes of every shape and color graced a variety of feet, hooves, flippers, etc., while outlandish hats were also the rage. Everything from twisty turbans to top hats and feathers, lots and lots of feathers, festooned these bizarre fashion statements.

An eclectic circus of the absurd had gathered on the forbidden island of Athulian for a day of fun.

· · · · · · ·

Meanwhile, from the secret entrance at the rear of the castle, a small squad of advance scouts from The Grinder's Elite Guard slipped from their quarters on a fact-finding mission. What was the troop size of the enemy, how were they armed, and where exactly were their striking forces positioned? Who was their leader and how did they intend to breach the castle's wall?

Sergeant Frompish was the Gootz squad leader. Physically strong, the completely bald Gootz soldier was shaped like a refrigerator. He wore a brushy mustache that covered his upper lip and ran all the way across his face to where it appeared to hook over his ears. He told funny jokes about some of the pompous Gootz officers and was generally well-liked by his squad. Frompish was also a notorious gambler and would bet on anything at the drop of a hat.

Using his telescoping monocular, Sergeant Frompish immediately recognized a problem. The invaders were just beyond the range of the arrows being fired from behind the castle's parapets. Yap arrows were falling harmlessly to the ground—harmless to the invaders, but as the squad leader was about to discover, not so safe for his advance scouts much closer to the castle.

The whining hum of an approaching arrow and then a sound similar to "thunk" gave pause to the small party of scouts. Frompish turned to find Margoth, a squat Gootz whose long, curly hair obscured the features of his face, the disappointed recipient of the arrow.

One of the yap arrows had found its way to Margoth's neck. That was quite a feat in itself considering it had been a long time since anyone had seen Margoth's neck, buried under multiple chins and an abundance of hair. The soldier's head seemed to sit squarely atop his shoulders without benefit of any type of a supporting structure.

If you weren't curious as to what was going on below his head, you would be hard pressed to know if Margoth was coming or going. Twirling his curly locks round his fingers while fingering his fresh wound, Margoth growled in an annoyed voice, "Rrrrrats!"

"OK," Sergeant Frompish said, "who's doing the counting?"

"I'll count," came a reply from a gaunt, wormy-looking Gootz standing off in the shadows behind Frompish.

"Twenty goya on eight seconds," called out the sergeant. Goya was the currency used on Athulian.

"Thirty goya on fourteen," Little Mumza shouted. He was a rather small Gootz and the son of Big Mumza, a notorious Gootz gangster. Big Mumza had an "economic arrangement" with The Grinder. The special deal allowed Big Mumza to steal from the poor and give to the rich, which would be none other than himself and The Grinder. The sweet deal also allowed Big Mumza to secure a position in the Elite Guard for his height-challenged son.

Margoth first slipped to a squatting position then fell forward, flat on his face.

"Take his pulse," Sergeant Frompish ordered anxiously. "How much time has passed?"

"Croaked," was the cold announcement from the unidentified Gootz holding Margoth's hairy, limp wrist.

"Twelve seconds," the skinny worm said.

"I won! I won!" Little Mumza did a combination shuffle and soft shoe dance around the lifeless body of his fallen comrade. "Didn't much care for you when you were upright, Margoth," Little Mumza said to the back of Margoth's head, "but I like you a whole lot better now that you're horizontal. Pay up, Frompish!"

"I only have a hundred-goya bill," said the sergeant, producing the single bill while glancing sideways at Mumza. "It's all yours if you have change." Frompish knew Little Mumza was flat broke because Little Mumza had lost all his money to him the previous night in a game of dice.

Thunk. A second poison arrow found a home, this time in the upper thigh of Little Mumza. He looked down at the shaft of wood protruding from his leg.

"Bummer," he said in disgust, "can you believe it? I mean, can't a guy catch a break?" His eyes glazed over and he fell to his knees. Looking up at Frompish and referring to his present economic condition, Little Mumza mumbled before kicking the bucket, "I'm a bit short."

"Good one!" laughed Sergeant Frompish, looking for a response from his squad. None was forthcoming. "Don't you get it? Little Mumza, who we all know was not very tall anyway and didn't have change for my hundred-goya bill, was down on his knees and he said, he was 'a bit short.' Always the jokester, that Mumza. Ya just gotta love the little guy."

Thunk.

Yet another arrow wound its way downward, this time sticking harmlessly into the ground just inches from Sergeant Frompish's boots.

Frompish looked up at the castle's parapets and, shaking a clenched fist at the archers high above, shouted, "IMBECILES!!!" Turning to face his soldiers the frustrated squad leader announced, "Mission cancelled!"

Doing an about face, off scuttled Frompish back up to the castle along with what remained of his squad.

Chapter 21
Elderwiser's Gift

Nitravoles came from out of nowhere, swarming Thorn Castle. Flashing up and over the walls then back down through a network of inside chambers surrounding a large central courtyard they flew.

The Gootz were caught off guard, totally unprepared to defend the castle from an enemy attacking from above. The cannons along the parapets were not positioned to fire into the sky, and there was simply no time for adjustment. The castle's archers were far too slow to react as the creatures from the Downunderworld darted this way then that through the castle's complex series of halls and all along the structure's four-sided battlements.

The timing was perfect. Suva and Ahneese stared into the eyes of the Gootz, temporarily blinding them. The sister suns were at the back of the nitravoles, who were now joined by Elderwiser's rawks, the vicious, bat-faced biters with their snub noses and piranha-like teeth. These creatures, the same ones released earlier by Elderwiser from under his cloak, had been nesting in the nearby trees waiting for the battle to begin. They turned out to be vicious fighters, gathering en masse to tenaciously attack their victims.

One after another flailing Gootz soldier was carried off in the talons of teams of screeching nitravoles, while Elderwiser's fierce rawks were relentless in their assault. The Grinder's Elite Guard was being picked apart and, for the moment at least, seemed defenseless to do anything about it.

Carter watched a continuous stream of Gootz soldiers carried screaming up and out from the castle. Turning to Elderwiser he asked, "Where are they taking them?"

The old wizard cocked his head considering the question. Pulling thoughtfully at the graying hairs rooted at his chin, Elderwiser answered, "Well, if I had to guess, I would say first for a long overdue bath, then possibly to the Downunderworld for some intensive education and reprogramming. But as I said, that is just a guess.

"The Gootz may presently possess the Circle of Power," he continued, "but it is quite clear that power does not ensure wisdom, intelligence, or good hygiene. I do not have insight as to the plans of nitravoles. If what I have heard about their history of punishing the forces of evil in the Downunderworld has a shred of truth, then there will be no safe place for the Gootz to hide. From far below ground, lost in a tangle of nitravole caves, the Gootz will be cut off from their source of power.

"Eventually, for some of the more fortunate," concluded Elderwiser, "there may be the option of redemption. Discovery of virtue is always a possibility. But based on the past performance of the Gootz, I don't believe conversion will come easily."

Elderwiser paused and looked thoughtfully up at the castle's parapet, where the number of Gootz archers had been thinned to such a degree as to no longer pose a threat. With Serene and Carter directly behind him, Elderwiser motioned to his unusual collection of unarmed confederates to follow him across the castle's drawbridge that spanned the moat.

The heavy wooden plank bridge, operated by a series of wheels and pulleys from within the castle's walls, had been lowered by the Gootz in anticipation of their assault against the invaders. The agitated swarm of flesh-eating fish swimming directly below hoped to get lucky today.

Carter watched several of Thorn Castle's Elite Guard climbing over each other in a disorderly panic while attempting to escape the wrath of the nitravoles. Most Gootz soldiers, however, remained loyal to their commander, Peggi, and of course to The Grinder.

Imalima and a mishmash of other Wimzicals came up quickly from behind, surrounding Carter and the Wiggwoggs to protect them. As only they could, the rest of the Wimzicals entered the castle in grand style. It looked like a circus had come to town with a loud assortment of colorfully costumed clowns leading the parade of performers. Their monocles, outrageous hats and shoes, and of course the feathers were worn with prideful splendor. What a hoot!

Musically handicapped Wimzicals blew noisily into the mouthpieces of their kazoos. Still other patriots of Wimzi, thoroughly enjoying the bawdy native rhythms played by the kazoosters, were not bashful in participating in their premature celebration. No one loved to dance more than a Wimzical, and in this parade they saw a perfect opportunity to get down and boogie. In their dancing orgy, the Wimzicals hooked arms with surprised Gootz soldiers, swinging them around wildly until the dizzy Gootz were totally disoriented. Faster and faster they spun. Eventually, no longer able to hold onto their partners, airborne Gootz would smash against the courtyard wall, knocking themselves unconscious.

Oh, it was quite the scene, and as you would expect in the throes of hand-to-hand combat, chaos ruled. The conventional military training manual of the Gootz army failed to include a section on this type of enemy behavior. These important omissions would have to be addressed in the next printing, but at the moment, there were more pressing issues at hand for The Grinder's Elite Guard.

Peggi couldn't believe his eyes. Bedlam had broken out within the castle's confines and his side was getting the worst of it. Jumping to the top of a low wall, he tried desperately to regain order amongst the Gootz soldiers. He commanded his forces, what was left of them, to pull back to the castle keep to protect the increasingly vulnerable Circle of Power.

Far under Thorn Castle, isolated soldiers from the Elite Guard were digging in. These were the best of the best of The Grinder's military and sworn to secure the Circle of Power at all costs, including the sacrifice of their own lives. They were aware the castle walls had been breached but had little more information than that.

Peggi hobbled down into the castle's keep joined by several other retreating soldiers where they quickly disappeared into one of the many underground hallways.

· · · · · · ·

Elderwiser's white robes flowed behind him as he raced along the dimly lit hallway just ahead of Serene and Carter. Cool dank air came up to greet them as they noisily descended a narrow circular flight of stairs.

"We are close now, my friend, can you feel the Circle's energy?" Serene asked Carter, who was running alongside her.

"I don't quite know what I feel at the moment. My mind feels separate from my body."

Carter had noticed how much older he felt since first arriving on Aeiea.

Perhaps "older" was not the right word, he thought. Perhaps "more conscious" would be a better choice of words. With his growing awareness of the natural world, Carter could now hear it whisper its secrets to him. Nevermore had opened his mind to observing things from the perspective of a wild animal. Carter could see, hear, smell, and sense things not of the world he was born into.

Now what he inhaled made the hairs on the back of his neck sting. Gootz were close and getting closer. In the confined quarters under the castle, he probably didn't need a highly evolved sense of smell to scent the presence of the odorous Elite Guards.

Arriving at the bottom of the stairwell, Elderwiser saw a swaying platform over a deep gorge. Suspended by heavy rope, the swinging bridge led to yet another long set of stairs. Where the stairs ended, a diffused light at the far end of a hall drew his gaze like a moth to a flame.

"I sense we are almost there," Elderwiser called out over his shoulder.

Just then Peggi's voice filled the hallway of the underground warren. "Yes indeed you are. With all the exercise you have been getting lately, old wizard, you must be quite hungry. I must admit my surprise at your having made it this far. For a bunch of misfits, your performance to date has been quite impressive. So impressive, as a matter of fact, that as a reward for your relentless determination, I will be your host at your last lip-smacking good meal.

"SOUP'S ON, SO COME AND GET IT WHILE IT'S HOT!!!" Peggi screamed in a manic voice. His high-pitched laughter echoed through the tunnel. It was in that moment that Carter realized it wasn't just the nasty Gootz he had smelled.

Suddenly the familiar flip-flop of the multi-web-footed Imalima was heard running up from the back of the tunnel. Imalima smelled soup. No one loved soup more than Imalima. When it came to a gourmet's appetite for culinary experimentation, the Wimzical stood second to none.

"Eat or be eaten," was a rule of thumb for this creature from Wimzi. Even the rank flavor and stringy texture of a Kenga spy bird had been enjoyed by Imalima as an exotic delicacy.

From a distance, it looked to Carter like the Wimzical had borrowed a hat from one of his buddies. The hat turned out to be anything but a hat.

Standing before Carter and Serene, Imalima said, "I would like to introduce you to my friend." Rolling his crossed eyes up and to the back of his head he continued, "This here little birdie is Frenk. You may find him rather arrogant and a bit full of himself, but I like him. His official full name on his pedigree papers is Frencis Narli Stine III, which someone shortened to Frenk N. Stine and I further shortened to just plain old Frenk. Since you selfishly wouldn't let me have your bird, I got one of my own. Bet my bird could beat up your bird," Imalima said to Carter.

Sitting atop a tuft of wool on Imalima's head was a giant black horsefly with huge unblinking eyes. The fly looked menacingly at Nevermore, who shuddered. Its tattered wings seemed to have seen some serious combat action and when the horsefly smiled at Carter, there were random dark gaps between exaggerated pointy biters indicating several missing teeth. Furthermore, Frenk's teeth were silver-plated.

"Scary," commented Nevermore.

"Scary indeed," Imalima agreed. "Your bird may have an element of *cute-itude* going for it, Mr. Penniless, but mine cut his teeth on the luscious leftovers left over in the lovely landfill wastelands of Wimzi. Frenk has other qualities going for him aside from honking mega-muscles, that, as you may recall from recent experience, make up for his *cutelessness*. Why, I believe I just invented two new C words," Imalima said.

Ignoring his friend's liberties with language and the abuse of his name, Carter Nicholsworth stared at Imalima's new friend Frenk and thought the gigantic horsefly looked vaguely familiar. Although not an expert on the facial features or the care and handling of pet horseflies, teeth like those are thankfully rare and not easily forgotten.

"Did you know they're cannibals?" Imalima asked. "My 'birdie' goes absolutely nuts for Gootz fly soup. He has a rather large extended family that also shares his fondness for this delicacy. It probably has something to do with the soup's delectable *fresh-flesh* dumplings."

Carter paled and considered throwing up. Imalima, totally insensitive to the Earthling's obvious state of revulsion, continued.

"You don't want to be stingy where these 'birdies' are concerned. No siree. They have the reputation of not having a sense of humor on matters such as these. I would imagine if denied their fill of Gootz fly soup, most likely they would go directly to the source of the problem to properly redress their grievance. With the overripe stinkiness being exuded by our Gootz hosts, the 'birdies' should have no problem locating a good replacement source of protein, if you understand to what I am alluding."

Imalima stood on his hindmost legs and whispered into Carter's ear, "Frenk and his buddies are not picky eaters, soup or a simple raw Gootz burger will do just fine. Condiments not required."

Rising in the air vertically from the head of Imalima, the giant fly with its filmy blue wings hovered for a moment over the assembled group of adventurers. He was immediately joined by scores of other flies that seemed to appear from out of nowhere. With his mouth gaping, Carter looked on with amazement at the gathering storm of flies.

"Probably not a good time to be standing with your mouth wide open," observed Serene. The hungry herd of horseflies, with Imalima's recently acquired pet in the lead, headed off down the corridor in the direction of the "dinner party" and the promise of hot soup.

Needless to say, the flies were *not* the intended guests to whom Peggi had extended his personal invitation. As you may recall, the Gootz have a love/hate relationship with the bothersome flitterers—the emphasis on hate. If not for their culturally cultivated appetite for the flies, either in the preferred form of soup or simply chopped then smushed with a little garlic and olive oil onto a sesame cracker, you could leave out the love part altogether.

In the cramped dining hall just off the entrance to the castle's keep, Peggi and the Elite Guard had gathered to host the falsely publicized dinner party. The actual purpose of the proposed banquet was an ambush of the trespassers.

From the interior of the dining hall came a great disturbance of splashing and smashing. Plates of soup, glasses of wine, and assorted dining utensils flew through the air as pandemonium was having its own party.

Initially, the flies were not faring well. The angry Gootz took out their frustration on the uninvited guests for their ruined surprise dinner party. Dead flies littered the banquet tables joining the mess of broken dinnerware and spilled soup that now covered the chamber's stone floor.

"Smash the little buggers!" shouted Peggi over the din.

Imalima's "birdie," Frenk, was now even angrier than his unintended host and was anxious to demonstrate his outrage at the unwelcoming tone of Peggi's reception. Circling the dining room, he led a diving swarm of his buddies in a counterattacking maneuver onto the melon-shaped heads of the Gootz. With fly swatters they swatted but with little success. The offended flies would not be denied a hot meal and, at the moment, had little concern from which source their protein came.

Elderwiser and the adventurers advanced. The howling screams of pain coming from just beyond their sight were something awful to hear and made Carter shiver. Rounding a corner, Elderwiser's followers looked down into a large dining hall that had erupted into mayhem.

The old wizard signaled for his army to follow him past the discombobulation into a second hallway leading off the first. In little time, they arrived at the end of the hallway where they found a heavy arched wooden door with a sign:

NO ENTRANCE. FOR EMPLOYEES ONLY.

Not surprisingly, the door was locked. Elderwiser reached to a sash tied around his waist where one ornamental key hung from a ring. Carter thought it strange that he had never noticed the key before. Inserting the key into the lock, the wizard pushed against the door. The old hinges complained as, slowly, the creaking door opened.

Another stairway.

Down they went. In the next moment, Elderwiser, Serene, Carter, Nevermore, Imalima, and an assortment of other Wiggwoggs and Wimzicals found themselves standing inside what they believed was Thorn Castle's keep.

"This must be it!" Serene announced with excitement. "Somewhere in this vault lies the Circle of Power."

The chamber was a large room with a low-hanging ceiling. A great assortment of chests filled with looted treasure spilled out onto the dirt floor. The available candlelight was dim and Serene was having a difficult time getting her bearings. Glittering jewels played games with her eyes, and she tried squinting to reduce the light's glare.

There was no sign of the Circle of Power.

From the opposite side of the chamber a wide second door was flung open. Peggi, along with his remaining forces of Elite Guard who had managed to escape the flies' fury, charged into the vault, their swords drawn.

Everything now seemed to be moving in slow motion for Carter. The long-anticipated face-to-face meeting of opposing forces was finally here, and he believed the Circle of Power had to be somewhere nearby. The confusion of confrontation was reduced in his ears to the muffled sounds of the whooshing of wind and ocean waves breaking onto some far-away distant shore.

Peggi abruptly stopped, as did the guards just behind him. Hostility stood silently still and staring for a moment on both sides of the room. Elderwiser, with Serene and Carter at his side and Wiggwoggs and Wimzicals behind him, looked into the faces of the enemy. And then Peggi, swinging his sword overhead, began to slowly advance, closing the distance between them followed closely behind by the Elite Guard. The two camps were now separated by a distance of just some thirty feet.

Once again Peggi halted, this time, however, not by his own choice.

It seemed he had somehow managed to step his pegged leg into a hole in the ground and found his limb stuck. Try as he would, the leg would not come free. Many small holes, none bigger than an orange, opened on the dirt floor below the feet of the Gootz. "What kind of trick is this?" shouted Peggi at Elderwiser. It was just about then that he sensed something chewing on the tapered end of his wedged wooden leg. His leg was slowly sinking into the ground. For the first time in his life, Peggi was introduced to feelings of fear. He didn't quite know what to do with his newfound emotion.

"Help me get this thing out of the hole!" he shouted to the Gootz guard standing closest to him as he smashed his fist against the wooden peg in an attempt to free his leg.

Hearing the panic in their leader's voice, the Gootz quickly moved to his side and tried without success to pull their leader free. Like Br'er Rabbit's educational moment with the Tar Baby, it seemed the harder Peggi tried to get unstuck, the more stuck he became.

From many of the other small openings in the ground the curious white heads of nitravoles poked up to assess the situation. Then just as quickly the mysterious creatures from the Downunderworld disappeared back into the holes.

Without warning, a crack appeared at the edge of the hole that had been holding tight to Peggi's wooden leg. Quickly the crack spread from that opening to a second. The fracture then raced from one hole to another like a game of dots as Peggi and the present guardians of the Circle of Power looked on with puzzlement. The Grinder's most trusted soldier and the remnants of his Elite Guard soon found themselves standing in the center of a large circle of connected holes, staring at each other.

Abruptly, and with a great roar, the place where Peggi and the other Gootz had just been standing fell away.

The ground shook and then the floor, which was within the circle, made a terrible grinding sound before it caved in, entirely devouring Peggi along with rest of his Gootz soldiers. A large cloud of dust rose up from the sinkhole then gently floated back down into the opening. As Carter stared wide-eyed at where a moment ago the enemy had stood, the open wound immediately healed over without leaving a scar. An eerie silence now filled the vault.

"What was that about? Where did the Gootz go?"

"A one-way trip to one of the many catacombs located far below the castle and throughout the Downunderworld would be my best guess," Serene answered.

Elderwiser spread his cloaked arms and held his staff high above his head. A round jewel affixed to the top of the wizard's staff glowed garnet red.

Suddenly the chamber convulsed and then it slid from side to side like a terrifying ride in an amusement park.

"Earthquake!" Carter shouted.

Serene, fighting to keep her balance, firmly took his arm and shook her head in disagreement. "No, I don't believe so. This is something else. Watch."

Within moments, the action slowed and the ground finally began to steady. From where Peggi and the other Gootz had just moments ago been standing, the vault's floor once again opened. This time the opening was much smaller.

Like the special effect of a motorized lift rising from under a theater's stage, an opaque green glass platform rose up with a transparent crystal pyramid sitting in the center. When the platform reached knee high to Carter, it came to an abrupt stop.

"Is that it? Is that the Circle of Power?" Carter whispered to Serene.

"Watch," she reminded. "Watch and listen."

Everyone closed ranks around the raised platform for a closer look then separated, giving Elderwiser a clear path as he slowly made his way through his brave army to the pyramid. They melted back into the shadows of the vault in order to give the great wizard a private moment of reunion.

Using his staff to steady himself, the old wizard approached. With some effort, he knelt at the platform. Inside the pyramid, the golden medallion, the Circle of Power, pulsed, seeming to recognize its long-lost steward.

Elderwiser placed his hands on the pyramid and closed his eyes. Time held its breath. Then, lifting the crystal pyramid and placing it gently off to the side, the great Wizard of Wiggonwoggen took the Circle of Power into his trembling hands. As the wizard clutched the chained medallion to his heart, a single tear rolled from one eye, only to vanish into the reddish-gray curl of his beard.

Serene looked at Carter. They were standing shoulder to shoulder. It was one of those rare moments that, if you are very fortunate, you might encounter once or twice in a lifetime, a peak experience the boy from Earth was sure he would never forget.

Elderwiser stood then turned to face his unlikely army. A broad smile spread across his ancient face, and he brought the open palms of his hands together in front of his chest. "Thank you," he said to those before him, bowing his head. "You have risked everything to bring Aeiea back into harmony with the natural order of the Universe. Your commitment to this cause shall not go unnoticed."

He approached Serene, whispered something in her ear, and then held her face in his large hands as he stared intently into her eyes. It was a moment that seemed to hang in eternity. Taking a step back, the aged wizard, whose form had begun to fade, took the necklace and placed it gently over Serene's head.

"Now the treasure has finally been returned for safekeeping. I have done what needed to be done. The responsibility of stewardship for the Circle of Power I lovingly pass on to you, Serene. The transition has been made. It is now finally time for me to return home."

Carter thought Elderwiser was talking about Wiggonwogge, but that was not the case.

In an instant of ethereal transformation, like the fine dust that had risen from the collapsed floor moments ago, the Wiggwogg wizard was gone.

"What just happened?" Carter asked, confused by the wizard's disappearance. "Where did Elderwiser go?"

Serene did not respond. She stood staring for a while in silence at the empty space where her father had been standing. Finally, "Come," she said to Carter, taking his hand, "there is much yet left to be done."

Turning to face the Wiggwoggs and Wimzicals, Serene said, "We have partially achieved what we came for, but we are a long way from safe. The Grinder and his army will no doubt have heard the news. They will do all they can to recapture the medallion and punish us. We must defeat The Grinder and the Gootz. Then we must escape Athulian. Before we return to Wiggonwoggen, there is the matter of Carter Nicholsworth. He has been my trusted partner on this journey, and without him we would not be here holding the Circle of Power."

Carter was so preoccupied with the disappearance of Elderwiser that he didn't pick up on the last words of Serene. "Wait, what about Elderwiser?" Carter asked. "We need him."

"I'm afraid we will not see Elderwiser again except in our memories. His form as we knew it is gone from Aeiea forever. Do you remember him saying 'the transition has been made'? He was referring to the transferring of the golden medallion and the transformation of his physical life. He had long prepared me for this moment. I knew if we were successful in our quest for the Circle of Power what the consequences would mean for Elderwiser and me personally," Serene said.

"Everything is in constant transition, Carter. Everything is impermanent except for impermanence itself. This was one of the great lessons my father taught me. Although Elderwiser's form may be gone, his energy continues. We will safeguard the Circle of Power for as long as we are able, knowing that our overseeing of the medallion is like all things, impermanent."

"Won't you miss your father?"

"Of course I will miss his physical presence, but my father's love and spirit are an eternal light I shall forever carry within me. I am comforted with this truth. Wiggwoggs are instructed on matters such as these from a very early age. It is what we believe. An ending is only a beginning, nothing to be mourned or feared. Try to remember that."

"So much to learn," Carter said, feeling totally overwhelmed.

"My friend, you have come so far from that first day we met. Every day that passes, you grow greater in my heart." Without thought, her words had simply tumbled from her mouth. Sheepishly she lowered her eyes to the ground.

Carter took the awkward single step that separated him from Serene. He put his hands on her shoulders and, not taking his eyes from her face, gently brought her to him.

Now, with a certain degree of embarrassment, it was the emotionally uncomfortable Wiggwoggs' and Wimzicals' turn to lower their eyes.

For Carter, it was one of those tricky moments. He had finally reached a place he intuitively knew existed but had never before visited. Now upon his arrival he didn't quite know what to do in this unfamiliar situation.

Serene did.

Raising her head, she looked deeply into Carter's eyes. Observing the drama unfolding below his nest, Nevermore closed his eyes. So did Carter. Time seemed to stop, and in that rare moment, Carter would have been fine if it never started again. Serene reached up and softly brushed her lips against Carter's mouth. It wasn't much of a kiss as kisses go, and certainly didn't measure up by Hollywood standards, but for Carter . . . it was a moment profound.

· · · · · · ·

Word had reached The Grinder that Peggi was dead. Even worse news, his entire Elite Guard was destroyed as well, and the Circle of Power had been taken—he preferred the word "stolen"—from Thorn Castle's vault.

"Impossible!" he raged. "How can it be that a hodgepodge army of children and a bunch of nut jobs has defeated my Elite Guard and stolen my treasure? What kind of evil magic is at work here? Well, they still have to get off this island, and to do that they will have to go through me. Let them try. I can hardly wait."

The Grinder had the entire main force of the Gootz army at his back. He was in one of his especially foul moods, knowing the only way now to recapture the golden medallion was to outsmart the enemy. His inflated ego short-circuited his ability to understand that "outsmarting" was not an area of Gootz expertise. If he were to come up with a workable plan to keep the Circle of Power on Athulian he was going to have to control his temper, and that alone was a great enough challenge.

This was not the time for fantasizing on the exotic devices of torture he would reserve for the thieves. He had the advantage of knowing the lay of the land like the back of his hairy hand. Without doubt he had the superior forces, although recently the invaders had somehow managed to overcome the odds stacked against them in their confrontation with Peggi and the Elite Guard.

Now, he assured himself, it would be a different story. He would use his geographical advantage to lay an inescapable trap for his enemy. Not even magic or trickery would save them this time.

Chapter 22
Strange Bedfellows

"One of the last things Elderwiser said to me was that getting off the island of Athulian will likely be more difficult than getting on. The Gootz know we are here, and they know what we have," Serene said to her followers, who sat in a circle just beyond the walls of the now-vacant Thorn Castle. "Ideas, anyone?"

After a moment, Retann spoke up. "Personally I am a bit uneasy just sitting here out in the open. It seems to me the longer we stay at the castle, the more vulnerable we become. It also gives The Grinder more time to work out his plans. This place feels like a trap ready to spring. I suggest we make a plan and quickly put as much distance between ourselves and the castle as we can."

The others nodded their heads in agreement. "I think it makes sense for us to take an alternate route back to the beach and see if we can hitch a ride with Arni and the sea serpents," said his brother Lohden. "Anyone have any suggestions on another way back to The Great Sea Valion?"

Puffing himself way up to give the appearance of being larger than he actually was, Imalima stepped into the center of the circle.

"Uh-oh," Nevermore warned. "This can't be good."

For dramatic effect, Imalima walked slowly past each Wiggwogg, staring sternly into their eyes before moving on to the next. One by one he methodically went, finally stopping in front of Serene and Carter.

"Who better to get you out of this mess you have managed to get us into than me?" he asked. "Have you so quickly forgotten who led us most of the way to wherever it is we presently are?"

"Imalima does have a point," Carter said to Serene.

"Indeed I do, and if you are smart you will follow me," advised Imalima. The free-spirited Wimzical was laying his reputation as a born leader on the line. Since his good name was pretty much in shambles anyway, it wasn't that much of a risk. "My intuition is that there is a shortcut if we go up and around The Grinder's maze. Boy-with-heron-on-head, do you think you can convince your friend to do a little advance scouting for us?" Imalima asked.

"Nevermore is his name," reminded Carter.

Imalima was bad with names. Actually Imalima was bad with most things requiring the use of his mind.

"What a dumb name. What does it mean anyway? Come to think of it," said Imalima, "*Anyway* is about as good a name as *Nevermore*. How 'bout from now on we call him *Anyway*?"

"No way," Nevermore said.

"If you prefer," said Imalima. "I personally like *Anyway* a lot better than *No Way*, but it's your call."

"We're sticking with Nevermore. If you want to change a name, change your own," Carter said angrily. "I found him, I named him, and he's my bird *anyway*."

"Well, guess who woke up on the wrong side of the sleeping bag this morning? I thought you were sticking with the name Nevermore. Will you please make up your mind? Is it *Nevermore* or *Anyway*? Anyway, you are really confusing me."

"Stop, Imalima. Stop right now or I will unscrew one of your legs and bonk you over the head with it," said a severely frustrated Carter Nicholsworth.

"No need to get testy. I was merely making a suggestion. *Anyway*," said the Wimzical, slipping in a brief, smiling glance up at Nevermore, "you never answered my question. How about we use the bird as a scout?"

"I think that can be arranged," Carter replied, taking a deep breath while calming down. In a moment, following a brief conversation with Carter, Nevermore flew off to see what he could see.

One of the Wimzicals had found a secret back staircase that led down through the stone tower to the ground. That was a good thing since Peggi had ensured the rope ladders would not be an option for escape.

Descending to the bottom of the circular stairs, the adventurers discovered Croaker and the toads, earlier left behind at the base of the column, were nowhere to be seen.

"What do you suppose happened to them?" Carter asked. "Do you think the Gootz have anything to do with their disappearance?"

"I'll take that one," spoke up Imalima. "Having the inherited genetic consistency of a Wimzical myself, I have no doubt the toads can take care of themselves. There are no signs of foul play, and since the toads haven't been much help, there is not much to miss. Now, as I said or didn't say, I believe there is another way back down to the beach. We may want to consider a change of plans in order to avoid the Gootz. The little black heron should be back shortly with directions."

"His name is Nevermore," reminded Carter once again, "and he's not a heron. He doesn't look anything like one. About the only thing he has in common with a heron is a beak, feathers, wings, and claws. What's your problem, Imalima?"

"Um, excuse me," Imalima responded. "When you think of a heron, which by the way I am constantly doing, exactly what other features are there? I believe if I'm not mistaken, and I never am, you just made my point. Your friend is indeed a pedigreed heron, perhaps some type of an extinct variety or possibly a bird with birth defects. He could even be wearing a clever disguise, you know, shortening his legs and neck then dyeing his feathers black to confuse us. But let there be no doubt, a heron he is."

Carter remembered an earlier conversation with Imalima involving the creature's uncle, a dead herring, and a heron. He remembered as well the failed pursuit of logic in that surreal conversation and how it felt like a spiraling descent into the wacky world of Wimzi. Not looking forward to a return visit made Carter determine that in the best interest of time and sanity, he would not further engage in this discussion.

"Right you are again," he said, trying unsuccessfully to focus on Imalima's crossed eyes.

Unprepared to have anyone other than a fellow Wimzical agree with his peculiar line of reasoning, for once in his life, Imalima was speechless.

. . . .

Before long, Nevermore returned with exciting news. He had indeed discovered an alternate route from Thorn Castle all the way back to Bludenbonz Beach. The obscure secondary trail was a bit roundabout and would not be the shortcut Imalima had promised after all. On the other hand, it would involve going around the back of the castle as Imalima had suggested.

The alternate route allowed the travelers to avoid getting lost in the deadly hedge of thorns as well as the likelihood of stumbling into a Gootz trap. It was also reasonable to believe the Gootz would expect the burglars to use the same familiar route they originally had taken to make good their escape. At the moment of decision, everyone felt they had reason enough to modify their escape plans and instead go with Nevermore and Imalima's proposal.

Retracing their steps through the same tunnel under the maze of thorns, they stayed close together, moving quickly through the passageway and exiting at the edge of the forest.

"Time to zippity doo dah out of here," Imalima advised Serene and the others. "Since the escape route is both the bird's and my plan, with the assistance of Mr. Feathers over there lounging on the boy's head, I volunteer to lead."

Frenk the fly, who had briefly lived atop Imalima's head, had made a personal decision that he was far too independent to remain Imalima's pet. He had rejoined his fellow horseflies in search of new adventures. Imalima had enjoyed his brief experience as a pet owner, and he dearly missed Frenk.

Turning to Carter, Imalima asked, "What do you think about giving the heron a little change of prospective? I would have a significant height advantage over you if I walked forward on my hind legs. He can navigate our way off this island from atop my curly horn. How about it?"

Carter and Nevermore reluctantly agreed to Imalima's request, and it was a done deal. "OK, troops," Imalima called out to his small army. "Get ready to toddle on down the road." With Nevermore perched precariously on Imalima's ivory tower, the woolly one gave the order, "Forward . . . go!" And off they went with the Wimzical in the lead.

They moved at a fast clip, first going in the opposite direction they would eventually need to take to get back to Bludenbonz Beach. Using the outer wall of the maze as a guide, they went around the back end of the thicket. When they came once again to another corner of the maze, they turned west toward Bludenbonz Beach. Here they moved quickly along a narrow, underused path that wove through a field of wildflowers serving as a graveyard for fallen trees. The meadow stretched to the horizon, and with Carter occasionally glancing over his shoulder, Thorn Castle soon faded from sight.

Eventually the grassland surrendered to a rock quarry, most likely the source of stone used to build Thorn Castle. The loose gray stones slipped easily underfoot, making the going slow. After walking for some time through the quarry, the adventurers came upon a great bowl-shaped depression that held a collected treasure of beautiful, various-sized glass marbles . . . some considerably larger than beach balls. Under their translucent surfaces, three-dimensional rivulets of color flowed.

Imalima was anxious to explore. The energy of Suva and Ahneese poured down into the irresistible bowl of marbles. Glass reflected shafts of brilliant sunlight, causing Imalima to squint. He pulled a pair of rose-colored sunglasses from a pocket that no one knew he had and put the glasses on.

"Yowza, I love marbles! I'm going in, but just for a quickie," he announced, replacing his glasses with goggles, which he also pulled from the same pocket.

Serene took Imalima aside and advised against rushing into the pit of marbles. "Something doesn't feel quite right here. I can't put my finger on it, but . . . " She scanned the quarry for signs of her concern and found none. Sitting cross-legged atop a boulder, Serene said she needed time to think.

Imalima was growing increasingly impatient. "We don't have a lot of time," he said, shifting his weight from his right side to his left. The other Wimzicals took their cue from Imalima, whispering nervously amongst themselves. Still, no one interrupted Serene's meditation. Carter and the Wiggwoggs sat quietly where they were.

Moments passed. The silence was finally broken by the unmistaken distressed voice of Imalima.

"Help me! I'm stuck! The more I try to unstick myself, the stucker I get."

Nevermore, who had abandoned Imalima's horn, returned to his familiar nest atop Carter's head.

Against Serene's counseling, Imalima was deep into the marbles. He had somehow managed to get several webbed feet wedged under the glass spheres.

"Don't anyone move," Serene ordered, "especially you, Imalima. I don't believe your entrapment an accident. The reason for my concern came to me in my meditation. These beautiful marbles are meant to lure the unsuspecting, but unlike the quicksand in the Gagmi Swamp, they intentionally trap the curious as well as those who don't listen."

"Not a good time for lectures." Imalima's voice was beginning to sound a bit shrill. "Get me out of here!" The marbles had started to roll, very slowly at first then picking up speed. Imalima was having a hard time trying to keep from slipping under the balls of glass.

Serene did a most surprising thing. She ordered everyone back to the meadow.

"Wait," called Imalima now in a panic, "don't just leave me here!"

"Carter, collect the thickest tree limbs you and the others can find from the downed trees, then bring them here," Serene ordered. "While you're at it, try and find something strong we can use for ties. I will stay with Imalima and try to keep him calm. Hurry, we're running out of time." The urgency of her voice moved the group into action.

Shortly two piles, one of heavy limbs, the other, much smaller one of sinuous reeds that bordered the rock quarry, lay at Serene's feet.

"We need to trim up the tree limbs. Next, take a dozen or so of them and lay them out lengthwise. Lastly, lash them together using the reeds. We are building three rafts," Serene informed her followers. "They must be strong and able to carry all of us. Tie hand straps securely to the rafts' sides for us to hold on to. We just might need them."

Rafts? What are we doing building rafts when there is no water in sight? Carter wondered. *Shouldn't we be trying to get Imalima free from under the rolling marbles?* Though he was unsure of Serene's motives, he had learned to trust her wisdom even when he had no idea where her thoughts or actions might lead.

Everyone moved at great speed to get the job done, not unaware of Imalima's loud and incessant blubbering for rescue. Wiggwogg and Wimzical, in the spirit of teamwork, worked efficiently shoulder to shoulder alongside Carter. In little time, the last of the three sturdy rafts was completed.

"Done!" Carter announced. He and the others were soaked in sweat.

"Has everyone forgotten about me?" Imalima wailed from the depths of his misery. He was standing as tall as he could on his hindmost legs, but still appeared to be growing shorter by the moment as he was slowly disappearing under the marbles.

"Not hardly," Serene called back. "I want you to be prepared to get wet and then swim as if your life depended on it, because it does."

"That's not funny!"

"It was not meant to be," she responded.

The rafts were hauled to the edge of the deep basin containing millions of marbles and one panicked Imalima. Serene approached, holding her hand to the Circle of Power around her neck. She pressed it tightly against her heart.

"Please," she said, closing her eyes and appealing to The Source. "We need help." She then repeated her words several times. Serene had faith that her father's recent entrustment of the Circle of Power and her commitment to protect the medallion at all costs would not be in vain. It was a decision Elderwiser wouldn't have made if he did not have great confidence in her.

The metal grew warm in her hand, and the Circle of Power began to quiver, causing her arm to shake. The vibration grew in intensity, testing her resolve to hold on. She was now feeling the energy of her father's mystical power transferred into her hand, and she let it flow into her heart.

The wizard's daughter knelt down and touched the medallion to one of the larger spheres of glass. The beautiful marbles immediately began to slow then stopped moving altogether. Perfectly solid round forms of glass softened, becoming first like gelatin then melted altogether into a thin, viscous solution. Growing puddles oozed together, forming into small pools, then a pond and then a lake. The sizeable depression of land filled with oily streaks of liquid color.

Imalima was free and swimming with all his feet operating as paddles toward an extended branch held by Carter. As it turned out, Imalima, with his duck-like feet, proved to be quite a strong swimmer. The grateful creature was pulled ashore as the crater continued to fill . . . and then overflow.

"Flood! Quickly, onto the rafts!" Serene ordered. Within moments they were bobbing along flowing ribbons of colorful liquid. While swirling past the rafts, melting beads of pigment reflected light from the faces of twin suns Suva and Ahneese.

Now Carter, the Wiggwoggs, and Wimzicals understood the wisdom of Serene's order to build rafts.

Without warning, the newly formed river deepened and grew wider. The rafts held together remarkably well under the river's rapidly increasing flow.

Before long and with mounting intensity, the slippery liquid washed up and over the lashed tree limbs. Down the noisy river they sped. Changing lead positions, the rafts bounced wildly along the rush of color like wayward corks.

A sudden swell tipped the raft Ferbert was riding atop, knocking him off balance. He hadn't seen the wave coming because he had lost his grip on his handhold and had been distracted while trying to locate another. Unsuccessfully trying to grab hold of anything and sliding precariously close to the edge of the floating platform, Ferbert screamed.

"Take hold of my hand!" called a voice from behind him.

It was his twin, Fermond, who at the last moment reached out and grabbed hold of his panicked brother. Fermond had both feet jammed up hard against the raft's thick limbs and with all his strength held tightly onto the sleeve of Ferbert's tunic. Ever so slowly, the frightened Wiggwogg was hauled back from the edge of disaster.

The wild ride lasted for several miles on the river, ending almost as abruptly as it had begun. Coming hard around a curve in the rapids, the rafters were whipped to the outside of a series of dangerous eddies. Skirting the swirling liquid, they soon found themselves pushed out from the main flow toward a sheltered cove. There, gratefully, the rafts finally slowed and floated listlessly down along the riverbank.

The hour was growing late and darkness was beginning to settle in as the rafts were put ashore. Wearily they climbed up the steep incline. Just up ahead, the trail picked up at the edge of heavily overgrown woodland.

"We will camp here," announced Serene. "It has been a long and memorable day. The Gootz defenders of Thorn Castle have been defeated. We are once again in possession of the Circle of Power. On the other side of joy is sadness. We have also heard the last words from my father, Elderwiser, the great wizard of Wiggonwoggen. I am exhausted, as I am sure you are as well. Much still remains to be done, and for what may lie ahead, we will need the gift of good fortune and a wizard's wisdom.

"First thing in the morning, we will head toward Bludenbonz Beach," she continued. "I am feeling a sense of urgency, and we want to be on the beach well before nightfall. I don't want to spend one moment longer on this island than we absolutely have to."

. . . .

For The Grinder, time was also an issue. With his precious medallion "stolen," he was obsessed to find those responsible and punish them before they had the opportunity to get away. He heard the sound of a clock ticking loudly in his mind. His focus went to doing whatever it was that needed to be done to locate and recover the Circle of Power. He would do anything to ensure the precious medallion didn't leave Athulian. Reports had been received from a lone Kenga spy that the miserable thieves carrying his treasure were traveling an alternate route in attempt to escape.

"There will be no escape!" he madly screamed at his cringing army. "They will pay the ultimate price for their foul deed . . . but not before I have me some fun inflicting a bit of pain on these crummy criminals. I want to personally put a great hurt on whomever it is leading the disgusting tribe of sneaky sneaks. Oh, I can't wait to get ahold of him."

The Grinder put one of his massive hands to the back of his head and the other to his jaw. In one swift move, he gave his head a hard twist that was immediately followed by a sickly crunching sound. His face was contorted, and an unnatural smile opened onto the side of his face. A few of the soldiers closest to The Grinder shifted uncomfortably and tried to return his smile without looking directly in his eyes.

The Grinder's plan was foolproof. He couldn't have chosen a better route for the thieves to take if he had personally picked it himself.

"This is just perfect," he said to a subordinate standing close by. "There will be no slipping out of my trap this time. The thieves have never faced the full force of my army. They are so outnumbered they don't stand a chance. I will make them pay dearly for the mischief they have caused."

The Grinder looked up at a cliff that ran parallel to its twin approximately fifty feet away. Two vertical walls of rock separated by a narrow neck of land supported the head of a lush forest just beyond. Stacked boulders lining the base of the cliffs ran the full length of the walls. From where he was standing, the view presented a perfect funnel that would deliver his prize straight into his waiting arms. If he had spent a fortune to design and build a trap for his trespassers, he couldn't have done a better job. Now he just had to be patient while waiting for the surprise party to begin.

"Oh, how I do hope it is one of the Wiggwogg children's birthdays and that they enjoy surprise parties as much as I do," The Grinder said insincerely. "Fiddlesticks, how forgetful of me. I forgot to order the cake. Oh well, it's the thought that counts, is it not?"

Much of The Grinder's army was working at a feverish pace digging a channel about four feet deep and wide along the base of both cliffs. Others were busy in the nearby forest cutting and stacking brush that would be laid over the soldiers in the dual trenches. Those who could fit into the trenches would wait in hiding under their camouflage while others would conceal themselves behind the large boulders staggered along the walls of the gorge.

Inside one of the two well-hidden channels at the wide opening of the funnel and at the opposite end of the canyon from the The Grinder stood Specialist Ernat Gob. The young, inexperienced Gootz soldier was not having a particularly good day. He was exhausted from a lack of sleep and now down with the sniffles, he was not feeling his best. He often had nightmares and on occasion, he found himself revisiting a familiar place of horror from a past bad dream.

Last night's dream, for example, did not end well, with Specialist Gob failing to survive the nightmare. Upon awakening in the middle of the night, he sat on the edge of his bed with a box of tissues and his eyes closed, hunched into a shivering ball of fear. For the remainder of the night, the miserable soldier was unable to get back to sleep.

Gob was not your typical run-of-the-mill Gootz. He was sensitive and for that reason was singled out by officers and his peers for persecution.

"No room for a pansy pants in our ranks," chastised his platoon sergeant, so Gob was given the most miserable jobs possible in the Gootz army. Anyone perusing his military records would find a history of discipline issues and forced work details reserved for misfits and the lowliest of the Gootz soldiers.

Meanwhile The Grinder had instructed his throne be carried all the way from Bludenbonz Castle to the site of the upcoming massacre. The throne was to be set upon a high platform that was built at the narrowed end of the funnel so that he would have a ringside seat to the slaughter. On the remote chance an invader or two survived the gauntlet of misery he had ingeniously prepared, they would then have to get past him. The Grinder snickered and thought aloud while absently fingering the jeweled handle of his sword, "There is just no chance of that happening."

It was a difficult choice for the leader of the Gootz whether to take an active role in the impending bloodbath or simply, from the comfort of his throne, savor a grand overview of it. In the end, as much as he was looking forward to the exercise, he decided not to get his favorite fur-trimmed robe dirty. He would watch the show from the luxurious comfort of his box seat, chalice of mead in hand along with a savory mixture of fly dip heaped on crispy crackers. If the temptation of action was just too much to resist, he always had the option of jumping in.

The captured leader of the sneaky invaders was to be personally delivered to him unharmed. It had been days since The Grinder had enjoyed a good night's sleep. His mind was preoccupied with devising increasingly painful means of torture for the leader of the intruders before formally introducing him to the full length of his sword.

When the Gootz had completed digging the trenches, they jumped in, dragging the camouflaging brush on top of themselves. Now all they had to do was sit quietly and wait. By a planned signal from a Kenga spy hiding behind a boulder at the funnel's entrance, they would not have to wait very long. The unsuspecting adventurers were traveling a path that would shortly lead directly into the wide end of the funnel and The Grinder's trap.

· · · · · · ·

It wasn't just the Gootz who were awaiting the arrival of the adventurers. A great assortment of nitravoles, rawks, toads, and an undetermined number of territorial wolf packs, not particularly known for cooperation, was amassed out of sight from eyes on the ground. All along the upper edges of the opposing cliffs and trees overlooking the narrow valley, an unlikely assembly of diverse forces anxiously anticipated the arrival of Wiggwoggs, Wimzicals, and a boy named Carter Nicholsworth.

It has been said that war creates interesting bedfellows. Indeed, not a more interesting combination of allies had ever been assembled on Aeiea. From their hiding place above, the enemies of The Grinder watched the Gootz preparing their trap. Word had been sent back to Wimzi calling for a substantial reinforcement of toads, promising the reward of a never-ending buffet of fat flies.

Wolves, which are by nature shy and secretive animals, were far more plentiful living hidden deep in the White Mountains than any Gootz had imagined. Upon hearing of the mistreatment of Lapis and his pack at the hands of the Gootz, the extensive population of wolves from the White Mountains was more than eager to accept the invitation to the imminent confrontation.

Ushi, Lapis, and Croaker had decided to share the leadership responsibilities and in the spirit of cooperation had worked out a plan that was acceptable to all three. The nitravoles, who up to this point had done a yeoman's work of the heavy lifting, hid in the many cracks and crevices etched along opposing canyon walls while the rawks were concealed along the upper northern ridge in the trees. In their separate hiding places, they waited to help out where help was needed.

The success of the plan would be, to a large extent, dependent on surprising the surprisers. Wolves lay as still as the long shadows cast by the boulders that hid them, while the toads came dressed for the occasion wearing their own built-in costumes of camouflage.

From above and below, all held their breath and waited.

· · · · · · ·

As planned, the adventurers had risen early that morning and were making good progress without encountering any opposition. That was until Serene sensed something was not right. She held up her arms, and her army behind her came to a quick halt. They were just within a cluster of trees that hid them from the valley's gaping mouth just up ahead.

"It is time to use Elderwiser's gift promised long ago at the base of Mount Maluuk," the Wiggwogg leader announced to those gathered around her. "My idea is to adjust the reality of the Gootz who believe they are dealing with nothing more than a small number of Wiggwogg children and a bunch of weird Wimzicals. My nose tells me The Grinder and his army are not far off. I want to confuse the Gootz to cause them to lose confidence in their plans."

Reaching around her neck for a strap, Serene removed one of several bota bags she always carried. The others were filled with water, but not this particular one. "Take just three drops into your mouths," she instructed her small and most unusual platoon, "then close your eyes while concentrating on the number twenty-three."

They all did as instructed. When the Wiggwoggs and Wimzicals reopened their eyes, twenty-three duplicates of each of them had enlisted into their now formidable army. Their small group had just increased to considerably more than a thousand, and now there was the appearance of a real army. Carter laughed. The whole bizarre scene reminded him of the county fair and the trick mirrors inside the carnival fun house.

"Now this is more like it!" Nevermore exclaimed to Carter just before flying off with his twenty-three new friends to get a lay of the land and scout out the possible location of the Gootz.

Nevermore and his "air force" shortly returned, reporting little success in locating the whereabouts of the Gootz. Feeling safe to proceed, it was the Imalimas who were the first to enter the valley. They were followed closely by the Carters, the Wiggwoggs, the Wimzicals, and finally the four and twenty black birds that had no intention of ever being baked in a pie.

"One Imalima is more than enough," the real Carter remarked to the real Nevermore, "but I'll bet twenty-three more Imalimas will drive even him crazy."

"Crazier," was the single word reply from Nevermore.

Meanwhile the creature from Wimzi was lost in reverie while humming his choice of best-loved nursery rhymes. Lamenting the unfortunate outcome of a flea's encounter with a bee, at least from the bee's perspective, Imalima was rudely wrenched back into the present when the wheels of war were suddenly set in motion.

. . . .

The Grinder's plan had been to trap the invaders as they entered the funnel. They would be forced from behind to fill the narrow channel that led to his concealed throne. This is where the real fun would begin. He wanted his experience of their painful suffering to be up close and personal.

The leader of the Gootz rubbed his hands together in excited antici-pation. He was not overly concerned by what he perceived as the spirited enthusiasm of his army to get the party started early. It was not enthusiasm, however, that motivated the Gootz soldiers down at the other end of the valley into action. Panic was their inspiration. They had been anticipating a small group of thieves, and this was anything but the few invaders of Athulian they had expected.

To make matters worse, from the cliffs on high overlooking the val-ley's floor came tons of toads a-leaping down onto the entrenched Gootz. The initial plunge was immediately followed by swarms of reserve toadies waiting eagerly for action just behind the first wave. Just outside the val-ley, thousands of toads, each with a single drinking straw in its mouth, imitated the sound of a rapidly flowing river. As Carter Nicholsworth could testify, creating the sound of running water was an old trick used by the toad that answered to the name of Croaker.

The purpose of this flimflam was to attract an unsuspecting thirsty creature into believing he was about to have his whistle wetted while par-taking in some liquid refreshment and perhaps, if invited, join the toad for a meal. Usually too late to do anything about it, the unsuspecting victim would be disappointed to discover his guest status was bogus. The deceitful invitation often offered by the mean, green, three-toed toad was an obvious hoax perpetrated and refined to perfection by Croaker, whose actual intent was the consumption of his guest.

The hungry toads of Wimzi waited impatiently for Elderwiser's prom-ise of flies. They were known to not be very discriminating when it came to their food selection, but the stinky old Gootz were definitely not on their menu. Anyway, on this particular occasion the toads' creative ploy with a straw had quite different intentions.

· · · · · · · ·

The Gootz forces situated farther into the valley and closer to The Grinder were hunkered down under their blanket of camouflage and were unaware of the toads' deception. They were growing increasingly uneasy, some even seriously concerned, by the growing sound of rushing water coming from just beyond the valley. An honorable death by sword was one thing, but the thought of a meaningless death by drowning in a flash flood was quite another.

At first slowly, then in greater numbers, the Gootz broke with The Grinder's orders and emerged from their place of hiding to check on the source of the sound of surging water. In that tactical act of poor judgment, the now-exposed Gootz left themselves vulnerable targets. The Grinder leapt from his throne in anger at the lack of discipline demonstrated by his army.

"Get back, you idiots! What is wrong with you?" The Grinder screamed at his soldiers, jumping furiously up and down on the platform supporting his throne. The quickly constructed structure was not built for such abuse. First it creaked then it crashed. The Grinder, who was thrown to the ground, swiftly regained his footing when his attention was drawn to movement above the opposing sheer walls.

From all along the ridge, it began raining toads. As luck would have it, the initial toad to reach a target, a fat boy named Weezer, landed squarely on Specialist Ernat Gob, who then became the first Gootz soldier ever to make the acquaintance of a toad from Wimzi. The toad smashed down hard against Ernat's chest, knocking him to the ground. Sitting on his stomach, Weezer looked curiously into the dull eyes of Specialist Gob. Already the poison was running from the toad's head down across its lumpy body and soaking through the clothing of the Gootz soldier.

"Splish splash, let's give the Gootz a bath," sang the toad.

Death for Specialist Gob was not all that dramatic. It was more like simply going to sleep, and in a strange way, by his peaceful expression, it almost seemed as if Gob was grateful.

Jumping from his viewing platform, The Grinder screamed as he ran toward his soldiers. "Idiots! Get back! Back into the trenches!"

But it was too late. Off in the distance at the entrance into the valley, the Gootz saw the substantial army of Wiggwoggs, Wimzicals, and Carters approaching. The surprisers had become the surprised. Everywhere up and down the valley much of the Gootz army was in complete chaos. Their swords managed to do some damage against the toads, but having been out-surprised, they now appeared at an uncorrectable disadvantage.

Nitravoles and rawks swooped from the canyon's crevices and trees along the ridge down into the valley. Wave after wave of the flying creatures attacked the surprised Gootz, and all across the battlefield bedlam ruled.

The Grinder, along with many of his soldiers, fought valiantly and in some pockets of conflict actually seemed to have the advantage. For quite some time the battle's outcome remained in dispute as it raged up and down and back and forth across the valley. That is at least until the wolves arrived on the scene. Hordes of wolves descended from the cliffs on their enemy with a vengeance. Showing no mercy, they went about finishing the job the toads and the others had begun.

When eventually the dust of battle had begun to settle, all the Gootz soldiers were either lying dead or were in the process of dying. Only The Grinder was left standing.

The nitravoles were happy to participate in the cleanup, carrying the limp bodies of dead Gootz soldiers in their talons for a proper burial at sea.

Circling the outraged leader of the Gootz, the pack of wolves led by Tamu, the tawny-streaked mate of Lapis, silently stalked around and around as The Grinder slashed out wildly with his sword. The wolves were genetically programmed for this kind of kill. They skillfully worked an ancient game of tag handed down from generations of ancestors.

The pack moved with linear precision, like the gears of a watchmaker's clock. In the hub of the revolving wheel of wolves, The Grinder tried his best to protect himself, turning repeatedly to face the attackers on all sides. Now and then he took an unsuccessful swipe with his blade at a wolf that had probed within range of his weapon.

He became a bit dizzy then grew disoriented. Twice stumbling, The Grinder quickly regained his footing.

"Think you're smarter than me, do you?" he shouted angrily. "Come on, you cowards. If you are hungry, I have my sweet blade I would like you to taste."

There were no takers. The Grinder's invitation was received with the continued cool discipline of single-minded wolves. Save for the pathetic moaning of some unfortunate Gootz soldiers who insisted on over-acting their death drama, the recent scene of battle and bedlam had been mostly reduced to a hushed valley littered mostly with the corpses of defeated Gootz.

Every now and again, a wolf that faced The Grinder's back leapt into the circle and tagged The Grinder with a bite from its sharp teeth then withdrew. This infuriated The Grinder, who always spun around a moment too late to respond to his attacker. He would curse the wolf loudly. This was precisely the effect the wolves wanted their tactic to achieve. Frustration is perhaps one of a soldier's worst enemies in battle.

With The Grinder facing the tagger who disrespectfully stared back licking his lips, from behind the Gootz leader another wolf would jump into the circle and take a nip at one of The Grinder's legs. And so it went. . .

Dirt and sweat mixed with blood soon stained The Grinder's favorite royal robe. He had worn the ceremonial robe specifically on this day to celebrate the defeat of his enemy, but things weren't working out particularly well for the weary son of Mother Putzer.

Unlike The Grinder, wolves are quite patient creatures. From the wolf pups' earliest days at the hunt, they have practiced working this exercise to perfection and seem never to tire of its repetition.

There is a pecking order amongst wolves and a respect for the pack system that ensures their continued survival. They are both efficient as well as relentless hunters, able to run at a high rate of speed for hours on end once in the chase. Wolves have been known to cover sixty miles in a single night. The fleeing Gootz soldiers never had a chance. And now, the focus of their attention had turned its spotlight on The Grinder.

Ushi and Lapis stood above the fray on a boulder where they could easily watch the younger wolves practice their hunting skills. The circle was closing. In the center, The Grinder's world was fading. He was growing tired of the game.

The wolves sensed the Gootz leader's increasing vulnerability. Smelling the kill, they became more emboldened, striking now at will. In the end, The Grinder simply dropped his sword then fell to his knees before disappearing under a stack of excited wolves. I shall spare the reader the gory details of The Grinder's demise.

"What the—" were The Grinder's last words. Not very memorable considering his impressive reputation and the long legacy of torture and terror dispensed at will wherever he went.

This was the horrible and bloody scene that the adventurers came upon as they entered the valley. They had missed all the action, and by the look on Carter's face upon scanning the carnage, it was obvious that he felt a deep sense of gratitude for his absence.

The toads had broken out the fly swatters, and the fly swatters were doing what fly swatters are intended to do. Throughout the valley a great gathering up by the toads of dead winged nasties was taking place. The flies' highly developed sense of decay had smelled dinner beginning to cook under the intense heat of Suva and Ahneese. Their ravenous appetites had become their undoing. Now the toads were occupied with quickly collecting and preparing for export piles of the deceased winged delicacies.

Not bothering to say good-bye or making a comment of any kind, the toads abruptly left the scene, moving off in the direction of The Great Sea Valion. With great effort, Croaker and company hauled behind them in big, black, bloody bug bags their bountiful day's catch.

The reunion between Ushi, Serene, and the other Wiggwoggs was quite emotional. The missing Wiggwogg had been given up for dead by nearly all of his fellow travelers. Only Serene had not entirely given up hope that she would again see her friend alive. And here he was. Ushi and his companion, the wolf named Lapis, along with the other wolves, with help from the toads of Wimzi, the nitravoles from the Downunderworld and Elderwiser's rawks, had defeated the mighty Gootz army and their leader. Incredible. Serene was overwhelmed with feelings of gratitude.

"You owe me an explanation," she said to her fellow Wiggwogg, "and I am anxious to hear your story, but for now, our priority is to get back home safely. Perhaps later over dinner we can catch up."

"I'm sorry, Serene. I knew you and the others would most likely think I had been captured or killed, but there was important planning and organizing needing to be done. I had no way of contacting you."

"What is important is that you are safe and were here when we needed you. I have always been able to count on you, Ushi."

The other Wiggwoggs were overjoyed with Ushi's safe return. They crowded around him waiting impatiently for their turn to hug and welcome back their friend.

Although she wore the Circle of Power against her chest, Serene knew their return journey to Wiggonwoggen from Athulian was still uncertain. Then there was also the matter of Carter Nicholsworth. The great

Elderwiser had helped her understand what still needed to be done and how to do it.

Painful as it would be for Serene, a promise had been made and a promise would be kept.

· · · · · · ·

The effects of Elderwiser's potion were beginning to fade, and before long, Serene's inflated army had shrunk back down to its original size.

"A celebration is premature," Serene cautioned those gathered around her. "First we must safely find our way back to Bludenbonz Beach, then manage a way off this island. We can't depend on help from the sea serpents. The Gootz army has been defeated, but we may still encounter some pockets of resistance from those who likely have not gotten the word. This is not a time to let down our guard."

Lapis and the other wolves paced nervously back and forth showing signs of discomfort. They were anxious to return to the familiarity of the mountains.

Serene, joined by Ushi, spoke privately to Lapis. She thanked the large wolf for helping defeat the forces of The Grinder. Ushi hugged the neck of his friend and looked silently into the wolf's penetrating blue eyes. There was communication without words. In the next moment, Lapis wheeled around and loped off in the direction of home with Tamu and the other wolves close at his heels. Joining the wolves' departure were the nitravoles for a return to their original homes in the cliffs of the White Mountains overlooking the sea.

The swarming rawks simply flew toward the two suns and a destination unknown on Aeiea.

· · · · · · ·

There was nothing left to be done here. The adventurers were more than ready to leave the scene of the recent battle. With Ushi once again at his customary place in the lead, and without argument from Imalima, Carter, the Wiggwoggs, and the Wimzicals headed toward Bludenbonz and The Great Sea Valion.

Later in the day while taking a rest break, Serene learned of Ushi's adventure. She filled him in on the details of their encounter with Peggi at

Thorn Castle and their recovery of the Circle of Power. Both were caught up in the drama of Serene's recollections when from out of the shadows of the nearby trees stepped the Gootz archers, their bows armed and drawn.

They were a company of soldiers who had somehow managed to get cut off from the main brigade and had not yet heard the news of the defeat of their army and the death of The Grinder. Even with Serene's earlier warning, the adventurers were caught totally off guard. Quickly the Gootz under the orders of their commander, an old military veteran who went by the name of Bopus, bound and gagged their prisoners.

Tied to long poles, the prisoners were carried a distance through the overgrown forest to a clearing that served as the Gootz staging area. A series of tents squatted on a mat of grass. Absorbed in conversation, a number of ugly Gootz females with coiled springs of hair growing from facial moles and wiry whiskers sprouting from their chins ignored their newly arrived guests. The greasy-haired females perched on low wooden stools and sat in a tight circle of hushed gossip. As they whispered, they peeled gnarled root vegetables.

Down a gently sloping bank toward a river went the Gootz with their captives. Using a shortened pole, deep holes were pounded into the bank along the river's edge. The poles, and the adventurers tightly bound to them, were placed into the holes with the captives upside down, facing the rushing water. Satisfied with the stability of the poles, the Gootz left their prisoners and returned to their camp.

The good news for the hostages was that because this company of Gootz soldiers had been cut off from word of The Grinder's fate, as well as the transfer of the Circle of Power, they were not overly agitated. Bopus had indeed captured the adventurers, and for that he imagined The Grinder would be generously grateful. It is quite possible that if Bopus had been aware of the actual state of affairs, the trespassers would most likely have been killed on the spot.

Looking up, Iat noticed a gathering of dark, bloated clouds beginning to roll into the afternoon sky. "I smell rain," he said. In moments, the first drops fell on bone-dry soil. Small explosions of dust rose from around the base of the poles mixing with the beads of sweat standing on Iat's face. "How will we ever get out of this?" he wondered.

The rain that had begun as a light drizzle intensified. A downpour quickly threatened the safety of the prisoners as the swollen river was rising rapidly. In no time it would reach them, and if the Gootz didn't return shortly, they would surely drown.

You could see the alarm in the eyes of some of the younger Wiggwoggs, not to mention Imalima, who had spent much of his life running backwards focusing on the past so as to avoid dealing with the occasionally disturbing present.

Less than a few inches now from the head of Lohden, the water slapped at the base of the pole he was tied to. No one was waiting to be rescued by the Gootz who had left the prisoners to fend for themselves. Fear in this case was a good thing as Lohden worked feverishly to loosen the cloth that bound him to his pole. With the help of the rain and mud that made his skin slippery, he finally managed to work his hands free from his restraints. The youngest Wiggwogg, using all his strength, doubled up as in a stomach crunch to reach the fabric that secured his feet to the pole.

Untying himself, Lohden fell hard to the ground, knocking the wind out of him. He lay there dazed in the slick muck trying to catch his breath. In a moment he removed his gag and went cautiously from pole to pole releasing several comrades who then reciprocated by helping to undo the bonds that held the other prisoners.

Wasting no time, Serene ordered everyone to follow the course of the river that she believed would eventually run to The Great Sea Valion. Without delay, off they went.

· · · · · · ·

The Gootz, dry in their tents and weighted down with dinner, felt little urgency to check on the status of their captives. As day was beginning its transition to dusk, Bopus took advantage of a lull in the activity to drift off into a light sleep. In a rambling dream, the Gootz commander had a vision that greatly disturbed him. He saw his hostages running free in the forest, fleeing from the Gootz camp. Awakening, the shaken Bopus ordered several scouts to immediately check the status of the prisoners.

When the scouts returned with the bad news, Bopus fumed. He blamed his soldiers for not doing a proper job of securing the captives. Everyone pointed their fingers at each other, and shortly a fight broke out.

Because Bopus was in charge, he took the brunt of the blame. One of his officers had wanted to kill the trespassers when they were first captured, but no, Bopus wanted to play hero and personally deliver the prize alive to the supreme leader of the Gootz. Now they had all escaped.

"Well, don't just stand there with a finger up your nose!" the Gootz company commander shouted. "Bring them back and do it quickly! I will accept no excuses. If The Grinder finds out they escaped under our watch, he will have my head. I promise you, if I lose my head over this, a fate far worse than mine awaits you. Well, what are you waiting for? AFTER THEM!!!" he screamed.

The escapees' footprints were freshly etched in river mud close to where the long poles, now partially underwater, stood empty. They were obviously headed in the direction of Bludenbonz Castle and probably the beach below. The rain continued to fall and was now coming down in torrents. The Gootz felt they were not far behind the adventurers, and they needed no further incentive than the threatening words of Bopus to kill the enemy on sight.

"Show no mercy to the wretched invaders!" cried out Bopus, urging his soldiers onward. "Crack their bones, peel their skin, put out their eyes!" Sprays of spittle mixed with rain flew from the twisted mouth of Bopus.

· · · · · · · ·

Ushi's feet barely touched the ground as he led the adventurers on a furious run for their lives. Carter felt as if his heart had jumped up from his chest to his ears. He had never run so fast in his life, but then again he had never been more scared in his life either. How long could they keep up this pace before the Gootz eventually overtook them?

And then, as if the overgrown forest had suddenly come up against an invisible barrier, a rolling green expanse of grassland cluttered with the remains of recently hewn trees took its place. At that precise moment, it was as if someone had reached over to shut off the valve controlling the torrential rains. The dark sky washed to a deep purple, and in the distance The Great Sea Valion opened wide before them in a gesture of welcome.

The greeting was short-lived.

Thunk. An arrow slammed into the ground, just missing Imalima whose astonished look said something memorable like, "Huh?"

Serene unconsciously reached through the neck of her tunic for the Circle of Power. Several more arrows fell, one quickly ending the life of a Wimzical standing near her. Holding the medallion tightly in her hand, Serene mouthed a name over and over. The name carried with it eternal trust and unconditional love.

Chapter 23
Reunions

A shadow mimicked the river's flow. Suva and then Ahneese peeked from behind a black cloud to see what they could see. Twenty or so feet above and ahead of the shadow, a magnificent red owl flew through the last remnants of the downpour, gracefully tracing the twisted line of the river. Ordinarily owls are not known to venture out by day, but this was no ordinary owl.

Up in front of the owl, the Gootz were closing in on the adventurers. No more than a hundred yards now separated the adversaries. Within short order, the owl had overtaken the Gootz and then flown past the heroes as well, landing in a tree overlooking the river. Spreading its great wings to full extension then rapidly flapping them, the owl called out, "Serene."

Immediately along the route the Gootz were taking, the river suddenly diverted its course. The raging water turned its aggression in the direction of the Gootz, catching Bopus and his company completely by surprise. The powerful surge easily brushed the Gootz from the banks, dragging the panicked soldiers into the center of the river. Turbulent rapids swept them like leaves downriver past the startled Carter, Wiggwoggs, and Wimzicals. All of the Gootz were caught in the rush . . . except for Bopus and his son, Ronkunkle.

From a tree limb above the head of a wild waterfall, the owl watched as one after another thrashing Gootz made the long, vertical plunge to the rocky basin far below. When the last had slipped over the rim's edge, the splendid owl again spread his wings and also slipped away. Following the flight pattern of his roarks, the spirit of Elderwiser flew off for a private meeting with the sister suns, Suva and Ahneese.

All had witnessed the appearance and disappearance of the red owl. They had also witnessed the river instantly change its course, finishing what hopefully was the final chapter in the history of The Grinder and his army.

Serene spoke to her hushed group of followers.

"The owl's presence represents and reinforces what we Wiggwoggs believe: form may change but energy is eternal. An ending is at the same time a beginning."

Lost in their thoughts, the adventurers quietly picked their way down from the bluff to Bludenbonz Beach. Unlike the chaos they had experienced on their previous visit, this time the beach was quiet and empty. With night descending, and exhausted from the day's drama, the weary travelers dropped their packs and joined their gear lying on the sand. After a light meal, one by one each drifted off into a deep and well-deserved sleep.

· · · · · · ·

Bopus and his son Ronkunkle considered the loss of their entire company as something of a blessing in disguise. Word of the capture of the band of Wiggwoggs, Wimzicals, and one odd being with a bird on his head, their subsequent escape, and the Gootz failure to recapture the invaders now would never find its way to The Grinder's hairy ears.

Bopus didn't trust his soldiers—and for good reason. There had been talk amongst them to squeal on their leader's bungled handling of his prisoners as soon as the opportunity presented itself. Now with his soldiers out of the way, no one would know the nasty little secret of incompetence that went over the falls with them. No one, of course, except for his son, Ronkunkle.

There was no love lost between these two. Bopus considered his only son totally lacking in character and loyalty. Someone who would easily sell him out at the drop of a hat if by doing so he had the opportunity to move up a notch in the military chain of command.

Ronkunkle, on the other hand, thought his father to be a hopeless drunk, an inept leader . . . and an overall bad dad.

Late that day, Bopus and Ronkunkle were walking their way back through the forest toward the Gootz staging area. Bopus suggested they stop for a brief celebration of their fortunate escape from what surely would have been The Grinder's wrath had their soldiers survived. Bopus was quite inventive in creating special occasions to celebrate and get drunk.

While Ronkunkle gathered wood for a campfire, two drinks were poured from the flask that permanently hung around his father's neck, resting on his chest. Into the one intended for his son, Bopus added a "special" white powder taken from a small pouch with enough kick to kill a cow.

It wasn't long after Ronkunkle's return that Bopus, who was well into his fifth drink, noticed his son had not yet touched his first.

"Not thirsty?" he asked.

"You know how I hate your sloppy behavior when you have had too much to drink, Father. I am actually far more hungry than thirsty and suggest before you get too drunk we have a short hunt for tonight's dinner."

Drinking his dinner sounded like a much better idea to the company commander, but he agreed to a short hunt to appease his son. He reasoned Ronkunkle would wash his dinner down with the specially prepared drink.

Perhaps hunting and drinking is not the smartest combination of activities. Bopus was sure he had a wild bearkie in his sights when he mistakenly shot an arrow into the thigh of Ronkunkle. The son of Bopus screamed in pain and cursed loudly at his father who he didn't think was showing the proper degree of concern or sympathy.

"I said I was sorry. Get over it!" Bopus shouted at his sniveling son.

Obviously the reaction of Bopus was less than acceptable to Ronkunkle, who promptly set an arrow in his bow and sent it flying directly between his father's eyes.

"See how that feels! Now, that is how to properly use a bow and arrow," said Ronkunkle, looking into the passive face of his dead dad.

Ronkunkle limped back to where they had originally stopped to rest. Removing the arrow from his thigh, he had a rare moment of remorse for murdering his father. Lifting his specially concocted beverage, the lone survivor of the Gootz company toasted the memory of his recently departed dear old dad.

Without giving it another thought, the son of Bopus drained his drink.

· · · · · · ·

Arni and his sea serpent pals loved to play. Whenever they had the opportunity, a game similar to water polo would break out somewhere in

The Great Sea Valion. Rules were ignored. Contests were always won by whichever team displayed the most creative skills in the practiced art of cheating. Remember, the sea serpents were the creation of Hoo-Ha, the Grand Wimzard of Wimzi. The serpents were highly competitive and could never be accused of not playing hard to win. In the end, however, they were all good sports as well as friends. No matter who won, they held no grudges.

It happened that on this particular morning, just off the island of Athulian, a spontaneous game of "dunker," the sea serpents' favorite water sport, had broken out.

It was Imalima who first noticed the creatures playing not far out at sea. Those of Wimzi genetics had an instinctive sense as to the proximity of one of their own. The adventurers lined up along the water's edge waving frantically, trying to get the attention of the sea serpents that were in the heat of a close match.

"Yo, Arni!!!" shouted Imalima along with the other Wimzicals while wading out into the surf. Carter and the Wiggwoggs quickly followed.

Arni, who had been on the lookout for the return of the adventurers, was the first to respond. "They're back! Game over, boys." The sea serpents headed toward the shore.

The reunion just out beyond the breakers brought words of praise and congratulations from Arni as well as the other sea serpents for the success of the mission. Stories were swapped and those told by Imalima and the Wimzicals were quite animated, somewhat exaggerated, and of course sprinkled with some pretty bodacious lies. They were, after all, fellow Wimzicals doing what Wimzicals do best.

Finally, with the heroes securely seated on the backs of the sea serpents, Arni and the boys set out across The Great Sea Valion for the shores of Wimzi. Songs were sung and waves of laughter spilled out across the water.

Carter Nicholsworth was happy for his Wiggwogg friend Serene. She now had what she came for, and it all seemed to be working out fine for the prospects of peace and harmony for all the inhabitants of Aeiea's territories. Yet Carter felt a gnawing uncertainty regarding his own future.

"Do we have a plan?" Nevermore asked, picking up on his friend's mood.

"Not one I'm aware of. Ever since we left Lake Mohegan, I've felt like a passenger on a bizarre trip with no idea as to our destination. I guess in some ways that's the way life is, if you are brave enough to fly in the dark."

"I do it all the time," Nevermore said. "It is my natural state of being. I think the word you use for it is *intuition.* Long ago, humans also had a highly developed sense of intuition just like any other wild creature. I guess over time, due to a lack of practice and trust, they have lost this skill. You could get it back, but it would take a good deal of practice and a renewal of trust. A bit tricky at first until you get the hang of it, but definitely doable."

"Would you help me, Nevermore? Thanks to you, while on Athulian I had a brief experience with the enhanced sensory awareness of a wild animal, but total intuition is quite different."

"Sure, what are buddies for?" the little birdie asked.

Since Carter's arrival on Aeiea, he had become aware of how the Wiggwoggs often seemed to communicate without words, how they made choices often without logical information. His latest lesson about how intuition works came through observing the wolves on Athulian. Their eyes, ears, and noses appeared highly developed, but even more than that, they seemed to be aware of the wordless communication of nature's voice.

Carter spent most of the trip across The Great Sea Valion lost in his thoughts. He imagined what it might be like to have the natural instincts of an animal. The images excited him, and small seeds of possibilities began to root in his mind.

"Land ho!" Nevermore called out from the crow's nest of Carter's hair. Indeed, the outline of Wimzi was sitting low on the horizon. From the spines of the sea serpents, the Wimzicals sat up straight, craning their necks to get a better view of their homeland.

The water was calm with barely a ripple, while sisters Suva and Ahneese did their part in helping to provide a warm welcome for the victorious return of the Wimzicals. Croaker and his fellow toads had arrived in Wimzi just hours earlier with news of the defeated Gootz army and the death of The Grinder.

For those of you with doubts as to the aquatic skills of toads, yes, they can swim but not, however, with the Olympic prowess of cousin frog. Good enough at least to make it across the channel between the mainland and Athulian.

· · · · · · ·

All of Wimzi was in a mood for celebration, and the returning adventurers, who were warmly greeted on the beach, were treated as celebrities. Banquet tables were laden with food and even the Grand Wimzard of Wimzi was there.

Imalima, who had been trying to make himself scarce by hiding amongst the other Wimzicals, heard his name called out. The Grand Wimzard's technical assistant with megaphone in hand was summoning the Wimzical, whom you may recall had previously fallen from grace and been banned from the territory of Wimzi for life.

With head low and raggedy ears dragging in the sand, Imalima made his way slowly through the crowd that filled the beach toward the Wimzard's assistant. Two of the Wimzard's personal guards intercepted him. Positioning themselves on each side of him, the guards walked Imalima toward the makeshift stage containing the throne of the Grand Wimzard of Wimzi.

"Well, well, well. Look what we have here," said Hoo-Ha. Imalima could feel himself shrinking. He cowered like a beaten dog. The guards took Imalima up the platforms steps and left him standing alone before the Grand Wimzard.

"Unbelievable, and therefore conceivable, information has come to me through A. Croaker the toadster, who prior to his well-publicized deportation was a respected, well-known liar and once trusted citizen of Wimzi.

"Because of services beyond the call of duty, I have decreed a complete pardon for A. Croaker. The toad told—oooooooh, I like the way that sounds, *toad told*. Bet you can't say *toad told* first forward then backwards, *toad told, told toad*, five times fast with your eyes closed while spinning in circles. But I digest."

An advisor leaned to the Grand Wimzard's ear. "That's exactly what I said . . . 'I digress.' Who cares, and stop interrupting! My fashion coordinator, A. Dufus, has suggested," continued Hoo-Ha, the Wimzard, turning his attention from the toad to Imalima, "that your skin would make a mighty fine hat for me to wear at your funeral. If you can say without hesitating *toad told* forward then backwards five times fast with your eyes closed and spinning in circles, I'll tell you what I will do. I, your beloved leader and revered hero, in the spirit of generosity, would be willing to forego my new hat and let you wear your very own skin at your funeral."

There was a polite smattering of applause from the Wimzicals in attendance who nodded in approval of the Wimzard's implied generosity.

Imalima's crossed eyes bulged and he shuddered. He was not particularly good at word games or, for that matter, performance under pressure.

"What has that got to do with the subject, you ask?" No one had asked because no one really cared or remembered the subject anyway. "Nothing of course," said Hoo-Ha, answering his own question, "and that is precisely why my words are so important." Another advisor standing close to the Wimzard leaned over and whispered in his ear.

"Ah yes," responded the leader of the Wimzicals, "I seem to have wandered off into the bushes." He then unfurled a document that first ran to the floor of the stage, then over the edge, and finally down to the ground. Hoo-Ha cleared his throat and put on his favorite prescription yellow-framed sunglasses, the decorative ones with the angel wings on the top corners.

"Good citizens and friends of Wimzi, we are gathered here today to honor and thank the incredible Mr. Imalima. A. Croaker the toad told us of the heroics of Mr. Imalima and his invaluable contribution in defeating those nasty-smelling Gootz. Yada, yada, yada—OK, that's it, let's eat."

Once again the official bent to whisper to the Grand Wimzard of Wimzi. "Oh, silly me, I almost forgot," said Hoo-Ha, dismissing the official with a wave of his hand. "Mr. Imalima, I was just having a little fun at your expense. The funeral stuff was not true, of course. As a matter of fact, after careful review of your case, I have decided to overturn your conviction and welcome you back as a full citizen of Wimzi. In your honor, there will be a road named after you. However, it is a rather short road—ten meters to be exact, and it is a dead end. Nothing personal, it is all we have available at the moment as all the important roads are, as they should be, named after me."

Imalima was thrilled. Not so much about the street naming, but that the announcement of his impending funeral was premature and that he once again would enjoy the privileges of full citizenship in his homeland of Wimzi.

The party was merry and lasted well into the night. Promises were made to ensure that in the future Wimzi would be safe for travelers. The possibilities of a lucrative tourist industry along with an amusement theme park were also discussed. The Grand Wimzard liked the name, "Wimziland."

Mercifully, as the hour was quite late, the volume of the festivities was turned down as one by one the exhausted revelers crossed over into the place of happy dreams.

Morning found all who had participated in the previous night's festivities in a strange mood. Transition was looming and there was an underlying edge of uncertainty that hung over the beach like a dark cloud.

Breakfast was eaten mostly in silence. There was the unspoken knowledge that Wiggwoggs and Wimzicals would soon be going their separate ways. Carter wondered when or even if he would ever see his almost business partner Imalima ever again. Feeling a bit anxious that the winds of change were once again blowing, he searched out his friend, knowing the Wimzical would be good for a little light diversion. Carter found Imalima sitting alone under a tree located just beyond the sand at the fringe of the beach.

"Okay for me to join you, Imalima?"

"I guess."

"What will you do now that you've been welcomed back into Wimzi?" Carter asked.

"Exactly what I was wondering. My entrepreneurial expertise is unquestionably ahead of its time. For example, my invention of the bus stop before I even thought to invent the bus. What is a bus anyway? Don't tell me, or it would not be my original idea and I could not claim full credit for its invention. The language in the Wimzi Book of Rules is quite explicit on this type of thing—even if the book has yet to be written. Perhaps I will be the developer of the Grand Wimzard's amusement park. The possibilities boggle one's mind."

"Where will the money come from to finance such a huge undertaking?" Carter inquired.

"I was wondering that myself when I had an idea. Remember when I asked you if you wanted to be my partner? I could see by your expression that being my partner was not something that excited you . . . I'm quite sensitive, you know."

"Well, I . . ." stammered Carter.

"No hard feelings, old chump. By the looks of you, you wouldn't have brought much to the table anyway. I have the ideas, but I need capital, lots of capital. You know, shlamolies?"

"I don't know from shlamolies, but I do know cash. Where did you intend to get shlamo . . . I mean cash from?"

"Here's the really good part. We all know what an incredible hot-shot salesman I am, right? So I go out and find some yoyos fat with shlamolies. I convince them to cough them up so I can start my business. I will pay them back at an interest rate higher than they could get from the Bank of Wimzi, which is why they would invest in my company. I would personally go to the bank myself, but my credit is a bit shaky at present. At past as well, but tomorrow is a brand new day. Now this is where it gets exciting. I am the owner of my private company, which is named Imalima's Ideas Incorporated, or III, not to be confused with *ay yi yi*. When I have built this baby into a shlamolie maker, I go public."

"What does that mean?"

"You know how when you go to a market and one stall has fruit, another has vegetables, while yet another may specialize in flowers? In my market, instead of stalls, there will be companies such as my own and buyers can buy shares in the companies. I will sell shares of my company with a contract that I am to remain in control and be paid an outrageous sum of shlamolies yearly. I will hire my own board of directors who I will pay very handsomely. They in turn will award me an excessive bonus every year, even if we don't do so well. If they balk, I will fire them. I can do that since I will retain the bulk of the shares in the company. Whatcha think?"

"I don't know," Carter said, shaking his head. "The whole deal has a rather unpleasant aroma, perhaps something similar to the herring that bit the green weenie while sun-tanning on your poor deceased uncle's head."

"Well, you are wrong. It's a great idea and I bet it catches on. I believe you can break your back working hard your whole life while managing to scrape together a few domas to put under your mattress or you can choose to get into the game and play golf with big shot winners such as yours truly. Well, I'm off to write a business plan."

"Serene and the other Wiggwoggs are getting ready to leave. I'll go with them and I have the sense that I won't ever see you again," Carter said solemnly.

"Nonsense," Imalima said. "You know I have difficulty remembering names, right? But you probably don't know why. The reason is I just don't give much importance to current names since they are always changing. For example, on the next occasion we meet, we may very well have different names, and each of us will most likely be wearing a different body. I won't have a hard-wired memory of this time we have spent together nor of our other past encounters, but I will sense that I have known you before. It takes time and great gobs of silence to develop this telepathic awareness. So let's just say 'See you later, friend.'"

With that, Imalima flashed a toothy smile at Carter, winked, and made a "click-click" sound with his tongue. Kicking up a cloud of dust, he headed down the road toward the heartland of Wimzi . . . backwards, of course.

"Yowza!" Nevermore declared from on high. "Finally . . . something from the mouth of that crazy creature worthy of memory."

Moments later, Serene and the other Wiggwoggs found Carter deep in thought and standing exactly where Imalima had left him.

"Time to go," Serene announced to Carter.

"And just where are we going?"

Instead of responding with words, Serene simply looked into Carter's eyes, and with secrecy written in her expression, managed a small smile.

Chapter 24
What Goes Around, Comes Around

A considerably smaller group than the one that had partied on the beach the night before headed into the woods of Wimzi. Even though they no longer had Imalima as a guide, Carter and the Wiggwoggs felt comfortable in their surroundings. The air was cool, and a strong breeze whistled through tree limbs that swayed rhythmically to the timeless melody. Wispy roots grew down from the branches of an odd, fragrant version of a fir.

"It's like tinsel on a Christmas tree," Carter said to Nevermore, remembering winters in Lake Mohegan. Wimzi was crackling with magic and Carter imagined what the forest might look like if it were snowing.

The day stretched out uneventfully. That was quite fine with Carter, who had far more excitement recently than most people have in several lifetimes. It was late in the afternoon when the forest suddenly ended its presence and with it went the breeze. As if stepping from one painting into another, Carter and the remaining nine Wiggwoggs now stood amidst a series of sand dunes that bulged from the ground. The various-sized mounds, some as tall as a two-story house, hoarded just enough moisture to sustain clustered clumps of scraggly thistle.

Scratching an itch on his finger, Carter took a moment to examine the rest of his hand. Something was different. His hand looked older than he remembered. How long, he wondered, had it been since last he looked into a mirror? How much time had passed since last he had walked the familiar floor of Wickedwood? Time had lost its meaning. One day simply blended into another. The Wiggwoggs had no concept of a calendar. There were no instruments to measure the passing of time. Had he been on Aeiea for the equivalent of an Earth month? A year? Longer? There was the separation of day and night on Aeiea, but how long did each last? Every new question that riffled through Carter's mind only hastened to open another. Time was a human invention that carried with it the illusion of order.

"How long have I been here?" asked Carter, abruptly turning to Serene.

"I don't know what you are asking," she answered, preoccupied.

Understanding the futility in pursuing his line of thinking, Carter dropped the subject. He remembered time is measured by Wiggwoggs in terms of the degree of urgency, not by mathematics. There was no dinner time or time for sleep. You ate when you were hungry and slept when tired. Everything regarding the element of time was determined on an "as needed" basis. He wondered how this system might work on Earth.

Carter and company struggled up a steep, high hill of slipping sand where a weathered sign leaned from the ground. The yellow sign depicted a silhouetted group of children holding hands. The words warned, *Caution Ahead . . . Children At Play.* With Carter now in the lead, they continued their climb to the top of the bank. Upon reaching the summit, Carter took a giant step backward, nearly causing an avalanche of Wiggwoggs.

Returning to the bank's crest, Carter looked down upon a vast sea of individuals, from children to adults. They filled a shallow cauldron-shaped valley that spread out all the way to the horizon.

Twisted chimneys of solidified lava rose from a dried crust of igneous rock. Plumes of sulphur mixed with fire drifted lazily from the chimneys, and steam hissed from vents on the floor's crust in a turbulent display of geothermal eruptions.

At mid-distance, countless spiraled stairways stretched upward from the cratered landscape before disappearing into a darkening plum-colored sky. Lightning etched its presence onto the purple backdrop. Flashes of electrical energy sizzled and snapped impatiently at the heels of those gathered below, urging them forward in long, snaking lines. Up the curling stairways, ever higher they went, until eventually the climbers were swallowed by clouds.

A rotting band shell rested in the left foreground of Carter's view, precariously housing on its rickety stage a quintet of large creatures that resembled a family of long-legged armadillos. The five musicians sat stiffly on metal folding chairs dressed in crisp blue military uniforms. A single red feather curled up from their helmets. Each had affixed to the left chest of their buttoned-to-the-neck jackets clusters of medals and ribbons while epaulets of gold braid decorated their shoulders. The musicians' collection of colorful ornamentation bragged of service and pride.

Puffed cheeks urged a sorry attempt at a military march into two trumpets, two trombones, and a blotchy green-stained tuba. The tarnished instruments belched out discordant notes in the direction of the expressionless climbers.

"Do you know what's happening here?" Carter asked Serene, who was standing just behind him. He was bewildered by the scene below. The other Wiggwoggs were huddled tightly together off to the side and looking away. They were talking amongst themselves in hushed tones.

"Yes," Serene replied in a soft, reassuring voice. "Watch, and soon you will know as well."

And that is exactly what Carter did. He watched in a state of hypnotic trance. The activity below overwhelmed his senses in its impossibility. With all that Carter had experienced in his brief life, nothing could have prepared him for the monumental event unfolding before him or for what would happen next.

· · · · · · ·

Carter turned to ask Serene what she meant by her last words. To his astonishment, it was not Serene's eyes he saw but rather the eyes of a child about his own size. Serene was nowhere to be found. When he looked just beyond the child for the other Wiggwoggs, they were gone as well, replaced with the innocent faces of countless other unrecognized children.

At that moment, with his heart throbbing in his ears, Carter realized he was now standing in one of the many lines, this one made up exclusively of children. It was the same line that just a moment ago had been a far distance below him. His mind went back to when he was standing at the edge of the cliff at Thorn Castle and The Grinder's war machines were bearing down on him. He remembered Serene standing next to him and then at the same time standing a safe distance away looking at him.

"Serene!" he called out, but there was no answer.

As he stood in the queue leading to the spiral stairs, he noticed many of the children in his line holding the hands of smaller children, some not any older than an infant. Not only were the infants standing, but they were walking with the other children up the stairs.

When Carter's eyes searched beyond the children to the hill where he had just a moment ago been standing, he saw the Wiggwoggs far off in the distance looking back at him. They seemed so small. He wished himself with them, but that did not change his situation. Carter's legs felt heavy, as if they were not a part of him. Only with great effort was he able to move them at all. His mind spun with confusion. Digging his knuckles into his eyes, Carter tried his best to rub away his unsettling reality.

The child directly behind him tapped his hand impatiently on Carter's shoulder, urging him onward toward the stairs. The musicians stopped playing. All of a sudden, it became remarkably quiet.

Silence, thought Carter. The theme of a distant dream floated lazily through his mind. He closed his eyes then reopened them.

"Where are we? What's happening, Nevermore?" he asked aloud. Not hearing a response, Carter reached for reassurance, but the bird was gone.

Now his foot went to the first step on the twisting stairs, and then he was climbing. Around and up he went. Before long, Carter began to feel lightheaded.

What would happen, he wondered, *if he fainted or just sat down on a step and refused to move?*

For what seemed an eternity, he simply followed the child just in front of him, matching the placement of the child's foot on the next step with his own. Higher and higher they climbed. Several birds, surprised at his presence, nearly flew into him. He kept hoping to find Nevermore, but each sighting of birds only brought another disappointment. Objects on the ground were now indistinct, and his breathing was becoming increasingly difficult.

Thin pools of moisture gathered on the stairs just ahead of him. In another moment, Carter noticed he was climbing into a cloud and having a hard time seeing the child who was rapidly disappearing right in front of him. This was an all too familiar memory as he recalled his last visit to the Hunters Hut in Wickedwood. Still, the stairs led and Carter obediently followed. Soon there was no one in front or behind him that he could see.

But still, he climbed. The word "trust" that was a gift given to him from Serene played over and over in his mind, but try as he might, the hand of fear still held him tightly in its grip.

· · · · · · ·

It was in this bleakest moment of uncertainty that Carter's ascent abruptly ended. Instead of another riser, Carter found himself stepping onto a platform, not unlike an old wooden railroad station platform. Trying to grasp the significance of his latest surroundings, he first noticed that day had become night. Countless stars surrounded and lit the platform that silently floated in a vast pool of black sky.

At the far end of the "station," a single door hung closed, supported only by a freestanding splintered wood frame. Suspended in air above the door was a clock, the first Carter had seen since leaving his home that fateful morning. The large round timepiece wore freckles of twinkling stars on its dark blue face. An open, smiling mouth revealed the moon in its many phases. The clock was absent of arms. Its numbers . . . some upside down, some larger than others . . . were not in proper sequence. Under the clock, a sign read *Departure Times.*

Carter felt compelled to walk the platform toward the door so he could closely examine the unusual clock. Upon reaching the closed door, he couldn't help but notice a folded card hanging loosely from a nail pinned to the door's frame. On the face of the card was a beautifully painted butterfly and underneath the butterfly, written in a female's fine, delicate script, was the name Nicky Bixx.

Curiosity got the better of Carter. Removing the card from the nail, he opened it.

RIDDLE:
WHAT BEGINS WITH AN ENDING AND ENDS WITH A BEGINNING?

Carter stood with his eyes fixed on the words as if there might be an answer forthcoming if only he stared long enough. He felt a strong sense of familiarity with the words, but nothing more.

"Get it?" asked a familiar voice.

· · · · · · ·

There is in a lifetime a continuous parade of consequences that are the direct result of personal choices. Then there are the circumstances that may have nothing to do with personal choices at all. A good example of the latter might be the exact moment in which Carter found himself standing.

Just behind Carter was Serene, the riddle master. Nevermore sat comfortably on her shoulder. If birds could smile, you would have to say Nevermore was smiling. "See you on the other side," said the black bird. Directly behind Serene stood the rest of the Wiggwoggs.

"Who is Nicky Bixx? And no, actually I don't get it. I don't get any of this, but it seems you're all in on it." Carter's frustration and confusion played out on his face. His narrowing eyes filled with tears as he unconsciously placed the card from the door frame in his pocket.

Serene moved toward Carter and took him into her arms. She held him there quietly for a moment and then, without saying a word, stepped back.

What Carter saw in her eyes was something entirely unfamiliar, something beyond friendship or love or anything he had ever experienced. Something that was profound, relentless, and timeless.

One by one, the Wiggwoggs approached Carter. Each came forward and hugged him, then stepped away. The last words he heard came from Serene.

"Our reality is limited only by the restrictions we place on our minds. We are, we have always been, and we shall always be."

The visitor from Earth stood silently for a few moments staring into the eyes of Serene. Finally Carter understood.

"I get it," he said. He moved his head up and down in agreement. "I get it," he repeated, smiling. After a moment of awkward silence he asked, "Now?"

Serene simply nodded.

Nevermore winked and nodded as well.

Carter took a deep breath, turned, and opened the door.

He stepped off the platform, out into the dark.

His next sensation was one of complete weightlessness. Floating in the total absence of light and sound was, to his surprise, not a frightening or disorienting experience at all but rather strangely comforting. It did not seem to matter whether his eyes were open or closed since there was absolutely nothing to see.

Is time moving? he wondered. *Am I moving, and if so, where am I going now?*

In a while, threads of a long-ago dream began to reemerge. It was the dream that woke him into that haunting day he had disappeared from Lake Mohegan.

· · · · · · ·

Carter realized he wasn't breathing. He could feel and hear his heart beating in his chest, but he wasn't breathing. At first he was alarmed but then thought, *well, if I haven't been breathing, then perhaps I don't need to be.*

It was in this moment that he became aware of his confinement. His shoulders felt scrunched and one of his arms was stuck behind his back.

"Hush," said a woman's voice forcefully from somewhere beyond.

Who's that? Carter wondered. *And where is she?*

He opened his mouth to call out, but he had no voice. *How can I hush when I'm not even speaking? What's this about hush?* he wondered. *Is this another of those riddles? I'm not very good with these riddles.*

The boy from Earth concluded he must be in some kind of enclosure—perhaps a shaft or tunnel, at least that was the best idea he could come up with. At the far end of the tunnel, a warm golden light invited. He felt pressure against his stomach and realized it was his knees. He tried to remember how he had gotten to wherever he was but could not. He tried to remember his name but could not. He tried to remember anything at all from his past . . . anything . . . but could not.

And then, he was on the move.

Once again came the woman's voice, this time with more urgency and clarity.

"PUSH!"

Into that implausible moment of brilliant light, transition, transformation, and miracles came three simple words:

"It's a boy!"

Epilogue

Her thick red hair was worn long and untied. Most women in these parts modestly wore their hair tucked up under unflattering bonnets. But not her. She chose to wear hers loose to cover an inherited pair of exaggerated ears. Complementing the color of her beautiful hair was a fine spray of freckles that glazed her high, prominent cheeks.

Like most of those who had settled their community, the religious members of her church were from a large city far across the sea. They were by necessity now farmers but unaccustomed to the exhausting demands of working a farm. However, this was to be their new start, a safe place where they could finally practice their spiritual beliefs without fear of persecution. Together they were willing to work especially hard to carve out a life from their dreams.

On this particular day in her bedroom, "working especially hard" took on a new meaning. Finally alone, she lay in her bed with her newly born infant tucked snug in her arms. She gazed out the window into a heavy afternoon fog that seemed to have consumed a promising sunny morning. A small black bird flew to the window, landing on the sill. The bird just stood there, staring across the room at the mother and her baby for what seemed an eternity. Unable to grasp the significance of the moment, she simply stared back. And then, finally, the bird flew off.

After a few moments, her attention shifted to the table at the end of their bed. On top of the simple, handmade nightstand were a candleholder and a clear glass vase stuffed with an assortment of cut, long-stemmed flowers. Not your traditional "straight from the garden" variety. Oh no, these beautiful flowers were more than simply different. These flowers seemed . . . what is the expression—unworldly.

Because they were a family of the land, she knew her flowers. But these flowers, these flowers . . . at a loss for words, her mouth tightened and she just shook her head.

An unsigned card with a small nail hole at the top lay propped against the vase with a beautifully painted butterfly on its face. Under the butterfly, written in a delicate script, was the name Nicky Bixx.

Reaching for the card, she opened it, and inside was a most peculiar riddle. She read the puzzling words over and over, trying unsuccessfully to make sense of them.

"What do you make of this strange mystery, Nicholas Bixx?" she whispered into the small ear of her infant son.

Nicky, obviously with other things on his mind, simply stretched and yawned.

· · · · · · ·

Less than a mile away, and across from the winding dirt road that ran past their farm on its way to the village, was a pristine cold-water lake jumping with fish.

The sweeping hilltop view from the farm sloping toward either the lake on one side of the road or the storied forest hunkered down in the valley on the other, was absolutely breathtaking—both ancient and timeless.

· · · · · · ·

Speaking of time . . . in what seemed like the blink of a wizard's eye, a number of years passed. Nicky, as he was now fondly called, had grown into a fine, strapping farm boy. He had inherited his mother's flame of wild red hair and a rousing case of freckles to match. Like his mother, he also had an inherited pair of exaggerated ears.

· · · · · · ·

It was the year 1683. All was good and as it should be in the small farming village of Godswell. That is until one day, cats began disappearing. Nicky's grandmother's own cherished pet, a tawny old female named Hazel, was just one of the many missing cats.

Nicky had awoken early that morning from a very frightening dream, the details of which flirted just beyond the reach of his memory. Late that same afternoon, Nicky was out searching for Hazel. He had been unsuccessful, and his search had taken him quite some distance from the farm. A surprising heavy bank of fog had quickly worked its way down into the valley he had been exploring. He thought he'd better start for home before the weather got much worse.

It was just about then that Nicky heard the pitiful sound of a mewing feline off in the distance. The relentless sorrowful plea led him cautiously toward, and eventually into, the rapidly fading woods.

The dark shadows of two women slid amongst the the fog shrouded trees and the wind whispered, "You Must Stay, If On This Day, You Come Our Way."

What Nicky Bixx found in that mysterious forest was not what he or anyone else would ever have expected . . . not even in their wildest imagination.

But I guess that's another story.

Made in the USA
Charleston, SC
16 February 2012